'Here she stands above the competition, creating complex characters who evolve more than those in most thrillers. The breathtaking plot twists are perfectly paced in this compulsive page-turner' *Publishers Weekly*

'[Tami Hoag] confirms that she can turn out a police procedural as gritty, grimy and engrossing as the best of them . . . Hoag is in a crowded procedural market but the quality of the writing makes *Dust to Dust* a standout novel' *Observer*

'Grisly tension is not the only commodity on offer here – the internal politics of the police investigations are handled with genuine panache . . . Hoag has demonstrated . . . an effortless command of the thriller technique, adroitly juggling the twin demands of character and plot. The set-piece confrontations will ensure that it will take quite a lot to distract the reader from Hoag's narrative' *Crime Time*

'A top-class follow-up to Hoag's bestseller *Ashes to Ashes*'
*Publishing News*

'Her books are cleverly plotted, feature strong female protagonists and are extremely – often emetically – violent . . . Hoag has the bestselling writer's way with a punchy sentence and keeps the surprises coming right up to the very last page' *The Times*

'First-rate procedural detail with a credible crew of homicide cops, spectacularly foul-mouthed and fending off the horrors with dirty jokes. Some ornate plotting . . . worth your while, though, if not for the faint-hearted' *Literary Review*

'Lock the doors and windows, and turn on all the lights – Hoag has crafted a knuckle-whitening, spine-chilling thriller' *New Woman*

'Accomplished and scary' *Cosmopolitan*

Since the publication of her first book in 1988, Tami Hoag's novels have appeared regularly on the bestseller lists, including seven consecutive *New York Times* bestsellers. She lives in California. Visit her website at www.tamihoag.com

By Tami Hoag

# THE ALIBI MAN

## TAMI HOAG

An Orion paperback

First published in Great Britain in 2007
by Orion
This paperback edition published in 2008
by Orion Books Ltd,
Orion House, 5 Upper St Martin's Lane,
London WC2H 9EA

An Hachette Livre UK company

1 3 5 7 9 10 8 6 4 2

A CIP catalogue record for this book
is available from the British Library.

ISBN 978-0-7528-8183-6

Printed and bound in Great Britain by
Clays Ltd, St Ives plc

The Orion Publishing Group's policy is to use papers
that are natural, renewable and recyclable products and
made from wood grown in sustainable forests. The logging
and manufacturing processes are expected to conform to
the environmental regulations of the country of origin.

www.orionbooks.co.uk

*For my parents*

*Acknowledgements*

Everyone is familiar with the saying 'It takes a village to raise a child.' Producing and publishing a book is not so different. My job – which is conception, gestation, and birth – is only the beginning. There is a large extended family that sees me through my process, then takes over from there, and turns the daydreams and nightmares of my imagination into the book you now hold in your hands. I want to take this opportunity to acknowledge and thank all of those people who make publishing a book and making it a bestseller a reality.

To the art department, where book covers are brought from concept to dust jacket; to production, where miracles are worked ASAP every day on behalf of overdue authors (mea culpa), my thanks. To publicity and marketing, where campaigns are launched to generate excitement and to position books for maximum exposure; to the awesome Random House sales force who man (and woman) the front lines to get books into the hands of the reading public, my thanks.

To my agent and self-proclaimed monkey in the middle, Andrea Cirillo; my editor, the unflappable Danielle Perez; and my publishers, Irwyn Applebaum and Nita Taublib (my long-suffering champion lo these many years since my days writing for Loveswept), my most sincere and heartfelt thanks.

# I

She floated on the face of the pool like an exotic water lily. Her hair fanned out around her head, undulating, a silken lily pad to drift on. The sheer layers of fabric that made up her dress skimmed the surface, backlit by the pool lights, purple and fuchsia, the shimmering skin of a rare sea creature that came out only at night in the depths along a coral reef.

She was a vision, a mythical goddess dancing on the water, her slender arms stretched wide to beckon him.

She was a siren, tempting him closer and closer to the water. Her blue eyes stared at him, her full, sensuous lips parted slightly, inviting his kiss.

He had tasted her kiss. He had held her close, felt the heat of her skin against his.

She was a dream.

She was a nightmare.

She was dead.

He opened his cell phone and punched in a number. The phone on the other end rang . . . and rang . . . and rang. Then a gruff and groggy voice answered.

'What the hell?'

'I need an alibi.'

# 2

I am not a cop. I am not a private investigator, despite all rumors to the contrary. I ride horses for a living but don't make a nickel doing it. I am an outcast from my chosen profession and I don't want another.

Unfortunately, our fates have little to do with what we want or don't want. I know that all too well.

That February morning I walked out of the guest cottage I had called home for the past year, just as the sun was beginning to break. The eastern horizon was color-saturated in stripes of hot orange, hot pink, and bright yellow. I like that hour before most of the world wakes. The world seems still and silent, and I feel like I'm the only person in it.

The broad-leaved St. Augustine grass was heavy with dew, and thin layers of fog hovered over the fields, waiting for the Florida sun to vaporize them. The smell of green plants, dirty canal water, and horses hung in the air, a pungent organic perfume.

It was Monday, which meant I had the peace and quiet of absolute privacy. My old friend and savior Sean Avadon, who owned the small horse farm on the outskirts of Wellington, had taken his latest amour to South Beach, where they would oil themselves and roast in the sun with a few thousand other beautiful people. Irina, our groom, had the day off.

All my life I have preferred the company of horses to people. Horses are honest, straightforward creatures without guile or ulterior motive. You always know where you stand with a horse. In my experience, I can't say the same for human beings.

I went about the morning routine of feeding the eight beautiful creatures that lived in Sean's barn. All of them had been imported from Europe, each costing more than the average middle-class American family home. The stable had been designed by a renowned Palm Beach architect in the Caribbean plantation style. The high ceiling was lined with teak, and huge art deco chandeliers salvaged from a Miami hotel hung above the center aisle.

That morning I didn't settle in with my usual first cup of coffee to listen to the soft sounds of the horses eating. I hadn't slept well – not that I ever did. Worse than usual, I should say. Twenty minutes here, ten minutes there. The argument had played over and over in my mind, banging off the walls of my skull and leaving me with a dull, throbbing headache.

I was selfish. I was a coward. I was a bitch.

Some of it was true. Maybe all of it. I didn't care. I had never pretended to be anything other than what I was. I had never pretended I wanted to change.

More upsetting to me than the argument itself was the fact that it was haunting me. I didn't want that. All I wanted to do was get away from it.

I had lost time thinking about it. The horses had finished their breakfast and were on to other things – hanging their heads out their windows or over their stall doors. One had grabbed a thick cotton lead rope left hanging beside his door and was swinging it by his teeth around and around his head like a trick roper, amusing himself.

'All right, Arli,' I muttered. 'You're it.'

I pulled the big gray gelding out of his stall, saddled him, and rode off the property.

The development where Sean's farm was located was called Palm Beach Point – which was neither a point nor anywhere near Palm Beach. All horse properties, it was common to see riders on or along the road or on the sandy trails that ran along the canals. Polo ponies were often

3

jogged along the road three and four abreast on either side of an exercise rider. But it was Monday, the one day in seven most horse people take off.

I was alone, and the horse beneath me didn't like it. Clearly I was up to no good – or so he thought. He was a nervous sort, high-strung, and spooky on the trail. I had chosen him specifically for that reason. My attention couldn't wander on this one or I would find myself in the air, then on the ground, then walking home. Nothing could be in my head except his every step, every twitch of an ear, every tensing of a muscle.

The trail ran straight with the road on my right and a dark, dirty, narrow canal on my left. I sat, bumped the gelding with a leg, and he jumped into a canter, pulling against the reins, wanting to run. A small group of white ibis browsing along the bank startled and took wing. Arli bolted at the explosion of bright white feathers, leaped in the air, squealed, bucked, and took off, his long legs reaching for as much ground as he could cover.

A saner person would have been choking on terror, hauling back on the reins, praying to survive. I let the horse run out of control. Adrenaline rushed through my veins like a narcotic.

He ran as if hell was closing in behind us. I stuck to him like a tick, sitting low over my center of gravity. Ahead, the road made a hard turn right.

I didn't touch the reins. Arli ran straight, leaving the road, staying with the canal. Without hesitation, he bounded across a small ditch and kept running, past the dead end of another dirt road.

He could have broken a leg, fallen on me, thrown me, paralyzed me. He could have stumbled hard enough to unseat me and dragged me by one foot caught in the stirrup. But it wasn't the horse that frightened me, or the potential for injury or death. What frightened me was the

4

excitement I felt, my euphoric disregard for my own life.

It was that feeling that finally made me wrestle for control – of the horse and of myself. He came back to me a little at a time, from a dead run to a gallop to a canter to a huge prancing trot. When he finally came more or less to a halt, his head was up in the air, and he blew loudly through flared nostrils. Steam rose from his body and mine, both of us drenched in sweat. My heart was racing. I pressed a trembling hand against his neck. He snorted, shook his head, jumped sideways.

I didn't know how far we had run. The fields were long behind us. Woods stood on both sides of the dirt road. Tall, spindly pine trees thrust themselves toward the sky like spears. Dense scrub choked the far bank of the canal.

Arli danced beneath me, nervous, skittish, ready to bolt. He ducked his big head and tried to tug the reins out of my hands. I could feel his muscles quivering beneath me, and it dawned on me that this was not excitement he was feeling. This was fear.

He snorted again and shook his head violently. I scanned the banks of the canal, the edge of the woods on either side. Wild boar roamed through this scrub. Wild dogs – pit bulls set loose by rednecks who had beat them into meanness, then didn't want them around. People had reported sighting the occasional panther in the area. Rumors always abounded that something or another had escaped from Lion Country Safari. Alligators hunted in the canals.

My body tensed before I could even process what caught my eye.

A human arm reached up out of the black water of the canal, as if stretching out for help that was far too late in coming. Something – a bobcat, perhaps, or a very ambitious fox – had tried to pull the arm out of the water, but not for any benevolent reason. The hand and wrist had been mangled, the flesh torn, some bone exposed. Black flies hovered and crawled over the limb like a living lacy glove.

There were no obvious tire tracks leading over the bank and into the water. That happened all the time – too much to drink, asleep at the wheel, no common sense. People plunged to their deaths in South Florida's canals every day of the week, it seemed. But there was no sign of a car here.

I took a hard grip on the reins with one hand, pulled my cell phone from my belt with the other, and punched in a number.

The phone on the other end of the line rang twice.

'Landry.' The voice was curt.

'You're going to want to come out here,' I said.

'Why? So you can kick me in the teeth again?'

'I've found a body,' I said without emotion. 'An arm, to be precise. Come, don't come. Do what you want.'

I snapped the phone shut, ignored it when it rang, and turned my horse for home.

This was going to be one hell of a day.

# 3

A pair of deputies in a white-and-green Palm Beach County cruiser rolled through the gate behind Landry. I had ridden back to the farm to eliminate the complication of a horse at a crime scene, but I hadn't had time to shower or change clothes.

Even if I'd had time, I wouldn't have gone to the trouble. I wanted to show James Landry I didn't care what he thought of me. I wasn't interested in impressing him. Or maybe I wanted to impress him with my indifference.

I stood beside my car with my arms crossed over my chest, one leg cocked to the side, the portrait of pissy impatience. Landry got out of his car and came toward me but didn't look at me. He surveyed his surroundings through a pair of black wraparounds. He had a profile that belonged on the face of a Roman coin. The sleeves of his shirt were neatly rolled halfway up his forearms, but he had yet to jerk his tie loose at his throat. The day was young.

As he finally drew breath to speak, I said, 'Follow me,' got in my car, and drove past him out the gate, leaving him standing there on the drive.

A short gallop on a fast horse, the location of my gruesome discovery was more difficult to find by car. It was easier to lead the way than try to give directions to a man who wouldn't listen anyway. The road bent around, came to a T. I took a left and another left, passing a driveway with a busted-out motorcycle turned into a mailbox holder. Debris from the last hurricane – three months past – was still piled high along the road, waiting for a truck to come haul it away.

Dust billowed up behind my car even as I stopped the vehicle and got out. Landry got out of the county sedan he had pulled for the day, swatting at the dust in his face. He still refused to look at me.

'Why didn't you stay with the body?' he snapped. 'You were a cop. You know better.'

'Oh, screw you, Landry,' I shot back. 'I'm a private citizen. I didn't even have to call you.'

'Then why did you?'

'There's your victim, Ace,' I said, pointing across the canal. 'Or part of. Go knock yourself out.'

He looked across the brackish water to the branch the human limb had snagged on. The flies raised up like a handkerchief in the breeze as a snowy egret poked its long beak at the hand.

'Fucking nature,' Landry muttered. He picked up a stone and flung it at the bird. The egret squawked in outrage and walked away on yellow stilt legs.

'Detective Landry?' one of the deputies called. The two of them stood at the hood of the cruiser, waiting. 'You want us to call CSI?'

'No,' he barked.

He walked away fifty yards down the bank, where a culvert allowed a narrow land bridge to connect one side of the canal to the other. I shouldn't have, but I followed him. He pretended to ignore me.

The hand belonged to a woman. Up close, through the veil of flies, I could see the manicure on the broken nail of the pinky finger. Deep-red polish. A night on the town had ended very badly.

Blond hair floated on the surface of the water. There was more of her down there.

Landry looked up and down the bank, scanning the ground for shoe prints or tire tracks or any sign of how the body had come to be in this place. I did the same.

'There.' I pointed to a partial print pressed into the soft dirt just at the very edge of the bank, maybe ten feet away from the victim.

Landry squatted down, scowled at it, then called to the deputies. 'Bring me some markers!'

'You're welcome,' I said.

Finally he looked at me. For the first time I noticed that his face was drawn, as if he hadn't slept well. The set of his mouth was sour. 'Is there a reason for you to be here?'

'It's a free country,' I said. 'More or less.'

'I don't want you here.'

'It's my vic.'

'You're not on the job,' he said. 'You quit that too. Remember?'

His words hit me like a fist to the sternum. I actually took a step back at the verbal blow, not able to prevent myself from gasping.

'You are such an asshole,' I snapped back, more upset than I wanted to show. More upset than I wanted to be. 'Why should I want to be hooked up with you? You don't get your way and the first thing you do is fight dirty. You really know how to sell yourself, Landry. I can't believe women aren't beating down your door, you fucking prick.'

My eyes were burning, anger trembling through me like the vibrations of a plucked wire. I turned to go back to the body, thinking that the woman below the surface of the filthy water had undoubtedly been put there by some man she shouldn't have trusted – as if there were any other kind.

The arm seemed to wave at me in acknowledgment, and I thought I was hallucinating. Then it waved again – violently – and I knew instantly what was happening. Before I could react, there was a terrific splashing and thrashing, and water came up at me in a sheet.

Landry shouted behind me, 'Jesus Christ!'

One of the deputies called, 'Gator!'

9

Landry hit me in the back and shoved me to the side. As I tumbled onto my hands and knees, a gun went off above me, the report like the crack of a whip in my ears.

I scrambled away from the bank and tried to regain my feet, the worn soles of my riding boots slipping out from under me on the damp grass.

Landry emptied his Glock 9mm into the churning water. One of the deputies ran along the bank on the other side, shouldering a shotgun, shouting, 'I got him! I got him!'

The blast was nearly deafening.

'Son of a bitch!' Landry shouted.

As I watched, the perpetrator floated to the surface on its back, a bloody, ragged, gaping hole torn in its pale yellow belly. An alligator about five feet long, with part of a human torso still caught between its jaws.

'Shit,' Landry said. 'There goes my scene.'

He swore and stomped around, looking for something to hit or kick.

I went to the edge of the bank and looked down.

Alligators are known for rolling with their prey in the water, disorienting the thrashing victim, drowning them even as the gator bites through tissue and bone, rupturing veins and arteries. This one had jerked his intended meal free of the branches she had become entangled with. The gator may have even stashed the body there himself earlier – another common practice: stuffing the victim away for later, letting the body begin to decompose while wedged under a tree trunk.

Nature is cruel. Almost as cruel as human beings.

I stared down into the muddy water, looking for the rest of the body to surface. When it did, I went numb from head to toe.

I mouthed the words *Oh, my God,* but I don't think I said them out loud. I felt like I was floating out of my body. I sank back down to my knees, and my hands covered my mouth – to stifle a sound, to keep from vomiting, I didn't know which.

The pale blue face that stared back at me should have been beautiful – full lips, high cheekbones. She should have had translucent blue eyes the color of a Siberian winter sky, but the small fish and other creatures that lived in the canal had begun to feed on them. More of Mother Nature's handiwork: a death mask from a horror movie.

Over the years that I had been a street cop and a narcotics detective, I had seen many bodies. I had looked down into the lifeless faces of countless corpses. I had learned not to think of them as people. The essence of the person was gone. What remained was evidence of a crime. Something to be processed and cataloged.

I couldn't do that as I stared at this face. I couldn't detach, couldn't shut down my mind as it flashed images of her alive. I could hear her voice – insolent, dismissive, Russian. I could see her walk across the stable yard – lithe, lazy, elegant, like a cheetah.

Her name was Irina Markova. I had worked side by side with her for more than a year.

'Elena . . . Elena . . . Elena . . .'

It registered somewhere in the back of my mind that someone was trying to speak to me, but it sounded as if the voice were coming from very far away.

A firm hand rested on my shoulder.

'Elena. Are you all right?'

Landry.

'No,' I said, moving away from his touch.

I fought to stand and prayed not to fall as I walked away. But my legs gave out within a few steps and I went down on my hands and knees. I felt like I couldn't breathe, and yet my stomach heaved and I vomited and choked.

Panic gripped me by the throat – as much from my fear of my own emotions as from what I had seen or from fear of aspirating my own vomit and dying. I wanted to run away from my feelings. I wanted to bolt and run, just as Arli had bolted and run away with me earlier, bringing me to this terrible place.

'Elena.'

Landry's voice was in my ear. His arm came around my shoulders, offering strength and security. I didn't want those things from him. I didn't want anything from him. I didn't want him seeing me this way – weak, vulnerable, out of control.

We had been lovers off and on for the last year. He had decided he wanted more. I had decided I wanted nothing. Less than ten hours previous, I had pushed him away with both hands, too strong to need him – or so I claimed. I didn't feel very strong now.

'Hey, take it easy,' he said quietly. 'Just try to breathe slowly.'

I pushed at him, wriggled away from him, got to my feet again. I tried to say something – I don't know what. The sounds coming from me weren't words. I put my hands over my face, trying to hold myself together.

'It's Irina,' I said, fighting to regulate my breathing.

'Irina? Irina from Sean's?'

'Yes.'

'Oh, Jesus,' he murmured. 'I'm sorry. I don't know what to say.'

'Don't say anything,' I whispered. 'Please.'

'Elena, you should sit down.'

He told one of the deputies to call in a crime-scene unit and ushered me not to my car but to his. I sat down sideways in the passenger seat, bent over my knees, my hands cradling my head.

'You want something to drink?'

'Yeah. Vodka rocks with a twist.'

'I have water.'

He handed me a bottle. I rinsed my mouth out.

'Do you have a cigarette?' I asked, not because I was a smoker per se but because I had been and, like a lot of cops I knew – Landry included – had never entirely abandoned the bad habit.

'Look in the glove compartment.'

It gave my trembling hands something to do, my mind something small to focus on. It forced me to breathe slowly or choke.

'When was the last time you saw her?'

I took a deep pull on the smoke and exhaled as if I was blowing out candles on a birthday cake, forcing every last bit of air from my lungs.

'Saturday. Late afternoon. She was anxious to go. I offered to feed the horses and take care of night check.'

Unlike myself, Irina had an active social life. Where it took place and with whom I didn't know, but I had often seen her leave her apartment above the stables dressed for trouble.

'Where was she going?'

'I don't know.'

'Where *might* she go?'

I didn't have the strength to shrug. 'Maybe Players or Galipette. Maybe clubbing. Clematis Street.'

'Do you know her friends?'

'No. I imagine they were mostly other grooms, other Russians.'

'Boyfriend?'

'If she had one, she didn't bring him to the farm. She kept her business to herself.'

That was one thing I had always liked about her. Irina didn't burden those around her with raunchy details of her sex life, or who she had seen, or who she had done.

'Has her mood been any different lately?'

I tried a weak laugh. 'No. She's been churlish and arrogant, like always.'

Not sought-after qualities in a groom, but I had never really minded her moods. God knew I made her look like an angel. She had opinions and wasn't shy about voicing them. I respected that. And she was damn good at her job, even if she did sometimes act like she was in forced labor in a Siberian gulag.

'Do you want me to take you home?' Landry asked.

'No. I'm staying.'

'Elena—'

'I'm staying.' I put out the cigarette on the running board of the car and dropped the butt into the ashtray.

I figured he would try to stop me, but he stepped back as I got out of the car.

'Do you know anything about her family?'

'No. I doubt Sean does either. It would never occur to him to ask.'

'She wasn't a member of the taxpaying club?'

I gave him a look.

Undocumented aliens made up a large part of the workforce in the South Florida horse business. They migrated to Wellington every winter, just like the owners and trainers of the five or six thousand horses brought here to compete in some of the biggest, richest equestrian events in the world.

From January to April the town's population tripled, with everything from billionaires to barely-getting-bys. The main show grounds – Palm Beach Polo and Equestrian Club – was a multinational melting pot. Nigerians worked security, Haitians emptied the trash cans, Mexicans and Guatemalans mucked the stalls. Once a year the INS would make a sweep through the show grounds, scattering illegal aliens like rats being run out of a tenement.

'You know I'm going to call this in and people are going to come out here,' Landry said.

By *people* he meant detectives from the sheriff's office – not my biggest fan club, despite the fact that I had been one of them. I had also gotten one of them killed in a drug raid three years prior. A bad decision – against orders, of course – a couple of twitchy meth dealers, a recipe for disaster.

I had not escaped unscathed physically or mentally, but I hadn't died either, and there were cops who would never forgive me for that.

'I found the body,' I said. 'Like it or not.'

*Not,* I thought. I didn't want to be there. I didn't want to know the person who had become a corpse ravaged by an alligator. But somehow this trouble had managed to find me, and there wasn't anything I could do about it.

Life's a bitch, and then you die.

Some sooner than others.

# 4

Murder victims are afforded very little dignity at the scene where their bodies are found. Someone finds them, is horrified by the sight of them, calls the cops. Uniformed officers show up, then detectives, then a crime-scene unit with a photographer, someone dusting for fingerprints, someone measuring the distances between items at the scene. The coroner's investigator arrives, examines the body, turns it over, looks for everything from lividity to exit wounds to maggots.

By necessity, the people who work these scenes – and have worked hundreds before, and will work hundreds more – aren't able to allow themselves to acknowledge (not openly, at least) the victim as someone's child, mother, brother, lover. Whoever this person might have been in life, they are no one as they lie there while the scene is being processed. Only when the investigation begins in earnest do they come back to life in the minds of these people as father, sister, husband, friend.

Bodies found in water are commonly referred to as 'floaters.' There is nothing worse than a floater that's been in the water a few days – long enough for decomposition to begin internally, filling the body with gases, bloating it to grotesque proportions; long enough for the skin to begin to slough off; long enough for fish and insects to feed on and invade the body.

I had last seen Irina Saturday afternoon. It was Monday.

I didn't look as she was pulled out of the water – not straight on, anyway. I could have let Landry take me home and leave me out of this process, but I felt an obligation to stay at least for a little while. She had been part of my ersatz family. I felt a certain strange need to protect her.

Too little, too late, unfortunately.

Uniformed deputies were ordered to drag the dead gator up onto the bank. The coroner's people oversaw the extrication of human tissue from between the reptile's jaws.

I smoked another cigarette. My hands were still shaking. I leaned back against the side of my car, too wired to sit.

In the old days, when I was 'on the job,' as the cops say, nothing got to me. I was numb. Ice water in my veins. There was no case I wouldn't tackle. I was a woman on a mission: to dole out justice – or at least to serve up the bad guys to the DA's office hog-tied on a platter. I went from case to case to case, like an addict constantly looking for the next fix.

The last murder victim I'd had on the job was someone I knew, someone I had worked with and liked. His murder had been my fault. I'd made a poor decision going into a meth lab in rural Loxahatchee. Jumped the gun, so to speak. One of the dealers, a wild-eyed, mulleted cracker named Billy Golam, had pointed a .357 directly in my face – then turned abruptly and fired.

I watched in horror as the bullet hit Deputy Hector Ramirez in the face and blew out the back of his head, blood and brain matter spraying the walls, the ceiling, splattering my lieutenant, who was standing behind him.

Three years had passed, and I still watched that scene play out in my nightmares. The face of Hector Ramirez floated through my memory every night.

I suspected that tonight Irina's face would supersede that of the man who had died because of me. It would be Irina's pale blue face that stared up at me through the fog of sleep, her ravaged eyes and lips. The idea made me feel ill and weak all over again.

How well had I known her, Landry had asked.

I had known her for more than a year, and I hadn't known her at all. Our lives may have revolved around the same center but otherwise never touched. I felt regret for that. The remorse of the guilty conscience – something all of us feel when we've lost someone from our lives we had never taken the time to really know. We always believe there will be time later, after this, after that. . . . But there is no time after death.

On the other side of the canal, Landry and the rest of them were engrossed in their task of evaluating the scene and collecting evidence. They would be at it for a long time. They expected – wanted – nothing from me aside from my statement, which Landry would take later.

Irina was dead. There was nothing I could do to change that. I was of no use to her standing there watching as people stepped around her remains like a sack of trash torn open by scavenging animals.

I hadn't made the effort to get to know her in life. Before this was over, I would know her well. That was what I could do for Irina. I knew even then that the journey was going to take me places I didn't want to go. If I had known exactly where, I might have made a different decision that day . . . but probably not.

As if he had sensed the direction my mind was turning, Landry looked over at me, frowning. I got in my car, turned it around, and drove home.

Irina and I had come to Sean's farm at the same time, for the same job. Happenstance, if you believe in that. Fate, if you believe something more. I didn't believe in anything at the time.

I had answered an ad in *Sidelines,* a locally based magazine for people in the horse industry. *Groom Wanted.* The person looking had turned out to be Sean Avadon.

Sean and I had known each other back in the days when I was a daughter, had parents, lived on the Island (Palm Beach proper). I was filled with rebellion and teen angst, and horses were my escape from the rest of my spoiled, privileged, empty life. Sean, older and wilder, had grown up a couple of mansions down the street. We had been friends, an odd couple, unrelated siblings. Sean was my sense of humor – and fashion, he claimed. What he got out of the deal, I never had figured out.

I had been in a very dark place when Sean came back into my life – or I into his – filled with anger and self-loathing and suicidal fantasies. The two years past had been spent in and out of hospitals while doctors tried to put me back together like Humpty Dumpty. On the day Hector Ramirez was killed in my stead, I had gone under the wheels of a meth dealer's 434 truck and been dragged down the road, the pavement breaking bones and stripping flesh and tissue from my body. Why I hadn't died, I couldn't understand, and I had punished myself for it every conscious day I had in the two years that followed.

Sean had given the groom's job and the apartment that went with it to Irina. He had taken me in like a wounded bird and put me in his guesthouse. When I seemed strong enough, he had put me to work helping to ride his horses, knowing the horses would be more help to me than I ever could have been to them.

Irina's apartment was located over the plush clubby lounge in Sean's barn. I went into the lounge, behind the bar, took a bottle of Stoli out of the freezer, and poured some into a heavy crystal tumbler. Leaning against the bar, I looked at the room as if it were an empty stage, remembering a conversation I had had with Irina in this room a year past.

She had just thrown a horseshoe at the head of a Belgian horse dealer who had come calling to tempt Sean into parting ways with substantial amounts of money. She would have killed the man on the spot if she could have. Her rage was a palpable thing, huge and hot and bitter. She had launched herself at him, pummeling him with her fists until

Sean grabbed her by her blond ponytail and one arm and pulled her off.

I had brought her into the lounge while Sean tried to smooth things over with the Belgian. She told me the story of a girlfriend from Russia who had gone to work for the dealer, who used and abused her. In the end the girl killed herself. Irina had wanted revenge. I'd admired her for that. There had never been anyone in my life I felt strongly enough about to seek revenge on their behalf.

Full of passion. The heart of a tigress. I wondered if she had fought as fiercely for herself. Was there a killer holed up somewhere with fingernail scratches down his face, missing an eye, unable to walk straight? I hoped so.

I raised my glass in salute and finished off the vodka.

Putting on a pair of thin, tight riding gloves, I climbed the spiral stairs that led to Irina's apartment. If Landry caught me doing what I was about to do, there would be hell to pay. Of course, the idea of negative ramifications had never stopped me from doing anything in my life.

A very private person, Irina always locked her door, but I knew where the key was hidden and I helped myself to it. The violence perpetrated on her had not happened here. The place looked lived-in, not tossed. A single coffee cup sat in the drain basket in the sink. The latest fashion magazines were strewn across the coffee table.

She had left her makeup out on the counter in the bathroom. I remembered she had been eager to go on Saturday. She had rushed off alone, dressed to kill. She could have been on the cover of one of the magazines in her living room as easily as working in a barn. Even in a T-shirt, baggy shorts, and muck boots, she had exuded an almost royal sense of confidence and elegance. I often referred to her as 'the Czarina.'

The drawers in the vanity yielded the usual stuff: nail polish, tampons, cotton balls, condoms. I wondered if she'd dropped a couple of the latter in her purse that evening, anticipating a conquest.

What kind of man would Irina go for? Rich. Very rich. Definitely good-looking. She would never settle for the money if the guy with the purse strings was some short, fat, balding toad with sweaty palms. She thought too highly of herself for that.

Wellington during the season had no shortage of gorgeous men with lots of money. Elite equestrian sports have been underwritten by the wealthy since the time of Caesar, probably longer. Privileged sons and daughters, the princes and princesses of America – and a dozen other countries – were a part of the scenery at the horse show grounds and the international polo fields here. They populated the parties and charity fund-raisers that filled the social calendar from January through March.

Had Irina planned to snag a scion that night? I could too easily imagine the raw, cold terror that must have come over her when she realized her life was about to go horribly wrong.

I went into the bedroom and there found ample evidence of the royal Russian attitude. The bed was strewn with clothes that had been considered, then cast aside, as she dressed for her night out.

She had a very pricey wardrobe for an illegal alien who groomed horses for a living. Then again, in Wellington a good groom could make six hundred dollars or more per month per horse, plus day fees for horse shows, and another thirty-five to fifty dollars per horse per day for braiding manes each day of a show.

There were eight horses in Sean's barn. And Irina's apartment was hers rent-free. Her living expenses were minimal – cigarettes (which she smoked outdoors only, away from the barn; there wasn't so much as a lingering whiff of smoke in the apartment) and food (for which she seemed to have only a passing fancy, from what I'd seen in her refrigerator). Her priority seemed to be clothes.

The tags spoke volumes: Armani, Escada, Michael Kors. Either she spent every dime she earned on clothing or she had an alternate source of income.

But Irina put in long days at the barn. The first horse had to be groomed and tacked up by seven-thirty a.m. Night check happened at ten p.m. Her only day off was Monday. Not a lot of free time for a big-bucks second career.

Among the items on the dresser: an Hermès scarf, several bottles of expensive perfume, silver bangle bracelets, a lint brush, and a digital camera the size of a deck of playing cards. That I took and slipped into my pocket.

I checked her dresser drawers. If-you-have-to-ask-you-can't-afford-it lingerie. Skimpy. Sexy. An array of T-shirts and shorts she wore to work. The big drawer on the bottom right held a burled-wood jewelry box, and in the box were some very nice pieces – several pairs of diamond earrings, a couple of diamond tennis bracelets, a couple of necklaces, a couple of rings.

I picked up a heavy white-gold charm bracelet and examined the charms – a cross studded with small, blood-red garnets, a green enameled four-leaf clover, a silver riding boot, a sterling heart. A sterling heart inscribed *To I. From B. B.*

A small table sat adjacent to one side of the bed, serving as nightstand and writing desk. Irina had left her laptop on in her haste to leave Saturday. The screen saver was a slide show of personal photographs.

I sat down on the chair and watched. There were snapshots of the horses she cared for, of Sean riding in the big arena at the Wellington show grounds. There was one of myself riding D'Artagnan, Sean's handsome copper chestnut, early-morning fog hugging the ground beneath us, making it look as if we were floating.

The more interesting photos were of Irina and her

friends partying, tailgating along the side of the polo field. The stadium of the International Polo Grounds rose up in the background. A polo match was in full swing.

No jeans and T-shirts at this party. Everyone was dressed to the nines. Irina wore a big pair of black Dior sunglasses and a simple black sheath dress that showed off a mile of leg. Her hair was slicked back in a tight ponytail. Her girlfriends were similarly turned out. Big hats, big smiles, champagne glasses in hand.

I didn't recognize any of them. Even if they had been other grooms from the neighborhood, I wouldn't have recognized them out of their barn attire. That's how it is in the horse world. At social events the first hour of the party is spent trying to recognize the people we see every day in breeches and baseball caps.

The photos were not limited to girlfriends. There were half a dozen shots of gorgeous Argentinian polo players, some on horses, some standing, laughing, an arm around one or more of the girls. I wondered if any of them was *B*.

I touched the mouse. The screen saver disappeared, revealing the last Web site Irina had been looking at: www.Horsesdaily.com.

Without hesitation, I put my gloved hands on the computer's keyboard and went to work, clicking and double-clicking until I located the files that contained the photographs. I wanted to e-mail them all to myself, but that would leave a trail that would bring Landry down on my head like a ton of bricks. Instead, I pulled Irina's digital camera from my pocket and simply took pictures of the snapshots as each appeared on the screen.

The desktop screen returned when I closed the file on the pictures. The AOL icon beckoned. If I was very lucky, Irina would have her account set up with the password saved so she didn't have to enter it every time she signed on.

She lived alone. There was no nosy roommate she needed to protect herself from.

I clicked to sign on and was immediately rewarded with the AOL greeting and the announcement that Irina had mail. Mail I couldn't open because no one should have been on this computer after Irina's death. The mail had to remain new. But I pulled a white note card out of the table drawer and wrote down the e-mail addresses of the senders.

Access to saved mail was another story. I brought that up and browsed through the list, opened everything from the three days before I last saw Irina, and printed them out. Later I would go through them carefully, looking for signs and portents of the evil that was to come. Now I couldn't take the time.

Also on the writing desk was a basket holding mail. A coupon for Bed Bath & Beyond, a doctor's bill, an offer to join a health club. On the back of one of the e-mails, I jotted down the name and address of the doctor.

The message light on the phone was blinking, but as much as I wanted to listen to her messages, I couldn't do it without being found out, for the same reason I couldn't open her new e-mail. I could, however, check the numbers of the missed calls without disturbing the voice mail itself.

The readout in the small window of the phone told me Irina had missed four calls. Using the tip of the pen, I touched the button to scroll through the calls, and jotted the numbers down. Two were local, one looked like a Miami number, one was *Unknown,* a blocked call. All had come on Sunday, the latest being logged at 11:32 p.m. A call from Lisbeth Perkins.

I wondered what the callers would feel when they found out Irina was dead, may have already been dead at the time they made their calls to her.

Who were her friends? Did she have any family? Had one of those calls been from someone she loved?

*To I. From B.*

I checked the drawer for an address book but couldn't find one. Irina had been addicted to her cell phone. I imagined she kept pertinent addresses and phone numbers in it and/or in her computer. The cell phone – which had become like a growth on the side of her head, she used it so constantly – would have been with Irina on the night of her death. I wondered if Landry and company had found a purse in the weeds or in the canal.

If I couldn't have the cell phone, the next best thing was the cell-phone bill, which I found in a plastic file box under the table. I took the last two statements, hurried downstairs with them, and made copies on the fax machine in Sean's office.

I looked out the end of the barn, nervous that Landry would come rolling in, even though I knew better. He would be a long time at the scene. There would be no sense of urgency to go through the victim's apartment. The first priority was to find evidence where the body had been dumped. A shoe print, a cigarette butt, a weapon, a used condom, something dropped by the perpetrator.

Landry was lead on the case. He would stay there and oversee every detail. And he would have to deal with the press, because the news crews, like bloodhounds, would have picked up on the scent of death by now and beat it out there.

Still, I hurried back upstairs and replaced the bills. The copies I folded and tucked inside the waistband of my pants.

The crunch of tires on the crushed-shell drive drew me to the window – the farrier come to replace a thrown shoe. The delivery truck from Gold Coast Feed rolled in behind him.

The world kept turning. That fact always seemed cruel to me. There was no moment of silent respect for the dead, other than within the minds of those she left behind.

# 5

'What a fucking mess,' Landry muttered as he watched the ME's people load the various pieces of the girl into a body bag. Everyone was sweating and swatting at flies. It had to be eighty-five degrees, with wet-blanket humidity. His hands were sweating inside the latex gloves he wore.

A floater, a dump job, no crime scene, and Estes was involved.

'Why was *she* here?' Weiss asked with an edge to his voice.

''Cause somebody dumped her here,' Landry said, purposely misconstruing the detective's question. Weiss was a pain in the ass, always with the chip on his overly developed shoulder. The guy spent so much time in the gym his arms stuck out from his sides like he was a blow-up doll.

'I meant Estes. What was *she* doing here?'

'She found the body. Turns out the DB was someone she worked with.'

'Yeah? How do we know she didn't do it?'

'Don't be an ass.'

'I don't like her being around,' Weiss announced.

'She didn't ask to find someone she knows dead in a canal.'

'She'll be a problem.'

Landry said nothing. Weiss was right. Elena would be a problem. She wouldn't stand back and let the detectives do their job. She knew their job. She'd done it herself, and she'd been good at it. Irina was someone she'd worked with every day. She was going to take the girl's murder personally. She was probably doing something she shouldn't be doing on Irina's behalf at that very minute.

Frustrating, maddening, difficult, attitude up to here. It pissed him off no end that he wanted to be with her. *Had* wanted – past tense. That was over. Thank God they had been discreet. No one in the SO knew (at least not for a fact) they'd been seeing each other, therefore no one knew they'd split.

'Did she call you?' Weiss asked. 'You weren't up. I was up. Why didn't I get the call?'

Landry rolled his eyes. 'Oh, for God's sake. You have a bug up your ass because you didn't catch this case? We got no murder scene, no evidence, no witness, no suspect, a dead body mutilated by an alligator. Say the word, Weiss. You can have this gem. And you can deal with Estes too. She'll be so glad to cooperate with you, I'm sure.'

'I don't want it,' Weiss said. 'I'm just saying. The call didn't come through the channels.'

'Well, you go tell the teacher on me,' Landry said sarcastically, as he went toward an evidence tech making a mold of the shoe print Elena had pointed out to him along the bank.

'Why'd she call you?'

Landry looked over at him. 'What's the matter with you? She called me because she knows me. If you found a friend of yours dead – assuming you have any – who would you call? You'd call someone you know. You wouldn't take your chances on getting the first incompetent moron up on the board.'

Weiss puffed up. 'Are you calling me incompetent?'

'I'm calling you a pain in the ass. Just shut up for once and get your mind on the job. Jesus, you act like some jealous woman.'

The shoe print. Landry looked down at it. Maybe it belonged to their perp. Maybe it belonged to some redneck who dumped his used motor oil into the water a week ago.

It didn't tell them anything, didn't give them anything to go on. The only good it would do to have the cast would be once they had a suspect and could get a warrant to look in the guy's closet.

'Looks like a boot,' the evidence tech said without looking up. 'A work boot. Round toe. Blundstones or something like that with a medium-deep tread.'

'Are you doing the tire tracks?' Such as they were. A few ridges in the powdered shell along the other side of the canal. A stiff wind would blow them away.

'Grant is on her way. She's better with the fragile ones.'

Landry jammed his hands at his waist and looked around. They had stretched the yellow tape across the road from his car to the bank. Behind the barrier was a bottleneck of white-and-green county cruisers, unmarked sedans, the ME's van. News vans had rolled in to further choke off the only way in or out of this backwater shit hole.

The reporters swooped in on a death scene almost as fast as the buzzards and were just as hungry and noisy. A corpse to feed on? Their favorite fodder. They didn't get that many in the Wellington environs, though the statistic climbed a little each year. The area was growing fast. Construction was constant. And with the influx of people came an increase in every kind of problem, including crime.

'The natives are getting restless,' Weiss said, nodding at the growing crowd.

'Fuck 'em.'

'Hey, Landry,' another of the detectives called from farther up the bank and back into the scrub. 'Got something here. A purse.'

The bag was small, cylindrical, gold encrusted with rhinestones. Landry snapped a photo of it with his digital camera. The crime-scene photographer took half a dozen shots from varying heights and angles. One of the crime-scene guys took measurements from the purse to where the body was found, and from the purse to the boot print.

When the evidence marker went down to mark the spot, Landry picked the purse up and opened it. A cherry-red lip gloss, a compact, an American Express gold card, three twenties, two condoms.

'Guess we can rule out robbery as a motive,' Weiss said, loudly enough to catch the attention of a reporter or two on the other side of the canal.

Landry gave him a look. 'Girls don't get dumped in canals because they carry too much cash.'

'I'm just saying.'

Weiss was always just saying. The man never had a thought cross his mind that didn't fall out of his mouth.

'There's no driver's license,' Landry said. 'No cell phone.'

'Haitians have been stealing cell phones,' Weiss said. 'They've got a racket going. My brother-in-law got a bill from Verizon that was twenty-seven pages long. Calls to Zimbabwe, the Ukraine, all over the world. The farthest he ever called was his mother in Astoria, Queens.

'So maybe some Haitians followed her out of a club, grabbed her . . .'

Landry tuned him out. Another couple of sentences and Weiss would be into his theory that Castro was behind the influx of criminal types from the islands to South Florida. Maybe he was, but Landry didn't want to hear about it. He had to deal in the present, the here and now, the corpse du jour. The anti-crime unit could worry about Castro.

He opened a little zippered compartment in the purse. Inside was a foreign-looking coin. The girl was Russian. It was probably something from the old country to bring her luck.

The ME's people came past with the body bag.

So much for that theory.

'All right,' he said on a sigh. 'I'm going to go deal with these people and get it over with.'

As he made his way to the other side of the canal, he dug in his pants pocket, came up with a couple of extra-strength Excedrin and choked them down without water, shuddering at the bitter taste left in his mouth.

Like hogs at a trough, the reporters tried to muscle one another out of the way for the honor of being the first to stick a microphone at him.

'Detective!'

'Detective!'

'Detective!'

The pushiest was the blonde from the NBC affiliate in West Palm. 'Detective, what can you tell us about the victim? What can you tell us about the murder?'

'I can't tell you anything about the victim, and we don't know yet that this is homicide,' he said. 'The ME will determine cause of death.'

'But clearly the body was dismembered,' the woman said.

'We don't know when that happened. We don't know how long the body has been in the water.'

'Are you saying this is another alligator attack?'

Excitement swept through the group, raising voices, as if some poor soul being eaten alive by a giant reptile was a better story than a regular person–person murder. The media seemed to want to promote the idea that the alligators were conspiring to take back their habitat, like something from a bad horror movie.

Three area residents had recently died in separate incidents with gators. One swimming in a pond, one walking a dog on a jogging path along a canal, and a drunk who had the misfortune of passing out on the bank of another canal within easy striking distance for the predator. Even if he'd been conscious, the drunk probably wouldn't have gotten away. An alligator can charge short distances as fast as thirty-five mph, nearly as fast as a thoroughbred racehorse running full out.

'No, I didn't say that,' Landry said.

'But it could have been?'

*It could have been aliens,* he wanted to say, but sarcasm was not looked on with a sense of humor in the sheriff's office.

'I can't speculate as to the cause of death' was what he said. 'At this point we have no idea how the young woman died or how she came to be here. The sheriff's office will be releasing a sketch of the victim later today, and we'll ask for help from the public in trying to ascertain her whereabouts the last few hours of her life.'

'A young woman?'

'How old?'

'Who was she?'

'Have you found the murder weapon?'

'Was she sexually assaulted?'

'We won't know that until the autopsy is complete,' Landry said.

The blonde leaned ahead of the pack. 'Who found the body?'

'A local resident.'

'Will you release his name?'

'No.'

'When will you be able to give us more information?'

'When we have some,' Landry snapped. 'Now you'll have to move the vehicles so we can get on with it. We're burning daylight.'

# 6

The SUV in the photo of the tailgating party had vanity plates. STAR POLO 1.

The best polo in the world is played in Wellington, Florida, during the winter months. Big-money-sponsored teams. Players with rock-star status. The ultrarich, the ultra-powerful, the ultrafamous filled the stands at the International Polo Club every Sunday. Early rounds of tournaments were played all week long on the fields stacked one after the next behind the main stadium.

I had a passing familiarity with the sport, having dated several completely inappropriate men involved in it back in the days when pissing off my father was a priority in my life. By reputation, polo players are wild, passionate, aggressive, hot-tempered, unfaithful, and their riding skills are not limited to polo ponies.

There were plenty of women in Wellington who believed a mad hot affair with a polo player was just the thing to spice up life. Perhaps Irina had been one of them.

Not interested in sticking around for the arrival of Landry and his team, I got in my car and drove into town, still in my riding clothes and smelling of stale sweat and horses. No one would look at me twice. Half the population of the town went around that way every day during season.

Still, I felt vulnerable and self-conscious, as if anyone looking at me would know instantly what had gone on that morning. I jammed a black baseball cap on my head and put on a pair of dark sunglasses and went into the Tackeria.

The Tackeria, located in a strip mall on Wellington Trace,

was a tack shop and social hub where horse people of all disciplines went to shop for essentials and catch up on the latest gossip. The specialty of the store was polo, with several aisles dedicated to polo equipment and clothing.

I was known there, stopping in from time to time to pick up the odd thing for Sean or to buy myself a pair of breeches. One of the clerks at the counter looked up and said hello as I approached.

'What can we help you with today, Elena?'

So much for my disguise.

'Just a question. I need to go out to Star Polo, but I'm not exactly sure where it is.'

'In the back,' the clerk said. 'Jim Brody. He's the owner. Your lucky day.'

'Yeah,' I said. 'Thanks.'

I went toward the back of the store but turned down one of the aisles of polo gear. Too many years as a narc. I always want to know what I'm walking into. Conversations were going on around me. Somebody was complaining about the price of gas. A woman wanted to know if the store carried a particular brand of gloves. Three people were in a discussion about the prognosis of an injured polo pony.

'. . . tore up the deep flexor tendon, right hind.' Voice number one. Strong, with the potential for bluster.

'How long will that take?' Voice number two. Quieter. Even.

'Too long. The season is over for her.' Voice number one again. 'She may not come back at all.'

'What a shame.' Voice number two.

'The team is so deep, you'll never miss her.' Voice number three. A smooth Spanish accent.

'Barbaro scored a lot of goals off her.' Voice number two.

'Barbaro could score off a donkey.' Voice number one.

I moved to the end of the aisle and checked them out while I pretended to look at horse halters. A big guy with a red face and a Tommy Bahama shirt. Fifty-something, gray hair, good-looking forty pounds ago. A tall, lean man in denim with a narrow face that looked to be carved from old leather. And a neat, tanned man in pressed khakis and a pink polo shirt with the collar turned up, his black hair slicked straight back. Handsome. In his fifties. Probably Argentinian. White-white teeth.

The tall man worked in the back, repaired equipment, fitted saddles. I had seen him back there different times when I was in the store, but I didn't know his name. That made Tommy Bahama the owner of Star Polo: Jim Brody. I didn't recognize him from any of the tailgating photos. The third man had been in the background of one of the shots, laughing, raising a glass of champagne, a cute twenty-something blonde at his side.

Brody slapped the denim-shirt man on the shoulder and said he'd see him soon.

I turned and made my way to the front of the store, careful not to be seen by the clerk I had spoken to. She was occupied with a customer. I slipped out the door and went back to my car. Brody and the other man came out. Brody got into a pearl-white Cadillac Escalade: STAR POLO 1. The Argentinian slid behind the wheel of a silver Mercedes convertible and followed the Cadillac out of the parking lot. I drove out behind them.

# 7

The main entrance to Star Polo on South Shore Drive (which is, of course, nowhere near the shore of anything but a drainage canal) looked like the entrance to a five-star resort. Stone pillars, huge trees, banks of red geraniums, clipped grass. The Cadillac and the Mercedes turned in. I drove past and went to the stable gate farther down the road.

A rider went past with three ponies tethered on either side, going for a jog. The farrier was banging on a hot shoe, shaping it to fit the foot of a horse being held by a barn hand. A groom was hosing the legs of a chestnut in the wash racks across the drive from the barn. Apparently there was no day of rest at Star Polo.

I parked my car in the shade and went to the girl in the wash rack.

Her focus was on the horse's forelegs and the cold water that ran down and puddled on the concrete. Lost in thought, she held the hose in one hand, and with the other toyed compulsively with a medallion she wore around her neck on a thin black cord. She looked sad, I thought; then again, maybe it was just the way I felt and I wanted to project that onto everyone around me. It seemed wrong that people should be going on in a normal way. But their reality was not mine.

'Boring job,' I said.

She looked up at me and blinked. Twenty-ish, I figured. Her curly streaked blond hair was up in a messy clip. She looked different in a faded tank top and baggy cargo shorts, but I recognized her from one of the tailgating photos. She stared at me with big cornflower-blue eyes.

'Hose duty,' I said. 'It's boring.'

'Yeah. Can I help you?' she asked. 'Are you looking for the barn manager?'

'No, actually, I'm looking for you.'

Her brows knit. 'Do I know you?'

'No, but I think we have a mutual acquaintance. Irina Markova.'

'Sure, I know Irina.'

'I recognize you from a photograph she has. From a tail-gating party at the polo grounds. I'm Elena, by the way,' I said, offering her my hand. 'Elena Estes.'

She shook it tentatively, still not sure what to make of me. 'Lisbeth Perkins.'

The friend from the caller ID.

'Have you seen Irina around?' I asked.

'She doesn't work here.'

'I know. I mean, just around.'

'We went out Saturday night. Why?'

'I work at the same barn as her. We haven't seen her for a couple of days.'

The girl shrugged. 'It's her day off.'

'Do you know where she would go? What does she usually do on her day off?' I asked, fishing for whatever information I could get about Irina's life away from the barn.

'I don't know. Sometimes we go to the beach when we're both off. Or shopping.'

'Where did you go Saturday night?'

'Are you a cop or something?'

'No. I'm just concerned. The world is a scary place, Lisbeth. Bad things happen.'

She gave a little involuntary laugh. 'Not to Irina. She can take care of herself.'

How I wished that had been true in the moment it had become clear that she could not.

'She was in a big hurry to leave work Saturday,' I said. 'Did you guys have plans?'

'Just to go out. No place special. We went to a couple of clubs on Clematis Street.'

'Which clubs?'

Looking annoyed, she turned to the faucets and shut off the water.

'I don't know,' she said impatiently. She was nervous with my questions. Whether she had reason to be or whether she was simply sensing something was wrong, I didn't know. 'What's the difference? We hit some clubs. We had a few drinks.'

'With anyone in particular?'

'I don't like all these questions,' she said. 'It's none of your business what we did.'

She unsnapped the horse from the ties and started toward the barn with him. I followed.

'I'm making it my business, Lisbeth,' I said.

She put the horse in a stall and busied herself with the door latch.

'Have you seen or heard from her since Saturday night either?' I asked.

'No. You're scaring me.'

'I sometimes have that effect on people.'

'I wish you would leave.'

She knew something bad was coming. She wanted me to go away before I set the bad thing loose. Then maybe it didn't really exist and it couldn't touch her life. Oh, to be twenty and still believe in innocence.

'Lisbeth,' I said.

She didn't look at me. She seemed to brace herself. I half-expected her to plug her ears with her fingers.

'Irina is dead. Her body was found this morning in a canal.'

The big cornflower eyes went glassy with tears. 'You're

37

lying! What kind of sick person are you?'

From the corner of my eye I could see one of the stable hands looking over at us, frowning. He started toward us with a pitchfork in hand.

I turned to him and told him in Spanish that everything was fine but that I had given Lisbeth some very sad news. The death of a friend.

The aggression went out of him and he expressed his apologies and went back to his business.

'I'm sorry, Lisbeth,' I said. 'It's true. And there is no good or gentle way to say it.'

The girl put her hands over her face and slid down to the ground, her back against the stall door. She drew in a shuddering breath and said, 'No,' the word weak and muffled. 'No, you're wrong.'

'I'm not. I wish I were, but I'm not.'

'Oh, my God!'

I squatted down beside her and put my hand on her shoulder. 'I'm very sorry. You two were close?'

She nodded and sobbed into her hands until she gagged.

'Can we go sit somewhere?' I asked quietly.

She nodded, pulled a dirty rag out of the cargo pocket of her shorts, wiped her face, and blew her nose. She held on to my arm as we rose. She felt as weak and shaky as an elderly person in poor health.

'What happened?' she asked, hiccuping air between syllables. 'Did she drive off the road? She's a terrible driver.'

'No,' I said, and said nothing more until we were seated on a bench at the far end of the barn.

'It's not clear yet what happened,' I said. 'There was no sign of her car.'

The girl looked at me, confused. 'I don't understand.'

'Her body was dumped there. She was probably murdered.'

I thought she might faint, she was so pale. But she got up

from the bench, ran around the corner of the barn, and retched. I waited, feeling empty, drained from telling her and, in telling her, reliving that horrible moment of discovery.

When she came back and sat down again, she put her head in her hands. She was shaking visibly.

'I can't believe this is happening!'

'Me neither,' I said.

'How can this be happening?'

I would have told her that life is cruel and unpredictable, but she had just discovered that for herself.

'Lisbeth, I need to know everything that happened Saturday night.'

'We hit some clubs on Clematis. Had some drinks, danced.'

'Any guys involved?'

'Sure. We have this contest . . . to see which one of us can get the most free drinks.'

'Did any of the men seem to think they should get something in return?'

'Ha,' she said with very little strength. 'All of them. They're guys.'

'Did Irina have any interest?'

'No. "Boys," she would say, and make a face. She didn't waste her time on boys.'

'Did any of them take that news badly?'

'All of them,' she said again. 'They're guys.'

'I mean a guy who got pissed off, maybe made a threat, made you uncomfortable.'

'No. Well . . .' She shook her head as if shooing away a thought she didn't want to have.

'Just say it. Maybe it's nothing, but maybe it isn't.'

'There's this guy we run into a lot. Irina dances with him . . . kind of leads him on. . . . He always wants her to leave with him, but she never does.'

'And Saturday night?'

'He called her a name. We were leaving. Irina laughed at him. He didn't follow us or anything.'

'What did he call her?'

'He told Irina she should go for a ride with him. She said he meant a ride *on* him and that she wasn't interested in riding a pony.'

'And he said what?'

'"You fucking Russian cunt," pardon my language. Irina just laughed and blew him a kiss.'

'What's his name?'

'Brad something. I don't know. He wasn't interested in me, I wasn't interested in him.'

'What club was this in?'

She rubbed her hands over her face and shrugged. 'Monsoon, maybe . . . or Deuce. I don't remember.'

'When you'd had the fun you could have at the clubs . . .'

'We came back to Wellington and went to Players for a while. It was Mr. Brody's birthday. There were a lot of people there. I left around one.'

'And Irina?'

'She was still there.'

'With anyone?'

'No one in particular.'

'And no one was paying special attention to her?'

The girl laughed, but her eyes were welling again. 'Everyone paid attention to Irina. Every *man*.'

Something dawned on her then, and she said, 'Wait,' and dug into another of the many pockets on her shorts, coming up with her cell phone. 'I took some pictures.'

She called the pictures up and scrolled through several, then stopped on one. 'This is that guy. Brad.'

The photo was cockeyed and the lighting wasn't great, but I could make out his face. A good-looking kid with the spoiled expression of a privileged youth.

'Can I send this to my phone?' I asked.

'Sure,' she said, and handed me the phone. 'There are a couple more.'

I scrolled through them. Irina dancing. Irina laughing with another girl. 'Who's she?'

'Rebecca something. She's a tutor for Sebastian Foster's kid.'

Sebastian Foster had been a hell of a tennis player in his twenties. The Wonder from Down Under – wild blond hair, tan, quick as a cat, with a massive serve – until his shoulder had given out. I had read in *Wellington Lifestyles* magazine that he wintered in Wellington so his daughter could for the most part skip her education in favor of riding in horse shows.

I had firsthand knowledge of that life. My mother had taken me out of school and brought me to Wellington more than one winter growing up so I could ride and show, the only activity that seemed to keep me out of trouble. I had routinely bribed my tutor to get out of doing work. Math? Why would I ever need to know that?

I clicked to another photo. Partying hearty at Players, a restaurant and club just outside the Palm Beach Polo and Golf gated community. Like most places in Wellington, Players was overrun all winter with horse people. It was the place pretty young grooms and riders liked to go to cut loose. Not surprisingly, many wealthy gentlemen went there with eyes for those pretty young things half their age.

'Who is this?' I asked.

Lisbeth looked at the photo. 'You're kidding, right? That's Barbaro. Juan Barbaro, the polo player.'

'I don't follow it,' I admitted.

'He's a ten-goal player. He's the best in the world.'

And he was gorgeous. Thick black hair, dark eyes that seemed to stare right out of the photograph with confidence and sexual energy to burn. Adonis should have looked like this guy.

'He rides for us,' Lisbeth said. 'For Star Polo.'

I had no doubt that Juan Barbaro did a lot of riding, and not all of it on horses. This guy probably had women tossing their panties onto the polo field.

Beside him in the next photo was Jim Brody with his arm around Irina, who was young enough to be his granddaughter.

And on Irina's other side was a face I hadn't seen in years, except in very bad dreams.

Time stopped. My body went numb. I stopped breathing but realized it only when black cobwebs began to encroach on my peripheral vision.

Bennett Walker. Still handsome. Dark hair, blue eyes, tan. Scion to the Walker family that owned half of South Florida.

Bennett Walker. The man I had meant to marry long ago, in a previous life, before everything about and around me changed.

Before I dropped out of college.

Before my father disowned me.

Before I became a cop.

Before I became a cynic.

Before I stopped believing in happily ever after – twenty years ago.

Before Bennett Walker asked me to give him an alibi for the night he raped and beat a woman nearly to death.

42

# 8

I was living in a condo in the Polo Club off and on that winter season, 1987. Taking a break from my second year at Duke, my father's alma mater.

I was not a good student – not because I wasn't capable but because it irritated my father, and that was important to me at the time. I had chosen Duke for that very reason, of course.

All my life I had considered Edward Estes to be a father in name only. Even in my earliest memories he was always off to the side, disconnected, present for the sake of appearance. He probably could have said the same of me and my efforts at being his daughter, but I was a child and he was not.

Children are uncanny little creatures. They read the subtext and see the complex subtleties in people. They adjust their own thinking, their actions and reactions, accordingly. Children are closer to, and more trusting of, their intuition, and none of the influences that block and distract us as adults have had a chance to cloud that clarity of instinct.

Edward Estes was not my biological father. I had been adopted as an infant by him and his wife, Helen Ralston Estes. A private and costly adoption I would be reminded of on – at least – a yearly basis, and always in a moment when it could do the maximum emotional damage.

They had been unable to have children of their own. He had been pissed off at his own lack of ability to produce a proper heir and had, through the amazing contortions of his psyche, managed to corkscrew that anger around to direct it at Helen and at me. At Helen because of her insistence to

43

adopt. At me because I was the living example of his physical shortfall.

Helen, a shallow, spoiled child of privilege, had found her life lacking the fashionable accessory all her friends were having at the time: a baby. So she found a baby broker, made a down payment, got her name on the list, and waited impatiently. The exercise would be repeated in exactly the same way, with exactly the same emotional depth, in the '90s when she had to have a money-green Birkin bag from Hermès.

Unlike the classic Birkin bag, my trendiness had come and gone with the fashions in Helen's life. The instant I discovered rebellion at age two, I was handed off to the nanny and was seldom seen in public until I reached the perfect age of cuteness: five. At five I once again became Helen's favorite doll, to dress up and take out to mother–daughter functions and other ideal photo-op activities, such as riding lessons.

To my good fortune, I was a natural talent on a horse. Not only was I cute as a button in braids with bows and a velvet-covered helmet, I could stick on a pony like a burr and was, in no time, bringing home blue ribbons.

Everybody loves a winner.

Even my father, as much as he disliked me, very much liked the accolades and attention I brought as a budding equestrian star. My talent on a horse became the bargaining chip that kept me from being shipped off to boarding school in Switzerland when I was fourteen and got caught smoking pot and drinking booze with the gardener's twenty-year-old son. The fact that my photograph would appear in many a magazine on every Palm Beach resident's reading list allowed me to blow off half a semester at Duke to show horses in Wellington in the winter of 1987.

That was the winter I fell in love with a man for the very first time in my life. I had seen no point in it before then.

In my experience and nineteen years of observation, I had only ever seen love go bad, crash, and burn. No one came out happy or unscathed. It seemed to me a much better idea to play around and have some fun and move on when the relationship started to head south, which they all invariably did.

I would have been so much better off if only I had stuck to that principle. But along came Bennett Walker. The day I fell in love with him, I knew that was the day that would change my life forever. I had no idea how true that statement would be, or how tragic.

The Walker family fortune had been made in the ship-building business during World War I. During the Depression, they bought up shipping companies and diversified into the steel business. The fortune was doubled, tripled, quadrupled through World War II and subsequent global conflicts. In the '50s they had branched into commercial development and real estate.

Most of my father's money he had made on his own as one of the country's highest-priced, most sought-after defense attorneys to the rich and infamous. He himself had become a celebrity of sorts over the years by getting guilty wealthy people off the hook for their sins, and was worth more socially because of that than because of the age of his fortune. Old-money Palm Beachers were disdainful of how he came by his wealth – behind his back, of course. When they found themselves in a jam with the law, however, he was always a best and dearest friend.

He knew, of course. And he was both amused by it and resentful because of it. Resentment was my father's forte. No one had ever carried a bigger chip on their shoulder than Edward Estes.

So imagine his glee when his rebellious daughter was seen on the arm of the most-eligible-bachelor son of the wealthiest old-money family in Palm Beach. His daughter, who was well-known for choosing wildly inappropriate boyfriends – polo players and rock musicians being my personal favorites. Outside of my riding accomplishments, falling in love with Bennett Walker was the first thing in my life I had ever done that pleased my father. It only stood to reason, I suppose, that it would be the thing that would ultimately destroy what relationship we had.

I left Star Polo in a daze and just started driving. I didn't think, didn't plan. I went on autopilot. It was a relief to be numb and empty. The bloody mess that had been the day sank into a dark corner of my mind as I drove. I didn't hear anything. My surroundings seemed unreal and distant.

My conscious mind had overloaded. Escape seemed like a good idea at the time. But my subconscious had its own agenda, and after miles of blur and strip malls, I found myself driving over the Lake Worth bridge onto the Island. Palm Beach.

Palm Beach is a world of its own, a sixteen-mile-long sandbar studded with palm trees and mansions. The southern half of the island is so narrow, there is only one road leading north. As it widens, side streets branch off and wind around, the exorbitantly expensive half to the Lake Worth side and the obscenely expensive half to the ocean side. The landscaping is so lush it is difficult from the street to get more than a glimpse of many of the grand homes, much less their grand views.

My parents' house was a pink Italianate villa behind tall iron gates. A cobblestone drive circled a fountain featuring a mermaid perched on a trio of sea horses, pouring water from an urn. More than once as a small child I had been hauled out of the fountain, naked as the day I was born, filled with the joy of freedom, God forbid.

I parked illegally across the street and just sat there. If I sat there another fourteen minutes, a squad car would come by and the uniform inside it would hassle me because I obviously didn't belong there. The right corner of my mouth quirked upward in what passed for an ironic smile.

I hadn't set foot in that house in nearly two decades. I hadn't even driven past. It felt so strange to sit there across the street, looking in the gate. Absolutely nothing about the place had changed. I could have been looking back in time. I half-expected to see myself at ten, at fifteen, at twenty-one, coming out the tall black double doors.

At twenty-one I had come out those doors one day and never returned.

One of my parents was driving a black Bentley convertible these days. It sat parked under the portico. Probably my father. My mother had always abhorred the sun and swathed herself in silk and chiffon to hide every inch of her skin, until she looked like a mummy designed by Valentino. My father was always tan and fit, played golf and tennis, and piloted his own vintage cigarette boat in races on Lake Worth.

I wondered what he would do if he came out of the house, drove his Bentley out the gate, and saw me sitting there. Would he even recognize me? The last time he had seen me I had a long, wild mane of curly black hair. My expression had been furious, and to my horror there had been tears swelling in my eyes.

A year past, in a fit of rage, I had hacked my hair off boy-short and had kept it that way. My expression now was the unchanging, carefully neutral expression the plastic surgeons had given me after nearly two years of reconstructive surgery. And I was now physically incapable of crying.

Self-absorbed narcissist that he was, I doubted he would even see me as anything other than a loiterer. He would have his cell phone out and be speed-dialing the police as he went down the street.

My mother had come to see me in the hospital after my

47

date with the asphalt under Billy Golam's 434. Not because I had called her. Not because she was my mother and had been keeping tabs on me. She had come because her housekeeper had seen my name in the *Palm Beach Post* when the incident was in the news and had asked her if I was a relative.

Helen had come to see me, but she hadn't known what to do or say when she got there. I gave her a point for trying to do the maternal thing, even though she had only a passing knowledge of the concept. I bore no resemblance to the daughter she remembered. Not physically or otherwise. I had been gone from her life almost as long as I had been in it.

She had been so uncomfortable that after fifteen minutes I pretended to fall asleep so she could leave.

I asked myself then why I had come here. Wasn't it enough to have those old memories crack through the scars that covered them? Did I have to come here in person to make the pain sharper?

Apparently I thought so.

What strange irony that Irina's death would somehow be intertwined with my past and that in wanting to help Irina I would have to face that past, something I had avoided doing my entire adult life.

I started the car and drove away. Drove home.

# 9

The day was nearly over by the time I got back to the farm. The horses, unaware and unconcerned with how my day had gone, were hungry. Cars from the SO were parked all over the place, including the one Landry had been driving. They were up in Irina's apartment doing the same thing I had done hours before them.

A deputy stopped me as I got to the barn.

'I'm sorry, ma'am. There's an investigation in progress. You can't go in.'

I looked straight in his face. 'I can and I will. I own these horses,' I lied, 'and they need to be fed. Do you want to be held responsible for the illness or death of any of these animals? Before you answer that, I should inform you that any one of them is worth more money than you'll see in five years.'

He was officially intimidated. The young ones are so easy.

'No, ma'am. But could you please wait here while I go inform the detective in charge?'

I sighed, rolled my eyes, and walked past him. He didn't stop me, but he did go into the lounge and, presumably, up the stairs to the apartment, where he would tell Landry about me. The man in charge.

As I went about feeding the horses their dinner, I tried to pretend the deputies and detectives and crime-scene investigators weren't there. If they weren't there, then I could pretend Irina wasn't dead. If they weren't there, I wouldn't have to interact with Landry.

He didn't come flying out of the lounge. That was a good sign. I went about my business, tending the individual needs of my charges. Witch hazel and alcohol on legs that tended to puff up overnight, carefully wrapped bandages — not too loose, not too tight. Lightweight sheets on all but Oliver, who thought it was hysterically funny to rip his expensive custom-made blankets to shreds. A few extra carrots for Arli, for his traumatic morning. A few extra carrots for Feliki, because she was the boss mare, and no one could get anything she didn't get too or she would throw a tantrum in her stall.

I went last into the stall of the new princess of the barn: Coco Chanel. Coco was amazingly beautiful, dark chocolate brown with a splash of white on her hind legs and a perfect blaze down her face. Ears pricked at attention, she looked at me with huge liquid eyes filled with happiness that I was coming in to visit.

I spoke to her in a quiet voice, touched her neck, scratched her withers. She arched her neck, sniffed my head, ruffled my hair with her nose, and started scratching my shoulder. Reciprocity with no strings attached, no ulterior motives.

I wrapped my arms around her neck, closed my eyes, pressed my cheek against her, and hugged her. To experience such pure innocence and trust at the end of that day felt cleansing. This sweet horse had never been mistreated, had never been anything but adored her entire life. She didn't know violence or hatred or the perversions that poisoned the minds of humans. I wished I could have said the same.

'Have you been in the apartment?'

I let go of the horse, turned, and looked at Landry. I wondered how long he had been standing there. The thought that he might have been there for a long time, watching me in an unguarded moment, irritated me.

'Yes,' I said. 'I imagine my prints are still on file with the SO. You won't need to take them again.'

'You shouldn't have gone up there,' he said without any kind of rancor. His face was drawn. His tie was yanked loose.

'You should know better than to bother telling me.' I slipped out of the stall, closed and latched the door.

'Did you take anything?'

'Of course not,' I said, as if highly offended. 'Do you think I'm an idiot? Do you think I don't know procedure?'

'I think you don't give a rat's ass about procedure. You never have. Why start now?'

'Is there something in particular you want from me?' I asked. 'Because, if not, I would like to go get out of these stinking clothes, have a shower and a drink, and go to bed. I've had as much of this day as I can stand.'

He was probably thinking the same thing. He'd been working this for ten hours without a break, I was sure. Without a meal, I was willing to bet. A steady diet of coffee, maybe a doughnut, or a candy bar, or some horrible fast-food beast on a bun that he would have eaten with one hand while he stood off to the side at the scene, continuing to direct people with the other hand. And now he would go back to the sheriff's office and start on the paperwork. He still had a long night ahead of him.

I didn't feel sorry for him. That was his job. Irina was just another DB (dead body) for him. He had known her well enough to say hello, that was all. Personal emotion would not be a factor in this for him, nor should it have been.

'What did you see up there?' he asked.

'The same things you did.'

'I mean, did it look like anything was out of place?'

'I wouldn't know. I'd never been in Irina's apartment before. She was a very private person.'

He nodded, then rubbed his hands over his face and down the back of his neck. The muscles there would be as tight and corded as ropes holding a great weight. His right

51

shoulder would have a knot in it the size of a tennis ball. He would groan like a dying man if someone started to work the kink out with a massage.

I had no interest in doing that. I just knew it was so because I'd done it many times.

'Where've you been?' he asked, the same as he would ask if we had been meeting for dinner. *How was your day . . . where'd you go . . . what did you do. . . .*

'I need to sit down.'

I walked out the side of the barn toward the riding arena. The landscaping lights had come on as the sun sank low. I sat down on an ornate park bench. Landry sat on the opposite end.

I told him about the photograph on Irina's laptop, the one from the tailgating party, and about finding Lisbeth Perkins at Star Polo and the things Lisbeth had told me about the encounter with the guy at the club on Clematis Street.

'She didn't have a last name for him?'

'No, but she has a photo of him on her phone.' I didn't tell him that I had the photos as well. I didn't want to show him, didn't want to deal with looking at that last photo again with an audience. 'She also has photos of Irina later in the evening at a birthday party at Players. Lisbeth left the party around one. Irina stayed.'

'Anybody of interest at the party?'

'A lot of wealthy men with shaky morals,' I said. 'Jim Brody, who owns Star Polo. A couple of hotshot polo players. Paul Kenner, Mr. Baseball—'

'Spitball,' he corrected me, scowling. Kenner had once hit on me, in front of him. Men.

'—A couple of Palm Beach rich boys. Bennett Walker.'

Somehow I expected Landry to have a big reaction when I said that name, as if he would instantly know all about my history with Walker. Stupid. Landry hadn't even

52

been living in South Florida at the time. And I certainly hadn't spilled my heart out to him about it. Our pillow talk had consisted of more current events.

'Bennett Walker,' he said. 'He races boats, doesn't he?'

'I don't know,' I said, even though I did. Bennett and my father had the sport in common. They could have talked boats for hours. For all I knew, they still did. 'He's into the polo scene.'

'Rich.'

'Filthy. You'll want to talk to him,' I said, dreading the thought.

He nodded. 'I'll want to talk to anyone who was at Players that night, down to busboys and valets.'

I should have told him about Bennett and the rape/assault charges back when. I should have told him I had testified at the trial.

I should have told him that I had loved Bennett Walker once. That I had loved him enough to say yes when he asked me to marry him. But I told Landry none of those things. He would find out soon enough.

Tearing all those memories out of the emotional and psychological scar tissue was going to be a terrible experience. I wanted to stall the inevitable as long as I could. I felt like Harrison Ford in the opening scene of *Raiders of the Lost Ark* when the gigantic stone is rolling after him as he tries to escape the secret temple. The huge ball that was my past and my pain was rolling toward me, and there was nothing I could do to escape it.

Landry reached over and stroked his hand over the back of my head tenderly. 'Elena,' he said softly. 'I'm sorry about this morning. About Irina. About the way I treated you when we first got to the scene. I'm not the most tactful guy when I'm angry.'

'You were cruel,' I said, looking straight at him. He looked away.

'I know. I wish I hadn't said what I did about you quitting. I didn't mean it.'

'Then why did you say it?'

He thought about his answer for a moment, weighing the truth versus something less.

'Because I wanted you to hurt . . . the way I hurt.'

I shouldn't have wanted him to touch me, but I did. If I could have gone back in time to Sunday night, knowing what was going to happen that Monday, I probably wouldn't have broken up with him. I probably would have put it off, just to give myself the luxury of turning to him. He probably expected that I still would turn to him.

I could have leaned forward and kissed him. He had moved that close. And then he would have wrapped his arms around me and held me tight. And we would have gone into my guest cottage, and we would have ended up in bed – because we always ended up in bed. And we would exhaust each other, and maybe I would be able to sleep and not dream.

Headlights turned in at the gate just then. Sean, back from his day at the beach.

'That's Sean?' Landry asked. 'You want me to tell him?'

I shook my head as I stood up. 'I'll do it.'

'I'll need to talk to him.'

'Can it wait until tomorrow?' I asked.

He looked at his watch. 'It can wait until later. I need to grab something to eat. I'll go and come back.'

'Thank you.'

He wanted to say something more but thought better of it. I walked away before he could change his mind.

The best thing to do in a weak moment: walk away.

I didn't look back.

Landry watched her walk away. He followed at a distance, until he was standing in the open doorway of the stable. Sean Avadon had pulled his black Mercedes in among the official vehicles. He got out, looking puzzled. Elena went up to him. They talked. Landry recognized the expressions, the body language. The confusion, the shock, the denial, the crushing weight of the emotion that came with realization of the terrible truth.

Sean put his arms around Elena and hugged her, and Landry felt a sharp cut of jealousy slice through him. Even knowing that Sean Avadon was gay didn't lessen it. It didn't matter that the embrace was not romantic or sexual. He envied Avadon for being allowed to touch her.

He turned away and went back upstairs to the apartment. Weiss was digging through Irina Markova's dresser drawers, checking out her lingerie.

'Where've you been?' he said, scowling at Landry, irritated.

'Why? You want me to go back out so you can have a moment of privacy to whack off with a dead girl's underwear?'

'Fuck you, Landry.'

'Fuck yourself.'

The latent-prints person didn't even bother to glance at them.

'You were with Estes,' Weiss said. 'Was she giving you a blowjob or what?'

Landry wanted to kick him. Hard. Then maybe shove him out a window. He checked the position of the windows. One overlooked the riding arena. He wondered if Weiss had been watching.

'She was giving me information, dickhead. About our vic's movements Saturday night.'

The telephone rang then, and everyone looked at it like it was a bomb about to go off. Landry went to the writing desk next to the bed and squinted at the caller ID. *Private.* No number. When the machine picked up, Irina's voice told the caller to leave a message, no cutesy girly greeting. After the beep came a whole lot of Russian. A man's voice.

Landry waited for a moment, then picked up the receiver. 'Hello?'

The Russian went silent.

'Hello?' Landry repeated. 'Who is this?'

'Who are *you*?' the voice demanded.

'Are you trying to reach Irina Markova?'

Another hesitation. 'Who wants to know?'

'This is Detective Landry, Palm Beach County Sheriff's Office. Who is this?'

'What are you doing on this telephone?'

'I'm talking to you. Are you a relative of Ms. Markova?'

'Why?'

'Are you?'

'Yes. She is my niece.'

Landry took a deep breath and let it out. 'Sir, I regret to inform you that Irina Markova is deceased.'

'What? What the fuck are you talking about?'

The confusion.

'Her body was discovered this morning in a canal outside of Wellington.'

'The fuck! No! You are lying! Who the fuck are you, sick bastard!'

The shock, the denial.

'I'm sorry, sir. The body was positively identified at the scene by an acquaintance.'

The man's breathing was shallow and fast. 'She is dead? You are telling me she is dead? Irina?'

'Yes.'

'This was car accident?'

'No, sir. She appeared to have been murdered.'

'Murdered? What? Who would do this? What kind of animal would do this?'

'We don't know. I would like to speak to you in person,' Landry said. 'You might be able to help us.'

Silence. A long silence. He mumbled something in Russian that sounded like a prayer, then, 'Oh, my God. Oh, my God. Irina.'

The crushing weight of the emotion that came with realization of the terrible truth.

'Sir?' Landry said. 'I'll need to get your name and address. I'll need to speak with you in person about the disposition of your niece's body.'

The line went dead.

Landry put the phone down and used his own phone to call the watch commander at the county jail, to get a line on a Russian interpreter. Drunks, derelicts, and criminals of all nationalities routinely passed through the jail. It was essential to have people available to translate their rights to them, tell them how to manipulate the system, and teach them all the English they needed to know: *I want a lawyer.*

Landry wanted to know what message the caller had begun to leave. He had no way of knowing whether or not the caller was in fact Irina Markova's uncle or if he was related by language only.

The Russian mob had put down roots in Miami in the '80s and, like kudzu, had spread all over the state, infiltrating every illegal and corrupted business there was. The Russians were smart and ruthless, a scary combination.

He had no reason to think Irina Markova had any connections to criminal types, but he did know she had very expensive tastes that no groom's salary could begin to pay for. Designer clothes, designer shoes, designer bags, a boxful of diamond jewelry.

'Did he give you a name?' Weiss asked.

'No.'

'Is he a relative or what?'

'Maybe. He said so.'

Landry sat down at the desk and grabbed Irina's phone to try the speed-dial numbers. The first number belonged to someone named Alexi.

He hit *dial*. The phone on the other end began to ring. No one answered. After four rings the voice mail picked up.

*'I can't take your call. Leave message.'*

'Bingo,' Landry whispered to himself. An instant winner. The voice was the same. Now he had a first name to put with it. Alexi.

The beep sounded.

'Sir, this is Detective Landry calling back. Your niece's body has been taken to the medical examiner's office at the Palm Beach County Criminal Justice Complex at 3126 Gun Club Road, West Palm Beach. An autopsy will be performed tomorrow. Her remains should be available for release by the end of the week. Please call me back at your convenience.'

He gave his cell-phone number and ended the call.

'Did you get his number?' Weiss asked.

'No.'

Landry crouched down and unplugged the phone cords.

'I'm going back to the office,' he said. He grabbed the phone and its base, wrapped the cords around it, and started for the door.

'What am I supposed to do?' Weiss said, irritated he was being shut out.

'Go home. I don't need you.'

Landry went down the spiral stairs and left the stable.

Lights were on in Elena's house but not in the main house. Sean was probably with her. They were probably having a drink. Avadon would be asking questions. Elena would give him the play-by-play. They would share their disbelief, their shock, their grief.

He knew he wasn't invited. She would be pissed as hell if he tried to join them. He hadn't known Irina more than in passing. He would have been a stranger intruding. Elena didn't want him there anyway. She had made that decision. She didn't want a relationship, didn't need him. He was surprised she had allowed him to stroke the back of her head as they sat on the park bench. A weak moment. He wished it had lasted longer.

Pushing the thought aside, he got into his car and started the engine. He had a job to do, and the night was young.

Alexi Kulak went out the back door of the bar and began to pace. Back and forth, back and forth, the same four strides over and over, like a caged animal. He couldn't hear the noise from the bar for the pounding inside his brain. He was unaware of his surroundings, except for knowing that it was night and the only light came from a bulb over the door to the bar.

Irina dead. That couldn't be. That could not have happened. He wasn't going to believe it. There had to be some kind of mistake.

He felt sick and angry and . . . and lost. Things like this did not happen to him. He was the one always in control. The world around him ran according to his rules, by his permission. It was inconceivable that some person had come into his world and done this terrible thing. It just couldn't be.

He pulled his cell phone out of his pocket with trembling hands and pressed the number for her cell phone. It didn't matter that he had already called that number twice and had been passed immediately to voice mail.

*'This is Irina. Please leave message.'*

He waited impatiently for the beep. 'Irina? Irina, answer the goddamn phone. Answer me! Answer me!'

He screamed into the phone, still pacing. Sweat ran down his forehead and into his eyes. His hair was wet with it. His heart was pounding.

'Irina? Irina!'

He called her name over and over, until finally the only sound that came out of him was a wild animal cry of pain.

Alexi Kulak was well-known for his mastery over his emotions. Most people would have said he didn't have any, but that was not true. In that moment he knew the kind of grief from which the only escape is death. In that moment he knew the kind of fury that could scorch the earth and everything on it. In that moment he knew the kind of hopelessness that crushed the spirit.

Irina was dead. He knew it now. He felt the absence of her life force. The emptiness was like an anvil pressing down on him.

His phone fell from his hand and bounced on the cracked pavement. He put his hands to his face, feeling the heat of his tears, and he dropped to his knees and slumped forward, heedless of the impeccably tailored suit he wore.

What did it matter, a suit? It meant nothing. Nothing meant anything. Irina was gone, dead, murdered, her life torn from her and crushed. Her body was cast aside like the carcass of an animal, thrown into a filthy canal.

What mattered now was that someone would have to pay for her death. He would find that person. He would find that person, and that person would suffer in every conceivable way until they begged and prayed for death.

This Alexi Kulak promised, and all knew that Alexi Kulak was a man of his word.

# II

The cell phone was encrusted with pink crystals. Very girl-ish, which surprised him. Irina had been in no other way a child. Old far beyond her years, he thought. Jaded in a way one didn't expect. An old soul, some would say.

He didn't believe in souls.

The ring tone the phone played when it was being called was classical, melancholy.

The thing had been ringing all evening. He waited for several moments after the song had played, then opened the phone. The screen told him there was voice mail. He touched the call button and listened.

There were three messages, all of them in Russian, all from the same man. The tone of the first message was casual. Tension crept into the second one. Tension and impatience. The third call was desperate, panicked.

He saved the messages, then scrolled through the menu to *settings* and to *voice message*.

'*This is Irina. Please leave message.*'

He hit the button again.

'*This is Irina. Please leave message. . . . This is Irina. Please leave message. . . . This is Irina. Please leave message. . . . This is Irina. Please leave message. . . .*'

# 12

I had the shower and the drink, but as exhausted as I was, I didn't go to bed after Sean left. What would have been the point of it? I would have slept fitfully for a couple of hours, if I slept at all. I would have been up prowling the house at two in the morning, avoiding even making an effort to go back to sleep, because I knew that nightmares were lying in wait for me.

A little wax to spike up the hair a bit. A pair of slim dark jeans, a simple black top, sexy sandals. Mascara, lip gloss, and a pair of diamond earrings. At least I looked presentable, even if I didn't feel fit for public interaction.

Landry's car turned into the drive, and he parked and stood beside it for several moments, looking my way. I watched through the barely opened plantation shutters in my bedroom. Then he turned and went to Sean's house.

I waited for a couple of minutes, then left, driving at a crawl, hoping no one would hear me leave.

Players was relatively tame on Monday nights. Everyone who had to have a job had to be at that job bright and early Tuesday morning. Hangovers were not a good idea for people who had to muck stalls and ride horses all day in the South Florida sun. Those who didn't have to have jobs were free to do as they pleased, but with a shortage of twenty-something girls looking for a good time, the club didn't hold the appeal it did on the weekend.

The entertainment for the evening was a Jimmy Buffett wannabe with a guitar, a harmonica, and a bad-looking aloha shirt (as if there is some other kind). He had a guy on keyboard who wore a captain's hat and a double-breasted blue blazer with shiny brass buttons, and a drummer who was young enough, and looked bored and embarrassed enough, to be the son of one of them.

I walked into the bar and skirted the dance floor, where a dozen people were drunk enough to have lost their inhibitions. I've always thought there should be a public-service ad showing video of middle-aged drunk people dancing. The rate of alcoholism would surely plummet, simply from the humiliation factor.

The bartender, a hunky young fellow with dark eyes and five o'clock shadow, came over as I took a seat toward the end of the bar.

'What can I get for you, ma'am?'

'For starters, you can not call me ma'am, you darling boy,' I said with a wry smile tucking up the right corner of my mouth. 'How do you ever expect to have a mad hot affair with an older woman if you treat them like your old aunt Biddie?'

He grinned. Excellent orthodontia. 'What was I thinking?'

'I can't imagine. Next, you can bring me Ketel One vodka with tonic and a big squeeze of lemon.'

'You got it.'

He turned away to see to it. Someone had abandoned a pack of cigarettes on the bar. I helped myself to one, feeling vaguely guilty, not that I had stolen it but that I was smoking at all. Filthy habit. When he came back with the drink, I asked him his name.

'Kayne Jackson.'

'Kayne Jackson. My God, you're a soap star waiting to happen,' I said. 'Kayne Jackson, I'm Elena Estes.' I took a sip of the drink, savored it, and sighed. 'It's a wonderful pleasure to meet you. Were you working here Saturday night?'

'Yeah, why?'

I had downloaded and printed the photos from Lisbeth

63

Perkins's cell phone. I showed him the one of Irina sitting between Jim Brody and Bennett Walker. 'Did you see this girl here?'

'Yeah. That's Irina. She's a regular with that crowd. Hot babe, but she wouldn't look at me twice.'

'Do you think she had a problem with her eyesight?'

'I think I don't have a big enough wallet.'

'Ahhh . . . One of those. Looking to snag herself a rich husband?'

He shrugged.

'Did you happen to see when she left?'

'No. I couldn't say. It was Jim Brody's birthday. It was a zoo in here. Why?' He looked a little suspicious. 'Are you a cop or something?'

I took another sip of the drink, another drag on the cigarette. 'Or something . . . Did she seem to be having a problem with anyone?'

'No. She was having a good time,' he said, then checked himself. 'She and Lisbeth Perkins got into it about something out in the hall. Lisbeth looked pissed and left. Must have been around one.'

'With anyone?'

'Alone.'

The band had decided to give it a rest. More people came to the bar. Kayne Jackson excused himself and went to serve people who wouldn't make him work so hard for his tip.

'Are you enjoying my cigarette?'

The voice was smooth and warm like a fine brandy, almost seductive, a little amused, accented. Spanish.

I looked at him from the corner of my eye as I exhaled a stream of smoke. 'Why, yes, I am, thank you. Would you like one?' I said, offering the pack to him.

His dark eyes sparkled. 'Thank you. You are too generous, señorita.'

'Señorita. You could give Junior here a lesson or two. He called me ma'am.'

He looked shocked and disapproving. 'No, no. This is unacceptable.'

'That's what I said.'

He smiled the kind of smile that should require some kind of permit to use, because of the impact it could have on unsuspecting women. 'I haven't met you.'

I offered my hand. 'Elena Estes.'

He took it gently, turned it over, and brushed his lips across my knuckles. His eyes never left mine. 'Juan Barbaro.'

Barbaro. The great man. Mr. Ten-Goal Polo Star. I didn't react, just to see how he would take it. He seemed not to care. The raw sexual magnetism that was his aura didn't diminish in the least.

'Estes,' he said. 'I feel I know that name for some reason.'

I shrugged. 'Well, you don't know me.'

'I do now.'

Eye contact. Direct, consistent, very effective. His eyes were large and dark, with luxurious black eyelashes. Many a Palm Beach lady paid six hundred dollars a pop every month to have an aesthetician glue on lashes like that – one hair at a time. He was tanned, with unruly black hair that fell nearly to his shoulders.

'What brings a beautiful woman here alone on such a boring evening?'

I looked down at the photos I had brought with me, losing the will to play anymore. 'I'm looking to make sense of something senseless,' I said.

I held up a photograph to show him, as if it were a tarot card.

Barbaro's broad shoulders sagged a little, and he looked sad as he reached out and took the picture from me. 'Irina.'

'You knew her.'

'Yes, of course.'

65

'She was found dead today.'

'I know. Our groom Lisbeth told me. They were very good friends. Poor Beth is devastated. It's hard to believe something so violent, so terrible, could happen to a person we know. Irina . . . so full of life and fire, so strong in her character. . . .'

He shook his head, closed his eyes, sighed.

'You knew her well?' I asked.

'Not well. Casually. At a party, to say hello, to exchange small talk. And you?'

'We worked together,' I said. 'I found her.'

*'Madre de Dios,'* he whispered. 'I'm very sorry for that.'

'Me too.'

The bartender brought him a drink without being asked, and he took a long sip of it.

'This was the last public place anyone saw her,' I said. 'Do you remember seeing her that night?'

'It was the birthday party of my *patrón,* Mr. Brody. Everyone was having a very good time. The kind of good time that makes memories vague,' he admitted. 'But I know that Irina was here. We spoke.'

'About what?'

'Party talk.' He gave me a long, curious look. 'For someone who works in the stables, you sound very much like a policewoman.'

'I watch too much television.'

'Lisbeth said Irina was murdered,' he said. 'Is that true?'

'That's what the detectives think,' I said.

'Murder. These things . . . They should not happen in Wellington.'

Wellington, Palm Beach, the Hamptons – the little Camelots of the East Coast wealthy. Where every day and evening should be filled with entertainment and pleasantry and beauty. Never anything so ugly as murder. Violent crime was a stain on the fabric of polite society, like red wine on white linen.

66

'A girl was murdered at the show grounds last year,' I said. 'Smothered facedown in a horse stall during an attempted sexual assault.'

'Really? I don't remember hearing of it, but then, my world is elsewhere. What goes on off the polo fields, I do not know. The crimes may be related, you think?'

'No. They're not,' I said.

'You knew that girl also?'

'Yes, actually. I did.' Jill Marone. A nasty pig-eyed girl. Liar, petty thief, shoplifter. A groom also.

Barbaro arched a thick brow. 'That is a very strange coincidence.'

I forced a half smile, though my mind had taken a sudden turn off the track. 'You may want to rethink becoming acquainted with me.'

'I don't think so, Miss Estes,' he said, taking gentle hold of my left hand. He raised it for closer examination of my naked ring finger.

The band was warming up again. The respite was over. Barbaro glanced at them, frowning.

'Come with me,' he said, moving away from his bar stool. My hand was still in his.

'That wouldn't be very wise of me,' I said. 'Considering there is a killer running loose.'

'I'm not taking you anywhere there won't be witnesses.'

He led me out into the hall and down the stairs to the restaurant, where at ten-thirty there were still several tables of diners. Everyone recognized Barbaro. I had no doubt that one of the many framed caricatures of famed polo stars on the walls was of him.

We went out onto the terrace. He whispered something to a waiter, and the waiter scurried away.

'This is better, yes?' he said, holding a chair for me. 'All that noise seems suddenly very inappropriate.'

'Yes. It's surreal: watching other people having a good

time. My tragedy hasn't touched their lives.'

'No,' he said. 'They cannot help their ignorance. A happy place isn't meant for mourners.'

The waiter returned with a bottle of Spanish red and two glasses.

'Not Argentine?' I asked.

'No. And neither am I. I am a Spaniard through and through.'

'That's interesting in a sport dominated by South Americans.'

He smiled. 'The Argentines do not find it so interesting. Pompous bastards.'

'As I'm sure they would say of all Spaniards.'

He grinned. 'I have no doubt.'

I sipped the wine. Very good. Warm, smoky, smooth, with a long, soft finish. 'Where in Spain? The south? Andalusia?'

'The north. Pedraza. Castilla.'

'Beautiful country. Not exactly a hotbed of polo.'

'You know España?'

'I was sent there for a semester when I was sixteen and had scandalized my family in some way or another. Somehow it never occurred to my parents I could be just as scandalous abroad.'

'And were you?'

I shrugged. 'If you count dancing naked with a diplomat's son in the fountain on the Plaza de Cánovas del Castillo.'

Barbaro laughed. 'I'm sure you were the toast of Madrid!'

'My misspent youth.'

'You are so different now?'

I looked out across a moonlit polo field, thinking that all that seemed more than two lifetimes ago, and I could barely remember even a ghost of how it felt to be that devotedly, joyfully rebellious.

'Forgive me,' he said quietly, reaching across the table to rest his hand on mine. 'This is not the night. . . .'

68

'I was just thinking Irina was not so different from me when I was her age. Headstrong, opinionated—'

'Passionate, determined,' he said. He raised a brow. 'I suspect she was not so different from how you are now.'

'That's true.'

'This is why you came here tonight. No matter you had the shock of finding her, no matter the weight of grief. You are here to find answers, to fight for her somehow. Yes?'

'Yes.' I took another sip of the wine. 'Saturday night – did you happen to notice a tall man, mid-fifties, dark hair, silver temples? Belgian.'

Barbaro shook his head. 'No. Does this man have a name?'

'I'm sure he has several. I doubt he would be so stupid as to use the one people would recognize: Tomas Van Zandt.'

'I've never heard of him. Should I?'

'No. He's someone Irina had a grudge against.'

The horse dealer she had tried to bludgeon with a horseshoe in Sean's barn a year past. Van Zandt, who had been a suspect in the murder of the girl at the show grounds, had simply vanished two days after the killing. Neither Van Zandt nor the rental car he had been driving was ever seen again. I had always suspected he'd ditched the car and gotten himself out of the country on a cargo plane with a load of horses – a shockingly easy thing to do, despite the media hype on Homeland Security.

What if he had come back? Irina knew too much about him. She had accused him of keeping a girl she knew as his sex slave in a camper trailer in Belgium. To Van Zandt's twisted way of thinking, the worst part of her charges had been the potential damage to his reputation.

Maybe he had decided to reinvent himself. He would never be able to show his face in Wellington without getting arrested, but if he was clever and very careful, and arrogant enough to believe he could pull it off, he might be able to weasel his way into a smaller market. The Midwest, the Northwest. He could still cheat people and swindle himself a small fortune among those not quite wealthy enough or connected enough to winter in Florida. But he would always know Irina was out there, lying in wait to ruin him. Grooms change jobs, move around, network. . . .

'Did you notice when she left the party?' I asked. 'Was she with anyone?'

'I couldn't say. I remember her dancing. I remember her dancing with Jim Brody. He danced with all the young girls.'

'Party animal. Does Mr. Brody have a Mrs. Brody?'

'Several. All in the past tense.'

'He likes the young ladies?'

Barbaro shrugged. Very European. 'He is a man.'

'How much did he like Irina?'

He frowned at me. 'You can't possibly think he would do such a thing.'

'Why can't I?'

'Señor Brody is a very powerful, wealthy man. He can have anything he wants.'

'You think a wealthy man won't commit a violent crime?'

His dark brows knit together in what seemed more like confusion or frustration than irritation. 'He doesn't need to force himself on women, or kill women.'

'What happened to Irina wasn't about need, Mr. Barbaro,' I said. 'What happened to Irina was about power and control. What animal knows more about power and control than a wealthy man?'

Barbaro shook his head and held up his hands to ward off my theory. 'No, no, no . . . Only a psycho does these kinds of things: kills a young woman, throws her body away like garbage.'

I put an elbow on the table and propped up my chin in

my hand. I watched his face, bemused by his discomfort at the idea that murderers might be hiding among the upper crust, even though I knew many people labored under the same misconception. I had never understood it, and I never would.

'What do you think a killer looks like, Mr. Barbaro?' I asked. 'Do you think a killer has matted hair and bloodshot eyes? Beard stubble? Scars? Tattoos? Do you think every killer, every rapist looks like a monster? I can assure you, that isn't the case. Dangerous creatures can be very beautiful.'

'Yes,' he said quietly. 'This is true. They can be. Tell me, Elena, are you speaking from experience? I hate to think of that.'

'That, my new friend, is a tale for another time. As fascinating as I'm sure you are, I've had a very long day.'

'You have.' He rose with me. 'Allow me to walk you out. As you said, there is a killer running loose in our town.'

'How do I know you aren't the one?'

'I am guilty of many things, Elena,' he said. 'But not that. I have an alibi.'

'Do you?'

'Yes,' he said as we walked back through the restaurant. He rested a hand against the small of my back in a gesture that was without thought or guile. 'I admit to having had too much to drink that night. I went to the home of a friend here in the Polo Club to sleep my sins away.'

'And she'll vouch for you, I'm sure,' I said as we climbed the stairs.

'*He* will vouch for me. Neither of us was sober enough to entertain ladies. I spent the night on his pool table, which I'm sure seemed like a good idea at the time. Not so much the following morning.'

'And this friend has a name?'

'Of course,' he said as we came up to the entry hall.

A Hollywood director couldn't have timed the moment

better. The front door opened, and Barbaro laughed and said, 'Speak of the devil!'

The devil indeed.

My body went cold and stiff as I stared at the face of Juan Barbaro's alibi:

Bennett Walker.

# 13

The autopsy suite in the Palm Beach County Medical Examiner's building was never a place Landry enjoyed visiting. It was a necessary part of his job. Mandatory, to his way of thinking, though he could have passed this part off on Weiss.

Weiss was like the weird kid in science lab who wanted to dissect everybody's frog – just because. But from the moment he was given the lead on a case, Landry became the victim's advocate. It was his job to get justice for that person. And in order to do that, he needed to know, to see with his own eyes, everything he possibly could about the victim – how she had lived, and how she had died.

He stood on the side of the table opposite the ME, in mask, cap, gown, gloves, and booties. All one could see of anyone in the room were their eyes.

The ME was Mercedes Gitan, acting chief medical examiner, to be precise. The defection of her predecessor to a cushy teaching job at the University of Miami had opened the spot for Gitan. If the powers that ran the county had any sense, they would give her the position permanently.

'See here?' she asked, pointing into the gaping wound where the gator had taken a large chunk of tissue out of Irina Markova's lower torso. 'It's a section of the head of the femur. The gator snapped it like a chicken bone. The power in an alligator's jaws is unbelievable: between fifteen hundred and two thousand pounds of pressure. Equal to the pressure of the weight of a small pickup truck.'

'I'd rather be under the truck,' Landry said.

'Amen to that. I did the autopsies on two of those recent alligator-attack victims. That's not a good way to go. I can't even imagine the terror those people felt. I suppose the good news here is that our victim was already well past feeling anything when she was attacked – by the second animal, that is,' Gitan added grimly.

She heaved a sigh and shook her head as she looked down at Irina Markova's face, the ravaged eyes and lips. 'These are the tough ones. I can slice-and-dice drug dealers and gangbangers all day long. They know what they're in for, doing what they do. This one is a pure victim. She didn't go out looking to cross paths with a killer.'

'I knew her a little bit,' Landry said. 'Enough to say hello. She was an acquaintance of a friend.'

'I'm sorry. You don't have to stay for this, James. I can call you later.'

'No. This is part of it. She's my vic. You know how I am.'

'Superstitious?'

He shrugged, still staring at the body. 'I need to see what happened to them with my own two eyes. I feel like . . . like I owe it to them to be here, at least for this part, you know? Crazy, huh?'

'Not so. Shows that you're still human. I always figure that the time I start just counting the bodies, not thinking of them as human beings, is the time I need to consider another career. I mean, I don't get emotionally involved. We can't do that and stay sane. But I do them the courtesy of knowing their names.'

'Thanks for coming in for this one, Merci,' Landry said.

He had called her personally to make the request. He'd known her for six or seven years, had watched her work her way up the ladder. She was very good and very thorough. This wasn't going to be an easy case. Gitan would garner every bit of information, no matter how insignificant it might seem. She wouldn't miss a thing.

'Oh, who needs to have a life?' she said. 'Besides, the mayor of Wellington, the mayor of West Palm, the mayor of

Palm Beach, the sheriff, the state's attorney, and half a dozen other big shots called me after you did.'

Landry gave a humorless laugh. 'Nobody cares when some Loxahatchee redneck gets his brains blown out. A beautiful young woman strangled and dumped – that's bad for tourism. Can't have a killer running around during season.'

Gitan glanced at her watch and huffed a sigh. 'Where the hell is Cecil? WHERE THE HELL IS CECIL!!'

'Just waiting for you to scream, boss.'

Gitan's assistant, a seven-foot-tall black transvestite, came into the suite. Even on the stool, Gitan had to crane her neck to look up at him.

The process began with the external examination of the body. Gitan spoke quietly into her microphone, identifying the victim, stating her age, height, weight, sex, color of hair. She couldn't state the color of her eyes, because there was nothing left of them.

Landry stared at the girl's hand, at her fingernails, still flawlessly painted a vibrant red despite her time in the water. A couple of them were broken. Hopefully she had sunk them into her killer. Hopefully Gitan would discover something to suggest that – skin cells, a microscopic bit of blood, enough of something for a DNA profile.

The body had been in the water for some time, but unless the fish had taken up giving manicures, maybe there was a chance that something lodged well under the nails could still be there.

The analysis of that kind of evidence took time. Serology, toxicology, DNA profiles. Real life isn't like television. Even with a rush put on the potential evidence, it would take days, even weeks to get results back. And even if they got a DNA profile on the perp, it would be helpful immediately only if the guy had offended before and was in the national data bank.

Gitan examined every inch of the girl's body. Every mark, every cut, every bruise was measured and photographed. Landry was hoping for bite marks. No defense attorney could argue away bite marks. They were as good as fingerprints.

'What do you think here? Bite marks?' he asked, pointing to several dark semicircular marks around the areola on the left breast. He had put his reading glasses on and bent down close to squint at them.

'Could be,' Gitan said. 'The shape is right, but I'm not seeing clear individual tooth marks. Maybe he bit her through something like sheets or a light blanket, to obscure the marks. Maybe he's smart.'

'Maybe he's done this before,' Landry said.

That was a very bad thought. They wouldn't be talking about some random horny bastard who didn't want to take no for an answer. The crime wouldn't be about a situation that had gotten out of hand. It would be about something done methodically, which required organized thought and enough cool in the heat of the moment to take precautions against self-incrimination.

Gitan moved on to the ligature marks around the girl's throat.

'What do you think?' Landry asked. 'A rope? A wire?'

'First,' Gitan said, 'we have thumbprints on either side of the larynx. See here? So we know her killer choked her manually at some point in the attack. But then we have the ligature marks as well. Not a wire. There's too much abrasion. It had to be something with texture. If it was a rope, it was quite thin. I'm not seeing any natural rope fibers, but she's been in the water. Fiber evidence is a lot to hope for. Or the rope could have been synthetic. Nylon cord, maybe.'

Looking through a lighted magnifying glass, she studied and studied the deep grooves cut into the girl's neck. The skin had broken in places.

'Huh,' she said, as she took a tweezer and very carefully plucked a piece of something out of the wound.

'What is it?'

'Dried coagulated blood. Look.'

Landry looked at the scab through the magnifying glass. Stuck in it were several fibers so small they were all but invisible to the naked eye. Short, superfine, dark. Almost like short hairs.

'The lab rats will have an answer when they can get it under a microscope,' Gitan said.

'I'm surprised you found anything,' Landry said.

'Sometimes we get lucky. Her killer didn't dump her right away. The wounds had time to dry and harden.'

When Gitan was satisfied she had examined every inch of the front of the body, Landry helped Cecil turn the girl over. Gitan moved Irina Markova's hair out of her way to examine the marks on the back of her neck. There weren't any.

'Okay,' Gitan said. 'Either there was something behind her and between her and the killer, or maybe the killer was on top of her, holding her down with the ligature.'

'In my experience, the kind of guy who does this kind of thing wants to watch the victim's face as he chokes her,' Landry said. 'The fear gets them off. Watching the lights go out in the eyes is a big power trip.'

'Looks to me like he strangled her to the point of unconsciousness, then let her regain consciousness, only to "kill" her all over again.'

'Sick fuck,' Landry muttered.

'He let her lie somewhere for quite a while before he dumped her in that canal,' Gitan pointed out.

With no heartbeat to move it through the circulatory system, the girl's blood had pooled down her back and the backs of her legs and arms in a huge purple stain. The body had remained on its back long enough that the blood had clotted and set, which took hours. No matter what had been done with the body after that, the lividity wouldn't move or change.

'Maybe he had to wait to dump her,' Landry said. 'Or maybe he's one of those freaks that likes to play with them after they're dead.'

Landry stayed until Gitan was ready to make the incision across the top of the girl's head. The scalp would be pulled back and the interior examined for evidence of trauma; the cranium would be checked for fractures. He didn't need to hang around for that. He didn't need to wait for Gitan to make the primary Y incision across the chest and down the torso. He didn't need to watch as Irina Markova's sternum was split in two and her chest was cracked open like a clamshell. He didn't need to watch as her organs were lifted out of her body and weighed.

He had seen it all before. Everyone had a liver. Everyone had intestines. Everyone had a brain. None of that was of interest to him. The organs were examined and weighed, and notes were written down, because that was procedure. But no internal disease or defect had killed Irina Markova.

Someone else's disease had killed Irina – whatever malignancy it was that took up residence in the minds of murderers.

With that thought foremost, he went across the parking lots to the sheriff's offices and Robbery/Homicide.

'The interpreter is here,' Weiss said.

They went into the interview room Weiss had exited. The older man standing at the end of the table wore no readable expression. His long face might have been carved from stone. Dressed in black, he was tall and narrow and wore a clipped-close white mustache and goatee that had been sculpted to a point just below his chin.

His left eye was piercing blue, the right milky white,

ruined but left bare for all the world to see. No patch, no glasses to hide behind. The old priest put it out there like he was proud of it, like it was an ugly badge of honor. A scar split the eyebrow above it.

Weiss introduced him. 'Father Chernoff, this is Detective Landry, who is also working on this investigation.'

Landry let the remark slide. He didn't need to whip his cock out and put it on the table in front of a holy man just to put Weiss in his place.

He held out his hand to the priest, who had quite a grip on him for a guy who had to be in his seventies. His fingers were gnarled and twisted like the branches of an ancient windblown tree.

'Father Chernoff. Thank you for coming in on such short notice. Unfortunately, that's the only kind of notice we get at the start of a murder investigation.'

The old priest looked down his nose at him as they took their seats. Landry flashed back on Catholic school, where he had spent much time on his knees, saying Hail Marys for one sinful infraction of school rules or another while Father Arnaud glared at him.

'This is a Russian girl who died.' His accent was heavy, but his English was crisp.

'Yes, sir. Irina Markova. She worked on a horse farm outside Wellington. Do you know of any Markovas in the area? If she has family here, we'd like to contact them.'

The priest ignored the question.

'This one,' he said, tilting his head in the direction of Weiss, 'played for me the tape from the answering machine.'

'Yes. Are you able to translate for us?'

Again, the priest ignored the question, as if Landry's agenda held absolutely no interest for him. 'This girl, she was a criminal?'

'Not to my knowledge. Why? What does the man on the tape say?'

79

'His name is Alexi, yes? This one told me.' Again he tipped his head at Weiss without bothering to even look at him.

'We believe so, yes. Why did you ask if the girl was a criminal?'

'Play the tape again, please.'

Weiss touched the button on the machine, and the Russian voice spewed forth in staccato bursts.

'He says, "Why the hell have you not called me? Are you too fucking good for me now with your fancy, soft American men? Don't forget who you are, Irina. Don't forget who owns you. I have a job for you to do. It will pay well, greedy girl."'

'Do you recognize the voice?' Landry asked.

'There are many Russian men called Alexi,' the priest said.

'Do you have any idea which one this guy might be?'

The priest looked around the room as if suspicious one or more of these men named Alexi might be hiding in a corner, listening in.

'Are you familiar with Russian organized crime, Detective Landry?'

'I know about it.'

'Then I don't need to tell you these are very ruthless and violent men. They are a disgrace to our community. Not all Russians are criminals.'

'But you asked me if I thought Irina Markova might be.'

'There is a man, a very dangerous man. His name is Alexi Kulak. He is a vicious wolf. This perhaps is his voice.'

'Do you know him?' Weiss asked. 'Do you know where we can find him?'

'I know of him. He is the kind of man who believes he "owns" people and can do with them what he will.'

The bitterness in the old man's voice seemed personal.

'Did he do that to your eye?' Landry asked.

The priest sniffed. 'No. KGB did this to me when I was a young man. They burned my eye because I would not be a witness for them. I watched a man steal two loaves of bread to feed his family. It was just after the war. People were starving.

'In my Russia we feared only KGB. There were no criminals. Now there are many criminals and no KGB. It is not a better place.'

'Do you know someone who may be able to help us find Alexi Kulak?' Landry asked.

'I know someone,' the priest said. 'But he will not speak with you.'

'If he's afraid, we can speak over the phone,' Weiss said. 'All we're trying to do at this point is locate this Alexi person.'

The old priest got up from his chair. He stood ramrod straight, a formidable figure in his black cassock and priest's collar.

'He will not speak with you,' he said again, 'because Alexi Kulak cut out his tongue.'

# 14

In my imagination I had always visualized that I would be prepared for this moment, that I would have the upper hand when this circumstance arose, that I would know exactly what to say. I pictured myself as being strong and in control, unaffected by the sight of him, and looking like a million damn dollars. And Bennett Walker would be the one taken by surprise, rattled and shaken, unable to speak. But that wasn't what happened.

He came through the door with a sense of purpose, his attention on his friend and alibi, Juan Barbaro. Time and lifestyle had chiseled some lines into his face but in a way women would find attractive. He still had all his hair – dark, wavy, falling in his eyes. He still had the body of an athlete – tall, broad-shouldered, trim hips. He was impeccably dressed – white slacks, black jacket, black-striped shirt opened at the throat. The dashing social scion, disheveled just enough to be sexy.

He glanced at me with not one shred of recognition in his eyes.

I was a very different person from the girl he had known. Gone was the wild mane of black hair, the ready-for-trouble smile, the glint of excitement in my eyes. I had been vibrant then, flush with first love, innocent – if not in fact, in spirit.

Twenty years is a long time. A whole lot of life had gone on since I had last seen him. Still, a part of me was offended he didn't know me on sight, that he hadn't stopped dead in his tracks, gone pale, started to stammer. Had I been so unimportant to him that he had never imagined this moment? Out of sight, out of mind. A bad memory best left in the past.

'Juan, my man,' he said, grabbing Barbaro's hand and pumping it like a politician. 'Could I have a moment—'

'Where are your manners, friend?' Barbaro asked. 'I have a lovely lady on my arm, if you haven't noticed. Why would I leave her for an instant to be with the likes of you?'

'I'm sorry,' Walker said at me, not to me. 'But I—'

Barbaro ignored him. 'Elena, this is my very rude friend, Bennett Walker. Bennett, my lovely companion for the evening, Elena Estes.'

He saw me then. He looked at me for the first time and saw me. There was the stunned, guarded look I had been wishing for.

'I've never known you to be at a loss for words, Bennett,' I said, as if I were calm.

'Elena.'

He wanted the floor to open and swallow me. He wanted to turn and go back out the door. Do-over, without the woman who had tried to put him in prison.

'You know each other?' Barbaro said. 'Why would I be surprised? Is there a beautiful woman within fifty kilometers you don't know, my friend?'

'Oh, I knew Bennett back when,' I said, enjoying the apprehension in Bennett's eyes. 'Or so I thought.'

'Elena,' he said again. 'It's been a long time. How are you?'

'Is that the best you can do?'

'Yes, at the moment.'

'To think you used to be so quick on your feet.' I glanced at Barbaro from the corner of my eye. 'Ben used to be able to talk his way out of anything. Isn't that right, Ben?'

He said nothing.

'I'm upset, to answer your question,' I told him. 'A friend of mine was found murdered this morning. Imagine my surprise to discover you were seen with her the night she went missing.'

'I don't know anything about that,' he said. He was pissed now. I could tell by the way he tilted his head, set his jaw, avoided looking at me.

'Well, some things never change,' I remarked.

'If you could excuse us for a moment, Elena, I need to have a word with my friend.'

He put a hand on Barbaro's shoulder, ready to draw him aside.

'Getting your stories straight?' I asked sweetly. Stupid of me, but there it was. Sometimes I can't help myself.

Barbaro seemed bemused but content to watch the fireworks, his gaze bouncing back and forth between us as if he were watching a tennis match.

Walker took a moment to compose himself, breathing in, breathing out. He was very aware of the two couples that had just come upstairs from the restaurant and stood talking not ten feet away.

'I don't need a story,' he said quietly, stepping a little closer. I didn't retreat. I wouldn't. I looked him in the eyes, knowing that would make him uncomfortable.

'You don't think so? An unconscious alibi witness?' I shook my head. 'Not good, Bennett. Although at least he can't dispute your version of events.'

'Elena, I understand that you're upset,' he said. 'But I didn't have anything to do with that girl's death, and I resent you implying otherwise, especially considering other people can hear you.'

I actually laughed. 'Oh, my, what would the neighbors think? Can't have me tarnishing your sterling reputation. You are just un-fucking-believable,' I said, lowering my voice.

'Twenty years and you still hate me.'

'There is no statute of limitations for what you did, Bennett. Not with me.'

'Despite what you choose to believe, I was exonerated.'

'What an interesting reinvention of history.'

'I'm not having this conversation with you, Elena. Not here, not now.'

'Well, when you find you have room on your dance card, do pencil me in. There's just nothing like reliving old times,' I said sarcastically.

I slid my gaze away from him to Barbaro. 'Now, if you gentlemen will excuse me. It's been a very bad, very long day. I'll see myself out.'

I walked away and out the door, past the valet stand. I had parked in the lower lot. A Glock 9mm lived in a secret panel in the driver's door of my car. I couldn't take the risk of the gun falling into the hands of a minimum-wage sixteen-year-old bored with waiting on rich people.

'Elena!'

Barbaro. He jogged to catch up with me. But when he did, he didn't seem to know what to say. He had the expression of someone who had come in on the middle of a conversation.

'I'm afraid I don't understand what just happened.'

'I'm sure your good friend will fill you in,' I said. 'A word to the wise, though: Don't invest too heavily in giving him an alibi. If I find out he had something to do with Irina's murder, I'll make very certain that he pays for it, and I won't care who gets in my way.'

'That's crazy! Bennett is a good friend.'

'How long have you known him?'

'Several years. He would never have anything to do with harming a woman.'

'Really? Why not? Because he's handsome? Because he's charming? Because he's rich?' I asked. 'For such a worldly man, Mr. Barbaro, you are terribly naive. When you go back in there and sit down to have a drink with your pal, ask him if the name Maria Nevin means anything to him.

'And whatever he tells you, know this: Bennett Walker is a liar and a rapist. I know, because I was his alibi once too.'

He didn't know what to say to that and wisely chose to say nothing at all.

I turned to open my car door. Barbaro put a hand on my shoulder.

'Elena, please don't leave angry.'

He was standing too close. I didn't turn to face him.

'I'm not angry with you.'

'You are angry with the world, I think.'

'Yes,' I whispered, feeling very beaten by the day. Physically beaten. Emotionally spent. His hand moved from my shoulder to touch the back of my head.

'Please don't try to comfort me,' I said. 'I really don't think I can take it right now.'

'You are always the strong one?'

'I don't have a lot of choice in the matter. If you'll excuse me now, I really have to go.'

He moved a step to the side so I could open the car door.

'May I call you?' he asked.

I laughed without humor. 'I can't imagine why you would want to. I haven't been the most pleasant company.'

'The death of a friend does not create pleasant circumstances. Still . . . This does not change the fact that you are a beautiful, complex, interesting woman, and I would like the chance to get to know you better.'

'Hmmm . . . You're a brave soul,' I said, looking at him. In the film-noir black-and-white light of the parking lot, he was starkly beautiful, and I could feel the sexual energy that rolled off him in waves.

'Fortune favors the brave,' he said, and he leaned forward and kissed me gently, briefly. Just long enough to make me think I might want more.

'You're naughty!'

The voice came from the far side of my car. A person of

indeterminate gender stood in back of the car parked next to mine, staring at us. A woman, I thought from the voice. But there were no other indicators. She was covered in what looked to be a black unitard that exposed only the features of her face, features painted on like a character from Cirque du Soleil. On top of her head was a conical black hat with a pom-pom at the end.

'You're very naughty!' she said. 'Like the others. Very naughty!'

Barbaro took a couple of menacing steps in her direction. 'Get away from here, Freak! Go! Go before I call the police and they arrest your crazy ass!'

The Freak curtsied and ran away awkwardly on high platform shoes. She crawled through the pipe gate that led onto the Palm Beach Polo development and was gone.

I turned to Barbaro. 'What the hell was that?'

'The Freak,' he said. 'Have you never seen the Freak?'

'No. I don't get off the farm much.'

'She hangs around town. I've seen her here before. She's crazy.'

'I got that.'

'Never mind her,' he said. 'Go home and try to get some rest.'

He reached up and touched the left side of my face, gently, I'm sure, though I couldn't really feel it.

I slid behind the wheel of the BMW and told him my phone number, and I drove away wondering what exactly I had just let myself in for.

I thought of Barbaro's kiss and felt guilty. I thought of Landry and the moment we had shared outside the barn, how I had wanted to turn to him but hadn't. And I felt guiltier. Not that I needed to. I had ended my relationship with Landry. He wanted something from me I couldn't give, wouldn't give. I'd done him a favor, whether he wanted to see it that way or not.

Maybe a fling with a hot polo star was a way to drive that point home.

*Don't read too much into it, Elena,* I told myself. Inasmuch as I planned to use my new connection to Juan Barbaro to dig into this case, for all I knew he was planning to do the same thing. He had been there the night Irina went missing, as had Bennett Walker, and Barbaro's *patrón,* birthday boy Jim Brody. Perhaps he planned on being the distraction that would take my attention away from his wealthy friends.

I had no doubt that Juan Barbaro could have his pick of wealthy women and gorgeous girls in Wellington. Why pick me?

The lights were out in Sean's house. I was glad. As much as I loved Sean, I didn't want to interact with one more person.

I walked into the cottage and didn't even bother to turn on a light. The moon was waxing toward fullness, giving off enough illumination for me to walk down the hall to my bedroom. I went into the bathroom, turned on the light, and started the shower running. The acrid smell of tension and stale cigarettes clung to me like a film.

I bent over the sink to brush my teeth. When I finished and looked up, I wasn't alone.

A man stood in the doorway behind me. For a stunned second, I just stared at him in the mirror, then I spun around to face him. He was disheveled but wearing a suit, and the whites of his eyes were red.

'You are Elena Estes.' His voice was accented. Russian.

'Who the fuck are you?' I demanded.

'My name is Kulak. Alexi Kulak.'

# 15

Magda's was a shitty bar in a shitty industrial part of West Palm, a dingy clapboard building that looked as if it should have been condemned ten years before. Parking was in the back, a cracked concrete lot studded with weeds. A chain-link fence crowned with razor wire locked Magda's patrons out of an auto salvage yard.

This would probably be an exercise in futility, Landry thought as he got out of the car. The old priest had named this bar as a possible spot to find Kulak. But the odds of anyone here talking to him were long. The Russian community was close-knit and tight-lipped. But he had to start somewhere.

He and Weiss had agreed to call it a day and start fresh in the morning. Landry glanced at his watch: 12:14 a.m. Morning. It would be hard enough to get these people to talk to one cop, let alone two. Particularly if one of the two was Weiss. Alexi Kulak was potentially too important a lead to screw up.

Kulak had a record of arrests but no convictions. He had been brought up on charges of assault and attempted murder, but nothing ever stuck. Witnesses developed faulty memories. Victims chose to let bygones be bygones. This was a man no one wanted to mess with.

Landry knew a guy who worked the organized-crime task force, but he hadn't called him. He might have gleaned a scrap or two of information on Kulak, but the OC detectives were notoriously paranoid and selfish. They sat on bad guys for months, for years, trying to piece together a case that could stand up. The last thing they wanted was some

Homicide dick walking into the middle of something and screwing up their work.

He had learned the basics about Kulak – what he looked like, his record, etc. Father Chernoff had supplied the information that the auto salvage yard behind Magda's was Kulak's legitimate business. But his last-known address, according to the DMV, was smack in the middle of the Baby Gap store downtown, and Landry had found no other notations of an actual address, nor had there been any mention of relatives.

But relative or not, Kulak had been close to Irina Markova. He had offered her a job, a well-paying job. Criminal enterprise paid a hell of a lot better than shoveling horseshit. That explained the pricey wardrobe. It also probably gave someone motive to do her harm. Maybe because she crossed somebody up. Maybe to get at Kulak. Maybe Kulak had killed her himself and the phone message had been an act to throw the scent off.

Landry went in the back door of the bar and down a narrow, dimly lit hall with an uneven floor. The place smelled of beer and boiled cabbage, and the smoke was so thick it stung his eyes and jammed in his throat like a fist. Conversations died as he walked in and took a seat at the bar. People stared at him openly, then glanced at one another and muttered in Russian.

He looked at the bartender, a massive bald man with blue tattoos inked all over his skull. 'Vodka. Straight up.'

'What you want here, Copper?' the bartender asked.

Landry repeated himself. 'Vodka. Straight up. You have vodka, don't you?'

'Do bears shit in woods?'

'You tell me.'

The bartender laughed loudly, poured him a shot, and set it on the bar in front of him. Landry tossed it back and fought the need to grimace and gag. The bartender poured him another and he repeated the process, on a mostly empty stomach.

The bartender laughed again. 'You Russian, Copper? You drink like a Russian.'

'What makes you think I'm a copper?'

'You're all the same. Big attitude, shiny shoes. We don't got nothing to tell you here, Copper.'

'You don't even know what I'm going to ask.'

'It don't matter.'

'You're not going to tell me where I can find Alexi Kulak?'

'No.'

'That's too bad. A relative of his was found dead today, and we need to know what to do with the body.'

The bartender made a sour face and shrugged. 'This person is dead. There is no reason to rush. They will be just as dead tomorrow and the next day.'

'So, I should come back tomorrow and wait until Alexi Kulak shows up?' Landry said. 'You know, I'm a busy man. I can't hang around like that. Maybe I should send a couple of squad cars over, put some uniformed officers in here. Is that what you want me to do?'

The bartender frowned, making his skull tats undulate.

A voice behind him laughed. 'Is joke! American police, you can't do nothing to make people talk.'

Landry glanced over his shoulder. The one behind him was nearly as large as the one behind the bar. Good. If he had to prove himself, this was the guy to do it with.

'You say please and thank you and let criminals get off with slap on wrist like naughty children,' the man went on. 'Is not like Russia.'

There were many murmurs of agreement.

Landry turned around on his bar stool. 'If Russia is so fucking great, what are you doing here, Boris? Did you get tired of standing in line all day for a roll of toilet paper? Do you even use toilet paper? Do they have indoor plumbing in that ass-backward country of yours?'

The Russian scowled darkly. His hair was thick and bristly, like the pelt of a bear, and came to a V just above his brows. A vein stood out in the side of his neck. 'You watch your mouth here, little policeman. There are more of us than you.'

'Did you just threaten me?' Landry asked. 'Did you just threaten a law-enforcement officer?' He turned back to the bartender. 'Did he just threaten me?'

'What you gonna do about it?' the bartender asked. 'Scold him? Take away his supper?'

'I have the right to defend myself,' Landry said. 'I might have to do this.'

As he said it, he came around with his left elbow and drove it into the solar plexus of the man standing behind him. At the same time, he pulled his weapon from his shoulder holster and ran the gasping Russian backward into a wall.

He pointed the gun in the big man's face and shouted, 'I might have to do that! How do you like that, asshole? Am I making my point clear? I might have to blow your fucking brains out! Is this like Russia now, cocksucker?'

There was shock and fear in the man's eyes as he tried to see the end of the gun barrel.

Just as quickly as he had turned on the guy, Landry let him go and backed away. The Russian slid halfway down the wall, bent over, his mouth working like a fish's as he tried to get air.

'Don't fuck with me, Boris!' Landry shouted, jabbing a finger at him. 'Don't fuck with me!'

Landry went back to the bar and ordered another vodka. He looked around at the crowd. 'What the fuck are you looking at?'

They seemed grudgingly impressed with him now. Still

wary, still uncooperative, no doubt, but there was a little respect where there hadn't been. That was the only way he was going to get anywhere with this crowd.

He took his vodka and tossed it back, hoping he wouldn't just puke it up there and then. From inside his sport coat he pulled out a photograph printed from Irina Markova's computer and held it up.

'This is Irina Markova,' he said loudly. 'She was found murdered today. She was Russian. Some of you might have known her. And I'm gonna work my ass off to find and apprehend her killer and make sure he never sees the light of day again.

'If anyone here has anything to tell me, I'm leaving my card on the bar. And if anyone can tell me where to find Alexi Kulak, I need to know. If he doesn't come to claim the body in three days, she gets buried in a pine box in potter's field.'

That was a lie, but Landry didn't care. He needed to know what he needed to know. He turned back to the bartender and put the picture of Irina down on the bar. She was sitting in a horseshoe booth, sandwiched between two well-dressed, wealthy men who had probably never set foot in a place like this. Her smile was dazzling. There seemed to be no connection between this girl and the corpse he had left lying on a slab in the autopsy suite.

The bartender was looking at the picture too, his expression pensive.

'The guy choked her, then strangled her with a garrote. Raped her, tortured her,' Landry went on, embellishing for maximum effect. Gitan hadn't been able to say for certain whether the girl had been sexually assaulted. There were no obvious signs of torture. 'Sick bastard even did her after she was dead. And then he dumped her in a canal so the fish could eat her eyes out.'

The bartender's mouth trembled as he stared at the picture.

'You don't want to rat out the piece of crap who did this?' Landry said. 'Me, I'd give the cops my own brother's head on a platter if I knew he did something like this. But then, I'm not a Russian.'

He tossed half a dozen business cards and a twenty-dollar bill on the bar and gave the bartender a little salute. *Do svidaniya.*

The vodka was starting to kick in as the adrenaline ebbed. He walked out the back door, turned, and puked. There was no one back there to see him. He leaned against the building and took a couple of deep breaths. He just needed a moment, a little air.

One of three things could happen now. No one would come out. Someone would come out, maybe talk to him, maybe not. Boris would come out and beat the shit out of him.

He rubbed his hands over his face, lit a cigarette to get the taste of vomit out of his mouth, wondered if Elena was sleeping. Then he cursed himself for wondering. There was no getting close to her. She just wouldn't allow it. He should be glad she'd cut him loose. It pissed him off that he wasn't.

He wasn't exactly Mr. Share My Feelings himself. It was a wonder they'd lasted as long as they had. They were like a pair of porcupines, the two of them.

Still, he felt like a bastard for what he'd said to her at the scene. If there was anything Elena wasn't, it was a quitter.

The door opened and a woman came out. Stacked, teased hair, too much makeup, skirt up to her ass. She stopped, posed with her profile to him, lit a cigarette, and blew a stream of smoke up at the moon.

Landry waited.

'Damn,' she said, looking at him. 'My cigarette went out. Do you have a light?'

He walked over, flicked his lighter. She looked up at him from under her brows as she took a deep drag.

'That's something,' she said on the exhale. 'You kicked Gregor's ass. About time someone did.'

'It wasn't that hard,' Landry said.

She gave a coquettish laugh and batted her lashes. 'You sure you're a cop?'

'That's what it says on my ID.'

'My name is Svetlana. Svetlana Petrova. You're looking for Alexi?'

'You know where to find him?'

She made a pouty frown and shrugged a shoulder. 'In hell, I hope.'

'You're not a fan?'

'He's a pig.' She turned her head and spat on the ground. Class.

'What'd he do?' Landry asked. 'Fuck you and dump you?'

The fire in her eyes told him yes. 'Hey!' she snapped, hitting him in the chest with the heel of her hand. 'No guy dumps me! I tell him take a hike. He's cheap, and he fucks around with whores.'

Landry bit his tongue and looked at the door. It was only a matter of time before someone else came out.

'Was one of those whores Irina Markova?'

She made a sour face. 'She led him around by his dick. He made a fool of himself.'

'You think maybe he got sick and tired of that? Maybe he decided to teach her a lesson?'

The thought had not occurred to her. 'Alexi? Kill her?' She warmed to the idea quickly. 'Maybe . . . He could have. He has terrible temper.'

'Did he ever knock you around?'

She hesitated and glanced down, then back. Whatever she was about to say was probably going to be a lie. 'Yes. Many times. But I hit him back.'

'So maybe you just want to make trouble for him.'

She tried to look innocent, something he was sure she

95

hadn't been in about two decades. 'What trouble? I don't tell you nothing.'

'No? Then I might as well go.'

She reached out and caught hold of his lapel as he started to turn away. 'You give up too easy.'

'I've got a murder to solve,' he said. 'I can't stand here and play grab-ass with you, honey. If you've got something to say, say it.'

She frowned and pouted again. 'You're no fun.'

'Yeah, people tell me that. Was Kulak here tonight?'

'Earlier, for a couple of hours.'

'What was his mood?'

'Pissed off. He's always pissed off.'

'When was the last time you saw Irina Markova?'

The sour face again. 'I don't know. I don't look for her.'

'Was she here Saturday night?'

He could see the sudden turning of the wheels in Svetlana's brain. She narrowed her eyes and fought the start of a smile. 'Yes,' she said. 'Saturday night.'

'Around midnight? One o'clock?'

'Yes. Yes. I looked at my watch. I saw them arguing.'

Landry turned and started for his car. Svetlana hustled after him, the high heels of her shoes *clack-clack-clack*ing on the concrete.

'What?' she said.

'You're a liar. Irina Markova wasn't here Saturday night. I don't want you if you're going to lie to me. You're wasting my time. You haven't given me one damn thing I can use.'

'Okay, okay. I tell you where he lives. You have paper? Pen?'

Landry handed her one of his business cards and a pen from the inside pocket of his coat. She put the card on the hood of his car, scribbled across it, and handed it back to him. He squinted at it.

'This had better be legit,' Landry said.

'I swear. And it's a big secret. Hardly anybody knows. Not even cops. Not even feds.'

'And this is his phone number?' he asked.

'No,' she said, looking up at him, moving a little too close. 'Is my phone number. Call me. I'll show you how to have fun.'

Landry stuck the card in his breast pocket, got in the car, and drove out of the lot, leaving his informant standing there hot and bothered. Some mope coming out of that bar was going to be a lucky man tonight.

# 16

'What are you doing in my house?' I asked, wondering what I could get my hands on to use as a weapon. Maybe I could hit him in the head with the stone soap dispenser, except I couldn't reach back far enough to get it without him seeing.

'You know Irina,' he said.

'What if I did?'

He looked dazed, maybe psychotic, or ill. For all I knew, he had killed her.

'She liked you.'

I said nothing. His eyes wandered away from me for a second. I eased a couple of inches to the right.

'Did you know Irina?' I asked.

He looked at me again. 'I loved her.'

Still a 50/50 chance he had strangled her. Maybe better. Nothing could drive people over the edge of violence more than love. He loved her but she didn't love him. He loved her but she cheated on him. He loved her obsessively and wouldn't let her go. There were a dozen scenarios.

'Did you know her in Russia?' I asked, shifting my weight from one foot to the other, inching a quarter step ahead.

'She was best friends with my little sister, Sasha.'

That name rang a bell. Sasha Kulak. The friend of Irina's who had committed suicide because of Tomas Van Zandt, the horse dealer Irina had attacked in the barn.

Kulak. Alexi Kulak. Russians . . .

'She spoke fondly of Sasha,' I said, slipping the fingers of my right hand into the drawer behind me. He didn't seem to notice.

'Did she speak of me?' he asked. Inside his open jacket I could see the handle of a gun.

'Irina was a very private person. She didn't talk about her personal life very much.'

Tears filled his eyes. He appeared to be in a great deal of pain. 'I was a ghost to her in this life she led. She shut me out.'

This wasn't sounding good with regard to motive. My fingers fumbled over something in the drawer. I grabbed hold. A small pair of scissors.

He turned in the doorway and leaned against the frame, eyes closed, his face red as he fought tears.

'What do you want from me?' I asked.

He wiped a square hand across his eyes. There were tattoos on the back of his hand. Prison tats?

When I was a narc, the Russians had taken over a substantial chunk of the heroin trade in South Florida. Rumor had it they had gotten in bed with the Colombians to edge into the cocaine market. They hadn't ventured into crystal meth then. Meth had still been – and still was – the bastion of white trash.

Alexi Kulak. Russian mob? Had that been Irina's second job? The job that subsidized her lifestyle among the rich and famous?

'She is dead,' he said. 'Murdered.'

He had taken hold of his emotions and locked them away somewhere. I could see him change, grow calmer, focus.

'Yes,' I said.

'She told me about how you helped that little girl.'

A year before, Molly Seabright, twelve going on Methuselah, had come to me, mistakenly believing I was a private investigator, to ask my help in finding her missing sister.

'You know these people she ran around with,' he said.

'These rich American playboy sons of bitches.'

'No,' I lied. 'I don't know them.'

Kulak pinned me with a look that made me feel like an insect on a display board. The energy coming from him now was focused and intense. 'You know them.'

I said nothing.

'I want to know which one killed Irina.'

'I'm not a private investigator, Mr. Kulak.'

He stepped into the bathroom, suddenly aggressive, intent on intimidating me. 'I don't care what the fuck you call yourself. I need to know who killed Irina.'

'That's a police matter,' I said. I couldn't back away. I was already against the vanity.

Kulak reached his hand up and grabbed me across the lower half of my face. I came underhanded with the small scissors and jammed it into his belly. I felt the blade hit a rib.

He howled and staggered back, looking down in astonishment as his shirt turned red with his own blood.

I clasped my hands together and swung at him from the side, hitting him hard in the cheekbone and temple.

Kulak staggered backward, stumbled, and fell.

I started to jump over him, but he caught me by one ankle, and I went down, my teeth biting deep into my lower lip. The taste of blood filled my mouth. I kicked at him to free myself. Arms and legs scrambling, I tried to pull myself forward, got to my knees, got my feet under me.

As I tried to lunge forward, Kulak caught me by the back of my neck, shoved me into a wall, and held me there with his own body weight.

'You bitch! You stabbed me!'

'Yeah. I hope you die of it!'

Kulak started to chuckle, then laugh, then laughed harder. 'You are like Irina, I think.'

I hoped not. I didn't want to think about water creatures nibbling at my face as I lay dead in a drainage ditch.

'You,' he said, dead serious once again. 'You will be my eyes, my ears, my brain. They will accept you. You are one of them.'

'I don't work for you,' I said. 'I want to know who killed Irina, but I don't work for you.'

He turned me around and held me up against the wall by my throat. My toes were barely touching the floor. He looked like it wouldn't matter to him one way or the other if he crushed my larynx.

'Yes, Miss Estes,' he said softly. 'I'm afraid that you do.'

I didn't argue. His voice and demeanor made me go cold beneath the sweat of fear and adrenaline. His eyes were flat and black, like a shark's. I swallowed hard beneath the weight of his hand around my windpipe.

He brought his face very close to mine and whispered, 'Yes, you do.'

# 17

The sun was not yet up when I left my cottage and went to the horses. I fed them, then went outside and sat on the same bench Landry and I had occupied the evening before. It seemed that weeks had gone by since then.

I had thought long and hard about Alexi Kulak. Most sane people would have called Landry and spilled the whole story, then got on the next plane to places unknown. Most sane people would have thought that the fact I didn't want to do that spoke volumes about the state of my mental health.

Alexi Kulak was a criminal. He was volatile and dangerous. The fact that he had loved Irina only made him more so. I had done some homework on him after he left – as I sat at my computer with an ice pack wrapped around my throat.

The Russian mob was nothing to mess around with. The fact that relatively little had been written about Kulak told me he was smart. No one needed to tell me he could be ruthless.

Even so, my gut told me to keep it to myself. I wanted to find Irina's killer. Kulak and I had that in common. If I could come up with results, he had no reason to hurt me. If I ratted him out to the cops, I was likely to end up in the trunk of a junker car going into the crusher at Kulak's auto salvage yard.

If Irina's murder had something to do with her connection to Alexi, then through him I would have access to a part of Irina's life Landry wouldn't be able to touch.

That's what I told myself, even though I knew full well

Kulak wouldn't have come to me if Irina's death had to do with him. That was the reason I gave myself for making a deal with a devil. There were others lurking in a dark corner of my mind. I refused to bring them to the surface.

I showered and dressed and made myself as presentable as I could. There was nothing to do about my fat lip but tell a lie to explain it. A short vintage Gucci scarf around my neck hid the bruises the ice pack had failed to prevent.

Billy Quint should have been a sea captain a hundred years past. It had been almost that long since I had met him when I was working Narcotics and he headed an OCB (Organized Crime Bureau) undercover team working the port of Fort Lauderdale along with the DEA. The teams from the individual agencies had a mutual agenda – to crack a drug-money laundering scheme that had been taking large sums of U.S. currency out of the country on cargo ships bound for Panama. The connection to Palm Beach County had been what had come back on the return trip: cocaine. Lots of it.

Quint lived in a bungalow along the intracoastal waterway, south of Lake Worth. Retired, not by choice. He had refused to speak to me over the phone. OCB guys learn early on to take every precaution possible. They have to deal with deadly animals every day, and they don't all survive. So I wasn't surprised when Quint wouldn't speak to me. Old paranoia dies hard. Especially for someone who almost didn't make it out of the game alive.

'I thought you were dead,' he said gruffly as I got out of my car and walked toward him.

'I'm like you,' I told him. 'I'm too mean to die.'

'Tough nut. You always were.' He rolled down the dock in his wheelchair and tossed some fishing gear into a beat-up dinghy.

'Is that thing seaworthy?' I asked, dubious.

He squinted up at me, one eye closed tighter than the other, a filthy old captain's hat jammed on his head. It was impossible to decide where his sideburns ended and his ear hair began.

'What's the difference?' he asked. His voice was full of gravel. He fell into a fit of wet, rattling coughing. When it passed, it took him a moment to get his breath back.

'Are you okay?' I asked like an idiot.

'Lung cancer,' he said by way of explanation, like it was nothing. Like he had a cold. 'The devil will catch up with me sooner or later. I've dodged him one time too many.'

'I'm sorry to hear it, Billy.'

He shrugged, waved it off. In that moment he looked ancient, even though he wasn't more than in his late fifties. His useless legs canted off to one side as he slouched in his wheelchair. His skin had a strange yellow cast to it.

I didn't have to ask him if he was in pain. I knew what it was to have your body broken in ways you shouldn't have survived – and often wished that you hadn't.

Quint's legs had been broken with a sledgehammer by a couple of Russian thugs in the employ of an ambitious mob lieutenant. He had been allowed to live for his value as part of the media circus that followed the brutal attack. Free publicity, advertising to one and all that the Russians were not to be fucked with – by anyone.

Arrests had been made, but nothing stuck. The lieutenant and his henchmen had vanished off the continent, probably literally. No one in the Russian community would talk. The police, the feds – all had been powerless to protect even one of their own.

A middle-aged Filipino woman built like the corner mailbox came out of Quint's bungalow and trundled to the dock. Her brows lowered and she started in.

'Your breakfast is ready. I don't make good food so you

can turn up your nose like Mr. Hoity-Toity and let it go to waste! Come in and eat!

'You!' she said, pointing at me like Uncle Sam on the recruiting poster. 'Come and eat. You're too skinny. What's the matter with you, you don't eat?'

Quint rolled his eyes. 'Simi. My keeper.'

'I thought you said the devil hadn't caught up with you yet.'

He barked a laugh and fell into another coughing fit.

I choked down Simi's greasy rice, onions, hot-peppers, hot-sausage concoction when she was watching and fed a handful to the Jack Russell terrier under the table when she wasn't.

'I see you,' she barked, facing away from me at the stove. 'You feed that dog, he gets gas. You gonna stay and smell his farts, Missy?'

'Oh, go on with you, woman!' Quint growled. 'Don't you have to go to church?'

'To pray for your soul!' she shouted at him.

'Why the hell would you want me in heaven?' he asked. 'You won't be there.'

I snuck the dog another handful under the table.

They swore and shouted at each other for another five minutes before Simi made a rude gesture and stormed out.

'Is she always like that?' I asked.

'Nah. She's on her party manners. We've got company,' Quint said. He took his plate off the table and put it on the floor for the dog. 'I don't care if he farts. He sleeps in her room.'

I put my plate down too.

'So what brings you, Elena?' he asked. 'You didn't wake up today and think you should, from the kindness of your own heart, go and visit an old cripple.'

'You think so little of me, Billy,' I said.

He laughed and coughed. 'Like you said, you're like me. Spill it.'

'Alexi Kulak. Do you know anything about him?'

He may not have been on the job anymore, but guys like Quint never really get out. They keep their eyes peeled and their ear to the ground. At one time, he had known more about Russian organized crime in South Florida than anyone else. I was betting he still did.

He made a sour face. 'Why? You're not dating him, are you?'

'No. But he was in love with a girl I knew. She was murdered over the weekend.'

'And you're going to ask me if I think he could have done it? From what I hear, that one could pluck your eyes out and have them for a snack.'

'He didn't kill her,' I said. 'He wants to know who did.'

'So he can cut the bastard's jewels off and shove them down his throat?'

'I didn't ask.'

'I can guarantee. And what do you care what Alexi Kulak wants? Did he give you that fat lip?'

'I tripped and fell and bit my lip.'

'Why don't you just try to tell me you ran into a door?'

'It's the truth,' I said, looking straight at him.

One advantage gained from my accident and the subsequent nerve damage: I had no problem telling a straight-faced lie. Of course, I had been a pretty good liar long before that.

'And Alexi Kulak wasn't there at the time?'

'What's he into?' I asked, pointedly ignoring his question.

'What isn't he into? He's a full-service mobster. Hijacking trucks, extortion, shylocking, prostitutes, drugs. This friend of yours, what was she into?'

'Wealthy men. She had expensive tastes.' I shrugged. 'The more I find out, the less I feel I knew her.'

'Was she working for Kulak?'

'I don't know. I got the feeling she led him around like a dog on a leash. But I know she wasn't buying Gucci handbags with what she made grooming horses.'

'How does a girl like that snag wealthy men?'

'By their libidos, I suppose. She was a beautiful girl.'

'Could Kulak have been using her to get to one of her rich friends?' Quint asked.

'If that was the case, what would he need with me? He would already know whose heart to cut out. He told me she shut him out of that part of her life,' I said.

'The same would be true if she had been working for him in some other capacity,' Quint pointed out. 'Those throats would already be cut.

'What made him think you could be useful to him?'

'Apparently, Irina – the dead girl – liked me,' I said. 'Though I couldn't say we were close. We worked together.'

'Doing what?'

'I ride horses.'

'That's a living?'

'The horse business brought sixty million dollars into Wellington last year.'

'Jesus,' Quint said, impressed. 'And you don't have to get shot at.'

'Not usually.'

'So Kulak knew you're in that world. Do you run in the same circles as the dead girl?'

'No.'

'Does he know you were a cop?'

'He knows whatever Irina told him. She told him I helped a young girl find her sister last year.'

'What makes me think there's a lot more to that story?'

'There is,' I said, 'but nothing relevant to this.'

'What are you going to do?' Quint asked.

I shrugged. 'I want to know who killed Irina too.'

'You didn't tell anybody on the job up there about Kulak?'

'No offense, Billy, but I'd rather not end up on the business end of a sledgehammer.'

'There's no guarantee that won't happen even if you do help him, Elena. He won't want a loose thread left hanging,' Quint said. 'This guy is the real deal. He's smart, ruthless. Alexi Kulak is as cold-blooded as a snake.

'Do you know how he came into power?' he asked.

'I'm here to learn.'

'The story goes he got off the plane from Moscow, went up to West Palm, where he was supposed to become a lieutenant under Sergi Yagoudin. Kulak, Yagoudin, and another lieutenant met. Kulak cut Yagoudin's throat from ear to ear. He killed the lieutenant, put the lieutenant's prints all over the knife. Then he got rid of that body, but he kept the guy's hands. I hear he still keeps them in his freezer and uses them from time to time to leave prints at crime scenes.'

'If it was only the three of them meeting, how do you know this isn't just a heartwarming Russian bedtime story?' I asked.

'It's true' was all he said. He wouldn't say more. He didn't need to. 'You're playing with a cobra, Elena. You will get bitten. It's just a matter of when and how badly.'

# 18

They sat around a mosaic-tile-topped table imported from Italy. It was three hundred years old and had come from the villa of a wealthy merchant in Florence. It weighed as much as any one of the polo ponies grazing in the irrigated field on the far side of the vast, manicured back lawn and gardens.

Jim Brody believed in living the good life, and he had more than enough money to do it. With nothing but a BA, a big ego, and a good bluff, he had started his own firm in 1979, representing professional athletes in contract and endorsement negotiations. In the beginning, his knack for picking up underestimated athletes about to become superstars had built his reputation. His reputation for big-dollar deals had then brought big-dollar players.

He often called his practice 'a license to print money.' And he had no problem spending it.

Two young Hispanic men in white jackets and black slacks served the breakfast. Omelets made to order, bacon, sausage, hash browns, pastries, fruit, three kinds of juice, champagne, and fresh-ground coffee Brody had flown in monthly from a private plantation in Colombia.

His friends gathered here weekly for breakfast. The Alibi Club, they called themselves. Men who shared his passions for money, polo, beautiful women, and assorted other vices. Sebastian Foster, forty-three, at one point the fifth-ranked tennis player in the world. Paul Kenner, forty-nine, former major-league-baseball all-star, one of Brody's early successes. Antonio Ovada, fifty-one, Argentinian, old money, owner of one of the top polo teams in Florida, breeder of top-dollar ponies. Bennett Walker, forty-five, Palm Beach, old money, Brody had known him for years. Charles Vance IV, fifty-three, CEO of a company that owned a fleet of luxury private charter jets. Juan Barbaro, thirty-three, Spanish, one of the top polo players in the world.

'Have the detectives spoken with you yet?' Ovada asked.

'No.'

'They will. And when they do, what will you tell them?'

Brody looked across the patio, not really seeing the lounge chairs or the pool. 'That she was at my party. I knew the girl. That's not a crime.'

'I suppose not.'

'What will *you* tell them?' Brody asked.

'That I saw her at the party. I didn't see when or with whom she left. I was with you, here, for the rest of the night, drinking your most expensive scotch and smoking illegal Cuban cigars.'

'Me too,' Kenner said.

'And the woman you were with?' Ovada asked. 'What will she say?'

'Nothing. She doesn't want her husband to know. I don't want him to know either. He's the size and temperament of a grizzly bear.'

'I've met him,' Foster said. 'You definitely need an alibi.'

'You slept with her too?' Kenner asked.

'Yeah. Nice piece of ass, but not worth getting my legs broken.'

Bennett Walker, in dark glasses, hungover, shifted restlessly on his chair.

Charles Vance sliced a piece of sausage on his plate and chewed enthusiastically. 'Home with my wife,' he said. 'The in-laws are visiting. I wasn't at the party more than an hour. I have witnesses.'

Brody looked down the table at Barbaro.

'I was passed out on my friend's pool table,' the Spaniard

said with a grin. 'You know how to throw a party, *Patrón*. Bennett was like a corpse himself the next day. Neither of us would have been of any use to a woman. Isn't that so, my friend?'

Walker looked at him, distracted, and lifted a hand as if to say, *whatever*, then got up from the table and went into the pool house.

'What's his problem?' Kenner asked.

Barbaro shrugged. 'Too much vodka at Players last night.'

'Is his wife having trouble again?' Vance asked.

'Who can know? She is always a fragile creature, is she not?'

'I'd wish him my sympathy,' Vance said, 'but considering what he gained marrying her, she doesn't seem like that much of an inconvenience.'

'You don't have to live with her,' Kenner said.

'Neither does he,' Vance pointed out. 'When was the last time Bennett crossed the bridge to the Island?'

Walker emerged from the pool house and came back to the table. His hair was wet and slicked back.

'How's Nancy these days, Ben?' Brody asked.

'She's fine. Helping her mother plan some charity event. Keeps her mind occupied.'

Walker's wife was the daughter of one of the wealthiest old-money families in Connecticut. A beautiful but emotionally unstable girl, Nancy Whitaker seemed to live in her own world much of the time, doped to the gills just so she could function, in and out of mental hospitals and sanitariums.

Some people had been surprised when it was announced the very eligible Bennett Walker was going to marry her. Other people looked at the net worth of the two families and saw a merger, not a marriage.

That was seventeen or eighteen years in the past. Brody hadn't yet made the Palm Beach scene, but he'd been aware of Bennett Walker. Walker's alleged rape and beating of a local girl had been in the national news. Privileged heir to a huge fortune accused of taking what he wanted and walking away scot-free in the end. The stuff of tabloid headlines.

The marriage to Nancy Whitaker a year later had given the impression that Bennett had settled down, that clearly he was a good guy, otherwise the Whitakers would never have allowed their daughter to marry him.

The reality was that the Whitakers had married off their problem child, the Walkers had gained business and political connections worth millions, and Bennett's wife's condition allowed him the freedom to do as he pleased. Not a bad trade-off, Brody thought.

'So, everybody's covered,' he said.

They always made certain of that, watched one another's back. That was what the club was all about. No man went without an alibi if he needed one. One of them always covered. Hookers, mistresses, drugs, booze, gambling – whatever the vice, one of them always covered for another.

It had seemed harmless for the most part, in the beginning. Who cared who fucked who? So what was the big deal, telling a little white one for a buddy with a small cocaine problem? Company money lost on a sure-thing bet in the fifth race at Gulfstream? Not a problem. They covered for one another.

As he sat there looking at his friends, all of them with secrets of their own, he wondered if any one of them had ever imagined covering for a murderer.

# 19

Kulak never showed at the address Svetlana had given Landry. At least not in the two hours he had sat on the place before going home to catch a couple hours of sleep. She had probably sent him on a snipe hunt, he thought. Svetlana and the gang back at Magda's would be having a laugh on him later.

Whether the woman had lied to him or not, he didn't consider his visit to the bar to have been a waste of time. He'd made an impression. He'd gotten his word out. That word was sure to pass to Alexi Kulak.

'You look like shit,' Weiss pointed out as they drove out South Shore to find Star Polo. Weiss was behind the wheel. It made him feel important. Landry was too hungover to care. 'What happened to you? Did you get dragged behind a truck or something? I thought you went home last night. You look like you slept in your car.'

'I went and got drunk,' Landry said. 'I stopped at that Russian bar and pounded down some vodka. You should do that once in a while, Weiss. Loosen up your sphincter.'

'You went there without me?' Weiss said in the Tone. 'We agreed we would wait until today.'

'It was today.'

'I can't believe you went there without me.'

Landry gave him a look. 'What are you? My new girl-friend? Are your latent homosexual tendencies emerging? Should I be watching my back, Weiss?'

'Oh, fuck you, Landry.'

'Not interested,' Landry said. Weiss snatched a breath to bark back at him. 'Don't miss the turn, sweetheart.'

'You never used to be this big an asshole,' Weiss said. 'You been taking lessons from Estes?'

'Don't try to be clever, Weiss,' Landry said. 'It just magnifies your inadequacies.'

Weiss leaned out the window and jabbed the button on the intercom for the gate. The person who answered had to go see if Mr. Brody was available to receive them.

Weiss huffed, 'Fat bastard's probably watching us over closed-circuit television. This guy's so fucking rich, he shits money. He reps Milton Marbray, NBA rookie of the year. He reps half the all-stars in baseball. Money for nothing.'

The ornate iron gates opened, inviting them in. A guy in black slacks and a white jacket greeted them as they pulled up in front of what looked like a Caribbean plantation house. The cars parked on the curved drive in front of the house looked like they had just come out of the exotic-car-dealership showroom – a Jaguar, a Ferrari, a Mercedes, a Porsche.

Landry got out of the car and introduced himself to the servant, showing his badge.

'Mr. Brody is on the rear terrace entertaining friends. Follow me, please.'

As they walked through the center of the mansion, Landry's attention wasn't on the dark teak floors or the white walls hung with art that was probably worth more than he made in ten years. His attention was already through the open doors to the terrace, where half a dozen men sat lounging around a table under the shade of an arbor covered in striped fabric.

He immediately recognized Paul Kenner, the ex-baseball player. Elena had told him Kenner was at the birthday party the night Irina went missing. Another guy sitting at the table did beer commercials – some Aussie tennis player from the last decade. The rest he didn't know.

A big man with an aggressive smile and a loud shirt got up from the head of the table and came across the flagstone, sticking out his hand.

'Detective. Jim Brody,' he said. His grip was like a can crusher.

'Mr. Brody, I'm Detective Landry. This is Detective Weiss,' he said, nodding in Weiss's general direction. 'We're looking into the death of Irina Markova, and we're speaking with everyone who may have seen her the night she went missing.'

'Terrible tragedy,' Brody said in a booming voice. 'Of course I saw it on the news yesterday. We were all just talking about it. Everyone here was at the party that night, at one point in time or another.'

'Really? Hey, one-stop shopping for us, Detective Weiss,' Landry said. 'Great coincidence, huh?'

Weiss looked at Brody like he was a piece of dog crap. The tough guy. 'And you were all just talking about it?' he said flatly. 'Then it's fresh in your heads.'

Landry looked around the table. A couple of them looked cool. A couple of them didn't.

Kenner stood up with a stupid grin on his face. 'Hey, I think I met you once.'

Landry gave him the cop eyes. 'Yeah? Did I arrest you?'

'No.'

'My mistake.'

'Detective.' A distinguished-looking man, probably in his early fifties, grass-green Lacoste shirt, khakis with knife-sharp creases, rose from his chair and handed Weiss a business card. 'I'm afraid I have to leave. I have a tee time with my father-in-law. But I'm happy to speak with you later, although I don't have much to contribute. I didn't see the girl. I was in and out of the party early in the evening. After that I was with my family.'

Another one pushed his chair back. Mid-forties. Dark

hair, wet, slicked back. Black wraparounds. Ralph Lauren shirt: collar open, sleeves rolled up neatly to mid-muscular forearm. He slid out of his chair and stepped to the side, like he thought he might be able to slip away unnoticed.

'And you are . . . ?' Landry said.

He was hungover, that was what he was, Landry thought. He had that look. Landry recognized it because he'd seen it staring back at him out of the bathroom mirror that morning.

Even slouching, the guy was tall. Good-looking, like a Kennedy. He turned his head to the side, as if he didn't realize he was being spoken to.

'Having a memory problem?' Landry prodded.

'Bennett Walker,' he said, and wiped a hand down the lower part of his face. 'I'm afraid I'm not feeling well, Detective. One too many last night.'

Landry shrugged. Be a buddy. 'Hey, me too. I've got a head like a medicine ball. If I can just ask you a couple of questions on your way out . . .'

Walker gave the smallest of nods and started toward the house. Landry walked beside him.

'Russian vodka,' Landry said. 'From real Russians. I think they made the shit in a bathtub. Nasty.'

Walker was breathing very carefully through his mouth. 'Me too,' he said. 'Vodka. But I don't know any Russians.'

'Sure you do,' Landry said as they went into the house. 'You knew Irina Markova.'

Walker's step faltered. 'Not really.'

'I looked at some photographs from the party that night,' he bluffed. 'You looked pretty friendly to me.'

'It was a party. I had a lot to drink.'

'Is that a habit of yours, Mr. Walker? Drinking too much?'

'No more than anyone else.'

'The party was Saturday night. Last night was Monday. I don't know too many people who tie one on every other night of the week,' Landry said. 'Do you?'

Walker stopped and held his head in his hands for a moment, a man in pain.

'It was a party,' he said again.

'And last night?'

'Drinks with a friend after a long day. Look, Detective,' he said, his patience fraying around the edges. 'I appreciate your concern, but my drinking habits are none of your business.'

Landry spread his hands. 'Hey, you're right. I don't know anything about you. Maybe you're under a lot of stress. Maybe you've got problems with your finances or your wife or your girlfriend, boyfriend, whatever. What do I know? I only know what you tell me . . . and what other people tell me – friends, enemies, observers. Wouldn't you rather tell me yourself?'

'There's nothing to tell,' Walker said. 'I left the party . . . I don't know . . . maybe two-thirty. Went home. Passed out.'

'Can someone vouch for that?'

'Yes. Juan Barbaro.'

'And where can I find Mr. Barbaro?'

Walker motioned back from where they'd come. 'He's at the table. If you'd excuse me now, Detective. I would really rather go home and be sick in private. If you have other questions, I can try to answer them later.'

Landry ignored him. 'Did you see Irina Markova leave the party?'

'No.'

'Did you see her with anyone in particular during the evening?'

'No. It was a party. Everyone was with everyone.'

'One big happy family.'

'There had to be a hundred people there,' Walker said, frustrated, 'probably more. I didn't have any reason to keep tabs on anyone. I can't help you.'

'Excuse me, Detective, but I have a quick question for my friend.'

Walker looked relieved. 'Detective, this is Juan Barbaro. My alibi, not that I need one.'

Barbaro held a hand out. Landry shook it. Strong, but not out to prove anything. The man looked him in the eye when he spoke, something Bennett Walker hadn't yet managed to do. Still, he seemed too slick to trust, too good-looking, too sure of his own charm. In breeches and brown riding boots, he looked like a male model in an ad for some cologne with a sporty name – Rider, Player, Jock.

'Too much partying that night,' Barbaro said, smiling, at ease. He sat down on the arm of a fat upholstered chair. 'It's a wonder we managed to find his house.'

'You both went there and crashed,' Landry said.

'Yes.'

'Just the two of you.'

'Yes,' Barbaro said. 'I am afraid we were both beyond entertaining.'

'You live together?' Landry asked.

'No, no,' Barbaro said. 'Ben's home was closer. I knew I could not drive.'

'Wise choice, then.' And convenient, Landry thought. He watched Walker, who was a very unhealthy shade of ash. Sweat began to bead across his forehead.

'I have to go,' he said, and turned again for the door. Landry didn't try to stop him.

'Are you playing later, Ben?' Barbaro called after his friend.

Walker didn't turn around. 'No.'

'He's not doing so well, your pal there,' Landry said as Walker hustled out the front door.

Barbaro frowned. 'My friend is a complex man with a complicated life.'

'Complicated in what way?'

'In the way of women, of course. His wife, she is . . . difficult.'

'Was she at the party that night?'

'No, no.'

'Was she at the house when you got there?'

'Mrs. Walker lives on "the Island," as they say. They have a lovely home on the ocean side. Ben and I went to his home in the Polo Club.'

'They're separated?'

'No,' Barbaro said. 'They are wealthy. The wealthy do not live like you and me, Detective. Bennett keeps a home here in Wellington, where he stays for the polo season. He is quite a good amateur player.'

'And the wife?'

'Has her charities and so forth in Palm Beach. Benefits and balls, and so on.'

'And it's fine with her that her husband is over here partying with twenty-some-year-old girls?'

Barbaro shrugged in that European way that made Landry want to smack him upside the head. 'As I said, the wealthy are not like you or me.'

'Maybe not,' Landry said. 'But in my experience, women are women, and women don't like their husbands off fucking around on the side.'

Barbaro smiled like a wise man to a moron. 'You have much to learn about these people, Detective.'

'Oh, I plan to learn everything about them. What about you, Mr. Barbaro? Did you spend any time with Irina Markova that night at the party?'

'To say hello, party talk. We may have danced, I think,' he said, looking up as if he might see the image of that on the ceiling.

'How well did you know her?'

Again with the shrug. 'Irina enjoyed the scene, as many pretty young women her age do. I knew her socially. It's a terrible thing that happened to her.'

'She was a groom,' Landry said. 'Doesn't seem like a groom would be included in this crowd.'

'Did you ever meet Irina?' Barbaro asked with raised brows. 'Aye yi yi! She was a beautiful, sophisticated young woman. Very self-assured, very sexy. A young woman like that is welcome everywhere she goes, is she not?'

'Did you have a relationship with her?'

'No.'

'Did Bennett Walker?'

'You would have to ask him that.'

'I'm asking you,' Landry pressed.

'Ben is a wealthy man,' Barbaro said. 'Irina liked wealthy men.'

'Was he sleeping with her?'

'I don't know. They were friendly. But she was friendly with other wealthy men as well.'

'She slept around.'

'I don't go into the bedrooms of my acquaintances, Detective. I find it unwise to know too much,' Barbaro said. 'I am a polo player, a professional athlete. I am an entertainer. I am very good at what I do, and because of this, I am desirable to know among these wealthy people. But I am not one of them. I make my living off their largesse. I am an employee.'

'I don't see any other hired help sitting at that table out there, Mr. Barbaro,' Landry pointed out.

'Nevertheless . . . If I was a player of no consequence, I would not be here. Inasmuch as these gentlemen may tell you otherwise, I know better.'

Strange, Landry thought. Barbaro was setting himself apart, distancing himself from the pack. Most people went out of their way to appear to belong to an exclusive social set.

'How long have you known these people?'

'I have been coming to Palm Beach and Wellington for four years, five years,' Barbaro said. 'I came here to play for Ralph Lauren when I was only a three-goal player.'

'What does that mean?'

'That is a rating system, a handicap. Players are handicapped, based on their statistics and abilities, from one goal to ten. The higher the number, the better the player,' he explained. 'When I was a three-goal player, Mr. Brody saw my potential and hired me away. I have now been a ten-goal player for three years.'

'Mr. Brody has a good eye.'

'Which is how he made his fortune.'

'You've earned your place at that table,' Landry said.

'I have been good for Mr. Brody. Mr. Brody has been very good to me,' Barbaro said, raising his hands. 'And now I must go to work, so that all of this remains the same.'

Landry took his phone number and let him leave. Weiss came into the wide hall from the back terrace, still looking pissed off.

'I hate these people.'

'Because they're rich?' Landry asked.

'Because they're assholes.'

'Turning on your own kind?'

'Very funny. They didn't see anything, didn't hear anything, don't know anything, and they all alibi one another. And,' Weiss said, 'they want to know where they can send memorials. I could puke. What did yours have to say for themselves?'

'Same,' Landry said as they walked out. 'Barbaro alibis Walker. Walker alibis Barbaro. They both knew the girl, but neither of them saw her leave the party. She's screwing everybody, but nobody's screwing her.'

'I don't like it,' Weiss said. 'I don't like it that they're all here. I don't like it that they were talking about the girl.'

'It's a fucking alibi club,' Landry said.

'So now what?'

Landry looked off toward the stables. 'We find someone who isn't a member.'

# 20

I decided not to think about Alexi Kulak. It wasn't denial. There just wasn't anything I could do about him. I wanted to find Irina's murderer. That was my priority. My priority happened to coincide with his. The rest I would deal with when I had to.

I wondered if Irina's autopsy was under way. I wondered what information the medical examiner would come up with: Had she been raped? Tortured? When had she died? How much had she suffered? Had they by some miracle been able to find anything on or in the body that could yield a DNA profile of the killer?

Mother Nature is a strange old bird. I knew of cases where there should have been no hope at all of finding the perp's skin cells under the victim's fingernails — and yet it had happened. It could happen. The odds weren't good, but . . .

I thought of the Laci Peterson case in California, where all hope of finding the woman's body had gone overboard with her and the concrete anchor tied to her body. But that body had defied all odds, not only washing up onshore where it could be found but washing up onshore literally blocks from the state crime lab.

I knew that if there was any way Irina could have, she would have gone down fighting. I could only hope the ME had found evidence that was so.

Of course, I would not be privy to that information. When I was a cop, all the technology available had been at my disposal, provided the county wanted to pay for it. As a civilian, I felt as handicapped as Billy Quint.

I still had contacts in law enforcement, the few people who had not judged me as harshly as my fellow officers had judged me – or as I had judged myself – when my career went nova with the death of Hector Ramirez. I had known Mercedes Gitan when she was just made assistant chief at the ME's office. I had stood and watched her perform more than one autopsy when I was on the other side of the badge.

It had been three years and a lifetime since I'd seen her. She had actually come to the hospital a couple of times in the first weeks following my near-death experience. I hadn't wanted to know anyone then, certainly hadn't wanted anyone to know me. The people who tried to support me, I had shut out, and they gave up. I wondered now if she would even take my call, let alone give me information only the sheriff's detectives were supposed to have.

I stopped at a drive-through Starbucks on my way back to the farm to pick up something chokingly sweet and artificially flavored for Sean and a straight-up double-strong espresso for myself. Sean was leading a horse to the barn when I drove in. He looked like a Ralph Lauren ad. Tall, handsome, chiseled, narrow-hipped.

'I got you a venti white-chocolate mocha with whipped cream and enough artificial sweetener to kill a dozen lab rats,' I said, offering his drink to him, as he put the mare in the cross ties to groom her.

He looked at me, wide-eyed. 'My God, El! What happened to you? What happened to your lip?'

'I tripped and fell. Don't make a big deal. Take your coffee.'

He took the cup and set it aside, never taking his eyes off me. 'I don't believe you.'

'Why not?'

'Because you're a known liar, young lady.'

'Nevertheless,' I said, 'that's what happened.'

'Elena, I'm a nervous wreck already. Please don't make me worry about you.'

'That's a very good outfit,' I said. 'The brown breeches, the matching shirt, the pinstripes. Very chic.'

He looked offended. 'Do you really think I'm so shallow you can distract me with compliments?'

'It's always worked before.'

Behind him, the small bay mare pinned her ears and shook her head from side to side, raised one front leg in a threat to paw the ground.

'I think the queen bee is ready to retire to her chambers,' I said.

He took the horse back to her stall, but the break in concentration didn't distract him from my split lip.

'Swear to me that is not the result of domestic violence,' he said, staring down at me.

I rolled my eyes. 'First: I broke up with Landry two days ago. So just who beat me up? My imaginary friend? I was home alone last night. Second: Frankly, I'm offended you think I would let some jerk do this to me. And I'm offended on Landry's behalf.'

'I didn't say you would let him get away with it,' he said. 'Is there a corpse in your house we need to dispose of?'

The words were barely out of his mouth before his eyes filled with tears. 'Oh, my God, I can't believe I just said that.'

Poor Sean. Unlike myself, he had chosen to stay floating along on the cushy cloud of the sheltered Palm Beach lifestyle. The sensitivity hadn't been ground out of him working drug deals and homicides, living day and night among the cruelties of a baser existence.

He looked away toward the door to the lounge. 'I keep expecting her to walk out that door and complain about something. I wish she would.'

'I know. I wish yesterday never happened.'

'Never in my life did I ever think I would know some-one who got murdered,' he said.

'What about me?'

'You're too mean to die.' He turned and gave me an uncharacteristically stern look. 'You'd better be. You're the bratty little sister I never had. I'd never forgive you.'

'I'll do my best,' I said, thinking that a year before I might not have said the same thing. Sean was thinking that too.

'I didn't save you from the gutter so you could check out on me,' he said.

'I have no intention of checking out.'

He reached out a hand to not quite touch my fat lip. 'That looks awful. Don't you know how to use concealer? And a little Preparation H would take the swelling down. You could create the illusion of symmetry with a neutral lip liner.'

'Are you a closet transvestite now?'

'Honey, there isn't a closet I haven't already come out of,' he said. 'I haven't spent a small fortune on personal trainers and diet gurus to cover this physique with women's wear. Let's drink our coffee.'

We went out of the barn to sit on the bench by the arena. Sean stared into the middle distance, where a couple of news vans were parked on the road.

'Have they tried to talk to you?' I asked.

'I've declined all interviews. I couldn't possibly be so tacky as to comment on the murder of someone I know. Of course, that doesn't stop them from standing out there with their cameras.

'"Look!"'he squealed, pretending excitement. '"That's the barn where the victim shoveled horseshit! That's the grass she walked on!"'

'It's news,' I said. 'Like it or not. People get engrossed in these stories in part to make them realize how lucky they are. Their lives might be shitty, but at least no one has murdered them. Yet.'

Sean took a long drink of his coffee and was silent for a moment. When he spoke again, he said, 'You're going to get in the middle of this, aren't you?'

'What? The media?'

'The investigation.'

'Of course. What else would I do?'

'What else *would* you do? Nothing else,' he said. 'What else *could* you do? Leave it to Landry.'

It was my turn to say nothing.

'Why did you break up with him?' he asked.

'God, that sounds so high school. What was there to break up? We didn't have a relationship. We had sex.'

'He wanted something more?'

I turned and looked at him, annoyed he had made the assumption that I was the one who backed away, even though I was.

'Well, I knew you wouldn't be the one pressing for commitment,' he said.

'I did him a favor. I can hardly stand myself twenty-four/seven; I wouldn't wish me on anyone else.'

Sean didn't comment. I was glad.

'What happens next?' he asked.

'They'll do the autopsy today, continue interviewing people who knew her, people who saw her Saturday night.

'Did you ever see Irina out on the town?' I asked.

'Once in a while. At Players. Once or twice at Galipette.'

'Having dinner or in the bar?'

'Dinner.'

'Was she on a date?'

'With girlfriends.'

'Pricey dinner for hired help.'

Sean shrugged. 'Irina made a decent living. What could she have had for expenses? She lived here rent-free.'

'She has a closet full of Worth Avenue,' I said.

He looked a little shocked. 'I didn't pay her well enough to shop on Worth Avenue.'

Worth Avenue was the Rodeo Drive, the Fifth Avenue, of Palm Beach. The hunting ground of old-money matrons and young trophy wives alike. Lunch on Worth Avenue could cost a day's pay for the average groom.

'Irina had a life we didn't know anything about, Sean. She hung out with the polo crowd, the high rollers. And she did some kind of work for a Russian mobster named Alexi Kulak.'

He looked at me, astounded. 'A Russian mobster? This is insane!'

'Do you know Jim Brody?'

'The sports agent? Not really. I've seen him at the polo matches, of course.'

'Irina was at his birthday party Saturday night. As far as I've found out, that's the last she was seen by anyone other than her killer. From the photos I saw, she was the life of the party.'

'You can't think someone from that crowd . . .' His words trailed off at the look I gave him. 'Who was there?'

'Brody, Paul Kenner,' I said. 'Polo players, of course. Juan Barbaro.'

'Oh, my God, he's gorgeous.'

I held my breath for a moment, trying to decide if I should say the next words in my mouth or choke them back.

'Bennett Walker.'

Sean's face went carefully blank as he watched me. 'Oh, El . . .'

'You had to know he was around, Sean. You have a box at the polo stadium. You have to have seen him. Your social circles overlap.'

'Of course I've seen him,' he admitted. 'I just . . . didn't want you to.'

'Too late for that. I saw him at Players last night.'

'Oh, Jesus . . . Did he see you?'

'Yes. I was on my way out. He was on his way in.' I didn't tell him the son of a bitch hadn't even recognized me. 'I was my usual charming self: snide, sarcastic, accusatory, and threatening.'

'And he was . . . ?'

I shrugged. 'Not happy to see me.'

There was so much to say, he didn't say anything. Sean had been there through all of it – my relationship with Bennett, the engagement. He had watched me fall in love and be in love. He had been my only support when Bennett came to me asking for an alibi and my happy fairy tale turned into a nightmare. Sean was the only person on earth who knew the whole truth of that story.

'Sean, he was there the night Irina went missing. I saw photos of Irina sitting between him and Jim Brody. They looked very chummy.'

'Elena, you're not saying Bennett killed her?'

'He has to be considered a suspect.'

'Why would he kill Irina?'

'Why did he rape and beat Maria Nevin?' I asked.

'That was twenty years ago.'

'What's your point?' I said, annoyed. 'He beat and raped a woman then, why not now? The best predictor of future behavior is past behavior.'

'He was what? Twenty-four? Twenty-five?' Sean asked. 'He's a grown man. He's married. He has responsibilities.'

'Ted Bundy was a Young Republican. What's that got to do with anything? He has a history of violent behavior toward women; he was seen with the victim the night she went missing.'

'Maybe he has an alibi.'

'Of course he has an alibi,' I snapped. 'Bennett always has an alibi. He's the Alibi Man. There's always someone willing to lie for a rich man. Juan Barbaro claims they left the party drunk, went to Bennett's house, and passed out. And I imagine the dog ate his homework too.'

'Did anyone see Irina leave the party with him?' Sean asked.

'Not that I've found. That doesn't mean it didn't happen.'

'And it doesn't mean that it did.'

I got up from the bench and faced him. 'Why are you being such an asshole?'

'I'm not! I just see you getting fixated—'

'Fixated? I was a cop for half my life. I know a viable suspect when I see one. He's a known violent sexual predator—'

'He committed one crime twenty years ago—'

'I can't believe you!' I shouted. 'He nearly choked that woman to death. Violent sexual predators who commit a crime and get away with it don't quit while they're ahead. They get a power rush, and they do it again.'

'And in the last twenty years he's been a serial killer and not gotten caught or even suspected of any crimes?' he said, also standing up from the bench, gaining the height advantage.

'I didn't say he's a serial killer,' I said. 'But how difficult is it to imagine him getting away with anything? If Bennett Walker had been a poor minority kid, he would just now be getting out of prison for what he did to Maria Nevin.'

'I understand all of that, Elena. I'm only saying, just because he was at the party doesn't mean he's the one. I imagine there were a hundred people there.'

'You know, I don't know why I'm having this conversation with you,' I said. 'I guess I thought I might get a little support from the one person who should understand—'

'I *do* support you! For Christ's sake, how can you say I don't support you?' he demanded. 'I'm supporting you now, you're just too pigheaded to see it. I don't want to see you get tangled up in something that's going to upset you and hurt you and take you down a road—'

I held up a hand to stop him. 'I think what happened to Irina is a little more important than me getting upset that I have to deal with an old boyfriend. But thanks for your input,' I said with a sharp edge in my voice.

Sean set his jaw and looked away from me, which was what he always did when he couldn't reason with me. I didn't want to be reasonable. I wanted to speculate that Bennett Walker had killed Irina, because that theory offered the possibility that he would finally have to pay for what he'd gotten away with all those years ago. And I wanted my best friend to support me in that, whether he thought it was reasonable or not.

One of us should have said something to break the tension, but neither of us did. My phone rang.

'Yes?'

I must have sounded impatient to be bothered. There was a beat of silence before the caller spoke. 'Elena, it's Juan Barbaro. Is this a bad time?'

It took me a second to register and to downshift the tension in my voice.

'Oh. Juan. No. I'm sorry if I snapped at you. I'm on edge with everything that's happened,' I said, staring at Sean.

'Then you must take some time to escape it, yes?'

'Yes. Absolutely.'

'Come, then, this afternoon. Watch a friendly polo match. We'll have drinks after. Dinner if you like.'

'Ah . . . sure,' I said. 'Who's playing?'

'Myself, Mr. Brody, some other friends. Not Bennett Walker,' he assured me. 'You have to promise not to accuse anyone of murder,' he added, but in a casual tone. Joking.

'I'll be on my best behavior.'

'Hmmmm . . . Now, what fun would that be?' he said, and chuckled deep in his throat. Like the purring of a panther, I thought.

We set a time to meet at the International Polo Club and ended the call.

I took a deep breath and let it go, trying to clear my head of the argument with Sean. I had been invited into a circle of suspects. I needed to be sharp.

'I have to go,' I said to Sean, and turned and walked away.

I should have apologized to him. He was the only person in my life I truly considered to be my friend, and I knew that he was. But I felt like being petty and childish, so I went with that instead.

# 21

The old yellow-painted Palm Beach Polo Club stadium, located a stone's throw from Players, had been *the* polo mecca of the world for many winter seasons. Everyone who was anyone had drunk champagne and stomped divots during halftime on that field, including Prince Charles and Princess Diana. But big-time high-goal polo had decamped from there several years before and moved farther out of town to the new International Polo Club Palm Beach, leaving the old stadium at the mercy of hurricanes and the zoning commission. Plans were in the works to knock down the venerable old facility and put up yet another strip mall. So much for landmarks.

The International Polo Club on 120th Avenue had become the place to see and be seen, a state-of-the-art facility with a stadium for thirteen hundred spectators and seven impeccably groomed polo fields, each spanning more ground than nine football fields.

I turned in at the main gate and went past the entrance to the stadium and club. The palm-lined drive led past tennis courts to the stadium, the pool-house pavilion, and the Grand Marquee ballroom, where brunch was served on Sundays. Beyond all that, horse trailers were parked on the shoulder of the road – big gooseneck aluminum stock trailers, with polo ponies tied along the sides. Grooms tacked horses up, cooled horses out. A farrier had his truck-mounted oven glowing red-hot as he prepared a new horseshoe to replace one lost in the heat of battle. Iron rang against iron. Conversations rose and fell, interspersed with laughter, with orders, with fits of temper in three different languages.

Several of the fields were in use, riders rushing up and down, mallets swinging, whistles blowing. Cars, trucks, and SUVs were parked down the sidelines with friends, family, and spectators tailgating and enjoying the day. The atmosphere was casual. No high-goal tournament matches were being played. These were less important contests, practice games, amateurs having a good time.

A line of small ponies walking nose-to-tail came down the road from one of the far fields. The kids riding them were so small, their helmets seemed to swallow their heads whole. They all wore numbered polo shirts and carried mallets. Pee Wee Polo.

Despite the elitist air about the game at its highest level, polo at the grass-roots level is accessible to anyone who can afford a horse and is talented enough not to fall off at high speeds. Young, old, man, woman, everyone is welcome to play or to watch. Pack a picnic, bring the family. Drive through a Wellington neighborhood where a lot of professional players live during the season and you will see their kids on bikes, swinging mallets, playing in the cul-de-sacs and parking lots.

I found a place to park and looked for the Star Polo trailer. Lisbeth Perkins was walking out a sweating, puffing polo pony. She stared at the ground as she walked, looking lost in sad thoughts, and jumped at the sound of my voice when I said her name.

She looked up at me, cornflower-blue eyes wide and rimmed with red. She seemed almost afraid to see me, as if I were the agent of doom.

'What happened to your lip?' she asked.

So much for Sean's theory on concealer and hemorrhoid cream.

'I fell. It's nothing,' I said, then turned the conversation to her. 'I'm surprised you're working today. Mr. Brody knows how close you and Irina were. Wouldn't he give you the day off?'

'I didn't ask,' she said, her voice raspy and raw. 'I don't know what I would do.'

I wondered if she meant that she would have felt lost or that she would have been afraid of what she might do to herself. The first was understandable, the second extreme.

'You're a private investigator, aren't you?' she said to me.

'No.'

'Irina told me about you. You found that missing girl last year. That's why you were asking me all those questions yesterday, isn't it? You're looking for the killer.'

I didn't deny it.

'You told that detective about me. Detective Landry.'

'Has he spoken to you?'

'He came to the farm this morning. I told him everything I told you.'

'I went to Players last night,' I said. 'The bartender told me you and Irina were arguing about something that night.'

'We were not,' she said, too sharply, a sure indicator that she was lying.

I shrugged. 'He says he saw the two of you in the hall having words, that you looked upset, and then you left. He doesn't have anything to gain by lying to me.'

'It wasn't anything,' she insisted. 'I wanted to go home and Irina didn't. That's all.'

'Did you go there in one car?'

'No.'

'Then what was the problem? She was having a better time than you?'

She rolled her eyes and sighed in that way perfected by teenage girls. She was a very young twenty-something, I thought.

'It doesn't matter. There was no problem,' she said.

'Then why did it look like you were arguing?'

She wanted to tell me to fuck off, but I suspected she had been raised not to do that.

'Where are you from, Lisbeth?'

'Michigan. Why?'

'Good Midwestern upbringing. Your parents were churchgoing folks.'

'So? What does that make me? A hick?' she said, offended.

'It makes you polite, reserved, responsible, private. You're a good and decent kid, I suspect. You know what it is to be a real friend to someone.'

She didn't say anything, just kept putting one foot in front of the other, walking the horse, doing her job. She rubbed the medallion she wore between thumb and forefinger, probably making a wish I would disappear.

'You were a good friend to Irina,' I said. 'You want to see her killer brought to justice, don't you?'

'Yes.'

'Then why lie to me about this? What the two of you argued about that night might be nothing or seem like nothing to you, but it could point the investigation in a direction that takes us to a lead or leads us to the killer. If it was nothing, why don't you just tell me?'

'I just thought she should leave too, that's all,' she said.

'Because . . . ?'

'It was late,' she said, still staring at the ground. 'And sometimes those parties get . . . a little . . . weird.'

'Weird-strange? Weird-creepy? Weird-sexual?'

She didn't say, but my imagination was already off and running. Wealthy men out for a good time, no wifely supervision, few morals, fewer scruples . . .

'Lisbeth, do you know what a material-witness order is?'

'No.'

'If Detective Landry thinks you're withholding vital information in a murder investigation, he can put you in jail and compel you to testify,' I said, twisting the law to suit my needs. 'All I have to do is tell him we had this conversation.'

She looked at me then, scared. 'Jail? I didn't do anything wrong!'

'You're doing something wrong in not telling all you know.'

Her gaze bounced around like a pinball, looking for a way to escape. She believed I was a private investigator. I had thrown around the royal *we* enough to imply the sheriff's detectives and I were working in concert. She felt trapped. I hoped she would do what most good Midwestern girls would do in this situation – yield to authority and tell the truth.

Lisbeth looked around for witnesses, then back at the ground, embarrassed or ashamed or both. 'Sometimes things get out of control. Everybody's drunk or high or something. And they take the party to someone's house, and there's sex.'

'Like an orgy?'

The Big Sigh again. 'Yes, like that.'

'And you didn't want to go, but Irina didn't care?'

'Something like that,' she said, her voice dropping off as we neared the Star Polo trailer again. She pulled the horse into his slot among the others and started to remove his tack.

I hung back, sensing I had pushed her as far as I could for the time being. I couldn't say what she had told me surprised me at all. When people know they don't have boundaries, they seldom set their own. Too much money, idle time, and the devil's workshop, etc., etc.

Was that what had happened the night Irina disappeared? The party had gotten out of control, the sex turned a little too rough, the game turned deadly?

Nothing fazed Irina. Combine her jaded sense of the world with her alleged desire to snag a wealthy American husband . . . It didn't surprise me that she would have joined in the games – or that Lisbeth, with her down-home sensibilities, would not. On the other hand, for Lisbeth to know what she knew, she could have been a past participant. That would account for the embarrassment and/or shame.

I looked for witnesses and stepped in beside the horse. 'Lisbeth, who went to those parties?' I asked quietly.

'All of those guys,' she mumbled, glancing nervously over her shoulder. 'The Club.'

'What club? The Polo Club?'

'No. Mr. Brody and his friends. They call themselves the Alibi Club.'

An unpleasant feeling slithered through me when she said it. The Alibi Club. I had called Bennett Walker the Alibi Man. Now there was a club. Wealthy bad boys covering one another's asses when there was trouble. There sure as hell was trouble now.

'Lisbeth!' Jim Brody barked from the back of a horse. 'What the hell's taking you so long? Manuel needs you over here.'

'Yes, Mr. Brody. Right away.' The girl took her opportunity to get away from me.

Jim Brody and I locked gazes for a moment. He was trying to figure out if he should know me, if he should bother to.

'Elena!' Barbaro jumped off a horse and tossed the reins to a groom. He was a vision of virility, in white breeches and tall boots. The animal in his element. 'I'm so glad you've come!'

His smile was wide and white, his hair tousled. But the smile stalled when I turned to face him fully.

'What happened?' he asked, gently cradling my face in his hands.

'I tripped and fell,' I said. 'I should make up a better story instead of admitting what a klutz I am, but there it is.'

'Is it very painful?'

His thumb brushed the outer corner of my mouth on

137

the right side – the side with feeling – and something like electricity skimmed over every undamaged nerve in my body.

'Only to my pride,' I said.

His gaze lingered on my mouth long enough to make me think he might kiss me, but he kissed my cheek instead – the one I couldn't feel.

'Elena, this is Mr. Brody, my *patrón*.' He planted a gloved hand on my shoulder to guide me toward Brody. 'Mr. Brody, my lovely new friend, Elena Estes.'

'Estes?' Brody said as he climbed off his horse. 'Any relation to Edward Estes?'

Here was the moment I had been dreading. With Bennett involved in all of this, I couldn't pretend to be someone else. And if Jim Brody knew my father, then my father was going to hear about me from one of his cronies. I hoped to God he didn't decide to play the wounded party, waiting for the return of his prodigal child.

'Not by choice,' I said sweetly, forcing the half smile, trying to look like trouble, the fun kind. 'He used to be my father.'

Brody's brows went up and he barked a laugh. 'Stick around for drinks. I want to hear the rest of that story.'

He climbed up on a mounting block and got on a fresh horse. Whatever his amusement at me, he wasn't going to let it get in the way of his polo match.

'He knows your father?' Barbaro asked, surprised.

'Small world.'

'Your father enjoys polo?'

'My father enjoys power. He used to race boats. Maybe he still does, I don't know.'

'How can you not know?' he asked, puzzled.

'I haven't spoken to my father in twenty years,' I admitted. 'Shouldn't you be getting on a horse?'

He waved a hand in the direction of the field. 'I'm sitting

out this chukker. These friends of Mr. Brody's, all are wealthy men who enjoy the game but are not so good with the mallet. They set up the match so in every other chukker each team gets one professional. The rest of the match they spend swinging at one another.'

He stopped talking and focused his full attention on me, taking in the look: Chanel ballet flats, slim white linen cigarette pants, a simple black ballet-neck top with three-quarter sleeves.

'Very chic,' he said, smiling. 'Simple, elegant, confident.'

'Well, that's just me in a nutshell.'

Barbaro chuckled. 'Elegant and chic, yes. Simple, I don't think so.

'Come, sit,' he said. 'My car is on the sidelines.'

His car was a British racing-green Aston Martin convertible with buttery tan leather interior and a flag of Spain decal on one corner of the windshield. He held the door for me.

'Nice ride,' I said, settling in.

'I leased it for the season. That way I get a new toy every year.'

'And what do you do when the season is over?'

'I go someplace else and lease another. I'm going to Europe to play for the summer. I have my eye on a Lamborghini.'

'Polo is very good to you,' I commented.

'Modeling has been very good to me. Polo is my passion,' he said. 'So, tell me why you have not spoken to your father in so long.'

'Because we don't have anything to say to each other. It's as simple as that,' I said. 'It's no big deal. It's not like we're related or anything.

'I was adopted,' I explained.

'But he is the only father you have known?'

'Edward Estes owned the house I grew up in. He had no

interest in me beyond how I might be useful to him. And I made a point *not* to be useful to him at all.'

Barbaro said nothing. He looked very serious as he tried to figure me out.

'I can't believe your good friend didn't fill you in on some of this last night,' I said.

'All he said was that the two of you were once engaged.'

I laughed. 'What a pretty liar you are. You even manage to look innocent. I outright accused him of being a rapist with the potential to be a murderer, and you're telling me neither one of you brought that up after I left?'

He dragged a hand through his hair and looked away, uncomfortable. 'He told me he was wrongly accused and you believed the worst about him; beyond that, I did not want to hear anything from him about you.'

I didn't really believe him, but it was an interesting position he was taking. I watched him openly and wondered what he was all about.

'What are you thinking?' he asked.

'That you intrigue me,' I said.

His eyebrows went up, and his mouth curved. 'This is a good thing, I think.'

'That depends on what I find out.'

He shifted in his seat, leaning toward me. 'You will find,' he said in a low, sexy voice, 'that I am a gentleman – as long as you would like me to be; that I am passionate. . . .'

He leaned a little closer and cupped a hand around the side of my neck, his thumb brushing seductively back and forth just along my hairline. My pulse quickened.

'I have only just met you, Elena,' he said, 'but already I have decided I have never known a woman quite like you.'

'Oh, I can guarantee that,' I said.

'Hey, Casanova!' The Aussie-accented shout came from a rider I recognized as Sebastian Foster, the tennis player. He sat astride not ten feet from the hood of Barbaro's car.

'You're up, mate! You'd better hustle.'

Barbaro looked annoyed as he sat back; his hand fell away from my neck.

'Last chukker,' Foster said. 'Seven minutes more and you're a free man.'

'You'll stay?' Barbaro said to me.

'Of course,' I said, but not for the reasons he wanted, at least not primarily. I was being brought into the fold of the Alibi Club, and I knew without question I would find Irina Markova's killer among them. It was like being brought into a den of lions. Lucky for me I was an adrenaline junkie. 'I wouldn't miss it.'

# 22

'Here's what I have for you so far,' Mercedes Gitan said. 'Have a seat.'

Landry sat. Her office was extraordinarily neat. The desktop could be seen with the naked eye.

'Cause of death: ligature strangulation.'

'What about the manual strangulation?'

'The hyoid bone was intact. I would expect that to be broken if the killer had choked her to death.'

'Time of death?'

'That's a tougher call because of the body having been submerged.'

'Guesstimate?'

'She'd been dead maybe twenty-four hours, give or take.'

'Rape?'

'I couldn't say. There was too much damage to the lower torso from the alligator.'

'What good are you?' Landry asked.

'I can tell you she had oral sex before she died and that she hadn't eaten any solid food,' she said. 'Her stomach contents were semen and a green-apple martini. Find out what time she had dinner and add digestion time. That'll get you something.'

'How much semen?' he asked.

'A lot. This didn't come from just one player, pardon the pun,' Gitan said. 'This girl did the whole club.'

# 23

'So how do you know my father?'

The best defense is a good offense.

I took a seat beside Jim Brody at a table in the 7th Chukker, one of the members-only bars at the International Polo Club. Located in the grandstand, it was smaller and more private than the Mallet Grille and Bar in the clubhouse. An unobtrusive panel door on one end wall led into the Wanderers Room, a small, private dining room with a five-star chef for those intimate dinners among the obnoxiously rich.

Brody hailed the waitress. 'We had a client in common a couple of years ago. Dushawn Upton.'

Dushawn Upton, aka Uptown. NBA all-star guard and known wife beater, on trial for soliciting the murder of a pregnant girlfriend. Another sterling character wealthy enough to buy the support and loyalty of Edward Estes.

I was aware of the case – not because my father had been in the news but because the case had *been* the news while I was a captive television audience, languishing in a hospital bed, recovering from being dragged down Okeechobee Boulevard like a rag doll caught in the door of a pickup truck.

'He's a hell of a lawyer,' Brody said. 'Hell of a poker player too.'

'It's easy to bluff if you don't have a conscience.'

He looked at me as if he wasn't sure what planet I was from. 'What did he ever do to you to make you such a loving daughter?'

'Nothing,' I said. 'Nothing at all. We have philosophical differences.'

'You didn't believe Dushawn was innocent?' He tried to look astonished, even amused. I didn't pretend amusement with him.

'No one believed Dushawn was innocent. The jurors didn't believe Dushawn was innocent, but they'd been beaten over the head with "reasonable doubt" until they couldn't see straight. Thanks to my father, another criminal walks away scot-free. A real tribute to our system of jurisprudence.'

Brody raised his eyebrows. He probably wasn't used to women who had opinions and could speak in compound sentences. This made me intriguing to him, which was a good thing.

'Should I give him your regards when I see him, then?' he asked.

'Only if you want to ruin his evening,' I said sweetly. 'And when will that be? I'll put it on my calendar.'

'Some disease-of-the-week charity shindig at Mar-a-Lago next week.'

How surreal it seemed, sitting there, suddenly one degree of separation away from my father after twenty years of living in an alternate universe. I didn't like it. I didn't like the idea of him knowing anything about me. I didn't want to be in his head.

I didn't want to imagine my mother thinking about me, wondering what I was up to. Which meant I had managed to convince myself that neither of them had ever had a thought about me in years. Out of sight, out of mind. It was easier for me to think that. Easier for me to stay away.

If they wanted to reach me, they had to know where I was. My name was in the papers the year before, connected to the Erin Seabright kidnapping case, connected to Sean. If they wanted me to be a part of their lives, they could have reached out then. They didn't.

'This is looking entirely too serious,' Barbaro said, taking a seat next to me. 'What has he done?' he asked, nodding his head toward Brody.

'We were just reliving old times,' I said.

'No sense in doing that unless they were the kind of old times that make us smile and laugh,' Barbaro said.

That would have severely limited my ability to converse, I thought, but I didn't say it.

The waitress delivered a round of drinks. Her eyes never left Barbaro. She managed to put her cleavage in his face as she bent over to get the cocktail napkins just right. He graced her with a polite smile as he said, *'Gracias.'* But his attention was on me.

Impressive. All the godlike playboys I had ever known wouldn't have shown that kind of restraint, no matter how much they wanted to retain my attention.

'Elena works with horses,' he said to Brody.

For a second, Brody looked a little confused, trying to put together the fact that I was the daughter of Edward Estes but worked in a stable. But he was at least as good a poker player as my father, and the confusion was hidden so quickly anyone else might have thought they had imagined it.

'I prefer to make an honest living,' I quipped, toasting him with my drink. 'I ride for Sean Avadon.'

'I don't know him. He's not into polo.' This said as if no one outside polo was worth knowing.

'No,' I said. 'But don't feel bad. I'm sure he doesn't know or care who you are either.'

Brody laughed, loud and from his belly. 'I like her, Juan,' he said to Barbaro, as if Barbaro was presenting me as a prospective concubine. 'She's got sass. I like sass.'

'It's your lucky day,' I said. 'I'm overflowing with sass.'

'Elena worked with Irina Markova,' Barbaro said.

Brody didn't miss a beat. He must have been something

145

at the bargaining table. 'Irina. Nice girl. Terrible shame what happened.'

'Yes,' I said, though it had become quite clear to me that 'nice girls' didn't run with this crowd. 'We'll miss her. I understand you saw her that night she went missing.'

Brody nodded as he took a sip of his thirty-year-old scotch. 'She was at the party at Players. I think she gave me a dance, but I have to say, as the guest of honor, I was having too good a time to remember much.'

'You don't remember if she was at the after-party party?' I asked. I could have been a hell of a poker player myself.

'There was no after-party that I know of,' Brody said. He looked away from me as he dug into the breast pocket of his aloha shirt.

'I must have misunderstood,' I said. 'I thought someone told me there was. I guess she could have said maybe there was an after-party.'

'Who's that?' he asked, glancing at me from under his brows.

I shook my head. 'Not important. Obviously I misheard.'

'Tony Ovada drove me home. We sat and smoked cigars,' Brody said, pulling one out of his pocket like a magician pulling a rabbit out of a hat.

'Are you sure you're not your father's daughter?' he asked. 'This is sounding a lot like an interrogation.'

'I'm sorry,' I said, sitting back. I took a sip of my vodka tonic. 'What can I say? That's what passed for conversation in our house. I grew up thinking cross-examination and redirect were normal components of social intercourse.

'Irina was a friend. I want to see her killer brought to justice.'

'So do I,' Brody said.

'I just think someone who saw her that night might know something, might have seen something and not even realized it.'

Brody made a motion with his cigar. 'Juan was there. Did anything strike you as odd, Juan?'

'Elena and I have already had this conversation,' Barbaro said. 'I wish I could say I saw something, heard something, but I was busy having a good time, like you, like everyone.'

Brody lit the cigar, took a big pull on it, and exhaled, looking up at the smoke.

The attraction of cigars is entirely lost on me. They smell like burning dog shit.

'Maybe we should establish a reward of some kind,' he said. 'Money talks – or makes people talk.

'I'll do that,' he said, making the executive decision. 'I'll call that detective. What was his name?'

'Landry?' I asked.

'What's a good amount for a reward? Ten thousand? Twenty? Fifty?'

'I'm sure that's up to you,' I said. 'That's very generous of you, whatever you decide.'

He waved it off. 'It's the least I can do. I feel responsible in a way. After all, she was last seen at my birthday party.'

'Except by her killer,' I pointed out.

The doors to the bar opened and Bennett Walker stepped in. His hair was slicked back, and he wore a pair of black Gucci wraparounds, despite the fact that the sun had already begun to slip over the horizon. He was halfway to our table before he realized I was sitting there. He hesitated, but I didn't give him a chance to escape.

'What interesting timing you have, Ben,' I said dryly.

Barbaro frowned at me.

Bennett sat down across from me. 'The joke's on me, I guess.'

'Something like that.'

He waved a hand at the waitress, and she turned and went back to the bar to get his drink without having to ask what he wanted. A regular. Maybe too regular. He looked a little rough around the edges.

'Surprised to see you here, Bennett,' Jim Brody said, his face neutral.

Bennett shrugged. 'A guy's gotta be somewhere. Why not among friends?' He looked directly at me and said, 'Exception noted, Elena.'

Brody raised an eyebrow. 'You two know each other?'

'In a past life,' I said.

I could see the wheels turning in Brody's head. He would be all over this. He hadn't made his fortune without knowing the background on every client – and every adversary – he had: their mother's maiden name, the date they lost their first tooth and their first job and their virginity. He had probably known before anyone that Dushawn Upton was capable of having a pregnant woman killed.

He would have the story on my relationship with Bennett Walker with the snap of his fingers. He now knew my father was Edward Estes. He probably knew that my father had been Bennett's defense attorney. Not hard to put the pieces together. My life was a jigsaw puzzle for ages nine and up.

'Mr. Brody has decided to offer a reward for information leading to the arrest of Irina Markova's killer,' I said to Bennett.

'Good thinking,' he said, glancing at his friend.

A vaguely strange response, I thought. Good thinking because it would help the case, or good thinking because it would take away suspicion? Was Jim Brody's generous offer tantamount to the Alibi Club version of O.J. hunting for the real killer? In that case he could make the reward as extravagant as he wanted, because he knew he would never pay out.

'You might as well write the check to Elena,' Bennett said. 'She claims to have a nose for this kind of thing.'

'What kind of thing is that?' I asked, not quite able to

keep the edge out of my voice. 'Knowing a criminal when I see one?'

The waitress arrived with his drink and gave him the same treatment she had given Barbaro. Bennett shoved his sunglasses back on his head and gave her his undivided attention, but there was a coldness in his eyes that made my skin crawl.

'Elena was a police detective,' he said, as the woman walked away, with his eyes on her ass.

'Are you surprised I would know that?' he asked, turning to look at me.

'I'm surprised you would bother to,' I said flatly. 'Am I supposed to be flattered?'

Brody set his cigar down and stared at me. 'A detective? What kind of a detective? Homicide?'

'Narcotics.'

'Oh, no,' Bennett said, without emotion. 'I've broken your cover.'

'I don't need a cover. I don't have anything to hide,' I said. 'Besides, I'm not in that line of work anymore.'

'Then why are you here?' he asked pointedly.

'I was invited for my charming company and witty repartee. Why are you here? Besides soaking your liver in vodka for the third night in a row – that I know of.'

From the corner of my eye I could see Barbaro looking unhappy or angry or both.

'I'm surprised you didn't go into sex-crimes investigation,' Bennett remarked. 'Rabid as you are on the subject.'

Barbaro leaned toward him, raising both hands in front of him.

'Enough,' he said quietly. 'None of us came here to have a bad time. Enough.'

'I didn't start it,' Bennett said, petulant.

'No. You're never responsible for anything,' I returned. 'You pass gas and it's someone else's fault.'

'Jesus Christ,' Brody said. 'The two of you sound like you're married.'

I looked away from Bennett, pulling in a slow deep breath, trying to rein myself in. I am and always have been my own worst enemy. I should have kept my cool with him. I should have at least pretended not to be affected by him. But my emotions regarding Bennett Walker had been held inside me like a festering abscess for a very long time. The person who said time heals all wounds didn't know jack shit.

'No,' I said to Brody, trying to force the half smile. 'I narrowly managed to escape that fate.'

'I should be going,' I said, sliding out of my chair. 'After all, I'm not a member of the club, am I?'

If any of them caught the double entendre, they didn't let on. I had taken a couple of steps toward the door before Brody spoke.

'Don't leave on his account,' he said, gesturing toward Bennett with his cigar.

'It's okay, Jim,' Bennett said. 'It's not the first time Elena's run away.'

I wanted to slap him. I wanted to choke him the way he had choked Maria Nevin twenty years past. The fury that seared through me was fierce. He wasn't more than two feet away. It took everything I had to keep my hands at my sides.

'Do you really want to do that, Bennett?' I asked quietly. 'Do you really want to push me? You, of all people, should know better. You, of all people, should know I don't give a rat's ass what other people think of me or of anything I do.

'You want to be back in the news?' I asked. 'You want to have the Maria Nevin case dug up and spread out for the media to feed on all over again? Because if you push me, I guarantee that's what will happen. You can put your family through that. You can have reporters camped on the doorstep of your house, following your wife everywhere she goes, hounding her—'

'Leave her out of this.'

'Don't fuck with me, Bennett,' I said, my voice low and vibrating with rage. 'I don't have anything to lose.'

I turned and walked out.

# 24

Outside, night had fallen. It was chilly enough to want a jacket. I didn't have one, but my residual anger was more than enough to heat me from my core outward.

What the hell would I do now? How could I take what had just transpired and turn it to my advantage? Had I just bought myself a ticket out of the inner circle, or would Jim Brody be the kind of man who kept his friends close and his enemies closer?

I was an ex-cop. I had an ax to grind with Bennett Walker, one of Brody's chosen few. I had just threatened to make trouble for him.

Nothing that had happened was a surprise, I told myself. Of course Bennett would show up. These were his friends. Of course they would all find out I had been a detective.

My guess – my gamble – was that Brody would want me where he could see me and try to influence me. And I suspected he would use Barbaro to do it.

'Elena.'

Bingo. I turned. He was still in his polo shirt and white breeches, saddle-tan boots to his knees. He looked every bit as sexy when he was serious as he did with the bright rakish grin. Maybe more so.

'I was just thinking damage control might be your assignment,' I said.

He pretended not to know what I meant.

'Your *patrón* sent you.'

'No one sent me,' he said, irritated. 'I am not a servant. I don't want to see you upset. I don't want our evening to be ruined by this . . . this bitterness between you and Bennett.'

'That's a tall order. You're talking about anger that's been contained and aged like single-malt scotch in a barrel for twenty years.'

'His behavior . . .' he said, searching for what he wanted to convey to me. 'He was not a gentleman. I apologize for that.'

'Why should you apologize? Besides, I was hardly a lady,' I confessed.

He raked a hand back through the thick, wavy mane. He should have been on the cover of a romance novel.

'I'm sorry, Juan,' I said. 'I don't know it for a fact, but I suspect I come from a long line of bitter, vindictive women.'

'What purpose does that serve?' he asked.

'What do you mean?'

'What purpose does it serve to hold that anger? What good does it do?'

'He beat and raped a woman,' I said impatiently. 'Someone should be angry about that.'

'The woman you say he raped.'

'*I say?* I say it because it's true.'

'And what does your anger do about it? Does it punish Bennett? Does he lie awake nights feeling the weight of your rage against him?'

Of course he didn't. If my anger had been able to bear down on Bennett Walker, he would have been crushed to death by it long ago.

'Hatred is like taking poison and expecting the other person to die of it.'

'Thank you, Father Barbaro,' I said sarcastically. 'Save the rest of your homily for someone who cares. It's easy for you to say let bygones be bygones. You weren't there. You never saw what he did to that girl.'

*Or to this one,* I thought, but I would never say that.

'You are not punishing him, Elena. You punish yourself.'

I didn't say anything. I didn't want to go down that road,

not even in my own mind. And I certainly had no intention of forgiving Bennett Walker for his sins. Why would I? Why would anyone? Why *should* anyone?

Barbaro touched my shoulder. 'I don't want to see you upset, Elena, over something you cannot change.'

'But those are the very things to be upset about, Juan,' I said. 'You want me to absolve him because that's just easier? The system failed. Oh, well. Nothing I can do about it, so I might as well pretend he never brutalized a woman while he was engaged to marry me, then expected me to commit perjury for him.

'I don't get that,' I said. 'I don't get how you can think that's okay. It's not okay.'

He looked away and sighed.

'If you can't see that, what am I supposed to think about you?' I asked. 'You just turn a blind eye to anything you find unpleasant? Did you turn a blind eye the night Irina was murdered? Someone got carried away, the girl is dead, so sorry, but there's nothing to do about it now. Might as well party on.'

'How can you think that of me?' he demanded.

'How can I not?' I returned. 'I've known you twenty-four hours. I met you because a girl was murdered. How do I know you didn't do it?'

'I told you I didn't.'

I laughed. 'Oh, and nobody's ever lied to me, so I should just take your statement at face value.'

'Do you trust no one, Elena?'

'No. I don't,' I said truthfully. 'I don't know one person who wouldn't lie to suit their own purposes if the situation arose.'

'That is a very sad state of affairs,' he said, pious. 'I'm sorry for you.'

'Oh, please,' I said. 'You're in the horse business, you run with this crowd – filthy rich, bored, spoiled, amoral, power-hungry. Life is a high-stakes game with no holds barred. Unless you're the Forrest Gump of the polo world, you know damn well at least half a dozen people have lied to you before lunch.'

Barbaro looked down at the sidewalk, his hands on his hips. He seemed to have nothing more to say, or else he was at a loss which direction to take to get what he wanted out of the situation.

'I'm going home now,' I said, and started to turn away.

'No. Elena, don't.' He took a gentle hold of my upper arm. 'Don't go. Please.'

'You can't possibly think I'm going back in there.'

'No. Let me take you somewhere for dinner,' he said, standing a little too close. 'Someplace quiet. Just the two of us.'

My instincts went on point. He must have felt the tension in me through his touch, but he didn't have time to react.

'Is there a problem here?'

Landry. Guilt washed over me like cold water almost before I recognized the voice. I knew how this had to look to him, like exactly what it was: an intimate conversation between his now-former lover and the most eligible hot polo star on the circuit.

'No. We're good,' I said. 'Detective Landry, this is Juan Barba—'

'We've met,' Landry said, with the kind of distaste that suggested he hadn't been impressed. 'Take your hand off the lady, José.'

'The lady doesn't object,' Barbaro said.

'Is that right?' Landry said.

I turned to face him, forgetting how I looked.

His eyes went wide. 'Did he do this to you?' he demanded, jabbing a finger at Barbaro.

He wouldn't have heard me if I had tried to answer. He

155

had already turned on Barbaro like an attack dog.

'Did you do this to her?'

Barbaro took a healthy step back and raised his hands. 'No!'

Landry didn't hear him either. He advanced aggressively. 'I don't know what they do where you're from, Paco, but you strike a woman here, we throw your ass in jail.'

'Landry,' I said, thinking I might have to hit him with something to get his attention out of the red zone. 'Landry! Detective Landry!'

Finally he glanced at me.

'I took a fall,' I said. 'If some guy did this to me, do you think he'd be alive to tell the tale?'

He didn't want to believe me. He wanted to pistol-whip Barbaro. But he looked at me hard and I lied to his face.

'No one hurt me.'

His gaze went from me to Barbaro and back and forth, not trusting either of us.

'No one hit me.'

Landry gave me the cop face. He was angry. I could feel it coming off him like steam. If he chose to believe Barbaro hadn't assaulted me, then he had to go back to the original issue: why Barbaro had his hand on my arm, and why I hadn't objected. It was a no-win situation all the way around.

'I need to have a word with you, Ms. Estes,' he said. 'Regarding the murder of your groom.'

'Elena?' Barbaro asked. 'Would you like me to stay with you?'

'No. Thank you, Juan. It's fine.'

He was frowning at Landry. Landry was glaring at him. Men.

I started backing down the sidewalk. 'I assume you would like to speak to me in private, Detective Landry.'

He didn't say, but he broke off the stare-down and followed me.

'Nothing like the smell of testosterone on the night air,' I commented.

'You think this is funny?' he snapped.

'I don't know what "this" is.'

'What the hell are you doing?' he demanded, stopping me with a hand on my arm.

I stared at the point of contact. 'Take your hand off the lady, Detective.'

He let go but didn't apologize. The concept was unknown to him.

'What are you doing here?' he asked.

'I was having a conversation with an acquaintance.'

'An acquaintance? Since when?'

'Since it's none of your goddamn business,' I snapped back.

'It's my business if it's been more than two days.'

I actually gasped in surprise, the statement was such a sucker punch.

'Why don't you just call me a whore to my face?' I suggested. 'Two days ago you thought we should move in together. Now you think I've been screwing a polo player on the side all along. You are such an asshole.'

'I think you already said that yesterday.'

'Oh? Has something changed since then?'

He started to say something, checked himself, took a step back, and regrouped. I just stared at him and shook my head.

'I don't want you hanging around with this crowd, Elena,' he confessed. 'It's not safe.'

'With what you apparently think of me, why would you care?' I asked. 'Why don't you just leave me alone? I know what I'm doing.'

'It doesn't matter. There are more of them than there are of you.'

'You think they're going to cart me off like a pack of jackals?' I asked, not that the thought hadn't crossed my mind in that instant Barbaro invited me to go somewhere alone with him. 'Do you know something I don't?'

'I know a lot of things,' he said cryptically.

I looked past his shoulder. Barbaro was hanging by the entrance to the stands, watching, waiting. He couldn't hear us, but I'm sure his read on our body language was that Landry and I were anything but friends. Good. I didn't want the Alibi Club thinking I still worked for the SO; bad enough that they knew what they knew about me.

'Really?' I said to Landry. 'Do you know that these guys are going to back one another up no matter what? Do you know their parties usually end up being clothing optional – which, by the way, I don't know from experience, as hard as that may be for you to believe. Do you know that they call themselves the Alibi Club?'

'The Alibi Club?'

Point to me. He didn't know. I had managed to one-up him. I still had that edge, that need to grab a lead, a piece of evidence before anyone else could. Once a cop . . .

I glanced past him again just as Barbaro went back into the building.

'Who told you that?' Landry asked.

'Lisbeth Perkins. She argued with Irina at Players that night because she didn't want Irina to hang around for the after-party.'

'But she did anyway,' Landry murmured.

He turned away from me, thinking, sorting out puzzle pieces in his head. I knew the look.

'What do you know?' I asked.

He didn't answer.

'What do you know?' I asked again, knowing he wasn't going to tell me. The autopsy, I thought.

'You know what happened to her,' I said. 'You know how she died, what the killer did to her. You know if there was one killer, more than one killer.'

He said nothing.

'She was my friend, Landry.'

He made a face. 'Don't call her your friend. You never did anything but complain about her attitude.'

'So? I used to complain about your attitude when I still considered you a friend. I guess since that's not the case anymore, I shouldn't expect you to tell me anything.'

He shrugged. 'You sure as hell didn't tell me anything.'

'About what? I've told you everything I know, everything I've been able to find out.'

'You didn't tell me about you and Bennett Walker,' he said. 'Why is that? You had to know I would find out.'

'I didn't tell you because it isn't relevant. It was twenty years ago.'

'I'll bet it's relevant to you.'

'Meaning what?'

'Meaning you're thinking Walker did Irina.'

'You don't know what I'm thinking,' I said. 'It's becoming more and more apparent that you don't know anything about me in any way that matters.'

'Maybe if you offered—'

'Why would I?' I demanded. 'Why would I do that? Why would I share anything with you? Why would I trust you, James? You've shown me you'll take anything I say and use it against me. If I learned anything being the daughter of Edward Estes, I learned not to do that. I have the right to remain silent.'

He touched my arm as I started to walk away from him. I jerked away from him and kept walking, wishing I could walk right out of my life and into another, where I had no past, and no one knew anything about me, and I could be whoever I wanted to be.

What a pleasant fiction that would be. If I could pull it off. But I didn't know how to be anyone other than who I was, and I didn't know what else to do but go on.

# 25

Weiss drove up and parked at the curb on the wrong side of the drive as Elena walked away, headed toward her car.

'There goes trouble,' he said, getting out of the car.

'Shut up,' Landry said, and turned for the building.

He wanted a drink and a cigarette and to be able to shut his emotions off, like a sociopath. Life had to be a lot simpler with emotions stripped away, no energy wasted on overreaction, anger, regret. The way things were, he was going to drive himself to an early grave.

'They're not going to cooperate,' Weiss said. 'These are the kind of guys who have three-hundred-dollar-an-hour attorneys standing around in Brooks Brothers suits just on account of they look good.'

'So they can call in the dogs,' Landry snapped. 'So what?'

'I'm just saying.'

'I don't expect them to cooperate. I want to rachet up a little tension. Refusing to give the DNA sample only makes them look guilty.'

'Of getting a group rate on blowjobs,' Weiss said. 'We're a long ways from proving a homicide.'

'They call themselves the Alibi Club,' Landry said.

'The Alibi Club? Where'd you hear that?'

'The Perkins girl,' he said. It wasn't exactly a lie. 'She said things get pretty out of hand at their parties.'

'Was she there Saturday night? I thought she left.'

'She tried to talk the Markova girl out of staying.'

Weiss stopped and looked at him. 'When did you get her to tell you all this? We could hardly get her to tell us her name this morning.'

'Maybe she just didn't like you, Weiss,' Landry offered.

'Up yours, Landry.'

'Let's go do this,' Landry said, and went into the 7th Chukker bar.

It was a far cry from Magda's. Beautiful antique bar, plasma-screen TV showing a polo match, a waitress who didn't look like she had to shave twice a day.

He went straight to the table where Brody, Walker, and Barbaro sat. Weiss took Sebastian Foster's table.

Landry looked hard at Barbaro. It should be illegal for a guy to be that good-looking. The mental image of the Spaniard touching Elena sent a rush of angry heat through him.

'Sorry for the misunderstanding, Mr. Barbaro,' he said without much sincerity. 'I've got a hot button when it comes to men abusing women. This murder has me on edge.'

'Understandable,' Barbaro said. He didn't sound very sincere either. 'You are a friend of Miss Estes?'

'I wouldn't say that, no. She found Irina Markova's body.'

'She used to be a detective,' Jim Brody said. 'The two of you must go back.'

'No,' Landry said. 'We don't. I'm sure Mr. Walker here knows more about Ms. Estes than I do.'

Bennett Walker frowned, sulky. Spoiled rich kid at forty-something. If they had been little kids, Landry would have knocked him on his ass on the playground. He wondered how Elena had ever looked at this guy and thought it might be a good idea to marry him. But then, he couldn't wrap his head around the idea of Elena marrying anyone. She was so wary, so cynical.

Bennett Walker had to be a big part of the reason why.

'What brings you here, Detective?' Brody asked. He pushed himself up out of his chair, the genial host, half a cigar stuck in one corner of his mouth.

'We don't pass for members?' Landry said. He looked over at Weiss; Weiss shrugged.

'No offense,' Brody said, 'but if either of you boys has seven figures or more in your bank account, you must have one hell of a second job.'

'We're trying to eliminate people from our list of possible suspects,' Weiss said.

'You can check us all off the list,' Brody said. 'I thought we covered that this morning.'

'Not that we don't believe you,' Landry said, 'but this is the age of forensics. We're collecting DNA samples from men Irina Markova spent time with the night she disappeared. It's just a little swab inside the cheek. No big deal.'

Brody's eyebrows went up. 'DNA samples? Sounds like a very big deal to me.'

'It's for elimination purposes,' Weiss said. 'If you didn't do anything to the girl, there's no problem.'

'My attorney will have a problem with it,' Bennett Walker said. He rose from his seat as well, ready to make a break for it.

'Why is that?' Landry asked. 'Because you're already a suspected sex offender?'

'Because of that attitude,' Walker said, jabbing a finger at him. 'I was never convicted of anything. And I don't have any intention of having my name connected in any way to this murder.'

'It's a little late for that,' Landry said. 'You were in Irina Markova's company in a public place the night she was killed. I'll be surprised if that isn't news at eleven tonight. You might want to call your wife and tell her to go to bed early.'

Walker was pissed. Landry could see an artery pulsing in the man's neck. 'You leaked that information to the media?'

'I have more important things to do with my time,' Landry said. 'The media does a pretty good job of digging up dirt on their own. You ought to know by now how that works.'

Walker spoke to Brody. 'I'm not putting up with this harassment. Are you?'

'No, of course not. I'm going to dinner,' Brody said, unconcerned. 'If you want to get a court order, Detective Landry, go ahead. Then you can speak with my attorney.'

'That goes for me too,' Walker said. 'I know too much about how evidence can be tampered with to make someone look guilty.'

Landry shrugged. 'Suit yourself. But you look pretty damn guilty as it is refusing the test, considering your past. Don't come crying to me when that hits the papers.'

Walker was red in the face, and sweat beaded on his forehead. He was used to getting what he wanted. He had clearly been accepted back into the fold of the filthy rich after he walked on the rape/assault back when. He had money and his victim did not. In the eyes of the Palm Beach crowd, that made him a target and her a liar out for hush money.

Landry had looked back over everything he could find on the case. He didn't think like a billionaire. He thought like a cop. And a cop's conclusion was that Walker had been guilty and had bought his way out of jail with no more concern than if he had been playing a game of Monopoly.

Walker wanted to hit him. He could feel it, could see it in the man's eyes. Landry found that perversely amusing, and he smiled.

'You want to knock me on my ass for that?' Landry said. 'Go ahead. I'll be all too happy to haul you in for assaulting an officer.'

Brody intervened. 'Bennett, let's go. The chef is waiting for us.'

The rest of them had been pulled in by the tension. No one said anything while they waited for Walker to respond.

When he didn't, Paul Kenner, the erstwhile baseball player, got up and slapped Walker on the shoulder.

'Let's go, my man, the steaks are calling my name.' He moved past Walker, turned around, and headed slowly backward in the direction of a door at the far end of the room.

Walker kept his stare on Landry. 'The sheriff will be hearing about your behavior from my attorney.'

Landry laughed. 'You're not on the Island now. This is the real world. You can't threaten me or buy me off for doing my job. If you're on the list, you're on the list, Mr. Walker. You're a potential suspect, like any other potential suspect. And your attitude isn't doing anything but moving your name closer to the top of that list.'

Rich Boy didn't have anything to say to that. Landry just stood there. He would have stood there all night, waiting for Walker to back down and retreat. He didn't have to, but he would have. Walker went with Kenner and Brody toward the door to what was probably some members-only secret dining room. The rest of the club followed.

'I guess that was a group no,' Weiss said.

Landry was watching Barbaro, who went for the exit. 'Maybe. Maybe not.'

They followed the Spaniard out. Barbaro turned a corner and went down the sidewalk toward the men's room, but he stopped and turned to face them.

'I will take your test, Detective,' he said to Landry. 'I have nothing to hide.'

'And your friends?'

'Are spoiled, wealthy men. As I told you earlier today: The wealthy are not like you or me. They have certain expectations in how they should be treated.'

'They're a pain in the ass,' Landry said bluntly.

Weiss had the plastic bag and sterile swab in his hand.

'You want to do this right here?' he asked. 'You don't want an attorney present? You don't think we're going to tamper with the sample? You're not going to sue us for violating your civil rights?'

'I have nothing to hide, Detective. None of your points apply, because you won't find my DNA to match whatever other samples you may have.'

It took only a matter of seconds. Swab in the mouth, rub the inside of the cheek, swab in the evidence bag, done.

When it was over, Barbaro turned and went back into the building.

Weiss turned to Landry. 'How do you like that?'

'I'd be happier if we had Walker's sample.'

'You got some kind of hard-on for that guy?' Weiss asked. 'What's that all about?'

'Twenty years ago he went to trial on a rape/assault. The case fell apart and he walked,' Landry said. 'It was a William Kennedy Smith kind of a thing. Rich kid from a prominent family, victim without a pot to pee in.'

'He said, she said.'

'In the end, she didn't say. She suddenly refused to testify against him.'

'He bought her off,' Weiss said.

'That's my guess.'

'That was twenty years ago.'

'Tigers don't change their stripes,' Landry said. 'Especially not if they got away with something once.'

'And in all these years he just hasn't gotten caught.'

'Who knows? Maybe he started paying outright for rough sex. Maybe he knocks his wife around, keeps it all in the family. I don't know,' Landry said. 'I know he sure as hell acts like he's got something to hide. I know that I saw a snapshot of him sitting with Irina Markova the night she went missing.'

'I don't like any of these guys,' Weiss said. 'I think they'd sooner lie than breathe. And they walk around with this big air of entitlement, like their shit don't stink. They should all have to go to jail just for being jerks. Let them see what they're entitled to in there.'

Weiss left with the sample to take it to the lab. Landry followed him but went back to Robbery/Homicide. At his desk – one of a collection of ugly 1960-vintage tan metal schoolteacher reject desks in the room – he put his reading glasses on, clicked a couple of keys, and brought his computer screen to life.

He brought up the archived newspaper articles about Bennett Walker's arrest and trial and scanned them again. When he had first dug up the dirt earlier in the day, his reaction to the fact that Elena hadn't been the one to tell him had been strong. He wasn't sure he could put a name to the emotions – anger, hurt maybe. He didn't like being shut out of her life.

Funny, neither one of them had done much talking about what their lives were like before they became involved. It had never bothered him. He hadn't really even thought about it. What was the point in talking about twenty or thirty years back?

Now he felt like she had been purposely holding back on him.

React first, think later. She had every right to be pissed off at him. He'd been a jerk.

He read back through the Bennett Walker articles, read between the lines.

He hadn't been living in Florida then. He had been aware of the case mostly from catching the odd newscast, and he hadn't retained what little he had known. Digging up the details had been full of surprises, not the least of which being that Elena was engaged to Bennett Walker at the time.

Walker's defense attorney had been Edward Estes, Elena's father. A man well-known for confusing juries by twisting facts and misdirecting focus, and getting his clients off, no matter how dead-to-rights guilty they may have been.

In Walker's case, Estes had gone with the tried-and-true blame-the-victim defense. The girl was promiscuous, liked rough sex, had an abortion when she was seventeen. She seduced Bennett Walker. She asked for it. She only brought charges against him in the attempt to get him to buy her off.

Landry looked at the photograph of the victim taken in the hospital two days after the attack. She looked like she'd been run over by a truck. Nobody asked for a beating like that. The girl was a bona fide victim.

He could only imagine how Elena would have reacted to her father's battle plan. She was a person who believed in justice. Her father believed in winning.

Elena had testified for the prosecution against her then-fiancé, which must have gone over well with dear old Dad. His own daughter sabotaging his high-profile case, shattering his client's alibi – that he had been with Elena at the time of the attack.

Stories had then been leaked to the press that Elena was nothing more than a woman scorned, out for revenge; that she had a checkered party-girl past; perhaps she wasn't mentally stable.

Landry didn't wonder where those stories had come from. They had come from Bennett Walker's camp, and the general in charge of Bennett Walker's camp had been Edward Estes.

Her own father had turned against her to win a case.

*'Why would I trust you, James?'*

Her fiancé turned out to be a rapist, and her father sold her down the river to suit his own purposes.

Why would she trust anyone?

She wouldn't.

She didn't.

Including him.

# 26

He was waiting for me, as I knew he would be, at the gate into the Palm Beach Point development. Alexi Kulak.

My headlights washed over him as he stood beside his car. He had pulled himself together since I'd seen him. He looked neat, dapper even, in a tailored brown suit. He had shaved and combed his hair. He looked like a businessman waiting for the auto club to show up and change his flat tire. Impatient.

I pulled my car over, parked it, and reached down into the hidden panel of my door. At least I was better prepared this time.

I got out of the car and walked toward him, my hands at my sides.

'Mr. Kulak,' I said, stopping just out of his reach.

'What have you found out?' he asked, skipping the social niceties.

'Nothing,' I said.

'Nothing? Don't tell me nothing,' he snapped.

'What do you want me to say, then? Should I make something up?'

'You have a smart mouth.'

'Fire me, then. I didn't audition for this job.'

I had left my headlights on. I kept my back to the light so I could see him clearly but the glare and my shadow would make it difficult for him to see me. I could see he didn't appreciate my chutzpah.

'Do you know how I fire people, Ms. Estes?' he asked quietly.

'Fifty-five-gallon drum and forty gallons of acid?'

He smiled like a shark and looked every bit as deadly. 'That is a good one. Perhaps I should add that to my repertoire. Would you like to be the first?'

'No,' I said calmly. 'Do you want to find out who killed Irina?'

'Yes.'

'Then let me do my job.'

'You spent half the day with those men.'

'Yes, I did. Did you expect me to just ask the group over drinks whether or not any of them killed her? And did you expect any of them to just stand up and say, "Why, yes, I killed her. Why do you ask?"'

He'd had it with my mouth. He took two aggressive steps forward, bringing a thick hand up to strike me or to grab me.

I pulled the 9mm from my waistband behind my back and planted it squarely between Kulak's eyes, stopping him in his tracks.

'Don't you fucking touch me,' I said, in a very different tone of voice.

My anger pushed him back a step, and then another. I stayed with him, never losing the contact between the gun barrel and his forehead. He backed up until he was trapped against his car. His eyes were wide with surprise or fear or both.

'You will never touch me again,' I declared, adrenaline humming through me like a narcotic. 'I will fucking kill you where you stand. Don't think for a second that I wouldn't do it. I would kill you and stand on your corpse and howl at the moon.'

He was breathing shallowly and quickly. He didn't think I was bluffing. Good. He needed to know he wasn't the only unpredictable one in this strange arrangement.

I backed off and lowered the gun to my side. A car was coming toward the gate. The driver opened it with his remote control, drove through and on, never so much as glancing at us in curiosity.

'Which one do you suspect?' he asked.

'I don't have a favorite, and I'm not a psychic. I need a lead, a witness, to catch someone in a lie,' I said. 'If you want a quicker solution than that, why don't you have a couple of your associates beat it out of them one at a time?'

He hesitated, looked a little away from me. Odd, I thought.

'This is my business,' he said. 'My personal business.'

Alexi Kulak was the boss in his world. He could have snapped his fingers, and no one would ever see Jim Brody, or Bennett Walker, or any of that crowd again.

I shrugged. 'Kill them all and let God sort it out.'

'That is what you would do?' he asked.

'No,' I said. 'I would do it all quietly, patiently. I would gather evidence and speak to her friends. I would speak to anyone who might have seen her that night, no matter how unlikely it may be that they would have an answer. By the time I went in for the kill, I would have absolutely no question who had murdered her. And I would have absolutely no mercy for that person.

'That's what I would do,' I said. 'That's what I am doing. If you want to do it another way, that's your business.'

He sighed and sat back against his car, his broad shoulders slumping. He rubbed his hands over his face. His head was bowed.

'This pain,' he said, rubbing a fist against his chest. 'It is a thing that never ends. I want to scream it out of me. It is like a fire, and it burns and burns, and there is nothing I can do to put it out. I am mad with it.'

I actually felt bad for him. What an odd moment. Here was a man so ruthless he probably started his day eating the eyeballs he had plucked from enemies and traitors, and yet he was just a man, and he was grieving and in pain.

'You feel like you're caged with a demon,' I said. 'You can't escape it. You can't run away. There's nowhere to hide.'

He looked at me, and his face shone with tears he had tried to wipe away. 'You've known this pain?'

'I know what it's like to want so badly to reverse the past that I would have turned myself inside out to do it,' I said quietly, thinking of the day Deputy Hector Ramirez had taken a hollow-point bullet in the face, blowing out the back of his skull and leaving his wife a widow and his children fatherless. Because of me. I knew what that pain was. The pain of guilt.

And I knew all about the pain of loss. Not of having a dream just fade away, but of having it yanked away and smashed before my eyes. I refused to let the faces surface in my mind. The pain came anyway, like an old friend who would just walk in the front door without knocking.

'Let me do my job, Mr. Kulak,' I said. 'Then you can do yours.'

Without waiting for him to say anything, I went back to my car, did a U-turn on the street, and drove back toward Wellington.

*I would speak to anyone who might have seen her that night, no matter how unlikely it may be that they would have an answer.*

My own words came back to me, as did the vision of the strange woman who had approached Barbaro and me in the parking lot at Players the night before.

*. . . no matter how unlikely . . .*

# 27

I swung into the drive-through at Burger King for sustenance to go, then continued on down Greenview Shores to South Shore. I pulled into the lower parking lot at Players and sat there for a while, trying to choke down a few bites of a chicken sandwich. I didn't feel like eating. I felt like drinking.

It had been a long and taxing day already, and the night was young. My head spun with flashbacks of Landry, and Barbaro, and Bennett Walker. I could see Billy Quint squinting up at me from his wheelchair. I could see Bennett's cold, flat eyes as he stared at the waitress in the 7th Chukker and the look he gave me when he said, *'I'm surprised you didn't go into sex-crimes investigation.'* Taunting me, and enjoying it.

In point of fact, I *had* gone into Sex Crimes when I got my detective's shield. It hadn't lasted long. My captain called me 'overzealous,' sent me for a psych evaluation, and transferred me to Narcotics, where everyone was a little bit crazy and overzealousness was considered a virtue.

I had secretly been relieved, afraid that if I stayed in Sex Crimes I would have ended up killing a suspect out of my own fury and hurt.

Fury and hurt. My emotions were bouncing between the two like the ball in a game of Pong. If I thought about it long enough, I would realize how exhausted I was, and I would start thinking about what a mess my life had been to date and how I didn't see it getting any better. And things would go downhill from there.

Instead, I took the Burger King bag and set it on the hood so that my car wouldn't have that nasty BO stench of cold, uneaten fast food when I got back into it later.

I looked around the parking lot, casually walked around, stared hard into the night, where the sodium vapor light faded to black and the parking lot gave way to grass and trees. Though I had the creepy feeling of eyes staring back at me, I couldn't see anyone. Maybe later.

As I approached the front of the club, I pulled a snapshot of Irina and Lisbeth out of my clutch and walked up to the valet stand. The kid working was tall and gangly and looked like a goose with acne. His eyes went wide at the sight of my fat lip.

'You should see the other guy,' I said.

'Huh?'

The future of America.

'Were you working Saturday night?'

'No.'

'Do you know anyone who was working Saturday night?'

'Yeah . . .'

He paused so long I thought he had gone catatonic.

'. . . Jeff was.'

Jeff looked up as he came around the back of a white Lexus, stuffing his tip money in the pocket of his baggy black pants.

'Jeff was what?' he asked.

'Working Saturday night,' I said.

He cut his friend a look like he had just ratted him out to the homeroom teacher. This one was a foot shorter than the other one, with orange hair and a cowlick.

'Yeah,' he said reluctantly, as if he would have much preferred to lie to me. Little weasel.

'Did you see this girl?' I asked. I folded Lisbeth's half of the photo back and showed him the other half, tapping a finger beneath Irina's face.

He barely glanced at it. 'No, I don't think so.'

'Maybe you should look again,' I suggested. 'For more than a nanosecond.'

He glanced at it again. 'I don't know. Maybe.'

'You don't know?' I said sternly. 'Are you gay?'

He looked me in the eyes for the first time, shocked that I might think so, particularly in front of his cohort, who started laughing. 'No!'

I held the picture up. 'A girl who looks like this comes prancing in here dressed to kill, looking like more money than you'll ever make in your lifetime, and you don't know if you saw her.'

'We were really busy,' he said, evading my gaze. 'It was some rich guy's birthday party.'

'She came out this door, late. The party was breaking up. Only the diehards were left.'

He was squirming like the kid who threw the baseball through the neighborhood witch's window and got caught.

'Do you know why I'm asking you?' I questioned.

A black BMW 7 Series pulled in.

Jeff started leaning toward it. 'I have to work.'

'It's my turn!' the goose protested.

'It's his turn,' I said. 'You have to share, Jeffrey.'

He wanted to snap his fingers and become invisible. I tried again.

'Do you know why I'm asking you if you saw this girl Saturday night?' I didn't wait for another stupid answer. 'Because she's dead, Jeff. She came here Saturday and had a good time. And then she left here, and someone took her somewhere and strangled her to death and threw her body in a canal to rot and be eaten by an alligator.'

The kid made a nauseous face. 'Wow. That's sick.'

'Yes, it is. Is your memory coming back to you? Did you see her leave here Saturday night?'

He stared at the photograph, then looked away, frowning. 'No,' he said. 'I didn't see her.'

A Porsche pulled into the drive.

'I've gotta go,' he said, and bolted like a skittish horse.

I watched him, imagining him working Saturday night. A busy evening, money walking in and out the door. Big tippers. Someone slips him a little something extra to lose his memory. Just between us men – wink wink.

The goose came ambling back, oblivious of any tension around. He glanced at the picture.

'Hey, I know her,' he said. 'She's so hot!'

'You've seen her around here?' I asked.

'Yeah. She comes here a lot.'

'With anyone or alone?'

'With some other girls.'

'Have you ever seen her with a man?'

'Sure.'

'Who?'

'I dunno.'

I wanted to reach my hand into his brain and pull the information out.

'Let's try it this way,' I suggested. 'Always the same man? Or different men?'

'Different guys.'

'Younger? Older?'

'Older. Old rich guys.'

'If I brought some photographs by, do you think you might recognize any of them?'

'I dunno. . . .'

Even I can beat my hard head against a brick wall for just so long.

'Do you have a cell phone I can call you on?'

'Yeah.'

I dug a small notebook out of my bag. 'What's your number?'

He recited his number to me. I thanked him and went into the club, thinking I deserved a drink after that.

The gorgeous Kayne Jackson was tending bar again. Eye candy in a painted-on black T-shirt, biceps rippling as he prepared a cosmo to send away with the waitress.

'So, Kayne Jackson,' I said, taking an empty stool near him. 'What are your goals in life?'

He glanced up at me and smiled. 'Ketel One and tonic, big squeeze of lemon?'

I gave him the half smile. 'There's nothing more valuable or more dangerous than a bartender with a good memory.'

He chuckled as he scooped ice into a tumbler. 'I'm not dangerous. Where did you get that lip?'

'They were having a sale at Wal-Mart. Lifelike, isn't it?'

'Looks like it hurts.'

'Nothing a little vodka won't cure,' I said.

'I've heard that story before.'

'Everybody confesses to their bartender. Considering this crowd, I'm sure you've got stories that would make the average person's eyes pop out.'

'I'm valuable because I'm discreet,' he said, pouring the Ketel One. 'Or I wouldn't have this job.'

'Hmm . . .' I wondered if he drove a Maserati. Blackmail could be a profitable little side job. 'I imagine some of your patrons value your discretion enough to pay you a little something extra on the side.'

'I have some generous customers,' he said, noncommittal as he squeezed the wedge of lemon.

He set the drink in front of me and went to the other end of the bar to take an order. I watched him pop the caps on a couple of beers.

'Back to my original question,' I said when he returned. 'What do you want to be when you grow up, Kayne?'

He shrugged as he rinsed out some glasses in the sink. 'This is it.'

'To be a bartender?'

'Do you think there's something wrong with that?'

'No. I'm surprised, though,' I confessed. 'You're a young, extremely handsome, and charming man. You could be a model, an actor. Nothing against your profession, but I doubt your tips raise you to the same tax bracket as a Ralph Lauren model.'

'You'd have to ask Juan Barbaro about that,' he said. 'I do okay.'

'You're not secretly a wannabe polo star? A spy? A high-priced gigolo?'

He smiled, and female hearts all around the room skipped a beat. 'Why do you ask?'

I laughed. 'I don't buy trouble, but you'd be worth your weight in gold in Palm Beach.'

He pretended to shudder. 'I don't need money that badly. And I prefer my ladies to be under retirement age.'

And who could blame him? The median age of the Island's residents was creeping up toward the speed limit. Plastic surgery was a growth industry.

'So draw the line at the bedroom door,' I said. 'Do you have any idea what a walker can make during season?'

'Escorting old ladies to charity balls isn't my idea of a good time,' he said. 'I enjoy what I do, the people I meet. It's fun.'

'You make a lot of friends here,' I said.

'Yeah.'

The waitress came by, gave him an order, and gave me the once-over and a dirty look. Little bitch.

'You said you knew Irina.'

'Yeah. She was something.'

'Do you know any of her friends? Girlfriends she might have confided in?'

He started to shake a martini. Muscles rippled in his chest and upper arms.

'My opinion: Irina had acquaintances and rivals, not friends. She didn't strike me as the kind of girl who would confide in anyone.'

'Rivals?'

'The girls that run with that crowd all want the same thing, and there are only so many multimillionaires and handsome polo players to go around.'

He gave me a funny look. 'You worked with her. You must know more about her than I do.'

'It's becoming clear to me that I didn't know her at all,' I said. 'What about Lisbeth Perkins? She was a friend.'

'Girl crush.'

'Lisbeth is gay?'

'No,' he said. 'It was more like hero worship. Irina was glamorous, exotic, sophisticated, self-assured.'

Everything Lisbeth was not.

'Did Irina ever come in here with a boyfriend?'

'Nope.' He poured the drink and added two olives.

'Did she ever leave here with a boyfriend?'

'Not that I noticed,' he said, 'but my vision gets poorer and poorer as people move toward the door.'

'Would an infusion of cash improve that?'

He shook his head.

'Did an infusion of cash cause that problem?'

'I have other customers,' he said, and started to turn away. His left hand was braced against the bar. I reached out and caught his wrist.

'She's dead, Kayne. If you know something, it's worth a hell of a lot more than a big tip off the books. It's one thing to turn a blind eye to an affair. Irina was murdered. If you know something about that but you tell the police that you don't, you're committing a crime. You could be charged as an accessory after the fact.'

He pulled away from my touch, frowning. 'I don't know who killed Irina. If I did, I would tell the detectives. Do you want another drink?'

'No, thanks.'

'Then that'll be six-fifty.'

He walked away. I finished my drink, left a ten on the

bar, and went back to the lobby. I was frustrated. There were people around who had information, but there was no getting it out of them. Selfish, conscienceless bastards. Maybe I should have given Alexi Kulak a list of their names.

I went downstairs to the restaurant on my way to the ladies' room and spied Sean sitting by himself, eating a pork chop and reading *POLO* magazine. He didn't look up as I approached his table. He didn't look up as I took the seat across from him.

'You look lonely back here,' I said.

'I didn't feel up to having company,' he said. The guilt trip. I guess I deserved it.

I sighed and leaned my forearms on the tabletop. My mother would have been mortified to see it.

'I'm sorry about this morning,' I said. 'I shouldn't have implied you weren't supportive. My God, you've been the only support I've had for most of my life. You know what that means to me.'

My eyes started to burn. I would have had tears in them if not for the damage caused by 'the Incident,' as my attorney liked to call it.

Sean's expression softened, and he reached across the table and put his hand over mine. 'I love you, honey,' he said sincerely. 'I don't want to see you have to open the door on all that misery.

'I hate Bennett Walker at least half as much as you do. If he was involved in Irina's murder, I want to see him in prison. But I don't want this to tear you up, El. I remember what it was like during Bennett's trial, what it did to you. It broke my heart.'

There was a lump in my throat the size of a crab cake. I had to look away from him to compose myself. My eyes went to the magazine he was reading, but I didn't really take it in.

'Yeah,' I tried to joke. 'Made me the neurotic mess I am today.'

He took my chin in his hand and turned my face sideways, scrutinizing my lip. 'If that scars, I have the perfect doctor to fix it.'

'Yeah?' I said. 'And where do you have him? In one of your closets?'

'New York, of course. He did my eyes.'

'What?'

'Blepharoplasty,' he specified. 'They take—'

'I know what it means.'

'Five years ago,' he said. 'You never would have guessed, would you?'

'No. I've just always thought you were a wonder of nature.'

'Honey, even wonders of nature can use a little tweak now and again.'

I laughed, looking down at the table. His magazine caught my eye again.

'What are you reading?'

'I'm not reading. I'm just looking at the pictures,' he confessed. 'I want to have some of these Argentinian polo players stripped naked, dipped in chocolate, and delivered to my house.'

'May I?' I asked, reaching for the magazine. Sean pushed it toward me.

'You need to lasso one of these young stallions for yourself, El,' Sean said. 'Forget Landry. He's cute, but he's too cranky. Grab one of these guys and ride 'im, cowgirl.'

I didn't respond. I barely heard him. As I picked up the magazine, I fixed on the cover. The banner read: *Fun in the Sun: Top Amateur Players in Florida*. The cover featured a photo of Sebastian Foster, Jim Brody, Paul Kenner, and Bennett Walker.

'Can I borrow this?' I asked.

Sean frowned. 'What for?'

I was already out of my chair. I went around the table,

kissed him on the cheek, and left the restaurant.

The goose was at the valet stand, staring out at nothing, with his mouth hanging open. He jumped when I spoke.

'Hey, kid, look at this picture,' I said, holding the magazine up in front of his face. 'Do you recognize any of these men?'

'I dunno.'

'It's not a trick question. You either recognize them or you don't.'

He looked at me like he thought I might do something to him.

'Well, do you? Know them?' I added, heading off an I-dunno at the pass.

'Yeah.' He pointed a finger at Jim Brody. 'He drives an Escalade most of the time. But he's got like three other cars. They're so hot.'

I pointed at Sebastian Foster.

'Jaguar, like in *Austin Powers*. Shag-a-delic!' He laughed at himself.

Paul Kenner.

'Ferrari.'

Bennett Walker.

'Porsche Carrera.'

I pulled Irina's picture out and held it up next to the magazine cover. 'Did you ever see this girl leave here with any of these men?'

'Yeah.'

'Which one?'

He shrugged. 'That one.'

I held my breath as he raised his hand, reached out, and touched the magazine cover with his finger.

'Porsche Carrera.'

Bennett Walker.

# 28

I started trembling. My heart was beating so fast I should have been frightened. A witness could put Irina with Bennett Walker, leaving the club together in his Porsche.

'When?' I asked. 'When did you see them leave together?'

He dropped his hand and shrugged. 'I dunno. Maybe a week ago.'

Not the night she disappeared, I realized. This kid hadn't been working Saturday night. Still, his statement put them together, established that they had spent time alone together.

Unless that was what Jeff the Weasel was hiding — that Bennett Walker was the guy Irina had left with, that Bennett had bought the kid's silence.

'And that one.'

His voice snapped me out of my speculation. 'What?'

'That one,' he said again, touching the tip of his finger to the magazine page. 'Escalade.'

Jim Brody.

'He gets a lot of girls,' he said. 'I don't know why. He's really old.'

'And really rich,' I said.

Jeff the Weasel came jogging back from the valet lot, looking suspicious.

'So, Jeff,' I said. 'Your friend here says he saw that girl leave with Jim Brody.'

'No, he didn't,' Jeff said. 'He wasn't even working Saturday night.'

'Not Saturday night,' the tall one said. 'Last week. Remember? You were here.'

Jeff stared at his pal, wide-eyed. 'You are so fucking stupid! Shut up! You're not supposed to talk about the customers!'

'Guess what, Jeff?' I said flatly. 'If one of these guys was the last person to see that girl alive, we're not talking about a customer. We're talking about a killer. And you're not part of the Wink-Wink-Boys-Will-Be-Boys Club. You're aiding and abetting in a felony murder. You don't get sent to juvie hall for that. You ask your mother to pack you clean underwear and a big tube of K-Y Jelly, because you're going away to live with the big dogs.'

I pulled my phone out of my bag and called Landry while I stood there. I wasn't sure whether he would pick up or not. To his credit, he did.

'There are two valets working the parking lot at Players tonight,' I said without preamble. 'You need to speak with them as soon as possible. They have information.'

I hung up. The boys stood side by side, Mutt and Jeff – literally – mouths hanging open.

'You'll be meeting Detective Landry from the sheriff's office shortly,' I informed them. 'Please give him my regards.'

I left them standing there panicking and walked down to my car. When I pushed the button on the remote to unlock the doors, the lights flashed and the car made a little wolf-whistle sound – and someone jumped off the hood and spun around to face me.

I don't know which of us was more startled: me, or the peculiar little character caught with her hand in the Burger King bag I had left on the hood.

We stared at each other. She was in the same strange getup as the last time – the black unitard that covered everything but her face, the conical hat with the pom-pom, the platform shoes. Only her makeup had changed. Tonight her face was painted a dark color – blue or purple, I thought, though I couldn't really tell in the poor light of the parking lot. The area around her left eye was outlined in silver. She had painted a trail of curving lines from the right corner of her mouth up diagonally across her cheek to the corner of her right eye.

'You're naughty!' she declared.

'*I'm* naughty? That's my dinner you're eating.'

She wadded up the fast-food bag and put it behind her back.

'No, I'm not.'

'Do you have a name?' I asked.

'My name is No Name,' she said. 'You can't put that on my permanent record.'

'I wouldn't dream of it. What should I call you?'

Her eyes darted to the left, as if she were listening to the counsel of an invisible friend. 'You may call me Princess Cindy Lullabell.'

'Cindy,' I said. 'My name is Elena.'

'I don't care,' she said bluntly. 'You're naughty. Like the others.'

'What others?'

She shook her head from side to side, pom-pom waggling back and forth at the top of her pointy hat.

'What does it mean to be naughty, Cindy?' I asked. 'If I know, I can try not to be.'

Princess Cindy Lullabell dropped the Burger King bag on the ground, turned her back to me, wrapped her arms around herself as a lover would wrap his arms around her, and started wiggling and giggling. She paused once to look over her shoulder at me and blow me a kiss.

'Are you talking about people kissing?' I asked.

'They'll put that on your permanent record, even if you have a special pass.'

'Thanks for the warning. Can I show you something, Cindy?'

She gave me a dubious look.

'It's just a photograph,' I said.

She looked sideways at her invisible consultant. 'Is it a trick?'

'No. I just want to know if you've seen this woman.'

I held the photograph out, hoping there was enough illumination from the sodium vapor light to allow her to see. She reached up into her pom-pom and turned on a pinpoint light. The mother of invention.

She took the photo from my hand and studied Irina and Lisbeth.

'Oh, yes,' she said. 'They're VERY naughty. They won't be allowed to graduate, and that will go into their files.'

I took the snapshot back and pointed at Irina. 'Did you see her here Saturday night?'

She thought about that, conferred with whatever voice she was hearing. When she turned back to me, she said, 'When is Saturday?'

'Three days ago. There was a big party that night.'

'I don't attend parties,' she said. 'There might be drinking and naughtiness. My adviser says I have to go now. Thank you very much. Dinner was lovely. Good night.'

She curtsied, then bolted and made for the pipe gate and the Polo Club development on the other side of it. She was surprisingly quick in those awkward thick-soled shoes. I followed her at a distance, not so much interested in catching her as in seeing where she went.

I didn't want her to be frightened of me. Who knew what kind of information was locked up with the butterflies in her head? I climbed through the gate and started to jog after her.

She ran on ahead of me, elbows pinned to her sides, her lower arms flailing up and down, as if she were some strange wounded bird trying to take flight. She turned onto a cul-de-sac lined with lower-end condos – *lower-end* meaning they rented for a mere $3,500 a month for a one bedroom, one bath.

As I turned to cut across the grass, the toe of my adorable Chanel ballet flat tripped me, and I fell forward onto my knees and elbows. When I got up and looked around, Princess Cindy Lullabell was nowhere to be seen.

Damn.

I retrieved my shoe and jogged down the cul-de-sac to the spot I had seen her before I'd gone down. There was a shed row of double garage doors, all closed. The growth of tropical trees and banana plants and giant ferns had created a dark corridor down the side of the last of the condo buildings.

I didn't have a flashlight and wasn't inclined to go in there even if I'd had one. The potential for a nasty surprise was enough to keep me out. The lush landscaping was a haven for rats and mice. Rats and mice attract snakes. On the other side of the thicket of trees was a canal. Canals attract alligators.

The image of the gator rolling with Irina's lifeless body in its jaws flashed through my mind.

I went between the condo buildings instead, where light spilled out from the windows, allowing me to see what I was stepping on, mostly.

Horse people populated Palm Beach Polo and Golf. Horse people and their multitude of Jack Russell terriers, Welsh corgis, Westies, Labradors, Labradoodles, cocker spaniels, and every other breed of dog known to man. The owners weren't always so conscientious about cleaning up after them.

I looked around for another fifteen minutes, checked the storage sheds. Tried the doors. No luck. I went down the street to the west-entrance guard shack, which faced South Shore. The guard was watching a movie on a tiny television set. I went up to the glass door and tapped politely. She turned and glared at me and made no move to invite me in. I pulled the handle myself and hoped she wouldn't pull a gun and shoot me.

'Excuse me,' I said. 'Sorry to interrupt, but did you see anyone run past here a few moments ago? A person dressed in black with a cone-shaped hat and big platform shoes?'

'The Freak?' she said, indignant that I had asked her a question.

'Yes.'

'No, I ain't seen her.'

The woman was the size of a baby hippopotamus. She had planted herself on that chair like Jabba the Hutt.

'Do you know anything about her?' I asked.

'No.'

'Do you know where she lives?'

'No. Why would I know that? Do I look like I would hang out with the Freak?'

'Not at all. But working here, I imagine you see and know about all kinds of things.'

Her name tag read *J. Jones*.

'You don't happen to know her name, do you, Ms. Jones?'

'The Freak,' she said impatiently. 'Are you deaf?'

'I don't imagine that her mother gave birth to her, looked at her, and proudly said, "Let's call her the Freak," do you?'

J. Jones made a face. 'You don't need to get flip with me,' she said.

'Apparently, I do.'

She looked me up and down, taking in the fat lip, the grass-stained white pants.

'Do you live here, ma'am?'

'No, I don't.'

'Then why are you here? You can't be here for no good reason. How did you get on the property?'

'I climbed through the gate from Players.'

'That's criminal trespass,' she said. 'And why are you running around looking like that? What do you want with the Freak, looking like that? All grass stains and dirt, like you been rolling around on the ground like an animal.'

'I tripped and fell.'

'Running after the Freak,' she said with disgust. 'What's up with that?'

I surrendered. 'Never mind. Thank you for all your help.'

She snorted. 'I didn't give you any.'

'Exactly,' I said, my attention no longer on the guard but on the TV screens showing cars coming in and going out through the gate.

Guests were required to stop at the gate to talk their way in. Residents drove through, bar-code stickers on their cars being read by a sensor, which opened the residents' gate as they approached. And all of it was caught on tape. I wondered how many of the residents were aware of that.

Barbaro had said he and Bennett crashed at Bennett's house in the Polo Club Saturday night. They had to have come through either this gate or the main gate on Forest Hill Boulevard. If Irina had voluntarily come in with one of them – or drove herself – that would be on tape.

Exhausted, I hiked back to the parking lot and to my car. I drove home, went into my cottage, and went facedown on the bed, past thinking about what to do next.

# 29

Landry looked through the photographs Lisbeth Perkins had taken with her cell phone the night Irina Markova went missing. He had sent the photos from the girl's phone to his computer, where he had the added advantage of making the pictures large enough to study.

It always bothered him – seeing the victims frozen in time in a happy moment. In that moment, the person had not been thinking they would be dead soon, that someone would end their life with an act of violence. And more often than not, the person who ended their life was someone the victim knew. What a feeling that had to be – to look into a familiar face and see death coming.

Gorgeous girl, he thought absently. The looks of a model, attitude to spare. A girl with a lot of life ahead of her, life she would have lived with intent.

Weiss had taken a print of the photograph showing the guy the Perkins girl said had been bothering Irina that night and headed to Clematis Street, downtown West Palm Beach, to try his luck at getting a name to put to the face.

Felt like a dead end to Landry, but they had to check it out. But he couldn't see some guy following Irina back to Wellington, to the party at Players, to wherever she had gone after that. Way too much effort. The clubs were packed belly-to-belly on the weekends, full of hot young girls looking for trouble and guys happy to provide it. More likely Brad Something had washed the bad taste of rejection out of his mouth with alcohol and moved on to a more willing piece of ass.

The photos from Jim Brody's party were much more

interesting. There were snaps of Irina doing what appeared to be some kind of hot fertility dance with Mr. Hotshot Barbaro; of her sitting between Jim Brody and Bennett Walker; of her dancing with girlfriends. Either Irina or Lisbeth had held the phone at arm's length and snapped one of the two of them, side by side, mugging like supermodels.

Juan Barbaro interested him. Partly because he was still pissed off at the idea of the guy touching Elena, he admitted, but mostly for legitimate reasons. Professional athletes are notorious for feeling entitled to have anything they want, including women – especially women.

He sent off a couple of e-mail queries to the FBI and to a contact he had at Interpol, requesting any information available on the Spaniard.

Bennett Walker interested him for the obvious reasons.

Jim Brody interested him. It had been Brody's birthday. Had Irina been a gift? Had she given herself freely? Had someone paid her? According to the ME, Irina had been a busy girl giving blowjobs before her death.

So far, it seemed she had vanished into thin air. Nobody admitted to seeing her leave Players. He didn't know if she had left in her own vehicle or with one of the men. There had been no sighting of her car anywhere.

It would have helped to know where the after-party had been. He was guessing it was at Brody's house, but guesses wouldn't get him a warrant to search the property.

Elena's phone call earlier in the evening had sent him back to Players to interview the two valets, but one had split before he got there, and the other one hadn't been working Saturday night. That kid had told him about seeing Irina Markova with different gentlemen in their cars, but that wasn't worth much.

He wondered what the other kid might have had to say. If it had been a big revelation, Elena would have just said so when she called. Maybe she thought if he leaned on the valet who had been working that night he would be scared enough to spill his guts.

Landry had taken the kid's name and phone number. Tried to call. No answer. He would try again in the morning. He was convinced one of Jim Brody's posse knew something about the girl's death, but until someone could put her leaving that club – or being seen later on – with one of the self-proclaimed Alibi Club, he had squat.

He had been through Irina's e-mails, but most of them were in Russian, and he had set them aside until they could get the old priest back to interpret. He had briefly considered the idea of recruiting someone from Magda's bar to do the job, but he had no doubt he would be lied to six ways from Sunday. If it happened that one Russian had killed another Russian, and the motive was written in Russian in one of those e-mails, no Russian was going to tell him about it.

He had checked the girl's phone records and discovered that she liked to talk to girlfriends on the phone. Not exactly a revelation. Interestingly, she seemed to have a direct line to some of the wealthiest men in the Palm Beach area.

Popular girl for a horse groom.

Landry thought of the expensive clothes in the girl's closet. If she hadn't gotten the money for those clothes from her mobster pal, Kulak, where had she gotten it? Were these guys she knew just generous, or were they clients? Did she have something on one of them? Blackmail made a good motive for murder.

There was probably plenty to be had on Brody and his crowd. Men who gave one another alibis as a hobby had to be guilty of something.

He looked back through the notes he had made in the victim's apartment, detailing everything he'd seen there. Nothing out of the ordinary. The usual junk mail. A couple of bills. No sexually explicit photographs of Jim Brody naked and trussed up like a turkey in full S&M regalia. A coupon for Bed Bath & Beyond, a bill from a clinic, and an offer to join a health club.

The bill from the clinic was written in what might as well have been Sanskrit. She was being charged seventy-five dollars for an alphanumeric code.

Landry made a note to himself to call the clinic in the morning. He pulled his reading glasses off and rubbed his hands over his face. Out of gas. Time to call it, get some sleep, come back fresh.

The last thing he wanted to do was answer his phone.

'Landry.'

'Detective Landry, there's a man here asking to see you.'

The girl at the desk downstairs.

'Who is it?'

'A Mr. Kulak. Alexi Kulak.'

## 30

'Mr. Kulak.' Landry offered his hand, the Russian accepted.

He was a very neat man – neat suit, neat hair, tie perfectly knotted, as Landry's had been twelve hours ago.

'Detective. I have come to see about Irina Markova,' he said.

'I'm sorry for your loss.'

Kulak nodded and Landry showed him out the door. 'We'll take my car over to the morgue.'

Neither of them spoke as Landry drove from one parking lot to the next. He buzzed the front door, and the security guard let them in.

As long as he had been at this business, Landry had never quite shaken the creepy feeling of being in the morgue at night. It was too quiet in the halls; the lights were dim. Kulak walked beside him, staring straight ahead, his face blank. The tension in the man's body was so strong Landry could feel it.

'You can view the body on closed-circuit television—' he started.

'No.'

'All right. Just to prepare you, your niece's body was submerged in water for some time, and there is some . . . damage . . . to her face, from fish and so forth.'

A thick muscle pulsed in Kulak's jaw, but his expression did not change.

'The medical examiner performed the autopsy last night. You'll see stitches.'

The jaw muscle pulsed again.

The night attendant led them into the cold room, with

its wall of drawers where bodies were filed away like old tax returns. Kulak stood square, his hands in front of him. If he'd had a blindfold and a cigarette, he would have looked like he was waiting for a firing squad. Landry nodded to the attendant.

Kulak jolted at the sight of Irina, as if he'd been hit with a powerful current of electricity. He caught the sound of pain in his throat. His entire body was trembling. Sweat popped on his forehead. His facial muscles began to contort.

When he finally pulled his eyes away, Kulak turned, and a terrible, wild animal sound of torment and grief tore out of his chest. He fell to his knees and held his face in his hands.

The man was considered one of the most ruthless bosses in the South Florida Russian mob. The things he had seen, the things he had allegedly ordered done to people, were horrific. All of it done – guaranteed – without batting an eye. That man sat crumpled on the floor, crying silently into his hands.

Even Landry had to feel for him, regardless of how black and white he preferred to see the world. Grief was a common denominator, crossing all boundaries.

He stood off to the side and left Kulak alone for a few minutes. When Kulak began to gather himself, Landry said, 'You'll have to call in the morning to make arrangements. The ME will release the body as soon as all the autopsy results have come back.'

They walked out of the room, and Kulak sat down on a fake leather chair in the viewing room. Landry took a seat perpendicular to him.

'I have some questions for you,' he said.

Kulak didn't acknowledge him.

Landry pressed on. 'When was the last time you heard from Irina?'

Kulak didn't respond, just sat staring, devastated.

'Do you know anything about her personal life? Can you tell me about her friends, boyfriends?'

'I am going to kill the man who did this to her,' Kulak said quietly.

Landry didn't bother to tell him that he would go to prison for it. Frankly, he didn't blame the guy. If he ruled the world, that was how he would have set it up – so that the loved ones of the victim could go into a room with the perp and not come out until they were through with him.

'Mr. Kulak, do you have any idea who that might be?'

Kulak looked at him with an expression that could have cut through steel. 'If I knew that, Detective, I would now be cutting his beating heart from his chest.'

With that, he stood and walked out.

Landry let him go.

# 31

Jeff Cherry had never known one valuable thing in his life until he had taken the job as a valet at Players. He had taken the job because it seemed pretty much like money for nothing and he got to drive cars he otherwise could only have dreamed about. But he had figured out pretty quickly that he could make an extra five or ten bucks off certain customers if he sucked up hard enough, complimented the ladies, offered to do little extras like clean out the ashtrays while the customers were in having dinner.

The more he began to pay attention to the customers, the more the customers expressed their gratitude. Then one night a gentleman slipped him a twenty to turn his head and pretend he hadn't seen a certain young woman – not his wife – leave with him.

Being an entrepreneurial sort, Jeff had built himself a nice little side business, turning a blind eye to all kinds of things. Then expanding to provide other services, such as getting small amounts of recreational drugs delivered while his clients were in the club.

His success relied on his discretion and on knowing things he shouldn't have.

Talking with the cops was not on his agenda.

He split as soon as the bitch with the questions and the cell phone was out of sight.

He made a call from his cell phone while sitting in the parking lot of Town Square shopping center on Forest Hill and South Shore.

The client didn't pick up, of course. None of these people were going to take a call from a valet. He waited for the beep, then blurted it all out.

'Hey, this is Jeff from Players. From the parking lot. So anyway, this woman called the cops and told them I might know something about that dead girl — like who she left with that night. So I split, 'cause I don't wanna talk to them, but I gotta figure they're gonna come looking for me. I can't just get out of Dodge. I have a lucrative business to run, but lying to the cops isn't a regular service. So I gotta charge extra for that, is what I'm saying. So call me back.'

He left his number and ended the call, out of breath.

Wow. What would that kind of lie be worth? Ten grand? Twenty? It would sort of depend, he thought, on whether or not the client had actually killed that girl. He couldn't imagine that was what had happened. These people were rich. Rich people didn't go around killing people. But they wouldn't want people thinking that maybe they did even if they didn't, so that was worth a lot.

Fifty grand? More?

And what if the client *had* killed that girl? How freaky would that be?

A hundred grand?

He went over to the gas station and bought himself half a dozen Krispy Kreme doughnuts and a quart of chocolate milk, went back to his car, and waited for his phone to ring.

## 32

'She's a problem.'

'She's a detective.'

'*Used to be* a detective,' Barbaro corrected.

'She's investigating the girl's murder, badge or no badge,' Brody said.

They had adjourned from an uneasy dinner and regrouped at Brody's house, in the game room, where an antique billiards table dominated the space and oxblood leather club chairs were scattered around on Persian rugs a hundred years old.

Walker paced back and forth in a not-so-straight line. 'I don't want her around.'

'What do you want to do, Ben? Knock her off?'

He wheeled and shouted, 'Fuck you! Just fuck you, Kenner! Fuck yourself!'

'You're the problem,' Kenner challenged, scotch slopping out of the tumbler in his hand as he gestured. 'You have to be an asshole every time you open your mouth.'

'She tried to put me in prison!' Walker shouted. 'She'll try to do it again! She's a fucking cunt, and she hates me!'

'Let's stay on point,' Ovada said calmly. 'How does she know about the after-party?'

'*What* does she know about the after-party?' Kenner asked.

'I saw her talking with Lisbeth this afternoon,' Brody said.

Foster made a face. 'Lisbeth? She wasn't even there that night. She doesn't know anything.'

'She's been to other parties,' Barbaro pointed out. He sat

against the back of one of the club chairs, looking bored and unhappy to be there.

'So what?' Kenner said. 'It's not against the law to have a party.'

'The party isn't the issue,' Brody said. 'The cops want DNA, for God's sake. That means they have something to compare it against.'

'It's not against the law for consenting adults to have sex either.'

'It's not against the law to own a gun,' Ovada said, 'but if you are seen with the gun and a murder victim before the crime, you become a suspect.'

Walker turned a dark look on Brody. 'She's your groom. Fire her. Get her out of here. Send her back to where she came from.'

'And give her every reason to make trouble?' Brody said. 'No. I keep my friends close, and my enemies closer.'

'Well, get her close and impress on her to keep her stupid mouth shut,' Walker said. 'Stupid little bitch. Does she have any idea how lucky she is? How many hick-town chicks from Bumfuck, Michigan, get to have the life she does? And she's so ungrateful, she's shooting her mouth off to someone she met yesterday. Fuck that.'

'She's hardly the only girl who has been to a party,' Barbaro said.

'No,' Walker returned. 'But she's the only one talking.'

'Maybe she's thinking she'll get her fifteen minutes of fame,' Ovada offered.

'Oh, great,' Walker said. 'Now we can worry about her going to the press, and they can descend on us right behind the detectives.'

'Here's a news flash, mates,' Sebastian Foster chimed in. 'That's a done deal – the cops, the press. And it's got nothing to do with the Estes woman or Lisbeth. The detectives came looking straightaway. The dead girl was at the party at

Players. That's no secret. There had to be a hundred people there to see her. Why wouldn't the detectives come looking at us?'

'And if we don't cooperate with them, we look guilty,' Kenner whined.

'If we *do* cooperate, we look guiltier,' Brody said. 'I don't know about the rest of you, but I'm not going to prison because I got a blowjob on my birthday.'

'What are you going to tell them?' Ovada asked.

'Not a damn thing,' Walker said.

'Deny, deny, deny,' Foster chimed in. 'What else is there? Tell them, oh, yes, we all had sex with her? No one would find that suspicious.'

Brody focused on Barbaro. 'You're awfully quiet, Juan. What are you thinking?'

Barbaro shrugged. 'Only people who were at the after-party know what happened at the after-party. All of those people are in this room – except one. There is no reason to talk about it that I can see.'

No one said anything.

'Excuse me, gentlemen,' he said, pushing himself away from the chair. 'I have a match to play tomorrow. I'm certain Mr. Brody would prefer me to be fresh for it.'

He walked out of the room and out of the house, stopping to stand on the front porch. Walker wasn't far behind him.

'You need a ride home, friend?' Barbaro asked.

'No. I'm fine.'

'Did you kill her?'

Walker started, gave him a look that slid away too quickly. 'No! I told you, no. She was dead when I found her.'

Barbaro just frowned and shook his head, looking out at the yard.

'What's the matter with you?' Walker said. 'You were at the party too. Did *you* kill her?

'You're letting Elena poison you,' he said. 'You're pissing me off with that. You're supposed to be my friend.'

'Yes.'

'You're as bad as that stupid little twat groom. You know Elena twenty-four hours and you believe her over me? What the hell is that? What kind of friend is that?' Walker demanded, his voice getting louder and louder.

Barbaro spread his hands and gestured for Walker to keep it down. 'You need to calm down . . . friend.'

'Calm down? Do you have any idea what happens to my life if the media gets wind of me having anything to do with a murdered girl?' he asked. 'It's a fucking nightmare. They'll dig up everything from back then, spin it around, make me look like Ted Bundy.

'And – and – what about Nancy?' he asked as an after-thought. 'None of this is fair to Nancy.'

Barbaro arched a brow. 'Somehow, my friend, I don't believe your concern is for your wife.'

'Well, fuck you too, Juan,' Walker snapped. 'You want to have your name put out there as a rapist?'

'No one said the girl was raped.'

'That's what they'll imply, that the girl was raped and killed, and it had to be me because—'

He caught himself short of saying it.

'Because you did it before?'

Barbaro stepped out of the way as Walker took a wild swing at him, lost his balance, and tumbled down the stone steps to the lawn, landing with a thud and a groan. When he struggled back up onto his knees, his lip was split and bleed-ing.

Barbaro descended the steps, put a foot on his shoulder, and knocked him sprawling again.

'Look at yourself,' he said with disgust. 'You're drunk, you're pathetic. What kind of man are you?'

Walker came up on one knee and wiped the blood from

his mouth with the back of his hand. He took a couple of deep breaths and composed himself.

'My father-in-law is pushing me to run for office,' he said, getting up. 'Imagine that.'

'You seem a poor choice,' Barbaro said.

'It's America, *amigo*. Anything can happen. Look at Bill Clinton. The guy nailed anything in a skirt, and he was a two-term president.'

'Was he also associated with a murdered girl?'

'You know,' Walker said with an edge in his voice, 'the thing about this club is that no one is innocent. You've needed an alibi before.'

'No,' Barbaro said. 'In fact, no, I have not. I have *been* an alibi many times. I have been *your* alibi many times.'

'Then once more won't kill you,' Walker said. 'We stick to our story. We left Players, went to my place for a nightcap. We didn't see Irina after the party.'

'And if the detectives get a warrant and go into your home and find evidence the girl was there?'

Walker looked at his watch. 'They'll never get inside my house,' he said. 'That's what lawyers are for.'

Only slightly unsteady, he walked to his car and drove away into the night.

# 33

I long ago ruined my ability to sleep like a normal human being. Prior to my accident, prior to my years working the streets as a Narcotics detective. Long before any of that.

Four or five hours – rarely consecutive, rarely restful, and jammed with complex dreams – had become normal for me. Post-accident, a certain level of chronic pain had made it even more difficult. And I refused (for a host of reasons, some good and some stupid) the kind of medication that would have eased the pain and allowed me to sink below consciousness.

A doctor once told me that my brain had decided sleep stages one, two, and five were essential to life, and that stages three and four were a waste of my time. My own theory was less industrious and more human: that after the dream stage, REM sleep, all I wanted was to escape what lay in my sub-conscious.

Whatever the theory, the upside of not sleeping is being able to accomplish more than the average working stiff.

I sat at the small writing desk in my living room, making notes. Just a couple of lamps on, Chris Botti's smooth, sexy trumpet on the stereo, a glass of cabernet to sip at. It would have been a pleasant scenario, if not for the fact that I was investigating the murder of someone I knew.

If Irina had left Players with Bennett or with Jim Brody, where was her car? If she had driven herself to the after-party, where was her car? Landry had made no mention of it, which made me think he hadn't found it yet.

I made a note: *Car?*

Had the killer used it to transport her body, then driven

himself back to town? That would have been the smart thing. No evidence of Irina in his own car. But there would have been evidence of him in hers. The smarter thing would have been to run the car into a canal.

And where had they gone for the after-party? Out of town to Star Polo? Or across a few acres of manicured lawns and golf course to Bennett's home in the Polo Club? They had all been drinking heavily. Quicker and easier to do the latter. Cops liked to prowl right around that intersection of South Shore and Greenview Shores around closing time, looking for some easy tickets. There would have been less risk of getting a DUI if they left the club and literally turned right in at the Polo Club's west entrance.

I made a note: *Cop Stop DUI?*

The officer on patrol might have seen something – Irina's car, Irina in someone else's car, but no one was going to tell me about it.

I wanted to know where in the Palm Beach Polo Club Bennett lived. The homes in the development ranged from efficiencies for grooms, to condos, to town houses, to bungalows, to out-and-out mansions. Bennett would take the big house, because he could afford it, because it was a good investment, because he was spoiled and used to having nothing but the best. Because it was private.

If the party had moved to Bennett's house, the party-goers had driven through one of the Polo Club's two entrances, and their comings and goings would be on tape. Tape that I had no access to. But if I could find his house, I could check out his neighbors. Maybe one of them would complain about a party Saturday night. Even money said Sean knew exactly where the house was.

I made a note: *Sean – Bennett's address?*

I picked through the things I had collected from Irina's apartment. The e-mails I had printed out from her computer were mostly in Russian. Some were order confirmations from online sources of horse equipment and veterinary supplies, things she would have ordered at Sean's behest. A couple of them were from Lisbeth Perkins: a question as to whether or not Irina wanted to go to a karaoke bar with a couple of other girls. One about where and when they would meet Saturday night.

Those e-mails seemed so innocent in the face of what had happened that night. Young women going out on the town to have some fun, never imagining what was to come later that night.

*Should be a great party. C U later. I can't wait!!* Lisbeth had signed the e-mail with a series of yellow smiley faces.

A very young twenty-something, I had thought earlier. Fresh off the farm. She was getting a hell of an education now, poor kid.

I thought about Molly Seabright, the twelve-year-old girl who had come to me a year before to find her missing sister. Molly had often seemed to me to be more of an adult than I was.

Life jades us all at different rates, in different ways.

I had been about Lisbeth's age when my life truly turned itself on its head. The sadly funny thing was, at that time I had already believed I was cynical.

We were supposed to go out that night, Bennett and I. But I hadn't been feeling well, and I begged off. He had been exceptionally sweet – brought me flowers, cheered me up, tucked me into bed. He had gone off to meet a couple of buddies for dinner and drinks. I had drifted off to sleep that night thinking how incredibly happy I was, how I was finally getting the one thing I had craved my whole life – someone who really loved me.

By the next day, everything had changed.

Fate delivers the ultimate sucker punch.

I took Irina's digital camera, which I had lifted from her apartment, connected it to my computer with a USB cable, and downloaded everything on it — twenty-two images from her other life, including the snaps I had taken of the screen-saver photos on her computer monitor.

Parties, polo matches, gal pals at the beach. There were a couple of shots of hunky bartender Kayne Jackson shaking up martinis and libidos from behind the bar at Players.

Big Jim Brody in a straw hat and swim trunks, smoking a cigar as he stood on the deck of a swimming pool. I could have gone my whole life without seeing that.

Brody in the same getup with an arm around Lisbeth in a purple bikini, Lisbeth doing her best not to cringe away from him and his big hairy belly. She wore the kind of smile that could have as easily been from gas pains.

Someone had shot a photo of Irina and Lisbeth sitting together shoulder to shoulder, cheek to cheek on a poolside chaise, each with an umbrella drink in hand, toasting the photographer. They could have been sisters with their matching blond hair, matching dark glasses, matching medallion necklaces, matching smiles. So happy.

Barbaro and a couple of other players in full polo gear, joking around on the sidelines. Bennett Walker raising a glass of champagne. Bennett on a polo pony. Bennett at the swimming pool. One too many photos of Bennett, I thought.

Despite the years I had spent wishing physical deformities on him, he had aged well, I had to admit as I clicked back to the swimsuit photo. He had bulked up with maturity — with muscle, not fat. As a male animal, he had every right to be arrogant. What female of the species wouldn't have wanted that body in her bed?

And what husband-hunting temptress wouldn't have added those looks to the money that backed them up and come up with a prime target? In the crowd that Bennett ran with, the fact that he was already married wouldn't have necessarily deterred women from trying.

From what I had learned so far, from the profile of Irina that had begun to come together over the past two days, I had to think a wedding ring wouldn't have bothered her in the least. The thing Irina wouldn't have been able to compete with was the financial and social clout of Bennett Walker's in-laws.

Bennett was a very wealthy man in his own right, but there is nothing wealthy men love more than more money. More money, more power. More power, more control of the world around them.

I got up from my chair and paced like a restless cat, stopping every so often to stretch out one knotted muscle and then another.

If Irina went to the after-party, she went fully aware of the nature of the party and the kinds of things that were likely to go on there. One would presume she had every intention of being a willing participant. So why did she end up dead? Was it a case of rough sex gone wrong? Or had one of those men killed her intentionally? Why? For the rush? Had she pissed one of them off? Had Jim Brody wanted to murder a girl for his birthday? Had Bennett Walker lost his temper, lost control?

I sat back down at my desk and made a note: *Motive?*

What had Bennett's motive been when he beat and raped Maria Nevin? He didn't have one. He'd never seen Maria Nevin before that night. He had no reason to attack her specifically.

The bartender at the last club Bennett and his pals had visited testified that Bennett had been drunk, loud, and obnoxious. In his statement to the police, the bartender said that Bennett's buddies had been ribbing him about getting married, that his skirt-chasing days were over, to which Bennett had replied that he could have any woman he wanted, anytime he wanted.

The bartender had recanted that statement before trial

and had watered down the rest of his testimony as badly as he watered down the overpriced drinks at the bar.

But even if the bartender had stuck to his story, nothing said that night could have provided a motive for what happened.

Maria Nevin had initially told the police – and had held to that version of events right up until the day before she was to take the stand – that Bennett had flirted with her. They had danced together, had a drink together. They had gone for a walk on the beach, had sat on the wet sand as the tide went out, had started making out.

A little too intoxicated, Bennett hadn't been able to sustain an erection. He became angry. He slapped her hard several times. She struggled to get away from him, scratching him in the process. He pinned her down and choked her, achieved an erection, and raped her.

Was that what had happened to Irina?

I didn't want any of those images in my head.

To distract my mind, I began to organize the paper strewn across my desk. Irina's e-mails. Some notes I had made while in her apartment caught my eye. The name of a medical clinic. I typed the name of the clinic into Google. The search engine came back with a list of Web sites. I clicked on the first one, and the Web site opened on my screen:

*The Lundeen Clinic:*
*Serving Women in the Palm Beaches Since 1987.*
*Obstetrics and Gynecology.*

I made a note to myself: *Motive.*

# 34

When she had come to Star Polo to interview for a groom's position, Lisbeth had driven past the mansion Jim Brody lived in three or four months of the year (it was a second home then, a weekend place) and thought to herself that one day she would live in a house like that. An incredibly wealthy, incredibly handsome, incredibly sexy man would pluck her out of the stable yard and she would be just like Julia Roberts in *Pretty Woman* – except that she wouldn't have to be a prostitute first.

How wrong she had been.

She had gotten the job, been given an apartment over the stables, had her magical entree to the lifestyles of the rich and famous. All of that had happened.

The polo players had taken a shine to her because she was cute and had a great figure. Mr. Brody had taken a shine to her, and suddenly she was invited to parties and getting attention from the kind of men she had dreamed of sweeping her away. But none of them had fallen in love with her, and she had certainly been made to feel like she was a prostitute.

She sat on her bed with her knees drawn up, looking at the rack of expensive clothes she had purchased with the generosity of her wealthy gentleman friends. She enjoyed looking pretty. She enjoyed parties.

So had Irina.

Lisbeth wrapped her arms tightly around her legs and rocked herself as the tears came. Her eyes were already nearly swollen shut from crying. She couldn't seem to stop.

It wasn't like she didn't have other friends, but Irina had

been so strong, so sure of herself. She had walked into the world of the wealthy as if she had been born to it. Lisbeth felt lost in her sudden absence, cut loose from her anchor. Now she felt like she was the only one who knew all the secrets, and that was a very scary place to be.

Irina wouldn't have thought so. Irina would have laughed at her. Irina loved to play games, to angle for power. Lisbeth had both admired and resented her for that. It was all a game for Irina. Nothing meant anything. Lisbeth wished she could have been more like that.

Irina would have been the one to end up living in a house like Jim Brody's with a husband like Bennett Walker, and she would have accepted it all as her due.

In contrast, Lisbeth believed she would never feel like anything more than a hanger-on, a hick kid from the rural Midwest. An outsider with her toe in the door.

The clock saved her from sinking even deeper into the pain. It was time for night check, and it was her night to do it.

She held a cold wet cloth to her face for a few minutes, as if that would really help. The horses were probably going to freak out at the sight of her. Her head felt like a water balloon.

The stables were dimly lit at night. The barn manager was rabid about not startling the horses when they were resting. Lisbeth went from one stall to the next, doling out flakes of hay, checking legs, adjusting blankets.

It was a peaceful job and one she normally enjoyed, but she was jumpy, and exhausted, and shivering uncontrollably. She went up and down the aisle, bent over like an old woman.

*So alone,* she kept thinking. She felt so alone.

She had to pull herself together, she knew. She thought about quitting Star Polo. Good grooms were always in demand during the season. But she was afraid to do it. She didn't want to call attention to herself. She didn't want Mr. Brody to think she was turning against him.

She tried to think what Irina would have done if the situation had been reversed.

Irina would have gone on as if nothing had happened.

Knowing that only made Lisbeth feel worse.

Finished with her chore, she stepped outside the barn and looked out at the night. She rubbed her medallion between her thumb and forefinger, wishing the habit would calm her. Moonlight shone on the pond that spread out like quicksilver between the stables and the canal running perpendicular to the road. A heron waded in the shallows on long stilt legs. It paid no attention to her.

*So alone . . .*

The bag went over her head so quickly, Lisbeth couldn't even react. One second she was looking at the heron, and the next she couldn't see, couldn't breathe. Some kind of cord tightened around her throat, choking off her air supply.

Lisbeth grabbed at it, tried to get her fingers under it to pull it loose. She wanted to scream but couldn't. She tried kicking at the person behind her, but he yanked her off her feet and shook her like a rag doll until Lisbeth didn't know which way was up.

Dizzy, disoriented, terrified, she vomited inside the bag the second the cord loosened around her throat. The man dragged her backward, Lisbeth kicking and twisting and flailing like a wild animal caught in a trap.

The cord went tight again. Tighter. Tighter. Colors burst before her eyes. *I'm going to die,* she thought, astonished.

It was the last thought she had.

# 35

What is death? Where does the soul go?

People brought back from the dead by resuscitation always talked about a bright white light, about friends and relatives who had gone before them beckoning with smiles and open arms.

Lisbeth saw nothing. Blackness. She reached out with her hands and hit something solid. She pushed at it, but it didn't budge. *Coffin,* she thought, and she began to panic. She wasn't dead, she'd been buried alive.

She hit her fists against the lid again and again, crying. When she tried to scream, she couldn't. Her throat felt raw and swollen, and her mouth was parched to the point that it felt as if her tongue had doubled in size and was made of cotton. She tried to pull the bag off her head but couldn't.

Then it began to dawn on her that she felt motion. And when the sound of her own pulse pounding in her ears receded, she could hear the hum of tires on pavement.

She was in the trunk of a car.

As she realized it, a new wave of panic rolled over her.

Who had taken her? Where were they taking her? For what purpose?

There were no good answers to those questions.

The car began to slow, then stopped. A car door opened, then closed. She waited for the trunk to open, but it didn't.

Her heart was racing. She was shaking. The smell of her own vomit burned her nostrils. She strained to hear voices, but there were none.

What would happen to her now?

Would she wish she had already died?

*SPLASH! SPLASH! SPLASH!*

Someone was throwing heavy objects into water.

Then silence.

The trunk popped open then, and Lisbeth was grabbed roughly, hauled out of the car, and put on her feet. Her legs felt like they were made of string. Her knees buckled beneath her, but her captor held her up on her feet by the rope around her throat, as if she were a dog on a leash. She scrambled to get her feet under her, but he still half-dragged her off the pavement and into grass. The ground was soft and wet.

'No,' she said, barely croaking out the word. 'No. No!'

She stepped in water, tried to turn around and run. He shoved her ahead of him.

Now the water was ankle deep, shin deep. . . .

He was going to drown her.

'No! No!'

A wild squealing sound rang in her ears. She didn't even realize it was coming from her. It didn't matter how she struggled and splashed, the water was at her knees, her thighs. . . . Mud sucked at her feet.

'No! Don't kill me! Don't kill me!'

Her captor said nothing.

'Please don't kill me!'

. . . her crotch, her belly . . .

She was sobbing.

He said nothing, just drove her farther into the water.

It came up over her breasts.

He put his hand on her head, shoved her under, and held her there.

Choking on water, she fought wildly, in a blind panic.

Her captor yanked her up to the surface. Lisbeth had to tip her head back to escape the water trapped inside the cloth bag. She had swallowed water, inhaled water, couldn't get a breath to cough it out. She clawed at the bag clinging like wet plaster to her face.

He shoved her under a second time. When he pulled her back to the surface, he dragged her ashore and dropped her on the ground like a sack of garbage.

Lisbeth coughed and choked and retched, trying to expel the water from her lungs and replace it with air. The taste and smell of it was horrible, like it had come from a sewer. She managed to push herself onto her hands and knees, although a part of her just wanted to lie down and give up. All the while her mind swirled with fear and panic, and questions. Who was doing this to her? Would he rape her? Would he kill her? Would he torture her first?

And during all this time, her assailant never said a word, which was in some way more frightening than if he had been screaming at her. It was as if there was no emotion involved on his part.

Lungs aching, Lisbeth lowered herself to the ground, feeling too weak to remain on her hands and knees, let alone get up and try to escape. She was totally at his mercy.

Off to her left, something groaned. Not a person, she thought. It groaned again. An animal. Then a loud hissing sound.

*Oh, my God.*

*Alligator.*

Lisbeth pushed herself onto her hands and knees again and started scrambling, but she couldn't see, couldn't know which way was safe or if she would be running into worse danger.

The panic seized her again. 'Oh, my God. Oh, my God!'

Then, like a marionette, she was plucked off her feet. Her kidnapper crushed a forearm across her rib cage, trapping her against his body. The tip of a knife blade caught hold of the bag, pierced it, nicked her cheek, and split the cloth open on the right side.

The harsh glare of headlights was blinding. Then he swung her around so she could see where that light fell – on a section of paved road that ended with a striped road-block sign; on the bank of a marsh; on three alligators spread over that terrain, two on the bank and one on the road, hissing at the car. Empty ham cans littered the bank, and Lisbeth remembered the loud splashing sound she had heard while she was lying in the trunk. Bait.

Her attacker grabbed a handful of the sack and her hair and pulled her head back as he started moving toward the alligator on the road. Lisbeth began to struggle, frantic to get free of him. He pulled harder on her hair and kept advancing on the reptile.

'No! No! No! No!' she screamed.

The alligator opened its jaws and hissed.

Her captor stopped within ten feet of it and spoke for the very first time, whispering into her ear, 'This is what happens to girls who talk too much.'

# 36

'Do you know why you're in here?'

Landry didn't bite.

Weiss smirked. 'Are we getting a commendation?'

Lt. William Dugan stared at him. Tall, tan, gray-haired, he cut a figure of authority. The boss of Robbery/Homicide stood behind his desk with his hands jammed at his waist, his shoulders set.

Weiss glanced at Landry. 'I guess not.'

'So far this morning,' Dugan went on, 'I've had the sheriff and half the politicos of Palm Beach County crawling up my ass. Plus the state's attorney and half a dozen designer-suit defense attorneys, not the least of which are Bert Shapiro and Edward Estes.'

'Estes?' Weiss cocked a brow at Landry.

'Shut up, Weiss,' Landry growled.

'What the hell are you doing out there?' Dugan asked. 'Why are you messing around with these people?'

'They're suspects,' Landry said. 'What are we supposed to do? Send them engraved invitations to come down here and talk to us? Maybe we could make finger sandwiches and have tea. Maybe if we ask pretty please one of them will make a confession.'

'I'll tell you what you can't do,' Dugan said. 'You can't barge into a private club and demand these people give you DNA samples. What the hell were you thinking?'

'*Demand?*' Landry asked. He glanced at Weiss. 'Did you *demand* anything from those pricks last night?'

'Not me. Did you?'

Landry looked at his lieutenant. 'Stop beating around the

fucking bush. Who exactly are we talking about here? Bennett Walker?'

'Among others.'

''Cause I'll tell you right now, he's a punk,' Landry said. 'He's a spoiled rich-boy prick, who thinks he can do any goddamn thing he wants to, including beating and raping women.'

'He walked on those charges,' Dugan said.

Landry rolled his eyes. 'Oh, well, he must be innocent, then, 'cause Christ knows the justice system never fucks up.'

'Can the sarcasm,' Dugan snapped.

'This is bullshit,' Landry said. 'You're going to tell us to tiptoe around these assholes because they have money to buy big-prick lawyers? That's bullshit.'

'Do you know what those big-prick lawyers can do to your case?' Dugan asked. 'If Bennett Walker had given you a DNA sample last night and it matched DNA in the victim, you could kiss that evidence good-bye. Edward Estes is going to get that thrown out of court so fast it'll give you whiplash.'

'Well, what do you want us to do?' Weiss asked. 'Call central casting and ask for a fresh crop of suspects? Maybe some drug dealers?'

'Are you looking beyond these men?'

'I followed up on a lead on a guy named Brad Garland,' Weiss said. 'He saw the vic that night, she rejected him, he was pissed off.'

'And?'

'And he wrapped his car around a light pole on his way from one club to another. He was in the ER for eight hours and admitted for observation with a head injury.'

'Irina Markova spent the last hours anyone admits to seeing her with Jim Brody and Bennett Walker and that pack of dogs,' Landry said. 'It's a waste of time to look elsewhere. You want to make it look like we're going through those motions, assign someone else to do that. We've got real leads.'

Dugan frowned. 'You're serious about Walker?'

'Dead,' Landry said. 'In private these guys call themselves the Alibi Club. They think they can get away with anything.'

'Murder is a stretch,' Dugan said.

'Why? A sociopath is a sociopath. It doesn't matter how big his bank account is.'

'And they all cover for a killer?'

Landry shrugged. 'Maybe they all had a hand in it. We know she had oral sex with multiple partners. Maybe that's why no one rats out anyone – because they're all guilty.'

'Jesus,' Dugan muttered. 'This is going to be a media freak show. Just the idea something like that could be going on . . .'

He turned and looked out his window, as if expecting to see reporters and news vans crowding the parking lot.

'Nobody hears it from you,' he ordered. 'One thing leaks from this office, you're both out. You'll be working security at Wal-Mart.'

'My dream job,' Weiss cracked.

'I'm serious. Not one word. Have you talked about this Alibi Club with anyone else? Where did you hear it?'

'Lisbeth Perkins,' Landry said, resurrecting the lie he'd told Weiss the night before. 'She's a groom at Brody's place – and one of the sweet young things running with that crowd. She was best friends with the dead girl. I doubt she's the only one who knows about it. Gossip is a full-contact sport with the money crowd. It's only a matter of time before that shit hits the fan.'

'So far you can't put the dead girl with any of these guys once they left Players?'

Landry shook his head. 'I went to talk to one of the valets last night, but the kid split before I got there. Maybe he can put her in a car with somebody. Weiss is tracking him down today.'

'This is going to be one hell of a shitstorm,' Dugan said.

Weiss's cell phone rang. Dugan waved him out of the office.

Landry turned to go.

'Tell me about Alexi Kulak being here last night.'

Landry shrugged. 'There's nothing to tell. Irina Markova was his niece, or so he says. He came to see the body, find out about making arrangements.'

'In the dead of night?'

'If you were Alexi Kulak, would you come strolling into the sheriff's office at high noon?'

'Is he a suspect?' Dugan asked.

'No.'

'Why not?'

'Alexi Kulak has someone clipped, he goes out for borscht or whatever the hell Russians eat,' Landry said. 'He doesn't go see them in the morgue. He doesn't fall down on his knees, break down sobbing, and vow revenge.'

'Weiss told me Elena Estes found the girl's body.'

'Yeah. So?'

'So you neglected to mention that to me.'

'It's in my report.'

'Which I have yet to see.'

'I've been a little busy,' Landry snapped. 'Besides, it's not relevant,' he said. 'She was minding her own business and she happened to find a corpse.'

'And the vic worked where she lives,' Dugan pressed.

'You want me to pin it on her?' Landry cracked. 'That'd make some juicy tabloid headlines. We could make it out to be a lesbian thing. Or we could spin it that she killed the girl to frame her ex-fiancé, to make him pay for the rape he got away with back when. And then her father represents the asshole in the trial again. All we need is Bat Boy and a nine-hundred-sixteen-pound man and we've got a complete edition of the *Weekly World News*.'

Dugan rubbed his hands over his face and groaned. 'That's right. Elena Estes is Edward Estes's daughter.'

'Yep.'

'I need some Advil.'

'You might as well drink,' Landry suggested, as his cell phone began to ring.

'Is she digging around in this case?' Dugan asked. 'I can't have that. Especially because of her father. There's no way it doesn't bite us in the ass one way or another.'

He checked the caller ID. Elena.

'I recommend vodka,' Landry said, backing out the door. 'It goes with everything.'

# 37

'Landry.'

He picked up on the third ring. I had been hoping for voice mail.

'If that party moved from Players to Walker's house, every car that went there is on tape in the guard shacks at the entrances to the Polo Club,' I said without preamble. I was beyond social niceties.

'But we don't know where the party moved,' Landry said. 'Polo Club management is making right-to-privacy noises. They aren't cooperating without a warrant.'

'Damn.'

'We're working on it,' he said. 'We'll get it. I'm sorry about last night.'

It took me half a minute to digest that.

'I was way out of line,' he said. 'It doesn't matter why.'

'No,' I said quietly. 'It doesn't.'

I hung up. Not out of anger, but because there was no point in continuing the conversation. He didn't try to call me back.

I drove out to Star Polo, to the barns, in search of Lisbeth.

'She's not working,' one of the hands told me in Spanish. 'No one has seen her today.'

'She went someplace?' I asked.

He shrugged.

'Is her car gone?'

'No. Her car is here.' He pointed out the end of the barn to a sporty little red Saturn convertible.

I thanked him and went to have a look at the car. Where would she have gone without a car? It was a fair hike back into town. I doubted anyone would choose to walk it.

Did she have a hot date the night before? Was she sleeping in with Bennett or one of his pals? I doubted it. Lisbeth was in over her head with these people, and she knew it. With Irina gone, I suspected she didn't know what to do, how to get out of being one of the girls with this crowd. She was probably scared. And rightly so. Her best friend had been murdered.

I wouldn't have been surprised if she'd quit her job. And like any horse person in Wellington during the season, immediately I wondered if I could poach her to take Irina's spot at Sean's. That would endear me to Jim Brody.

'Elena!'

And there he was in a blue button-down shirt and riding breeches, his belly spilling over at the belt.

'Good morning – I hope,' I said, feigning apprehension. 'I was coming to look for you.'

'Well, here I am,' he said, jovial as ever.

I walked away from Lisbeth's car to where he stood on the drive. 'I want to apologize for last night,' I said.

'There's nothing for you to apologize for,' he said. 'Ben was out of line.'

'Nevertheless—'

'I didn't know him back then,' he said. 'But I've known him for quite a few years. He can be a real prick, but under that he's a decent guy.'

A decent guy who openly cheated on his mentally unstable wife with girls half his age. Someone had apparently lowered the bar on decency since I last checked.

'We just shouldn't be allowed within twenty feet of each other,' I said. 'There's too much history.'

'Well, that shouldn't preclude the rest of us from enjoying your company,' he said. 'You don't really think he had anything to do with Irina's murder, do you? I can tell you he was quite fond of the girl.'

'Fond?' That came out exactly how it shouldn't have.

Brody didn't take offense. In fact, he chuckled. 'Maybe that's not quite the right word. Irina liked to have a good time. She was strong, knew what she wanted. She would have made something of herself. She was hungry.'

'That's not always a good thing,' I said, thinking of the bill from the Lundeen Clinic and what that might have been about. 'I guess it all depends on what one wants. Maybe Irina wanted too much.'

His brows lowered ever so slightly. 'There's no such thing,' he said. 'You know what they say: Nothing succeeds like excess.'

'Who did say that?' he asked. A twitch of a brow, a twinkle in the eye. He was trying to move me off topic.

'Oscar Wilde,' I said. 'It didn't work out so well for him. He died destitute in a rented room.'

'Well . . .' He frowned. Tough to find a snappy comeback for that.

'Live 'til you die, that's what I say,' I said, forcing the happiness aura. 'Grab the gusto and all that.'

'I'm all for that,' Brody agreed. 'That's what we all should do. That's what we can learn from this tragedy.'

'I would rather learn who killed her first and hope I have the luxury of time to reflect on the moral to the story later,' I said.

He didn't like that. Life would have been so much easier for him if he could have distracted me with a shiny piece of jewelry or a trip to Bermuda. That's the trouble with women: We're so less easy to impress once we're past the age of blushing and giggling.

'I can't help you there,' he said, quickly losing all patience with me. 'In fact, I've been advised not to talk about the girl at all.'

'Advised? By whom?'

'My attorney,' he said, looking me square in the eye. 'Your father.'

That news should have come as no surprise, yet it still delivered an unwelcome kick. My father had just come one step closer into my life.

'Well,' I said, 'you're paying dearly for that advice. You'd better follow it.'

'I have a feeling you never did,' he said.

'No,' I said. *And I paid dearly too.* 'But then, no one ever looked at me as a possible murder suspect.'

'I'm heading that off at the pass,' he said. 'The best defense is a good offense. I didn't have anything to do with that girl's death, and I'm not allowing anyone to make it seem as if I did.'

I wondered what had happened to precipitate that move. Had Landry or Weiss pushed that button? Had the media?

The news hounds would be catching up to speed soon. I was surprised it hadn't happened already. The instant they got wind of the men last seen with Irina, they would be rabid, particularly when Bennett Walker's name surfaced. I knew for a fact that would be happening even while I stood there in the driveway of Star Polo with Jim Brody.

I knew because I had made the phone calls myself.

It's never too late to be bitter or vindictive.

'Was there anything else I can help you with?' Brody asked. 'I don't mean to give you the bum's rush, Elena, but I'm due to be somewhere.'

'No, no,' I said, glancing back at Lisbeth's car.

'I brought some things for Lisbeth,' I said, lifting my purse for him to notice. 'Some photographs I thought she might like to have from Irina. I know they were close.'

'Haven't seen her,' he said, looking around. Pretending to look for her, I thought. 'I don't think she's here.'

'Don't you find that strange?' I asked. 'Her car is here.'

'She probably went somewhere with a friend,' he said, and started moving away from me.

'You're probably right.'

I thanked him for his time and went to my car. He climbed into his Escalade. I followed him out the driveway. He turned left, I turned right. When I had gone a mile or so, I turned my car around and went back.

I went inside the barn, found the same hand I had spoken with earlier, and told him I had something to give Lisbeth and wanted to leave it outside her door. Did he know where she lived?

Oh, yes, she lived upstairs, over the stable. Go out of the barn and take the stairs on the left. He would show me. I told him that wasn't necessary and thanked him.

No one paid any attention to me as I went up to Lisbeth's apartment. From the landing I could see a rider going down the driveway with three polo ponies tethered together on either side, taking them out for a jog. I was out of sight of the wash racks. In the other direction, a thick row of trees screened the stable area from the view from the big house.

I tapped on the glass in the door and waited. Tapped a little harder and waited. I tried the doorknob. Locked.

Through the glass and a sheer curtain, I could see the living area of the tiny apartment. A couch, a chair, a messy TV cabinet, a coffee table strewn with magazines. A breakfast bar dividing off the minuscule kitchen.

I tapped on the glass one last time, then pulled a couple of simple lock picks from my bag and invited myself in.

# 38

'I have some news for you, Detective Landry,' Mercedes Gitan said as she stuck her head out the door of the autopsy suite.

'Good news?'

'Depends on your point of view,' she said. 'Come on in. We just finished up a drowning victim.'

'Hell of a way to start your morning,' Landry said.

Gitan pulled her cap off, setting free a mop of curly black hair, and tossed the cap and her gloves in a laundry bin. 'Sad. A young woman with her whole life ahead of her.'

'So was Irina Markova. What's the word?'

'Toxicology came back.'

'Drugs?'

'Ecstasy. A lot of it.'

'That's no big surprise, considering what kind of party she was at. A lot of X, a lot of sex.'

'She was an active participant. No date-rape drugs.'

'Anything under the fingernails?'

'Actually, yes. Her own skin,' she said. 'She was probably trying to dig her fingers under whatever it was she was being choked with,' she said, pantomiming the action.

'Anything else?'

'Some tiny bits of leather fibers. I think she was strangled with a thin leather strap or cord. The fibers I removed from the neck wound also appear to be leather.'

'But nothing that might give us a clue to her killer.'

'Sorry, no. Are you desperate?'

'No. I've got a couple hot prospects, but my life would be a lot easier if I could say "You did it. And here's the proof."'

226

'My life would be easier if George Clooney would sweep me away to his villa in Italy,' Gitan said.

'Ha-ha. I'd better get out there and face the lions,' Landry said. 'It's going to be a long, bad day.'

'My office has taken a half dozen calls from the media already this morning and another half dozen from the powers that be telling me not to talk to the press. These hot prospects you have, I take it they're not the usual suspects.'

'Not by a long stretch. Big bucks, social standing, pains in the ass.'

'Oooh . . . an honest-to-goodness juicy Palm Beach scandal,' Gitan said, pretending excitement.

'Move over, William Kennedy Smith. You ain't seen nothing yet.'

'Well, here's your bonus of scandalous dirt and motive: your vic was pregnant.'

'Shit,' Landry whispered. No need to decipher the bill from the Lundeen Clinic after all.

'Showed up in the blood tests,' Gitan said. 'There was so much damage to her lower torso from the alligator, there was nothing for me to find in the exam.'

'Let's keep that to ourselves for now,' Landry said. 'I can still use the DNA threat.'

'My lips are sealed.'

Landry thanked her and walked out into the sunshine. It was hot. He unbuttoned his shirtsleeves and rolled them up as he walked back across the parking lot to the justice center.

From a distance he could see the news vans and reporters scattered in individual spots that gave good background. The shit had officially hit the fan. Someone had ferreted out or passed along the information as to who the suspects might be in Irina Markova's murder. There was no other big case going on that would warrant this kind of attention.

Landry took a detour and went to his car, still far enough

227

away that no one was paying any attention to him. He backed out of his spot and drove slowly down the row toward the building to get a closer look. As he sat there, a black sedan with a driver and a man sitting in the back rolled past. The license plate read: ESTES ESQ.

Edward Estes. Elena's father.

The great man had arrived. Now the show would begin.

Landry's phone rang.

'Landry.'

'Weiss. We've found Irina Markova's car.'

The show would go on with one less in the audience, Landry thought as he turned left and headed out of the complex. He had more important things to do than watch Edward Estes shoot his mouth off – like proving Estes's client was a killer.


'This guy's a deputy,' Weiss explained as Landry got out of his car. 'He works security here on the side. So he got the BOLO on the car, and here it is.'

'You called CSI?'

'They're on their way.'

Irina Markova's car was a sporty little dark-blue Volkswagen Jetta. The windows were closed. It sat parked among a few hundred cars in the lot of the Wellington Green mall.

'Are there cameras out here?' Landry asked, looking up and around at light poles.

'No.'

'All right. Did you look inside the vehicle?'

'Through the windows,' Weiss said. 'I didn't touch anything. There are no visible signs of blood or anything. There's sand and dirt on the floor mats. And a partial footprint. It's faint, but it's there.'

'Yeah, I see it,' Landry said. 'Let's make sure they get a photograph of it before anyone touches the mat.'

'What do you suppose the odds are the guy left us any prints?' Weiss said.

'Slim and none if it was one of Brody's crowd. Those guys are too smart not to have wiped it down. Maybe we'll get a couple of head hairs. Better than nothing. Damn, I wish they had cameras out here.'

# 39

Hooves pounded the turf as the two horses ran. Maintaining a distance of about ten yards apart, one would advance, then the other, as the ball was struck and chased, struck and chased.

Barbaro swung his mallet with a casual ease that belied the strength behind it. The forehand shot went to Bennett Walker, who miscalculated his angle and distance. He yanked his horse back and twisted in the saddle to make an awkward offside tail shot.

Barbaro had to circle back at a lope to pick up the ball, now traveling at half speed. Just for practice, he brought his mallet across his body to the left side, reached forward and beneath his horse's neck, let the ball roll across his line, and tapped it back across to his friend.

Again Walker's timing was wrong. The ball crossed his line five strides ahead of him. He swore loudly, spurred his horse unnecessarily, then hauled back on the reins with such force that the animal's front feet came off the ground as her eyes rolled back and her mouth came open.

Barbaro rode over and jabbed him hard in the side with the head of his mallet.

Walker glared at him. 'What the fuck?!'

'It's not the mare's fault you can't play for shit!' Barbaro shouted. 'Don't punish her for your mistakes!'

He called Walker a few choice names in Spanish and jabbed at him again.

Walker took a vicious swing at him, and Barbaro blocked him with a forearm to Walker's wrist, driving Walker's arm up and back.

'You want to fight with me?' Barbaro shouted. 'I will kick your ass! I am not some little girl you can knock around!'

They were horse to horse, the polo ponies muscling against each other, ears pinned, the men knocking knee pad to knee pad.

They had this end of the field to themselves. The morning sun was bright and hot, horses and men all sweating, breathing hard. This was supposed to have been a practice, a lesson for Walker, a chance for Barbaro to hit some balls before the afternoon match – the first round in a big-money tournament that would conclude on Sunday on the championship field in front of the grandstand with a thousand or more spectators.

Walker threw his mallet down, staring at his friend and teacher. He looked back down the field. At the far end, a bunch of little kids were milling around on their ponies, gathering for lesson time. There was no one within earshot. Still, he kept his voice low.

'Why don't you just come out and say it, Juan? You think I killed her, no matter what I say. You think I just go around in the dead of night killing girls.'

Barbaro sat back. His horse settled but remained alert, sensing the tension. 'Brody tells me this morning that I need an attorney, that he has hired one for me – Elena's father.'

'Well, that should narrow down your chances of fucking her,' Walker said. 'Too bad for you.'

'I told him no.'

'So you'll get someone else.'

'No. I will not,' Barbaro said.

Walker digested that, looked down the field at the kids, looked back. 'If the rest of us have attorneys and you don't, that makes it look like we did something and you didn't. The cops will think they can turn you against us.'

Barbaro said nothing.

'Can they?' Walker asked.

'I don't want to be a part of this. It disgusts me.'

'Ha! *Disgusts* you? Like you haven't done your share of partying. Jesus, you've screwed more women than most men ever see in their lifetime. You've snorted your share of blow. You never looked to me like anyone was twisting your arm.'

'No one ever died because of it,' Barbaro said.

'Look,' Walker said. 'You're a part of this. You think the cops are going to believe you're a virgin? Take the damn lawyer. We stick together in this, everyone comes out fine.'

Barbaro rested his hands on the pommel of his saddle and sighed, looking down the field to the kids wearing helmets that seemed bigger than they were. Life was still shiny and new for them, filled with innocence and possibility.

'She was dead when I found her,' Walker said. 'I don't know what happened. I was passed out, remember?'

'You were the last man with her,' Barbaro said. 'I remember that. I remember you were angry because of it. I remember Irina making fun of your pouting. I remember you didn't take it well.'

'So that means I killed her?' Walker asked, offended but not quite able to meet Barbaro's gaze. 'She was a cunt. So what? She could suck the white off rice. That's all I cared about. That's all you cared about too.'

'I wasn't with her,' Barbaro said. 'You took her, and I left. Remember?'

Walker narrowed his eyes. 'No. I don't. You were there. I saw you. Everyone saw you. Do you have someone who can say you weren't there?'

Barbaro let that one go. 'Then who killed her? Everyone else had gone by then.'

'Hell if I know,' Walker said.

'Why can you not look me in the eye when you say that, friend?'

Walker didn't answer.

'If you don't know who killed her,' Barbaro said, 'maybe

232

it is because you don't remember what you did. You were the last man with her, then she was dead. Maybe you don't know you didn't do it. Maybe you think you did. Maybe you *did*.'

Bennett Walker still wouldn't look at him.

'Did you choke her during sex?' Barbaro asked. 'That is a dangerous game I know you like to play. You were angry. You are always angry with women. You like to get rough—'

'So did she—'

'How do you know you didn't kill her?'

The seconds seemed to tick past in slow motion.

Finally Walker looked at him. His eyes were flat and cold, like a shark's.

'What difference does it make?' he said. 'The girl is dead. I can't change that. And I'm not going to prison for it.'

He turned his horse and left the field, leaving Barbaro to stand alone.

# 40

I slipped inside Lisbeth's apartment and quietly closed the door behind me.

'Lisbeth?'

Nothing. Which meant I was free to violate her privacy.

I didn't go looking for anything in particular. I had learned as a cop that narrowing my focus too much caused me to ignore things that might prove important later on. That was especially important as a Narcotics detective – the ability to absorb every detail around me, to be aware of everything, no matter how insignificant at a glance. That skill had saved my life more than once and saved a case many times.

Lisbeth owned the usual fashion rags, plus a couple of polo magazines – Barbaro on the cover of *Sidelines* – and a selection of tabloids. She drank a lot of Diet Coke, had a bowlful of hard-boiled eggs, ate a lot of tuna – solid white albacore packed in spring water. There was a bottle of Stoli in the freezer.

She didn't strike me as a vodka drinker. I pictured Lisbeth drinking a piña colada, a margarita, a drink with a cutesy name that was sweet and colorful.

Irina had been her friend, though. Irina could pound down vodka like a Russian stevedore. Maybe it was for her.

Like so many people, Lisbeth kept a collection of snapshots taped to the refrigerator door. Many looked the same as what had been on Irina's computer and in her digital camera. Photos from parties, from polo matches, from clubs. Girlfriends, polo players – several of Barbaro, social players – Brody's crowd.

Only a few photos of Lisbeth herself. One in shorts and T-shirt, a candid of her holding on to a polo pony by a tangle of reins. One of her in a little black dress and Dior sunglasses, looking very glam.

There was the same photo of Lisbeth and Irina sitting side by side on the poolside chaise as had been in Irina's camera. And another of the two of them at a tailgating party.

There were several of Irina only. Irina in profile, speaking to someone out of the frame. Irina sitting at a bistro table, having a glass of wine. Irina sitting on the lap of a man whose face had been overlapped by another photo. I turned the corner up. Bennett Walker. I put the corner back down.

I stood there for another moment, thinking: Just as Irina had a few too many photographs of Bennett, Lisbeth had a few too many photographs of Irina.

'*Girl crush,*' Kayne Jackson had said. Hero worship. Irina had been everything Lisbeth was not – sophisticated, exotic, worldly, bold, adventurous. My eyes went from the photos of Irina to a photo of Lisbeth with Paul Kenner and Sebastian Foster, a photo of Barbaro and a couple of other players, back to the photos of Irina.

I moved on from the kitchen, down a short hall. The small bathroom was littered with wet towels. A wadded wet T-shirt and a pair of cargo shorts had been shoved into the wastebasket. They smelled of swamp and vomit.

The bedroom was a comfortable size, the walls painted lavender. The bed was a tangle of sheets. The wastebasket was full of discarded crumpled tissues. From crying, I thought. Lisbeth had lost her best friend, felt lost herself. A good bet: She was scared. She knew more than she was telling anyone. That was a big load to carry for a little girl from Nowhere, Michigan.

Along the far wall of the room stood a portable clothes rack hung with a condensed version of Irina's designer wardrobe. Her purse sat on the dresser. Inside: her wallet, her cell phone.

Where would she have gone without her wallet? What girl her age didn't have her cell phone Velcroed to the side of her head?

A sense of unease filled me and trickled down my spine like water. I turned to face the door.

The closet door stood slightly ajar. I pulled it open to reveal more clothes hanging on the rod and piled in a heap on the floor. And staring out at me from the corner, obscured by long hanging garments and covered by a blanket, a pair of blood-red eyes.

I jumped back with an expletive, then caught myself and tried to refocus.

'Lisbeth? Oh, my God, what happened to you?'

I shoved the hanging clothes out of the way and squatted down to meet her at eye level. She looked like something from a horror movie. The whites of her eyes were filled with blood, making the cornflower blue of the irises seem to glow. Her hair was matted in an insane tangle, studded with dead grass and dried leaf fragments. Her face was so swollen, she was all but unrecognizable.

'Lisbeth,' I said again. 'Can you hear me?'

I reached out toward her, wondering if she was dead. But she flinched as I pulled the blanket away.

'Come on. Get out of there.'

I offered my hand and she took it. Her fingers were like icicles. She started to cry as I pulled her from the closet. Wrapped in a long terry robe, she was trembling so hard she could hardly stand and, in fact, crumpled to the floor, curled into a ball, and started coughing – a hard, deep, rattling cough.

I knelt beside her.

'Lisbeth, have you been raped?' I asked bluntly.

She shook her head but cried harder; the sounds from her throat were raw and hoarse.

'Tell me the truth.'

She shook her head again and mouthed the word *no*.

I didn't believe her. She'd been strangled. I could see the ligature mark on her neck where her hair had fallen out of the way. She'd been strangled so hard the blood vessels in her eyes had burst.

'I'm going to call an ambulance,' I said.

She grabbed hold of my arm. 'No. Please,' she croaked, touching off another fit of coughing.

'Then I'm taking you myself. You need to go to the hospital.'

She squeezed my arm so hard, I imagined there would be bruises later.

I pulled the coverlet from the bed and put it around her. I didn't know what had happened to her, but I recognized what she was feeling now – fear, shame, disbelief. She wanted to wake up and realize she'd been in the middle of a terrible nightmare.

I reached down and stroked a hand over her hair. Lisbeth tried to push herself up into a sitting position.

'. . . so . . . scared . . .' she whispered.

She fell against me, shaking and sobbing, and I put my arms around her and just held her for I don't know how long, thinking how many times in my younger life I wished someone had done that for me. How nice it would have been just to have someone there, offering support and a safe place to fall.

'You're safe,' I said quietly. 'You're safe now, Lisbeth. No one is going to hurt you again.'

As we sat there on Jim Brody's property, I hoped to God what I said would prove true.

'Who did this to you?' I asked.

She shook her head.

'You have to tell me, Lisbeth. He can't hurt you now.'

'. . . don't know . . .' she said, and started coughing again.

237

'You didn't see him?'

She didn't answer me but pulled away, falling onto her hands and knees and coughing until she choked and gagged. I rested my hand on her back and waited for the fit to pass.

When she quieted, I said, 'I'll be right back, and then we're going to the hospital.'

I grabbed her purse off the dresser, then went into the bathroom and dug her wet clothing out of the garbage in the bathroom and stuffed it into a laundry bag that hung on the back of the door. I took the stuff downstairs, went and got my car, and pulled it around the side of the barn, parking at the base of the stairs.

A couple of stable hands watched me. One dropped what he was doing and walked toward the other end of the barn.

I took the keys, grabbed my gun out of the box in the door, and ran back upstairs.

Someone had attacked this girl, brutally, viciously. And the odds of this being a random act, all things considered, were long. She had been involved with Brody's club, friends with Irina; she had been seen talking to me, and I was not to be trusted.

Brody had tried to give me the bum's rush, had tried to tell me Lisbeth was gone even while we stood beside her car. I had to get her out of there. Certainly Brody hadn't attacked Lisbeth himself. He wouldn't be that careless, but there was no reason not to think he might have paid one of the barn hands to do it.

For all I knew, whoever had done this to her might have believed he had left her for dead. God knew she looked like she shouldn't have survived.

When I got back to her room, Lisbeth was curled up, chin on her knees, leaning against the foot of the bed.

'Come on, Lisbeth.'

She didn't respond, just stared at the floor.

'Come on!'

She shook her head slowly. 'No,' she whispered. 'Leave me alone.'

'That's not happening, Lisbeth. You can get up and come with me, or I can drag you out of here by your hair. Get up.'

She said something so softly, I couldn't make it out. She said it again, and again.

*I should die? I should have died? I could die?* I wasn't sure.

'I don't know what you're saying,' I told her. 'But it's not happening on my watch.'

I grabbed her by the upper arm and started toward the door, dragging her.

'Goddammit, Lisbeth. Get up!' I shouted. A strong sense of urgency began to fill me, like a balloon growing larger and larger.

She started to cry again and pulled against me.

'Stop it!' I snapped.

I could hear voices outside. Two men speaking Spanish. I glanced out the window and caught a glimpse of two men down by my car.

As threatened, I wrapped a hand in Lisbeth's thick wet hair, my fingernails biting into her scalp, and yanked her toward the door.

She cried out but stumbled along beside me. Tears streamed down her swollen face as I marched her down the stairs.

The men looked up at me.

'Hey! What you doin' with her?' one shouted at me. He was stocky, neatly dressed in pressed jeans and a Western shirt. He wore a cowboy hat and a Fu Manchu. The barn manager, I assumed.

'I'm taking her to a hospital,' I said.

'She don' wanna go with you.'

'That's too bad,' I said. 'I'm not going to let her die. Are you?'

'I think you better let her go,' he said, bringing up some attitude, trying to block the passenger door of my car.

'I think you better get the hell out of my way.'

'I'm callin' Mr. Brody,' he said, pulling out his cell phone.

'Yeah? You call Mr. Brody. You do that. How about I call the sheriff's office? And they can call the INS. How about that?'

The other guy got nervous at that.

'How about I tell the detectives you did this to her?' I said.

'I didn' do nothin' to her!' he shouted.

'Yeah, *jefe*? Who do you think the cops will believe? You or me?'

The nervous one had taken a couple of steps to my left, to Lisbeth's left. He took a couple more, angling over but edging in toward the girl. The boss took a step in the other direction.

I reached behind my back, curved my hand around the butt of my gun.

'Back off!' I shouted at the one closest to Lisbeth, drawing my weapon and pointing it at his face. His eyes went wide.

From the corner of my eye, I saw the boss make his move toward me. Without letting go of Lisbeth, I swung my arm around and backhanded him across the face with the gun. He dropped to his knees, putting his hand to his cheekbone, where the gun's sight had cut him.

The nervous one ran as I swung back toward him. Off to get reinforcements.

I yanked the car door open and shoved Lisbeth into the passenger seat, then ran around to the driver's side, got in, dropped the gun, started the engine.

Dust flying, gravel spewing, the BMW fishtailed around the end of the barn. A horse being hand-walked toward me reared and bolted sideways, kicking out at the groom. The horse got away. The groom shouted obscenities at me as I roared past.

Rubber squealed and burned as I swung out of the driveway onto the road and put the pedal down. I was past the white Escalade coming from the other direction so fast, Jim Brody's face didn't register until a half mile later.

# 41

I hate hospitals. I especially hate emergency rooms. No one working there ever believes what is wrong with you is an emergency. They never believe your story of how you came to be there. They never believe you might actually be dying, unless you have an obvious gunshot wound, arterial bleeding, or exposed brain matter.

I'd had two out of three when I was rushed in by ambulance the day meth dealer Billy Golam's 434 dragged me down the pavement. It was the only time in my life I had gone to an ER and hadn't been stuck in a room and abandoned for hours on end, only to later be treated like an annoying hypochondriac.

Lisbeth had none of the Big Three. They stuck her in what seemed to be a utility closet with a bed wedged into it along with a lot of surplus equipment. She sat in a little ball, still wrapped in her bathrobe. I paced, chewing at a ragged thumbnail.

'Why don't you lie down, Lisbeth?' I suggested. 'Try to rest a little. When the detective gets here, he'll want to ask you a lot of questions. You'll need to answer them.'

I had managed to get her to tell me at least part of the story as we waited. Someone – she didn't know who – had put a bag over her head, choked her, hauled her out into the wilderness, and held her head under swamp water until she nearly drowned.

I was willing to bet that didn't happen to people back in Buttcrack, Michigan. The kid was as traumatized as anyone I'd ever seen.

A girl in scrubs stepped into the room, looked at me like

I was a bad piece of cheese, went to Lisbeth, and took her pulse without so much as saying hello.

'Excuse me. Who are you?' I asked.

She gave me a dirty look.

'A nurse? A doctor?' I said. 'A twelve-year-old playing dress-up?'

'I'm Dr. Westral,' she snapped.

'Of course. I should have known that through mental telepathy. I'm off my game. Are you a real doctor,' I asked, 'or are you still saving your Lucky Charms box tops until you're old enough to cross the street to the mailbox all by yourself?'

'I'm a first-year resident,' she said, as if that elevated her above the great unwashed like myself.

'So the answer is B: not a real doctor.'

She tipped Lisbeth's head back, and blasted her light into one of Lisbeth's bloody eyes.

'This is Lisbeth Perkins,' I said. 'She's a human being.'

Snake eyes. 'Please be quiet.'

She listened to Lisbeth's chest with her stethoscope while Lisbeth coughed and wheezed.

'Someone tried to drown her,' I said.

The look again. 'Can *she* speak?'

'Why don't you ask her? She has a brain and a tongue and everything.'

'Who *are* you?' the child doctor demanded. 'Her mother?'

'I'm a friend,' I said. 'That's a person who is kind and has concern for another's well-being. I only explain this because I'm sure you don't have any friends, you snotty little bitch.'

Landry stepped in and looked at me. 'Making friends?' he asked.

'Detective Landry,' I said. 'This person claims to be a doctor. I suspect her name is Brittany, or Tiffany, or another of the popular -*ny* names.'

Westral abandoned Lisbeth, turned, and introduced her-self to Landry, who flashed his badge. She shook his hand, smiling politely, the perfect professional. I rolled my eyes.

She turned to me. 'Ma'am, you need to leave now.'

'You think so?' I said. 'I think you need to kiss my ass.'

Landry intervened. 'Dr. Westral, I need to ask you to step out now. You can complete Miss Perkins's examination after Special Agent Estes and I have finished questioning her.'

I narrowed my eyes at her as she passed me on the way to the door.

I turned to Landry. 'Special Agent? I'm moving up in the world.'

'Don't let it go to your head.'

'You're not going to ask me to step outside?'

'No,' he said.

'Good for you.'

He stepped close to me, his back blocking Lisbeth. 'We recovered Irina's car,' he said quietly.

'Where?'

'In the parking lot of the Wellington Green mall. It's being processed. We have a pretty good partial footprint on the floor mat. I've got a rush on getting a comparison to the footprint at the dump site.'

'Fingerprints?'

'Not when I left.' He tipped his head in Lisbeth's direc-tion. 'Has she told you anything?'

I filled him in on what I knew.

'So, whoever killed Irina did this to Lisbeth to shut her up,' Landry said.

'And so far, it's working.'

'Weiss is checking into getting access to the video from the guard shacks at the Polo Club for Saturday and Sunday. If we can get our hands on the tapes for last night, maybe we can get a look at Walker coming home that night, what he was driving. If it was him.'

Lisbeth had started coughing again. I went to her, sat on the gurney, and put my hand on her back. 'Lisbeth, Detective Landry needs you to tell him everything you can about last night. I'm going to go find you a real doctor. If I don't get thrown out of the hospital, I'll be back in a little while.'

She was trembling as if she was freezing to death. 'Don't l-leave me a-a-alone. Please.'

'You won't be alone,' I promised. 'Detective Landry will be right here or right outside the door until I get back, okay?

'He's a good guy,' I said, glancing over at him. 'He can be a real butthead, but he's a good guy.'

Landry followed me into the hall. I stayed close to the door. Landry stayed near me so we could keep our voices down.

'Taking in another stray?' he asked, his expression softer than I would have liked. God forbid someone should accuse me of being kind.

'I feel sorry for the kid. Shoot me.'

'You think they'll keep her here?'

I shrugged. 'It's the age of managed care. These places usually manage not to care one second longer than they have to.'

'And if they don't keep her?'

'I'll take her home with me,' I said without hesitation. 'She can't go back to Brody's.'

He frowned. 'I don't like you taking her with you. Someone tried to kill her, Elena.'

'No. Someone tried to scare her,' I corrected him. 'If they had wanted her dead, she would be dead.'

'Semantics,' he said. 'Someone nearly killed her. She's in danger, you're in danger.'

'Well, guess what? It's not your problem.'

He jammed his hands at his waist and blew out a sigh. 'Elena—'

'Don't. It's a dead horse. Leave it alone.'

He opened his mouth to try to say something, stopped himself, looked away, tried again, couldn't.

'Unless you have something germane to the case,' I said, 'I have to go find that girl an actual doctor past the age of puberty.'

'They all lawyered up,' he said. 'Brody's crowd.'

'I know. I ran into Brody this morning.'

'Then you know who his lawyer is.'

'Yes.'

'How is that going to be for you?'

'Shitty,' I said, irritated with him for bringing it up. 'I get to relive one of the worst times of my life, have the press dig it all up like a compost heap. And my esteemed father – who is more of a bastard in practice than I am by definition – will get to knock me around and tell the world that I'm mentally unstable, a pathetic, bitter woman who might do anything to wreak havoc on the life of the man who betrayed her twenty years ago.

'How would you feel?'

There was nothing he could say to that. Landry had grown up in a normal middle-class blue-collar family. He didn't know what it was to have to feel like a stranger, out of place in the only home he had ever known, betrayed by the only people he should have been able to count on unconditionally.

*How would you feel?* How did I feel? Upset that those memories still had so much power over me.

Landry's pager went off. He checked the number and frowned.

'You'd better go outside to answer that,' I said, glad for the excuse to get rid of him. 'Before you have every pacemaker in the building going haywire.'

He clipped the thing back onto his belt.

'I'll call you when I know something,' he said.

246

The olive branch, I thought. Or bait. Or a thin thread to keep us connected.

'All right,' I said softly. 'Thank you.'

He started to walk away, then turned back, cupped his hand around the back of my head, and kissed me with restrained frustration.

'Please don't get yourself killed,' he said.

Surprised, I stood flat-footed and watched him leave the ER, wondering if I was pushing away one of the few people in my life who might have stood behind me in what was to come.

# 42

Edward Estes was a distinguished-looking man: neat, lean, elegantly dressed. His face seemed to arrange itself quite naturally into a look of disapproval.

Alexi Kulak sat in his office in the back of Magda's bar, watching Edward Estes on the television screen with an intensity that would have frightened the man had he been able to see it.

*Estes.*

Alexi's blood boiled harder every time he read the name at the bottom of the screen.

This was not a common name, he thought. He knew from different things Irina had told him that Elena Estes came from a wealthy background. She knew these men with whom Irina had entangled herself. And now these men were being represented by an expensive lawyer of the same name.

Just how much a part of this group was the woman he had chosen to find out who had killed his Irina?

With every passing moment he became more and more convinced that she would never give him the name of the murderer. She would lie to him. She would lie to protect her own kind.

A single knock sounded against his door before it opened and Svetlana Petrova stuck her head in.

'I brought for you lunch,' she said, slipping into the office.

Every move she made was like a reptile slithering, Alexi thought. There was always that look in her eye as well: cold, sly. His brain, twisted with grief and lack of sleep and the

248

pills he was popping to stay awake, superimposed an image of Irina over her. Irina, tall and elegant, proud. Irina, slender and graceful, her eyes large and watchful, her lips as full as ripe berries. Then the image melted away and once again he could see only Svetlana. Svetlana, short and stubby, calculating. Svetlana, with her piggy little eyes and garish makeup, her clothes too tight, her hair too big and brittle with spray.

She came around the desk and took a seat on the desktop.

'You are too sad, Alexi,' she said. 'You torment yourself. It was not your fault. Irina did as she pleased, and this is what happened.'

Kulak stared at her, hating her more with each passing second. She wasn't worthy to have kissed Irina's feet.

She leaned forward so he could see her breasts inside her sheer blouse. She reached out a stubby little hand and touched his cheek.

'Let me make you feel better, Alexi,' she whispered. 'Let me take your grief away, if only for a short time.'

'You told me you brought me lunch,' he said bluntly.

She smiled her sly reptilian smile. 'But of course I did.'

Her feet braced on the arms of his chair, she leaned back, raised her skirt, and allowed her legs to fall open.

Alexi stared at her as she touched herself, opened herself. Her pussy was wet and red. He could smell her. Heat filled him.

Heat, but not the heat of sex.

The heat of rage.

'You fucking cunt!' he shouted, coming out of his chair.

He backhanded her hard across the mouth, the force of the blow knocking her off the desk.

'You dare do this!' he shouted, rounding the desk. 'You dare debase my grief! You are nothing but a whore!'

Svetlana was on the floor, dazed. She looked up at him as he came toward her, bore down on her, and she tried to turn

249

onto her hands and knees to scramble away.

Kulak grabbed her by the front of her flimsy blouse, which tore away as he tried to lift her to her feet. She landed hard on her backside and tried to push herself backward, but as she started to turn, she ran into the old file cabinets.

This time he grabbed her by the hair and pulled her to her feet.

She tried to say no, but her jaw hung slack, and all that came out of her were animal sounds of fear.

'You dare think you can take her place, you stupid, filthy cow?'

Still holding on to her hair, he made a fist with his other hand and punched her in the breast as hard as he could – once, twice.

She was crying now, hysterical, trying to pull away. Her nose was broken and bleeding, the blood running into her mouth.

Alexi shoved her roughly to the floor, where she landed in a heap, half naked, mascara running twin black rivers down her face, making her look like a ghoulish clown. She glanced toward the door, looking for someone to come and save her, knowing no one would.

He made to strike her again, and she cringed and cowered like a dog.

'I should kill you!' he shouted. 'I should kill you!'

And he might have, had something on the television screen not caught his eye. A photograph of a man, handsome, arrogant. Beneath the photograph a name: *Bennett Walker*. And beside it a photograph of a woman. Much younger than she was now, with a wild mane of black hair. Beneath the picture a name: *Elena Estes*.

He looked down at Svetlana and spat on her. 'You are not worth my effort.'

He had more important things to do.

Once more he stared at the television screen. A photo-

graph of Irina filled the frame beneath the title: MARKOVA
MURDER.

He went back around his desk, took a gun from a drawer, and left.

# 43

'I got the warrant. I'm at Palm Beach Polo,' Weiss said. 'We've got the girl's car driving in the west entrance at two-thirteen a.m. Sunday.'

'Can you see her in the car?'

'The tape isn't that good.'

'And Walker?' Landry asked, getting that old familiar tension in his belly. He could practically smell Bennett Walker's blood.

'And Walker and Barbaro in Walker's Porsche. And Brody's Escalade with a passenger. Ovada, maybe. And a couple of other cars I've got a deputy running plates on, but even money one is Paul Kenner and one is Sebastian Foster.'

'Jesus,' Landry breathed.

He stood on the far end of the sidewalk from the entrance to the ER. If he walked back inside and had a nurse take his pulse, they'd probably admit him.

He had the addresses of all the men in Brody's clique. Of them, two lived in the Polo Club development: Paul Kenner and Bennett Walker.

'And going out?' he asked.

'Brody leaves via the west gate around three-thirty; the car I think belongs to Foster goes out behind him. Not Kenner, not Walker.'

'And the girl's car?'

'Drives out the west gate Sunday night, late.'

'Can you see the driver?'

'No.'

'Shit,' Landry said. 'Go to Walker's place and canvass the neighborhood. See if anyone was aware of a party going on there Sunday morning. Kenner lives in the Polo Club too. If you don't hit pay dirt in one place, try the other.'

'If we can place the cars at either house, I'll get a search warrant,' Weiss said. 'In the meantime, should I get Walker and Kenner picked up for questioning?'

'No,' Landry said. 'We wait until we've got enough for an arrest warrant. Picking them up now will only piss off their lawyers – and give Dugan another excuse to chew our asses some more.

'I'll talk to Dugan about having someone sit on them from a distance.'

'Right.'

'Did they get any prints off the car?'

'A couple of partials is all.'

'Better than nothing.'

'My money's on the footprint,' Weiss said. 'What's up with the Perkins girl?'

'I haven't interviewed her yet. She looks like an extra from a horror movie. And she's scared shitless, but she claims she doesn't know who attacked her.'

'I thought you hadn't interviewed her yet.'

'I gotta go,' Landry said, and ended the call.

Immediately he called Dugan and updated him on the guard shack videos.

'Is there any way we can freeze these guys' passports?' he asked. 'They have access to private planes.'

'I'll call the state's attorney,' Dugan said. 'I'm guessing no. If you don't have enough for an arrest warrant, they're free to do as they please.'

'Can we sit on them?'

'And have Estes and Shapiro screaming harassment?'

'From a distance.'

Dugan hesitated.

'Jesus Christ,' Landry snapped. 'Do we have to ask please and say thank you when we slap the cuffs on them? Do we have to ask permission from their lawyers before we arrest any of them for murdering a girl and feeding her to the fucking alligators? Whoever did this is a goddamn criminal. I don't give a rat's ass how much money he has in his bank account.'

'Yeah, that's all very socially conscious of you, James. But the reality – which you know as well as I do – is rank has its privileges. Life isn't fair. If anyone past the age of six hasn't figured that out by now, they need to get their heads out of their asses and look around.'

'So the answer is yes,' Landry said. 'I'll have to go home and get my white gloves and party manners before I arrest one of these assholes.'

'And when the time comes, Landry, every *t* crossed, every *i* dotted on the affidavit, or Edward Estes will chew up your warrant and shit motions to dismiss. Got it?'

'Loud and clear.'

'Where's the other Estes in all this?' Dugan asked.

'Why would I know?'

'You have a way of coming across her. Do I have to worry about that?'

Landry didn't answer right away, considering the ramifications one way or the other. If he told Dugan that Elena was at the hospital with the Perkins girl, Dugan would try to do something to get her out of the way, to contain her. Taking her out of harm's way, Landry thought. But preventing Elena from doing any damn thing she wanted was no easy task.

If she thought Landry was behind Dugan's actions – and she would – whatever small scrap of trust she might still have in him would be gone, probably for good.

And while she didn't carry a badge anymore, this case was hers in all the ways that mattered. This was her vendetta, if in fact Walker had murdered Irina. Could he take that away from her? Should he?

'Landry?'

'Yeah. I'm here. My phone cut out. What did you say?'

'The media is digging up everything from twenty years ago,' Dugan said. 'She was involved with Bennett Walker. Testified against him on a rape/assault. Now here she is again, in the middle of it. Edward Estes's daughter. This could be the fucking Rubik's Cube of conflict of interest. Do you know where she is?'

'No,' Landry said. 'I don't.

'Look, I have to go interview the Perkins girl,' he said. 'She's in the hospital. Someone beat the crap out of her last night.'

'Does she know who?' Dugan asked.

'You'll be the first to know.'

He closed the phone and went back inside to take Lisbeth Perkins's statement.

# 44

A nurse practitioner, who was both competent and compassionate, examined Lisbeth and did the rape kit, finding nothing. Landry allowed me to stay while he interviewed the girl – as if he could have gotten rid of me. I listened to her story for the second time, thinking she had been through one of the most terrifying experiences I could imagine: blind, helpless, completely at the mercy of a ruthless, faceless demon.

Physically, Lisbeth would be all right. The blood in her eyes would recede over the next few days. The swelling in her throat would abate. She was on a heavy dose of mega-antibiotics to fight off any infection that might take hold in her lungs from inhaling the filthy, stagnant swamp water. Psychologically, she was in a far worse place.

She stared at the dashboard as we drove from the hospital to the farm, saying nothing, sitting so still she might have been catatonic. I let her be. The last thing she wanted to hear was someone crowing at her to buck up and count her blessings for being alive. Alive probably didn't seem like such a great thing just then.

Having been there myself, I knew enough to keep my mouth shut. People who have never experienced anything more devastating than a head cold are always the ones with the big Hallmark-card platitudes and wisdom. If I had a dollar for every time I wanted to tell one of those people to fuck off, I could have bought and sold Donald Trump three times over.

Sean was riding D'Artagnan when we pulled into the drive. He had the rock-solid seat and perfect upper-body position years of training with German masters had developed. He and the chestnut were one, springing across the diagonal line of the arena in a huge trot that seemed barely to touch the ground.

I wished I could be out there with him, the outside world receding as I focused on every footfall of the horse beneath me. In our sport, there is no time for the intrusion of external thoughts. In perfect moments, there is no conscious thought at all, only a oneness with the animal, only being. Communication is the simple exchange of pure energy. There is no process; no idea, plan, action, reaction, result. There is only intent and realization.

How unfortunate the rest of life is seldom that free of complications.

I parked in front of the cottage, went around the car, and opened Lisbeth's door — otherwise, I thought, she would have just sat there indefinitely, staring at nothing.

'Come on, kiddo,' I said. 'Let's get you situated.'

I had to put a hand on her shoulder to keep her moving, or she would have simply stopped and become a lawn ornament. Inside, I took her to the guest suite and showed her how to operate the shower. While she was at that, I set out a pair of my own sweatpants and a T-shirt for her, then went to the kitchen and heated some udon soup.

Elena Estes, Domestic Goddess.

No one who knew me would ever have imagined it (which was the way I wanted it), but there was a part of me that could have too easily been a nurturer.

The quality was not hereditary. My birth mother had sold me to the highest bidder before I was even out of the chute. Nor had I learned by example from Helen, my adoptive mother.

I had learned by longing, and wishing, I supposed. By imagining how I would be, and how I would not be, when I had children of my own.

We were going to have three, Bennett and I. A boy, a girl, and a bonus baby. I had been overjoyed at the idea, had chosen names, and had mentally mapped out the things we would do together as a family.

But then there was never a marriage, never a baby, never a family.

Somewhere in my thirties I had made a kind of peace with it. I had a different calling. I was dedicated to my career. Never the most social of creatures, I was long since used to my own company. That worked for me. I didn't have to conform to someone else's idea of perfection or endure their unending disappointment. I was able to find some satisfaction within myself. Contentment – or as close as I was ever liable to come.

I had grown used to being as irresponsible as I wanted to be, to being as spontaneous as I wanted to be. I could be as selfish and headstrong as I wanted. I resented ever having to compromise my time, my plans. I didn't have to be considerate of someone else's schedule or expectations.

That was my trade-off.

But there were times – when twelve-year-old Molly Seabright came to me and began to rely on me, for instance; and then with Lisbeth, who was in many ways younger than Molly ever was – that the old longing crept up on me and I wondered how differently I would have turned out if only. I never allowed it to last very long. It hurt too much and served no purpose.

I put a bowl of soup on a tray and took it to the guest room, tapping on the door before I let myself in.

Her curly hair was a wet tangle but clean at least. She had put on the clothes I left out for her and had assumed her favorite position of the day – sitting backed up against the head of the bed with her knees drawn up to her chin. Her fingers worried at the little medallion she wore.

'Eat a little bit of this if you can,' I said, setting the tray on the bedside table. 'It'll soothe your throat. I was choked myself just the other day, so I know.'

She looked at me, not sure what to make of what I'd said.

I shrugged and took a seat on the bed. 'The world is going to hell on a sled. What can I say?'

Lisbeth closed her eyes and shook her head. 'I don't know how any of this happened,' she whispered. 'I don't understand.'

'I guess people don't get murdered and beat up and treated like shit where you come from.'

She wasn't listening to me. She put her hands on her head, as if to hold it together.

'It's all my fault,' she murmured.

'You must think highly of yourself,' I said.

Confused and offended, she opened her eyes and looked at me for an explanation.

'To think you have the power to control the universe and everyone in it,' I said. 'You think if only you could have convinced Irina not to go to that party . . . You and I both know there was no stopping Irina from doing anything.'

'I begged her not to go.'

'Then you did all you could.'

She looked away and stared out the window. 'I wish . . . I wish . . .'

'If you're going to say you wish you'd died instead, save your breath. It wasn't your call, and that's just how it works sometimes. Take your breaks when you get them, Lisbeth. Life will turn on you soon enough.

'I made a bad choice once and a man died who shouldn't have,' I said. 'I stood right there and watched him get shot in the face. He had a family, and now they don't have him, because of me.'

'Don't you feel guilty?' she asked.

'Yes, terribly. But it hasn't brought him back, so what good is it? I've wasted a lot of time punishing myself. No one's given me a gold star for it. The world isn't a better place.

'Nobody likes a martyr, Lisbeth,' I told her. 'Now I try to get up in the morning and be a decent human being, do something good with myself, help somebody. I figure that's the best I can do to make up for my mistake.

'Save yourself the years of self-loathing and substance abuse, and just get on with it.'

Lisbeth stared at me, not knowing what to say.

'What a hell of a mother I would have made,' I said sarcastically. 'Donna Reed would be rolling in her grave.'

'Who's Donna Reed?'

I gave her a look. 'You *will* go to hell for that.'

She didn't ask me why. Trying to avoid another sermon from the crazy middle-aged lady.

'What I'm saying, Lisbeth, is work off your guilt. Don't wallow in it.'

'How?'

'Help me find out what happened to Irina.'

'But I didn't go to the after-party,' she said, looking away, staring at the wall as if the memory of that night was playing there on a movie screen visible only to her.

'Where was the party?' I asked firmly. 'And don't tell me you don't know.'

A big fat tear rolled down her cheek.

'At Bennett's,' she whispered.

I wasn't surprised, but still, that hard, electric jolt hit me in the stomach. A conditioned response to the sound of his name. Or the weight of boxed-up bad emotional memories banging into me. And even though it was essentially what I wanted to hear, I felt sick inside.

'Just how involved with Bennett was she?'

'I don't know what you mean.'

'Was she in love with him?' I asked bluntly.

Another big fat tear.

'No,' she said, but there was a note of uncertainty in her voice. 'She didn't love him.'

'They were lovers,' I stated without any care for Lisbeth's feelings. Cold hard fact.

She nodded. Two more tears.

'Did she have an agenda?'

'I don't know what you mean,' she repeated.

'I've heard from more than one person that Irina was angling for a wealthy husband.'

She inhaled a trembling breath. Through all of this she wouldn't look at me.

'Lisbeth, I know Irina was seen recently by a doctor at a women's clinic. Could she have been pregnant?'

More tears.

'Was she?'

The nod was almost imperceptible.

'She didn't love him,' she said again.

'Are you trying to convince me, Lisbeth?' I asked gently. The change-up pitch meant to throw her off balance: 'Or are you trying to convince yourself?'

She didn't answer. I sighed and waited, letting the emotional pressure build inside her. I played back the memories of the photographs I had looked at over the past couple of days. Lisbeth in the pained smile and the purple bikini, standing next to Jim Brody in his swim trunks. Lisbeth and Irina sitting shoulder to shoulder, cheek to cheek on a pool-side chaise, each with an umbrella drink in hand, toasting the photographer, all smiles.

'You miss her a lot,' I said softly.

Her shoulders were shaking as she tried to contain the emotions.

I thought about the vodka in her freezer. Out of place. The snapshots on her refrigerator. Too many of Irina.

'She was your best friend.'

She squeezed her eyes shut tight.

'Lisbeth?' I asked, then paused. 'Was Irina more than just your friend?'

'I don't know w-what you m-mean.'

'Were you in love with her?'

Now she looked at me, shocked, offended . . . guilty. 'I'm not a lesbian! Irina wasn't a lesbian!'

I had put together enough of a profile to know that Irina was whatever she wanted to be at any given time. There was no doubt she was into guys, but it wouldn't have surprised me to hear she swung the other way when it suited her. It certainly wasn't hard to imagine that at those Bacchanalian orgies of the Alibi Club, girl-on-girl action would have been a popular spectator sport – and Irina had loved the limelight.

'You've had a rough go of it, haven't you?' I said softly. 'You came down here thinking you were going to get a job, make some good money, meet people, have fun. Maybe you thought you'd meet the love of your life, I don't know. But you got something very different from what you bargained for.

'You got sucked in with Brody's crowd, you got overwhelmed. You're a good kid, Lisbeth. You didn't know anything about that world. Fast, shallow, amoral. In a way, you had the clearest vision of what it was, and how wrong it was. You come from a normal place populated with normal people. There's nothing normal about how these people live. Everything is a game, and they're entitled to have whatever they want until they don't want it anymore. And then they just throw it away, like it never meant anything to them.'

From the outside looking in, to people who have to worry about paying their mortgage and their electric bill, the world of the wealthy seems easy and wonderful. But every kind of life has its price and its pitfalls. In a lifestyle where there are no boundaries, it becomes a challenge to find one's true self. If everything comes easily, there is no way to establish worth. And if nothing has real value, then there is no way to gauge satisfaction or accomplishment or contentment.

That was Bennett Walker's world. He had everything anyone could possibly want, yet he was never satisfied. He had taken everything there was to take – except perhaps a human life. And in a world where nothing meant anything, why not take that too, just to see what it might be like to play God?

Bennett had always believed the world should run according to his plan. What if Irina had decided to disrupt that plan? What if she had decided she could get what she wanted by getting the upper hand on Bennett? What if she had told him she was pregnant, and that she expected him to marry her?

I could imagine the wrath that would set loose in Bennett Walker.

'Did you think something might happen that night, Lisbeth?' I asked. 'Is that why you tried so hard to keep Irina from going to the after-party?'

'I'm really tired,' she whispered. 'I want to go to sleep now.'

I considered pressing her harder but decided against it. Emotional battery was a good start. I would save sleep deprivation for later.

I didn't allow myself to feel guilty about it. Lisbeth was alive, Irina was not. Lisbeth would recover. The best I could do for Irina was vengeance. If I had to further manipulate, deceive, and abuse this girl to get it, so be it.

'One last question,' I said. 'Did you ever see Bennett Walker – or any of the rest of them, for that matter – hurt Irina physically?'

She didn't answer me. Either she was faking it or she had in fact fallen asleep. It didn't matter which. I didn't need

Lisbeth Perkins to tell me Bennett Walker was capable of hurting a woman.

I knew that firsthand.

# 45

'I knew he was up to no good,' the gate guard said. J. Jones. She pursed her lips and shook her head as she narrowed her eyes at the photograph of Bennett Walker. She was the size of a small upright freezer.

'How's that?' Landry asked.

'Because men that good-looking are always up to no good,' she said, looking at him like he was stupid. 'And he never drives that car. What's he doing in that car? He's always Mr. Big riding around in his Porsche or his this or his that. He ain't ridin' around in no Volkswagen. Him and that dark-haired foreign guy. Ooooh! I got to say, I do like lookin' at that one.'

'You're sure it was him?' Weiss said, tapping at Bennett Walker's head with his ballpoint pen. 'You're sure it was Sunday night?'

'Am I sure?' she said, offended by his obvious stupidity. 'Am I *sure*? That's my job. That's what I do. Are you *sure* you're a detective?'

'I have to ask that one every once in a while myself, Miss Jones,' Landry said, straight-faced.

Laughter exploded out of her like a cannon shot. Her massive chest rose and fell like a ten-foot sea. 'You got a sense of humor,' she declared.

'No,' Landry said. 'Not really.'

The guard turned back to Weiss. 'Honey, I'm working here in the middle of the damn night. Someone comes, someone goes, I'm gonna know it. That's what passes for excitement here. You think I'm just sitting around doing my nails all night? You think I'm just watching movies?'

'Were you here Saturday night?' Landry asked, pressing on.

'No. I was off Saturday. I have a life, you know. I'm not just sittin' in this place my whole life like a veal.'

'Doesn't matter,' Weiss said impatiently. 'We've got the tape. Let's go.'

Landry thanked the guard and left the booth behind Weiss, who was already halfway to his car.

'So?' Weiss said. 'That's gotta be enough for a search warrant for Walker's house. Videotape and an eyewitness who puts him in the dead girl's car.'

Landry's phone rang. Elena. He held a finger up at Weiss and took the call. 'Landry.'

'The after-party was at Bennett Walker's house in the Polo Club. Lisbeth told me.'

'Got it. Thanks.'

He clicked the cell phone closed and said to Weiss, 'The party was at Walker's house. *Now* we have enough for a warrant. Let's go nail his ass.'

# 46

I prowled around my living room with my cell phone in my hand, trying to decide what to do next. I could go to Bennett's neighborhood in the Polo Club and ask around to see if anyone saw him murder a girl Saturday night. That would go over big.

I could see it: security handing me over to Landry to be arrested for criminal trespass while he was executing a search warrant at Bennett's house. How convenient.

He didn't need me asking the neighbors anything. He would have uniforms doing KOD duty (knocking on doors) while he oversaw what went on in the house.

He would be trying to get a search warrant, I knew. If I had been in his position, that was what I would have been trying to do. I wondered how far he would get before my father stuck a wrench in the wheels of justice.

If he hadn't already at some point in his career, Landry was about to find out that there was a different set of rules for men like Bennett Walker and Edward Estes. The iron hand of justice would put on the kid glove. People who would have been ready to jab the needle in the arm of any other murderer would suddenly back down. The district attorney would be more willing to accommodate a deal.

Hard time? Surely, Mr. Walker — whose father-in-law footed the campaigns of practically every Republican candidate in the state — hadn't intended to strangle the girl. It was probably an accident. Perhaps time in a minimum-security facility with a good tennis court in exchange for a plea to involuntary manslaughter . . .

But what was I thinking? My father would never entertain the idea of a plea. He would run the state ragged in a full-blown CourtTV trial. He would reach deep into Bennett's coffers and call expert witness after expert witness. The state's budget for the trial would be pocket change by comparison. The state's attorney would be begging for five bucks to get ink pens and legal pads for the table. Edward would be forking over five or ten grand a pop for people with degrees to take the witness stand and convince the jury to buy a nickel for a dime.

At least this time the victim couldn't recant her testimony in exchange for a six-figure payoff.

Restless, I went to look in on Lisbeth. Whether she had been faking it or not when I left the room, she was well and truly out now. The lamplight from the bedside table touched her face with an amber glow. She looked about twelve, with her thick, wavy mane spread out across the pillow. A little girl still dreaming about becoming a princess.

I went in and covered her with a cashmere throw and touched her forehead to check for any sign of a fever.

Elena Estes: Mother Earth.

The cell phone vibrated in my hand. I walked out into the hall and answered it.

'Elena? It's Juan. I need to speak with you.'

'Here I am,' I said. 'Have at it.'

'No, no. Not this way. I want to see you.'

'Why?'

'You are not making this easy for me,' he said.

'Well, I know that's how you like things, but I'm not in the mood for it, Juan. Lisbeth Perkins has been beaten, strangled, and half-drowned.'

'What?' he asked with what sounded like genuine shock. 'Lisbeth? When did this happen? How did this happen?'

'Last night. She did night check, then someone grabbed her.'

'Oh, my God.'

'I'm trying to decide if I should be upset about that or if I should just shrug it off,' I said sarcastically. 'Especially seeing as she isn't dead, she just wishes she was. What do you think?'

'I think you are trying to make a point I've already taken.'

That gave me pause.

'I've been doing a lot of thinking, soul-searching.'

'It's good to know you have one.'

'I suppose I deserved that,' he said.

'I suppose you did.'

He heaved a sigh and tried to regroup. 'Please, Elena. Meet me. Or I can come to you. Whatever you prefer.'

I preferred not to have him come to my home, where my only witness was passed out cold in the bedroom. I had no reason to trust him. Even money said someone in that clique had attacked – or paid someone else to attack – Lisbeth. There was no doubt in my mind they had put their heads together the night before, after finding out about my past life with the sheriff's office. Brody knew I had been pumping Lisbeth for information. So did Barbaro.

Instead of trying to take me out of the equation, they did the easier thing and turned on Lisbeth. Easier to turn off the faucet than to make the bucket disappear.

'What's it about?'

'Bennett.'

I said nothing.

'Meet me downstairs at Players. I want to speak with you before I go to the detectives. Please, Elena, give me that chance.'

He was going to turn on Bennett. I couldn't have been more shocked . . . then hopeful, then suspicious.

'A soul *and* a conscience,' I said. 'Seems too good to be true.'

'Meet me, please,' he said.

'I'll be there in twenty,' I said, and closed the phone.

# 47

A couple of TV news vans had taken up residence in the main parking lot at Players. Python-size tangles of cord had been snaked from the vans up to the prime exterior-shot spots, where blinding white lights and screens stood on spider legs, ready for the on-camera talent to step in front of them.

Irina's murder was Big News again, with the rumors about the Alibi Club and its members. This was the last public place Irina had been seen Saturday night, a natural choice for a backdrop. As I watched, a blond woman with a very serious expression stepped into one of the setups to do her thing.

The tall gangly kid was working the valet stand. His hair was sticking up. He looked overwhelmed, which I imagined happened all the time, considering the slow-turning wheels of his brain.

'Where's your pal Jeff?' I asked.

'I dunno,' he said, breathing a little fast. 'He's late. I know that. And it's real busy.'

He hustled off to open the doors of a cream-colored Bentley. I went inside the club, took the stairs down, and told the maître d' I was there to meet Mr. Barbaro.

We were just far enough into the dining room that I couldn't gracefully back out when I saw the real focus of the media attention: Bennett Walker and my father having dinner. A publicity stunt that had my father's fine hallmark all over it. He wanted the public to see Bennett – handsome, well-dressed, well-behaved – having a serious discussion with his handsome, well-dressed, well-respected attorney.

Only my father could have bullied club management into allowing cameras into the dining room.

My feet stopped moving forward and I couldn't seem to help but look right at them.

My father was holding court and had yet to notice me. His hair had gone entirely gray and his face was a little drawn, but otherwise he looked exactly the same to me: arrogant, intelligent, and in his element in front of cameras.

The mix of emotions that bombarded me in that moment were diverse and upsetting. Just as I had with Bennett, I wanted not to feel anything when I saw my father for the first time in all these years. But of course that couldn't happen. The emotional memories of the first twenty-one years of my life rose up like a tidal wave inside me.

Anger, rebellion, guilt, that devastating sense of inadequacy I had always felt when he looked at me with that cold, disapproving stare. The stare that met my eyes now as he sat at a table with the rapist and probable murderer who had shattered my world twenty years past.

'Elena,' he said, with that same subtle hint of condescension as always, as if he were a king deigning to speak to a commoner.

The backs of my eyes burned, and I was furious with myself for it. But I had only that split second to think about it, because the couple of still cameras and video cameras there to make my father and Bennett Walker the news at eleven swung toward me with the realization of who I was.

I was trapped. I could leave and look like a coward or stay and face them both. There really wasn't a choice at all, considering the options.

I reached somewhere very deep inside me to hold my composure.

He wasn't ten feet away. I took a step, and another, toward him.

'Edward,' I said, echoing his tone of voice exactly.

I saw the almost imperceptible tension in his jaw. I had stopped calling him Father when I was twelve, a defiance he hated. I wouldn't be subservient to him. He had punished me time and again for my disrespect. I had never wavered. The only currency that meant anything to me had been the horses, and I knew he would never take them away from me, because it would reflect badly on him and make him look like the tyrant he was.

I glanced at Bennett, then back at Edward.

'Just like old times,' I said. 'Bennett destroying a woman's life, you defending his actions, and me on the side of right.'

He was furious with me, but he would never show it in public. He rose, as any gentleman would. Bennett stayed seated and pouted.

'Be careful, Elena,' my father said very quietly.

'Be careful?' I said so everyone could hear. 'Of what? Are you threatening me?'

'You wouldn't want to say anything slanderous,' he said, in that same quiet voice he might use to speak to a small child.

I laughed and smiled the sardonic half smile. 'It's only slander if it isn't true.'

Shutters and motor drives went mad.

He shook his head sadly. 'It's a shame you became so bitter.'

The benevolent monarch. My ass.

'How can you be disappointed?' I asked calmly. 'I'm exactly what you made me.'

He sighed the sigh of the long-suffering parent. 'You shouldn't upset yourself, Elena. It isn't good for you.'

Implying that I wasn't psychologically stable.

'Well, *Father*,' I said, with such venom he would never want to hear the word again, 'just when I think you can't possibly disappoint me more than you already have, you manage to find a way. Congratulations.'

I turned my back to him and walked away.

'I'll give your regards to your mother,' he said. 'If you want me to.'

I just kept walking. I certainly didn't care if people thought I was an ungrateful child. People had thought far worse things about me.

'Ms. Estes!'

'Ms. Estes!'

I held a hand up to indicate I had no intention of speaking to the media. They didn't try to follow me into the ladies' room.

The dizziness hit full force then, the shaking, the sweating. I threw up, rinsed my mouth, splashed cold water on my face. I didn't look at myself in the mirror for fear of what I would see in my eyes – vulnerability. I would hate myself for it.

I rinsed my mouth again, then dug an Altoid out of my purse.

When I finally stepped out into the hall, I was alone. The jackals had all run back to try to pull some meat off my father.

As I turned toward the terrace, there was Barbaro looking at me.

My vision flashing red, I went straight at him and into his face. 'You rotten son of a bitch!' I said, struggling to keep my voice down. 'You filthy, rat-bastard, son of a bitch! You set me up!'

'No! Elena, I swear!' he said.

I gave him such a look of disgust, he should have died from it.

'Elena! Please!' he said, and made to grab my arm as I turned away from him. I jerked out of his grasp. My pulse was roaring in my ears. I slammed out the side door to the external staircase and started climbing.

I knew he was behind me. I kept walking.

'I didn't know they were here,' he said, hustling alongside me as I went toward the parking lot.

'Oh, please. You can't come up with anything better than that?'

'That's the truth! I swear! I wouldn't do that to you!'

'Why not?' I asked, finally stopping and turning to face him. We were well away from the building now and half hidden by trees.

'Why wouldn't you, Juan? Jim Brody is your bread and butter. I'm supposed to believe you wouldn't set me up if he asked you to? Bennett is your best friend. You wouldn't help him if he asked? You already have, in something far more egregious than blindsiding me.'

'I didn't—'

'Or did my dear old dad put you up to it himself?' I asked. 'I'm sure you've met him. You've probably been out on one of his boats with Ben. Christ, he's probably your lawyer too.'

'I refused,' he said. 'Brody offered, I refused.'

'So, you're a rat leaving a sinking ship. Is that it? Trying your luck on your own?'

'I'm not guilty of anything but looking the other way.'

'Yeah? Well, a girl died in that time you turned your head,' I said. 'That makes the person looking away an accessory.'

'I wasn't there,' he insisted.

'That's your new story?'

'It isn't a story. Listen to me,' he said. He looked over his shoulder, checking for cameras and microphones. No one had noticed us.

'I was not there with Bennett all night,' he said.

I stilled my temper and studied his face in the poor light. It had been a long time since I'd learned to spot a liar. I was very good at it. If Barbaro was trying to scam me, he was very talented.

'Where were you?' I asked.

'I went to Bennett's house after the party, but I didn't stay. I didn't want any part of it.'

'Any part of what?' I asked, my mind running rampant with sordid and terrible possibilities.

He looked away. 'I am not a Boy Scout. I've partied a lot. That's not a secret.'

'Spit it out, for Christ's sake,' I snapped. 'I'm a big girl. And you, as you said, are no Boy Scout. Don't waste my time pretending to be embarrassed or trying to break it to me gently. I was a cop for a long time. Nothing you have to say is going to shock me.'

'Irina . . . was high, she'd been drinking,' he began. 'Everyone was on something or another. Irina told Jim Brody she wanted to give him a very special gift for his birthday.'

He was clearly uncomfortable with the memory. I waited.

'Irina was the only girl who came back to Bennett's house that night,' he said.

I felt sick at the possibilities for the rest of the story. Irina, brash, high, full of herself, and half a dozen men with one thing on their minds.

'She wanted to—'

I held up a hand to forestall any details he might have been about to give me. The details of the debauchery didn't matter. Only one thing did.

'Who killed her?' I asked.

'I don't know. I told you, I left. I walked back here for my car.'

'Did anyone see you leave the party?'

'They were otherwise occupied.'

'Did anyone see you walking?'

'No, but I saw Beth – Lisbeth – when I got to the parking lot.'

275

'Try again,' I said. 'Lisbeth left the party at Players around one.'

Barbaro shrugged. 'I thought it was her. It looked like her. I was sitting in my car. She walked past. She looked at me. I remember thinking, how strange to see her there. Then again, I had been drinking. I suppose I may have been mistaken.'

'I suppose you may have been.'

'You could ask her,' he suggested.

I made a noncommittal sound. I remembered Barbaro's handsome face staring up at me from the cover of *Sidelines* magazine on the table in Lisbeth's apartment. I remembered the snapshots of him and his buddies on the refrigerator in her kitchen.

He may have figured she would back him up because he was who he was or because she had a crush on him. Or he might have been counting on her silence because it had been assured the night before when someone whispered in her ear: *'This is what happens to girls who talk too much.'*

'No one else,' I said.

'I saw the Freak creeping around,' he said.

'How did you get your car keys?' I asked. 'I know you use the valet. They were gone by then.'

'I give them only the valet key. I keep my keys.'

'And no one was here to see you,' I said.

'No.'

'You have no one to corroborate your story.'

'No,' he said, growing impatient with my line of questioning while he was trying to do the good and noble thing.

I didn't care. *Good* and *noble* were two words with which none of his cadre had more than a passing acquaintance.

I shrugged. 'I'm only asking you the same questions the detectives will.'

He still took offense. 'I wish I had seen ten people, but I did not. I didn't know I would need an alibi later.'

'And it wouldn't have mattered if you had, would it?' I said. 'All you had to do was pick up a phone, right?'

Barbaro said nothing. He had no defense for that, and he knew it.

'Who killed her?' I asked again.

'I don't know.'

'Who do you *think* killed her?'

He rubbed his hands over his face and walked around in a little circle.

'I had a call from Bennett,' he said. 'Just before dawn.'

'He needed an alibi?'

'Yes.'

I remembered that call myself. Not a phone call, a personal call. Twenty years ago. Four in the morning. I had been sound asleep. Bennett had let himself into my condo. The sound of the shower in the guest bath woke me – and confused me. Why would he shower in the guest bath? When I went to ask him, the door was closed and locked.

Still feeling unsettled, I had gone back to bed. Some time later, he slipped under the covers next to me, warm and naked, and when I stirred, he told me he had been there for hours.

*'No, you haven't,'* I whispered, a strange apprehension stirring inside me.

*'But you'll say that for me, won't you, baby? You'll say that for me. . . .'*

I felt sick at the memory.

'Later he told me Irina was dead,' Barbaro said. 'That she was dead when he found her in his pool. He said she must have drowned.'

'And you believed him,' I said.

'I wanted to believe him. He's my friend. I couldn't imagine it hadn't been an accident.'

'If it was an accident, why didn't he call 911?'

'She was dead,' he rationalized. 'He was afraid of the scandal. He's a very visible, wealthy man, from an influential family. His wife is a fragile person—'

'I wonder if he ever thought of that while he was busy fucking twenty-year-old girls,' I said. 'And so, because Irina was already dead, and out of his touching concern for his invalid wife, he – *and you* – thought it was a perfectly acceptable idea to dump her body in a canal so aquatic organisms could feed on her eyes and her lips, and an alligator could stick her corpse under a sunken log to rot until it was just right for dinner.'

Barbaro squeezed his eyes closed, as if that would stop him from seeing the image I had just painted for him. His voice trembled a little when he said, 'I didn't know. I swear, I didn't know what he did with her until I heard on Monday.'

'And would it have made any difference to you if you had, Juan?' I asked. I shook my head and held my hands up to prevent an answer. 'Don't answer. Don't bother.'

Neither of us spoke for a moment. Barbaro stared off in one direction, thinking I don't know what. I stared off in another direction, thinking about the vibrant, promising young woman Irina might have been if not for a couple of twisted priorities and a half dozen men who believed the rules of decent society didn't apply to them.

She had made a couple of stupid, careless choices. It was nothing short of tragic that she had paid for them with her life.

'Did Irina think Bennett would marry her?' I asked.

Barbaro looked at me, confused. 'Why would she think that? She knew he's married.'

'I think she might have been pregnant. She had set her sights on him. . . . All things considered, I don't think it would have occurred to her that his wife would be an obstacle.'

She was young, beautiful, vibrant, exciting, sexy.

Unfortunately, she didn't realize those are qualities a wealthy man looks for in a mistress, not a wife. And the two things she was lacking were the only things that counted to a man like Bennett Walker: money and connections.

'I never thought anything like this would happen,' Barbaro said softly.

'Yeah,' I answered in kind. 'It's all fun and games – until somebody loses their life.'

'What happens now?' he asked.

'You talk to Landry.'

I took my cell phone out of my bag but hesitated before hitting Landry's number.

'You could have called him yourself,' I said. 'Why did you want to talk to me first?'

'I'm doing this because of you, Elena,' he said, the big brown eyes earnestly on me. 'Because of the things you said to me last night. That's not the kind of man I want to be.'

What a pretty line, I thought. But I didn't believe him. And I didn't trust him.

'I'm flattered,' I said without sincerity, then opened my phone and called Landry.

# 48

'What the hell do you mean we have to call his attorney before we execute the search warrant?' Landry was incredulous at the suggestion. 'That's un-fucking-believable!'

'It's a courtesy,' Dugan said, the way he might say, *It's ulcerative colitis.*

'A courtesy?! Since when is courtesy our job?'

Dugan shot a glance at the three-piece suit standing beside his desk. Who the hell wore three-piece suits anymore? Landry thought.

'Assistant State's Attorney Paulson here can fill you in,' Dugan said.

Landry glared at Paulson, a soft, doughy guy with pretentious little round glasses. 'How many search warrants of murder suspects' homes have you executed?'

'Well, I—'

'I'll tell you how many,' Landry said. 'None. Not one. So I'll fill you in, Paulson. We don't send out engraved invitations. We tip our hand, the suspect has time to hide things, get rid of things – *like evidence.*'

'This isn't just any murder suspect,' Paulson said. 'The Walker family is very prominent in Florida, as are Mr. Walker's in-laws.'

Landry stared at Paulson, stared at Dugan. 'Can you believe this guy? Can you believe this bullshit? Bennett Walker looks good for murdering a girl and throwing her body to the alligators. He probably assaulted the other girl to shut her up. I don't give a rat's ass who he is, or who his family is—'

'The governor does,' Paulson said.

Landry was so angry he couldn't speak. He walked out

of Dugan's office to his desk, grabbed two photographs from the stack of paperwork accumulating regarding Irina Markova's murder, and marched back into Dugan's office. He held up the 8310s from the autopsy and advanced on Paulson.

'This is what you're protecting,' he said. 'The man who did this.'

Paulson took a step back, recoiling from the sight of the mutilated face.

'We're not protecting him,' he argued. 'We're taking precautions. No one is saying to turn the other way because of who Bennett Walker is—'

Landry rolled his eyes. 'Right—'

'Look at it this way, James,' Dugan said. 'If Edward Estes is standing right there, he can't accuse you of planting evidence.'

'Why not?' Landry said. 'The man is a known liar who sold out his own daughter to get Walker off before.'

'Videotape everything,' Dugan said. 'Including Estes himself.'

'So now we have to wait for a camera crew,' Landry complained. 'Do you want Steven Spielberg to direct? I can make some calls. Or, hell, maybe the Walkers know him. Maybe we should ask our suspect.'

Dugan scowled at him. 'Can it. Do we know where Walker is right now?'

Landry gave an elaborate shrug. 'How would I know? You wouldn't let me put a unit on him.'

'Put a unit on the house,' Dugan said. 'Get everything in place. We'll call Estes at the last second.'

'I'll go with you to serve the warrant,' Paulson said.

'Serve coffee while you're at it,' Landry said. 'I'll have mine black with two sugars. Or maybe an espresso. It's going to be a long night. Maybe the Walkers could call Starbucks and have it catered.'

He left the room before Dugan could order him out and went back to his desk. After all his big talk to Walker at the 7th Chukker about hauling his ass in, throwing him in jail, nobody caring who he was, etc., etc., he felt like an asshole. Of course it mattered who Bennett Walker was and who he knew.

The world played a different ball game with guys like Walker – a rigged game.

Reading glasses perched on the bridge of his nose, he checked his e-mail to try to get his focus back. Nothing from Latent Prints, nothing from Gitan. One caught his eye. He clicked on it.

The shot-in-the-dark inquiry he had made to Interpol the night before had been answered. He frowned as he read it and read it again.

Weiss came in, looking jazzed. 'We have a 'probable maybe' match on the shoe print from the scene and from the car. Did you get the search warrant?'

'Yeah,' Landry said, without looking at him. 'We have to put a unit on Walker's house right now. Some asshole state's attorney is going with us, and we're waiting on a couple of videographers.'

'One big happy family,' Weiss said. 'Who else is coming? Walker?'

'And his attorney.'

'You're shitting me.'

'A courtesy from the Palm Beach County Sheriff's Office,' Landry said.

'Will there be coffee and cookies afterward?'

Landry didn't answer him.

'What are you looking at? Porn?'

'Get this,' Landry said, pointing at his computer screen. 'Juan Barbaro was questioned in relation to a rape/murder outside London in 2001.'

'And?'

'Nothing. Questioned and released. Some other guy was tried for it in '03 and walked.'

Weiss raised his eyebrows. 'What was his alibi for Saturday night?'

'He was with Walker,' Landry said. 'And Walker was with him.'

'Cozy.'

'Yeah.'

'He's the only one of the bunch who gave us his DNA sample,' Weiss said. 'He had to know we wouldn't match it to the girl. 'Course, that just means he didn't have unprotected sex with her, it doesn't mean he couldn't have killed her.'

'But why would Walker deal with the girl's body if he didn't kill her?' Landry said. 'The gate guard ID'd him in Irina's car. Nobody is that good a friend, especially not a guy like Walker. He's all about himself. Fucking sociopath. He expects other people to lie for him. He's not going to stick his neck out for anybody.'

'We need to get the boots,' Weiss said. 'If we can put him in the car and put him at the canal dumping the body, he can stick his head between his legs and kiss his ass goodbye.'

Landry grabbed his cell phone as he rose from his chair. He had a message.

*'It's me.'* Elena.

*'Bennett Walker's alibi just went away. Juan Barbaro is recanting his statement.'*

'Every man for himself,' Landry muttered as he scribbled down Barbaro's phone number. To Weiss he said, 'The Alibi Club just lost a member. Barbaro is recanting his statement.'

Weiss chuckled maniacally. 'I love it when they turn on each other.'

Landry grabbed his sport coat off the back of his chair and pocketed his phone. 'Let's go get the party started.'

# 49

'You don't believe me,' Barbaro said.

'I don't trust you,' I corrected him. 'It's a conundrum. If you've just told me the truth, then you've admitted you're a liar.'

'I don't want to believe Bennett killed Irina,' he said. 'Why would I tell you his alibi is a lie if it was not the truth?'

'I've known you three days, Juan,' I said. 'As I keep reminding you, I met you only because a girl was murdered and you're one of the involved parties. I don't know anything about you, aside from the obvious. You could have your own agenda. For all I know, you leave a trail of victims everywhere you go. Bennett could be a convenient scapegoat.'

'That's ridiculous.'

'Is it?'

'But you believe Bennett killed Irina,' he pointed out.

'I want to believe he did it. I want him to go to prison and sit there for the rest of his life, knowing that he didn't get away with anything in the end,' I said. 'But if I want that so badly, I overlook a truth I don't want to see, then Irina doesn't get justice.'

He stared down at me in silence for a moment, as if he were trying to decipher a piece of modern art. Finally, he said, 'I see that you are one of the most extraordinary women – people – I have ever met. You make me want to be a better man, Elena.'

'Wow,' I said. 'I guess I should think more highly of myself.'

He reached out and touched the right side of my face, and it seemed each of his fingertips contained a slight electrical charge. I wondered if he had any idea how powerful his touch was, how strong that animal magnetism. Even not quite trusting him, I felt the warm rush of attraction.

'He hurt you very badly,' he whispered.

I didn't tell him that Bennett Walker wasn't the first man to hurt me, or the last, or that there was scarcely a man in my life who hadn't – or that the ones who hadn't yet had the opportunity would be headed off at the pass by me pushing them away. Or that he would be the next to join that club if he came too close.

'What goes around, comes around,' I said. 'I'm a firm believer in revenge.'

His fingertips brushed the fine hair at the nape of my neck, and a chill went through me.

'I could make you forget him, Elena,' he said, his voice warm and soft, lowering his head until he was close enough to kiss me.

'I'm sure you could make me forget my own name,' I said, moving just out of his reach. 'But not tonight.'

I could feel his eyes on my back as I walked away from him. I could feel his touch on my skin long after that.

## 50

'So much for that last-minute phone call to notify Estes,' Weiss said, walking up to the front door of Bennett Walker's little weekend house: six thousand square feet of stone and marble that looked like it had been uprooted from Europe and replanted in South Florida, gardens and all.

Edward Estes's black Town Car pulled around the circular drive, and the attorney got out of the back, his face taut and drawn. Pissed off, Landry thought. Good.

'Hell,' Landry said, 'I thought he would have been here an hour ago having the rugs shampooed.'

'This is an outrage,' Estes snapped, his anger directed at the assistant state's attorney. 'The governor will hear about this.'

'He already has, Mr. Estes,' Paulson said. 'These are Detectives Landry and Weiss. They'll be conducting the search.'

Estes ignored the cops and looked down his nose at the papers in Paulson's hand. 'That warrant is invalid on its face. I have a call in to Judge Beekman to—'

'Do you have a key to this place, or do we have to let ourselves in?' Landry asked, unimpressed with Edward Estes and his attitude.

'You're going to proceed with this?' Estes said to Paulson. 'When this warrant is thrown out, anything taken during this search is fruit of the poisonous tree.'

Landry raised his eyebrows and looked at Weiss. 'Did you hear that? Mr. Estes seems to think we're going to find something here to incriminate his client.'

'That isn't what I said, Detective.'

'Maybe he knows something we don't,' Weiss suggested.

'Yeah,' Landry said. 'Like how many bodies Bennett Walker has gotten rid of over the years that we don't know about.'

'Make a remark like that in front of the press, Detective,' Estes said, 'and you'll be looking for a new profession.'

Landry shrugged as if it made no difference to him.

'Professional poker,' Weiss suggested. 'Money for nothing.'

'I thought maybe I'd become a defense attorney,' Landry said to him. 'How hard can that be?'

'You're a very amusing comedy act, Detectives,' Estes said. 'Unfortunately, being a buffoon isn't a trait that will impress a jury.'

'I don't know,' Weiss said. 'Seems to work for most of you guys.'

Paulson cleared his throat. 'Mr. Estes, our office notified you as a courtesy. As you can read in the warrant, we have sufficient grounds for the search. Why don't we get on with it, so it can be completed with the minimum amount of fuss?'

'I would prefer we wait for my client,' Estes said.

'Where is he?' Weiss asked. 'Out burying the murder weapon?'

Estes turned to him. 'Mr. Walker is an innocent man. He is to be presumed innocent. If you have an obvious bias, Detective—'

'Not at all, Mr. Estes,' Landry said. 'We only go where the evidence leads us.'

'What evidence?' Estes said. 'You're here on a fishing expedition.'

'We can put the victim here the night she died,' Landry said. 'We have a witness who puts your client in the victim's car, leaving the premises, less than twenty-four hours later. We can connect the car to the site where the young woman's body was found, and I'm betting we'll be able to put your client's foot in the boot that left a print both in the car and at the dump site.'

'My client has a very solid alibi for the night Miss Markova went missing.'

'Mr. Barbaro has recanted his earlier statement,' Landry said.

He had to imagine it wasn't very often anyone got to surprise Edward Estes, but he had just managed to do it. With information Elena had given him. She would have been pleased.

'That's news to you, isn't it, Mr. Estes?'

Estes didn't respond. He pulled his cell phone from the inside breast pocket of his tailored suit and stepped aside without a word.

Landry smiled like a shark. 'Tell your client Elena sends her regards.'

# 51

Jeff Cherry already had his money spent. He knew a guy who worked at a salvage yard that sent a lot of 'pre-owned' luxury cars to Russia. The guy had pretty much promised he could get him a sweet little Mercedes convertible for 25K, with a clean VIN.

Sure, he could have put the cash in the bank or paid back the half dozen or so people he owed, but what the hell. He worked hard for his money. Well, yeah, there was a certain right-time-right-place element to it, but on the flip side, he was providing customer service by keeping his mouth shut. *Information management,* he called it.

He had chosen a public place for the payoff because he wasn't stupid. He watched enough TV to know better. So he had picked the parking lot at Town Square shopping center. He parked on the side closest to Sal's Italian Ristorante because he liked their pizza, and he didn't know if his client was going to be on time or what, so he might as well have something to eat in the meantime.

He was a man with a plan. This payment would be Installment One – to keep quiet about the Russian girl Saturday night. Then he would go for Installment Two, which was really the more crucial piece of information he held. He had kept it in his pocket for a long time – almost a year – and now he finally had found the guts to make it pay off.

With the aroma of tomato sauce and Italian sausage filling his car, and thoughts of his new ride filling his head, he settled in to wait.

# 52

Bennett Walker drove around, thinking, his head spinning with questions of what he should do, questions about what had happened, what must have happened; imagining scenarios of what might happen, of where it all might fall apart. He had to stay calm. From experience, he knew he couldn't panic. As long as he kept his wits about him, winning was always possible.

That was how he had to look at it – as winning, not as surviving. That was what Edward had told him years ago.

Easier said than done.

The pressure was on. The press was on the story. Their focus was on him. Never mind that he hadn't been the only man seen with Irina Markova that night. He was the only man named Walker, married to a Whitaker, who had been on trial for rape and assault in the past.

His voice mailbox had been full for hours with calls from the many people in his life who were angry with and/or disappointed in him. And all of them would be asking him the same question he had been asking himself: How the hell had this happened?

He didn't have an answer.

If Irina Markova hadn't challenged him. If she hadn't been the whore she was. If they hadn't done so much X. If he hadn't been drunk . . .

If Elena hadn't found the body.

He still couldn't believe that had happened. Of all the people in the world . . . No one should have been on that road. No one should have found that body. That the person who *had* was the one woman on the face of the earth who hated him most was incredible to him.

If Elena hadn't found the body, none of this would be happening. Everyone would have just gone on with their lives. He wouldn't have done what he had done to that stupid cunt Lisbeth. He wouldn't have to do what he was about to do.

He wasn't a criminal. None of this ever should have happened.

*'Damage control,'* Edward had said. *'Contain and minimize the damage.'* It would all depend on what the detectives had, on what they found at the house.

The idea made him sick. It never should have come to this. They didn't have anything on him. How had they gotten a warrant?

*Stick to the plan. Damage control. Contain and minimize.*

That was why Edward had gone to the house. That was why Bennett had not. Edward had drawn the attention away with him, blustering about the search warrant. Bennett had stayed, finished his dinner, had a drink, chatted with acquaintances, then left. He had driven out to Brody's, to the stables where his own string of ponies resided, and changed out of his dinner clothes into jeans and a T-shirt, and his old Blundstone boots. He had a job to do.

He had to concentrate on the things he could do something about.

He turned right off Wellington Trace onto Forest Hill.

His stomach was churning.

His memory of Saturday night was fragmented – the early-evening images were vibrant, bright, electric; the hours after leaving Players were cloudy, dark. He could remember the sex – the smell of it, the taste of it. He could remember the heat, the rage.

He remembered his hands around her throat, the defiance in her eyes.

He remembered the feeling of dread in his gut when he

saw her body floating in the pool.

He must have killed her. She was dead. He didn't remember.

He turned off Forest Hill into the parking lot and spotted the car.

*Stick to the plan. Damage control. Contain and minimize.*

# 53

I watched through the foliage that divided Bennett's property from the yard of the house next door. The house behind me was dark and vacant. People moved in and out of Bennett's house, carrying things in, carrying things out.

My father was kept at bay outside the front door. I could tell by his body language he was angry. I could easily imagine how he had managed to insert himself into the situation. The Walkers, the Whitakers, the governor, my father. That all added up to privilege.

As I watched the people come and go from the house, I imagined Bennett's cronies and Irina going up the sidewalk and disappearing inside on Saturday night. And all the dark scenarios of what had played out in that house swirled through my head like a toxic gas.

Not for the first time in my life, I wished I had been adopted by a couple of CPAs in Middle America and had grown up to do my four years at a state college, get a job, get a husband, have a couple of kids. People who had that life didn't know the things I knew about the darker side of life. I envied them.

Because I needed to focus on something tangible, I moved toward the back of the property and peered through the branches to catch a glimpse of Bennett's backyard. The interior lights of the house spilled out through French doors onto the patio and across the dark water of the pool. Deck chairs were scattered around.

I thought of the photograph of Irina and Lisbeth sitting on the chaise together, looking happy and silly. Sitting here, at this pool, in these chairs. I recognized the background and the stripes on the cushions.

Lisbeth had tried to prevent Irina from coming here that night. They had argued. *'I begged her not to go,'* Lisbeth had said.

*'. . . he told me Irina was dead . . . that she was dead when he found her in his pool . . .'* Barbaro had said.

I wondered why he had turned his story around. Why, really. I was just too cynical to believe it was because I had somehow awakened a conscience in him.

But if it was simply to take himself out of the picture of what had really happened that night, if what he had decided to do was hang the murder on Bennett and exonerate himself, why tell a story with a component he couldn't control?

*'I saw Beth – Lisbeth – when I got to the parking lot. . . .'*

Why say that? Unless it was part of the power trip. Unless he knew he could control Lisbeth, because he had seen to it that she would be too terrified to do anything other than what he told her.

That would mean it was a game for him, that he was a monster.

I couldn't see that, but I hadn't seen it in Bennett Walker either.

I would have said I was well past being surprised by anything in this life, but in that moment I thought I wasn't so sure of anything anymore. Maybe that was what came with time and bad experience – the ability to know that no matter what I'd seen, things could always get worse.

And so they would.

# 54

Bennett Walker buzzed his window down halfway, looked at the kid in the car beside him, and said, 'I'm not doing this here. I'm not being seen with you.'

He lifted a small duffel bag off the passenger seat. 'There's twenty-five thousand dollars in this bag, just like we agreed. If you want it, come and get it.'

The kid stared at him, his mouth hanging open. There was pizza sauce on his face. For some reason, that image would stay with him: the idiot kid with pizza sauce on his face.

He drove slowly around the end of the buildings, going behind the shopping center, and made his way toward South Shore, checking his rearview mirror.

The kid followed. Of course he did. Greedy little shit.

He took a right on South Shore and drove past Players, then took a left and another left onto the grounds of the old polo stadium, via what had been a service entrance. Abandoned now for several years, the stadium stood sagging, in a shambles from hurricane damage, waiting for progress to come along and flatten it.

Bennett pulled in at the far end of the stadium, parked his car, and got out. Creepy place, he thought. Not like it was in the old days, when the barns were full and the place was electric with the energy that surrounded high-goal international polo. The outdated security lights were lit, but they gave little in the way of light or security and did nothing to dispel the feeling of being in a ghost town.

The kid pulled in beside him, parked his car, and got out. Neither of them noticed the third car, which killed its lights and stopped just off the road.

'Hey, man,' the kid said, his tone too familiar, like they were contemporaries, friends even. 'I can understand you not wanting to do this in front of people. Believe me, I don't want to make this difficult for you. I'm providing a service. I want my clients to feel comfortable.'

Bennett stared at him. 'What the fuck are you talking about, you slimy little shit? You're a blackmailer.'

The kid held his hands up and made a pained face. 'No, no, no. That's such an ugly word. That's not what this is at all. You're paying me a fee to manage some information for you. That's all. It's business.

'A man like yourself, you have a name to protect, yet you want to live a certain lifestyle. . . . Think of me like a personal assistant.'

'I don't want to think of you at all,' Bennett said flatly. 'Let's get this over with.'

He set the duffel bag on the trunk of the kid's car and unzipped it. 'Twenty-five thousand. I'm not sticking around while you count it.'

'That's cool, Mr. Walker,' the kid said. 'I don't want to put you out.'

Bennett turned and stared at him again. Unbelievable. What was there to say?

'Now, I'm sure you understand this only covers Saturday night,' the kid said.

'What?'

'The information specific to Saturday night,' he clarified. 'There's the other thing we haven't discussed.'

'What other thing?'

The kid made the pained face again. 'I hate to bring it up. I really do. But in light of recent events—'

Bennett advanced on him, towering over him. 'What the hell are you talking about?'

The hands went up again. 'Last April. End of the season.

During the big Super Bowl or whatever you call it in polo.'

'The U.S. Open? What about it?'

'There was a night at Players . . . a girl . . . in your car . . .' the kid prompted. 'She wasn't very happy. . . .'

Everything went cold inside Bennett. A fan, a polo groupie . . . She came on to him. . . . She wanted it. . . . They went outside. . . .

'She was crying,' the kid reminded him. 'You told me I didn't see anything.'

He had paid the girl ten grand to shut up. She had been all over him in the club. No one would have believed her – without a witness to back her up.

Funny, Bennett thought, he had been agonizing over what he was going to have to do. Now he just acted. He put his hand into the duffel bag, curled his fingers around the short crowbar, pulled it out, and struck Jeff Cherry with it as hard as he could, burying the thing in his skull.

The kid's head cracked like an egg. Blood and brain matter splattered, but not as much as Bennett had imagined. One hard overhand stroke, and that was it. He didn't even have to bother to pull the crowbar free to give him a second whack.

Bennett stepped back and stood there as the kid dropped to his knees and fell over dead.

As simple as that.

He popped the trunk on the kid's car, put the body inside with half a dozen mostly empty boxes from Sal's and numerous crumpled Krispy Kreme bags. From the duffel bag he took a couple of small bags of cocaine and planted them among the rest of the trash, making certain to get a little drug residue on the kid's fingers.

He closed the trunk. When the car and eventually the body were discovered, no one would find it hard to believe the kid had been on the wrong end of a drug deal gone bad. Everyone knew he supplied Players' customers with recreational substances. Jeff Cherry would be considered just another fatality in the war on drugs.

*Damage control.*

'A pity it will not go so easily for you.'

He startled at the sound of the voice and spun around.

A square, neat man in a brown suit stood pointing a gun at him.

'You are wondering who I am,' the man said.

His accent was Russian. That realization sent chills through Bennett Walker like shards of glass.

'I am Alexi Kulak,' the man said. 'I loved Irina Markova. You killed her. And I have come to kill you.'

As simple as that.

# 55

'The boots aren't here,' Weiss said. 'Either he got rid of them or he's wearing them right now.'

They stood in front of the house, taking a break, allegedly clearing their heads. Landry wanted a cigarette; the adrenaline was running full-bore. But he forbade anyone to light up within a hundred yards of a scene he was running. He wanted no chance of contaminating the scene in any way that could be prevented. Especially with a defense attorney standing right there watching every move.

'You're not going to find anything, because there's nothing to find,' Edward Estes announced.

'We know the girl was here Saturday night,' Landry said.

'You're not going to find evidence of a murder here,' Estes said.

'Yeah, that's the smart thing about choking the life out of someone,' Weiss said. 'No smoking gun. No spent casings. No bloody knives.'

'You allegedly have the testimony of one man that the girl was ever here,' Estes said. 'Has it occurred to you to wonder if that individual might have his own reasons for implicating my client in this? His own guilt, for instance.'

'Why would he bother?' Landry said.

'You might want to ask Scotland Yard that question.'

He'd done his homework, Landry thought – or someone had done it for him. Estes knew about Barbaro's connection to the case in England. But if Barbaro had killed Irina, why bother to change his story? Barring a surprise witness coming out of the woodwork, no one would have broken the alibi he shared with Bennett Walker.

Maybe this was how he got his kicks, Landry thought: kill a girl, pin it on a friend, watch the fireworks. His friends were all wealthy, influential men. Wealthy, influential men didn't go to prison for crimes they didn't commit. It seemed they hardly ever went for crimes they *did* commit.

'You have not one shred of physical evidence the girl was here, in this house, on the night in question.'

Landry said nothing. Even if they came up with trace evidence — hair, bodily fluids, whatever — they wouldn't be able to say it had been left the night of the murder. Estes would parade a bunch of hired guns into the courtroom — if they ever got the case to trial — and pound reasonable doubt into the minds of the jury.

They needed something irrefutable. Something that couldn't have been in Bennett Walker's house before the night of the murder, something personal to Irina. It wouldn't surprise Landry to find out Walker videotaped his sexual conquests. He had that kind of ego. But even with a videotape, it could be difficult to prove the when of it unless the date and time feature of the camera had been turned on.

He thought about Irina's things they had picked up that day along the canal: a small, cylindrical handbag, gold encrusted with rhinestones. Inside the bag: a cherry-red lip gloss, a compact, an American Express gold card, three twenties, two condoms. No cell phone.

Estes was droning on. The usual defense-attorney crap about how his client was going to sue the sheriff's office for harassment and how they would all live to regret fucking around with him and his big ego.

Landry pulled his phone out of his pocket and called Elena. She answered on the first ring.

'Elena. It's Landry,' he said. 'Your father is one colossal asshole.'

Edward Estes shut his mouth for the first time in hours and stared at Landry, suspicious.

'Tell me something I don't know,' Elena said. 'Has he threatened to ruin your career yet?'

'A couple of times. Weiss thinks we should take up professional poker.'

'Money for nothing.'

'Listen, what's Irina's cell phone number?'

She gave it to him. He thanked her and ended the call.

'Hell of a girl you raised there, Mr. Estes,' Landry said. 'Though I have a feeling she is who she is in spite of you, not because of you.'

He turned and went back in the house, dialing the number Elena had given him. Weiss followed.

'It's a long shot,' Weiss told him. 'What are the odds that the battery still has juice?'

'Fuck the odds.'

'I'm just saying.'

Bennett Walker was into power, adrenaline, conquest. A man like that liked to have reminders of his prowess. Souvenirs.

As he walked through the house, Landry saw those souvenirs all around: photographs of Walker playing polo, racing boats, downhill skiing. Tanned, good-looking, the big white victory grin, one hand raised in triumph and a hot babe presenting him a trophy on the other.

The phone on the other end of Landry's call rang and went to voice mail. He dialed again. The same thing.

He went into the master bedroom – a stark, modern space at odds with the traditional European style of the house. The bed was dressed in crimson silk on white cotton sheets, but it looked as if it hadn't been properly made in days. Clothes were strewn over chairs and dropped on the floor. There were dirty drinking glasses on the nightstand, and the place stank of sweat and stale sex.

'Unless he's doing her,' Weiss said, 'the maid hasn't been in this room for a while.'

301

Landry shushed Weiss and hit *redial* on his phone.

The sound was faint. Muffled. But it was there. Landry didn't know one piece of music from the next, but Elena would later tell him the song was by Beethoven – *Für Elise*.

Walker had sandwiched the phone between his mattress and box spring near the head of the bed, handy for a bedtime lullabye.

Edward Estes was still ragging on Paulson when Landry walked out the front door again.

'What kind of evidence do you think would be convincing, Mr. Estes?' Weiss asked. 'To prove Irina Markova was here the night she was murdered?'

Estes didn't even glance at the detectives. His eyes went straight to the cell phone covered in pink crystals Landry held in his gloved hand.

'How about a voice from beyond the grave?' Landry suggested, hitting the button to play the phone's greeting.

*'This is Irina. Please leave message. . . .'*

## 56

I had already started walking back to my car by the time Landry called to ask for Irina's phone number. What a Perry Mason moment that would be, I thought: showing the victim's found cell phone to her killer's attorney. Aside from the obvious incriminatory value of the phone being at the house, there would very likely be photographs from the evening's festivities stored in the phone's memory.

I hoped Landry had that moment of victory right in front of my father.

*Bang, bang, Daddy. There goes another nail in Bennett's coffin.*

He would probably mourn the loss of Bennett going to prison more than he had ever mourned the loss of me walking out on the family. And why not? Bennett was the son he should have been able to sire for himself: handsome, intelligent, ruthless, without conscience. A chip off the old block.

That was what my marriage to Bennett would have meant to my father: that he gained Bennett as a son-in-law. My happiness was irrelevant to him. I had been a means to an end. He should have thanked me for leaving. With me out of the picture, he had Bennett all to himself.

Now he would see Bennett on visiting days in the state penitentiary. Provided my father didn't get him off. There was no doubt that he would call into question every scrap of state's evidence. He would cast a shadow of doubt over every aspect of the investigation. I fully expected him to try to throw me under the bus, imply I had somehow interfered with the investigation.

Even as the thought occurred to me, a chill went down

my back. Landry had called me for Irina's number. If he had done that in front of my father, I could already hear the spin on the woman-scorned excuse. He would have me planting Irina's phone in Bennett's house, then telling Landry where to find it.

Before it was all over, he would have the jury believing I had killed Irina for the sole purpose of setting Bennett up, or out of a jealous rage that Bennett was with my groom or that my groom was with Bennett. He had already impugned my mental stability, why not take a crack at my sexuality as well?

I could see the tall, gangly kid still working the valet stand on his own as I retrieved my car from the lower parking lot. His friend Jeff the Weasel was probably off selling his story to the *National Enquirer:* I PARKED FOR A KILLER.

There was no sign of Barbaro's car. Was he even at that moment sitting in an interview room in Robbery/ Homicide, laying out his latest truth of what had happened the night Irina died?

*'I saw Beth – Lisbeth . . .'* he'd said.

*Beth.*

I wondered.

*To I. From B. . . . ?*

A little sterling silver heart on a charm bracelet. Something sweet, innocent, touching.

It was none of my business. I just felt bad for Lisbeth, that was all. She'd lost her best friend. She felt alone and afraid. I had never been as innocent as I suspected Lisbeth was before she came to South Florida, but I knew what it was to feel abandoned.

*My God, Elena, are you in danger of growing a heart?*

I certainly hoped not. No good could come of it.


Sean's house was dark. He'd gone off to one of the Disease du Jour charity balls that dominated the season. I went into the cottage wondering what to do with myself for the rest of the night.

The question was answered for me as I turned on the lights and found Alexi Kulak standing there waiting for me, gun in hand.

'Shouldn't we be past this by now?' I asked.

Kulak was unamused. He came toward me, pointing the gun in my face, backing me up, as I had backed him up the night before.

The cold kiss of steel touched my forehead as I backed into the wall. He stepped so close in I could feel the heat of his body, smell his sweat. His eyes were wide and glassy. The pupils pinpoints of black.

'Now you find out,' he said in a low voice, 'what happens to women who betray me.'

# 57

'I don't know what you're talking about,' I said, genuinely afraid because I really didn't know what he was talking about. That was always a much stronger line when I was lying.

Kulak looked as crazy as he had the first night he came to me. The significant difference was that his insanity that night had been driven by grief, and this rage was being given extra fuel by drugs. Raw emotion and chemical reaction – a volatile mix, the kind of combination that got people killed every day of the week. Especially when the vessel containing that mix was holding a gun.

'You lying whore,' he said, pushing the barrel of the gun into the skin just below my left cheekbone. 'I saw you. I saw you on television.'

'What are you talking about? On television?'

'You and your lover. He killed my Irina. You would protect him. You would never tell me.'

I swallowed hard and tried not to shake as I looked him in the eyes. 'Alexi. I don't know what you're talking about. You have to believe me.'

'I don't have to do nothing,' he said. 'I do what I want. I'm thinking I want to kill you.'

'How can I help you if you kill me?'

'You are of no use to me, you lying cunt.'

He grabbed me by the neck and marched me across the room, toward the French doors onto the back patio. As we passed the hall to the guest suite, I wondered what he had done to Lisbeth. She was of no use to him either. Had he killed her? Or was she in bed, still blissfully unconscious, unaware of the danger just beyond her door?

Kulak had begun to mutter in Russian. He shoved me out the door. I could see his car parked at the far end of the barn, out of sight from the driveway.

If he got me in the car, I was as good as dead.

I pretended to stumble, throwing Kulak off balance, then came up with an elbow, hitting him in the Adam's apple. He tumbled backward, choking, grabbing at his throat with one hand.

I bolted sideways, started to run.

I felt the sting almost before I heard the shot. The bullet cut through the flesh of my left upper arm like a hot, sharp knife. I grabbed my arm just as Kulak barreled into me from behind, knocking me flat on the flagstones, my right arm caught beneath me and no way to break my fall.

My breath burst out of my lungs, and stars swam before my eyes.

Alexi Kulak stood, grabbed me by the scarf I had tied around my throat to hide the marks he'd left from choking me, and hauled me to my feet.

He had to half-drag me to his car. Not because I was fighting him, but because I couldn't. Stunned, semi-conscious, and bleeding, I was no match for him.

When we reached the Mercedes, he popped the trunk and shoved me inside.

I had only a second to register the fact that there was already a body in it.

Bennett Walker.

# 58

Edward Estes declined to speculate as to the whereabouts of his client.

'You might want to give him a call,' Landry said in a voice filled with magnanimous sarcasm. 'Give him the heads-up. As a courtesy from the Palm Beach County Sheriff's Office.'

He left Paulson to deal with the attorney.

'Every cop in the county is looking for Walker's car,' Weiss said as they walked away from the house. 'We've got the airports covered.'

'What about the marinas? Walker races boats. If he can get to a marina, he can be down the coast in a hurry.'

'I'll notify the Coast Guard,' Weiss said. 'You know Estes is gonna try to say the phone was planted.'

'He can say whatever he wants. We've got the discovery on videotape. No jury in this neck of the woods is going to believe the poor-little-rich-boy routine a second time around.'

His phone rang. He grabbed it. Dugan.

'I'm just saying,' Weiss went on.

'Save it,' Landry said, snapping the phone shut. 'Let's go break his alibi. Barbaro is waiting for us.'

The Spaniard sat in the interview room, waiting. Landry watched him through the one-way glass. He appeared calm and relaxed, not like a man about to rat out his best friend on a murder. He ran a hand back through his hair, checked his watch, casually drummed his fingers on the table.

He looked confident.

Landry turned to Dugan. 'You got that thing working?'

The voice-stress-analysis machine – it had a yard-long name Landry had never bothered to learn – would pick up on the voices in the conversation and determine whether or not any of the parties were feeling stress or anxiety. A poor man's lie detector of sorts, and a good tool if the interviewee was easy to rattle.

Landry had to think it would be of little use here.

'Press him on the London case,' Dugan said, adjusting a knob on the machine. 'He won't be expecting that.'

Landry nodded, picked up a file folder with case notes, and went in.

'Mr. Barbaro. Thank you for coming down.'

Barbaro made a small dismissive motion with his hand. 'I felt an obligation.'

'To whom?'

Barbaro studied him for a second, making up his mind. 'To Irina, of course.'

'You didn't seem to feel any obligation when you gave your first statement, saying that you and Mr. Walker were passed out at his home that night and never saw Irina Markova after you left Players. Why is that?'

He sighed like a man burdened by a great disappointment. 'I never imagined what had happened. That my good friend could have killed the girl.'

'Really?' Landry said. 'That seems strange to me, seeing how you went through virtually the same experience in London a couple of years ago.'

The Spaniard's dark eyes met his. 'That was something very different.'

'A young woman, raped and murdered. How is that different?'

'The man who perpetrated the crime was not a friend of mine.'

'He got off. Did you know he was guilty too?'

Barbaro shrugged. 'I was not surprised.'

'Another wealthy guy,' Landry said. 'Into the polo scene.'

'A sponsor, yes.'

'Scotland Yard tried to pin it on you.'

'Prosecuting a foreign polo player would have been much easier than prosecuting a wealthy member of British society.'

'The wealth-has-privilege thing.'

'Money is the universal language, is it not?'

'So here you are, years later, in the States,' Landry said. 'Playing polo, minding your own business, and son of a bitch if a girl you know isn't murdered. You must have thought that was a hell of a coincidence. I know I do.'

'I came here of my own volition, Detective,' Barbaro said. 'I came to tell you the truth.'

'As opposed to the lie you've been telling me.'

'I don't excuse my behavior.'

'That's good. What changed your mind?'

'I've been accused of growing a conscience.'

'Is that right? Have you?'

'I'm here, aren't I?'

'Do you have anyone who can corroborate your story – that you left the party at Walker's house?'

'I thought I saw Lisbeth Perkins. I don't know whether she saw me.'

'Lisbeth Perkins told us she was home in bed shortly after one. Why wouldn't she tell us she saw you later?'

'You would have to ask her that question.'

'Are you aware Lisbeth was attacked last night and threatened?'

'I heard, yes.'

'Do you think she might be more apt to tell us she saw you now than she would have before the beating?'

'I resent that implication, Detective,' Barbaro said, rising from his chair. 'I came here to set the record straight about that night. If you're not interested in that, I'll take my leave.'

'You didn't see anyone else going back to your car?' Landry asked. 'No one saw you?'

'I saw the Freak,' Barbaro said.

'What freak?'

'The Freak,' Barbaro said impatiently. 'That's what she is called. She is a crazy woman. She is always around the parking lot there.'

'And this freak is your alibi?'

Barbaro sighed. 'Detective, if I was going to simply make up a story, do you not think I would come up with something less ridiculous?'

Landry sidestepped the issue. 'Do you think Bennett Walker murdered Irina Markova?'

Barbaro looked suddenly very weary. 'I think, Detective Landry, that for some men who have too much, there is never enough.'

'I guess what I'm wondering, Mr. Barbaro,' Landry said, 'is, are you one of those men too? This happened before in your life. You were suspected, denied it, came around and talked, and an acquaintance of yours almost went to prison. Maybe that's your idea of tipping the scales.'

'And maybe,' Barbaro said, 'you can go to hell.'

As he reached to open the door, someone knocked, and Weiss stuck his head in, looking to Landry.

'We've got Walker's car – and a dead body.'

# 59

'He's going to kill us,' Bennett said, terror in his voice. 'He's going to kill us, isn't he?'

'Shut up!' I snapped.

It was pitch-dark in the trunk. The smell of diesel fuel, sour sweat, and fear gagged me. I lay half on top of him. When I tried to move away, I cracked my head on the trunk lid.

'He's a Russian,' he said. 'He's that gangster Irina talked about. He's killed people.'

'Shut up!' I snapped again. My arm was burning like hell and still bleeding.

'Oh, my God. I can't believe this is happening.'

'Shut up!' I screamed, and kneed him as hard as I could. 'Shut up! Shut the fuck up! Yes, he's going to kill us! He's going to kill you, and he's going to torture you first, and I'm going to watch, you son of a bitch!'

'Jesus Christ, Elena! Do you hate me that much?'

'It's nothing less than you deserve for the lives you've ruined.'

'Oh, my God,' he said again. 'I can't believe this is happening to me.'

To *him*.

'Can you move?' I asked. 'Are your hands free?'

'No. They're tied behind my back.'

'Roll over,' I ordered. 'I'll try to undo the rope.'

'It's duct tape.'

'Roll over!'

Bennett struggled to move, to turn away from me. I struggled to get my hands in position. My injured arm was throbbing like the beat of a bass drum. I could move my fingers, but they felt swollen and clumsy. I couldn't find the end of the tape. I broke a fingernail trying to scratch through it.

'Fuck!'

The hell with Bennett, I thought. He would be of no use getting away, because he would think only of himself and end up getting us both killed in the process.

I started trying to feel around the trunk for anything that I might be able to use as a weapon. There was nothing.

The car made a sharp left, then a sharp right, then sat for a moment as something rattled and screeched outside.

A gate.

The car moved forward. The gate screeched and rattled shut.

When the trunk opened, the first thing I saw was the barrel of Kulak's gun. I held my breath and waited for Kulak to pull the trigger.

'Get out,' he said. 'Get out!'

I got out, a little dizzy, legs wobbly.

Hands bound behind his back, Bennett struggled out and stood doubled over for a moment.

'Stand up!' Kulak ordered.

Bennett rocked once on the balls of his feet, then bolted forward, hitting Kulak like a battering ram. He knocked the Russian sideways and kept running for the gate.

Alexi Kulak very calmly got his balance back, aimed, and fired.

I watched, horrified, as Bennett's right leg buckled beneath him, and he went down, crying out.

In the distance I could hear police sirens, but I knew with a terrible sinking feeling in my gut they wouldn't be coming here. We were locked inside the gates of Alexi Kulak's auto salvage yard, and we were at the mercy of a madman.

## 60

'So who is this guy?' Landry asked, shining his Maglite into the trunk of the car.

'Jeffrey C. Cherry,' the deputy said, reading from the victim's driver's license. 'West Palm Beach; 06-20-88. He's got an employee parking sticker from Players.'

'Jeez,' Weiss said, poking at the trash around the body. 'If he didn't have that crowbar in his head, I'd say he died from eating this shit.'

'There's a couple of dime bags of coke,' the deputy said. 'Could have been a drug deal gone bad.'

Landry looked over at Bennett Walker's Porsche. 'Could have been. But what was Bennett Walker doing here, and where is he?'

'And what drug dealer wouldn't steal that car?' Weiss asked. 'The keys are in it.'

Landry took a pen out of his pocket and pushed open the small black duffel bag that sat on the victim's chest. A couple stacks of bills – singles topped with a twenty – and what looked like some coke residue.

'This sucks,' he said. 'This is some kind of setup. This kid works at Players—'

'Valet,' Weiss said, peering in the open driver's door. 'He's got a name tag in here.'

Landry walked away from the car and called Elena. Straight to voice mail. He didn't like that. She would have been waiting to hear news on what the search warrant had gained them.

She had told him to talk to the valets. He guessed this was the kid who had split before he'd gotten there. Elena had known him, then. And Walker had been here.

'I've got a bad feeling about this,' he said.

Weiss flashed his light at the crowbar planted in Jeffrey C. Cherry's skull. 'Imagine how he feels.'

# 61

Kulak left Bennett lying on the ground, bleeding, and dragged me inside the building by my injured arm, digging his thumb into the wound every time I slowed down.

He took me into a large, open garage space with hydraulic lifts and drains in the concrete floor. Lights hung from a ceiling of open steel trusses. On one side of the space was a row of old beat-up red metal lockers with iron-mesh fronts. He dragged me to them, pulled one open, shoved me inside with my back to the wall, shut the door, and locked it.

I was in a cage. Literally a captive audience for whatever horror show Kulak might want to play out in front of me.

The cage was not much taller than I was and not much wider or deeper. I could get my hands in front of me, but I couldn't get any leverage or power to try to push against the door.

It seemed a very long time before Kulak returned. I began to think perhaps he had taken Bennett elsewhere to torture and kill him and that I would be left standing in that cage for hours and hours, wondering what would happen to me when he finally came back. Then I heard them – Kulak shouting at Bennett to move, a scuffle of footsteps, someone falling, Kulak shouting.

Bennett came sprawling through the doorway, landing on the floor near one of the drains. Kulak walked over, gun in hand. He seemed very calm, relaxed even, as if he had flipped the switch on his emotions.

'Take off your clothes,' he said.

Bennett looked up at him. 'What?'

'Take off your clothes, Mr. Walker.'

'Why?'

Kulak gave him a savage kick in the ribs, an action weirdly at odds with his demeanor.

'Take off your clothes, Mr. Walker. You are going to know how it feels to be vulnerable.'

When Bennett still didn't move, Kulak kicked him twice more, once in the back, once in his injured leg. Bennett struggled then to sit up, grimacing. His face glowed with sweat as he stripped off his T-shirt and jeans. He had trouble moving the injured leg, trouble bending that knee.

It seemed to take forever for him to complete his task. All the while Alexi Kulak just stood there, waiting, gun in hand. He smoked a cigarette, watching dispassionately as his victim struggled.

When he was naked, Bennett curled on his side on the concrete, and just lay there, breathing hard. His back was to me, and I could see the entrance wound in the back of his thigh – a small innocuous-looking hole that belied the damage the bullet had most surely done inside the leg.

Kulak dropped his cigarette butt on the floor and put it out with the toe of his wingtip shoe. He produced a pair of handcuffs, closed one around Bennett's left wrist and the other around one of the iron bars of the drain.

He walked over to a workbench, set his gun aside, and chose a tool from a rack hanging on the wall. He chose it carefully, like a musician choosing an instrument or a sculptor choosing a chisel.

It was a bolt cutter.

Bennett watched him. I could see the abject terror in his face. Like an animal trying to flee a predator, he threw himself as far away from Kulak as he could – a pathetically short distance – before the cuffs rattled and he strained against the unyielding iron bar of the drain.

'Why did you kill my Irina?' Kulak asked him with eerie calm.

'I didn't,' Bennett said. 'I didn't kill her.'

Kulak took a step closer and stomped on Bennett's wrist, making him cry out.

'Why did you kill my Irina?' he asked again.

'I-I didn't,' Bennett said. 'I barely knew her.'

Just like he was snipping a weed from his lawn, Kulak leaned over with the long-handled bolt cutter and cut Bennett Walker's left index finger off at the knuckle.

A wet hot sweat washed over me from head to toe. The screams were horrible. I closed my eyes for a moment but opened them again to abate the dizziness.

Bennett was sobbing. Blood ran from the stump of his finger.

With the toe of his shoe, Kulak knocked the detached digit into the drain. He stepped away, lit another cigarette, smoked it down halfway. After a moment, he went to Bennett, squatted down, and applied the red-hot tip of his smoke to Bennett's mutilated finger, cauterizing the wound.

Bennett screamed. The sound went through me like a razor blade.

'Why did you kill my Irina?' Kulak asked softly.

'I don't know,' Bennett whimpered.

'You don't know?'

'I can't remember.'

'You murdered this exquisite girl,' Kulak said, 'and she meant so little to you that you don't even remember why?'

'I don't know.'

Kulak looked at the butt of his cigarette, then casually leaned over and pressed the red-hot ember to the thin skin on the inside of Bennett's wrist and held it there.

Bennett's body jerked wildly, convulsively. His screams came from a place inside him so primal there was nothing human in them.

I tried to look away, but I could still see him in my peripheral vision. If I closed my eyes, the dizziness and nausea would wash over me and I would be sick. It was important I not appear weak. I knew that.

The stench of hot feces filled the air, and I tried not to gag.

Kulak waited for the screams to die, for his victim to lie still in his own waste.

But panic was a luxury I couldn't afford. Alexi Kulak could smell panic. He fed on it. He savored it like a fine wine.

'I loved her,' he said. 'I would have done anything for her. I *will* do anything for her. Why would she want you, Mr. Walker? You are weak. You are no man for a woman like Irina. She would have run you around like a trick pony. Is that why you killed her?'

Bennett shook his head. 'No.'

'Because she was too strong for you?'

'No.'

'Why, then?' he asked, as if he was asking a sweet small child. 'Why did you kill her?'

'I-I must have been angry.'

'Yes.'

'She made me angry.'

'Yes. And so you killed her?'

'I swear to God,' Bennett whimpered, 'I don't remember killing her. I don't remember anything. I must have blacked out.'

Kulak pointed at the stump of Bennett's index finger. 'This hurts quite badly, doesn't it?'

Bennett nodded. He was flat on his belly on the floor, his face pressed to the concrete.

'Let me take your mind off that pain,' Kulak said.

He stood up, took the bolt cutter, and snapped off half of the middle finger beside it.

I wanted to put my fingers in my ears to block out the screams, but I couldn't fold my injured arm that tightly. I wanted to throw up. I wanted to cry. Panic swelled in my throat like a balloon.

Kulak stood there watching Bennett Walker sob, watching the blood run from his mutilated hand and drip down into the drain in the floor.

'I'm sorry!' Bennett cried. 'I'm so sorry! I don't know what happened!'

I listened to him. I watched him lying there. Many times in my life I had told myself there was no punishment on this earth too severe for him. But all I could think in that moment was that he didn't do it.

Bennett Walker was a bully, but he was also what Alexi Kulak had called him: weak. There was no way he could take what Kulak was doing to him and not spill his guts. He didn't have it in him.

'You don't know what happened,' Kulak said. He turned then and looked at me.

'If you don't know,' he said, 'then perhaps your lover can tell us.'

# 62

Landry parked on the road fifty yards from the driveway of Sean Avadon's farm.

The main house was dark.

There was one light visible in Elena's cottage. Her car was parked out front. The front door was ajar.

Drawing his weapon, he went around the side of the house.

The French doors stood open.

Landry slipped inside. The only light was in the living room. Nothing was on – no television, no ever-playing jazz on the sound system.

He worked his way through the cottage, his anxiety growing. The guest suite was empty. Elena's suite was empty.

His cell phone rang.

'Landry.'

'Detective?'

The accent was Russian. The voice was heavy and male.

'I call from Magda's.'

'Yeah?'

The bartender, Landry thought. The big bald guy with the blue skull tats.

'You want Kulak?'

He almost said no. He almost said he didn't care anymore about Kulak, but then he didn't.

'That guy on the news,' the bartender said. 'The one they say maybe killed Irina.'

'Bennett Walker?'

'Kulak has him. At the salvage yard.'

'Why tell me?' Landry asked.

'I tell you for Svetlana,' he said. 'Kulak has that man, and a woman.'

'A woman?' Landry said, a chill washing over him. Alexi Kulak had Elena.

'You come and get Kulak,' the bartender said. 'You tell him Svetlana sent you.'

# 63

'He's not my lover,' I said with as much bravado as I could scrape together. If I could manage to stand up to him, I might at least buy a little time and in that time find a way to take him or get away from him.

Big talk from a woman in a cage.

'What would I want with him?' I said, as Kulak came closer. 'He's nothing to me. He's a piece of shit on the sidewalk.'

'I saw you on television,' he said. 'You were lovers. Your father is his attorney.'

'I don't have a father,' I said.

Something ugly flashed in his eyes. 'Have you not learned, Ms. Estes, that I do not like to be lied to?'

'Well, I'm not exactly thrilled to be called a liar, Mr. Kulak. So I guess we're even.'

He didn't know what to make of me.

'Edward Estes,' I said, 'stopped being my father the day he wanted me to lie under oath and give Bennett Walker an alibi, knowing he was a rapist.'

Kulak stood just outside the locker, very close, studying me like I was a specimen in a museum.

'You are very bold for a woman in your position.'

'I might as well be,' I said. 'You'll do whatever you want to do. I'll at least keep my pride.'

He turned and looked at Bennett lying on the floor, crying.

'You would not tell me,' he said. 'You knew it was him, but you would not tell me. You think I am a fool. I came to you for the truth and you told me you knew nothing.'

'Because I didn't. You wanted the truth. I hadn't found it yet. Believe me, he's the last person on earth I want to protect. He's a rapist at best and a murderer at worst. Why would I risk my life for him?'

Bennett could hear me. He looked up at me, pleading. 'For God's sake, Elena!'

'Shut up!' I shouted at him. 'You're exactly that and you know it.'

Kulak's interest went from me to Bennett and back again.

'All right, Ms. Estes,' he said, unlocking the door to my cage. 'You believe he is a rapist and a murderer. Show me.'

He opened the door and pulled me out of the locker by my injured arm. Black spiderwebs shot across my vision, and my legs swayed beneath me.

Kulak pulled me over to where Bennett lay bleeding. His skin was pasty white and gleaming with sweat. He was going into shock.

Once again Kulak kicked him in the ribs. 'Turn over! On your back!'

'Oh, my God. Oh, my God,' Bennett whimpered. Tears ran from the corners of his eyes as he turned to lie on his back.

Kulak put the bolt cutters in my hands, then pulled a .38 from a belt holster and put it against my head.

'You want justice, Ms. Estes?' he said. 'You want revenge? I want revenge. For Irina. Give him the justice a rapist deserves. Castrate him.'

# 64

The bolt cutter was heavy. The sharp steel pinchers hovered over Bennett Walker's genitals. The cold steel of the gun barrel rested against my temple.

'Is there a problem, Ms. Estes?' Kulak whispered.

'No,' I said. 'I've been waiting a long time for this moment.'

Bennett cried, mumbling my name, saying 'please' over and over.

'I'm just . . . a little dizzy,' I said, swaying against Kulak.

'Do it,' he said.

I pretended to try to open the bolt cutter without success.

'I feel really weak,' I said.

'Do it!' he shouted. 'Do it!!'

Abruptly, I dropped to my knees and elbowed Kulak in the groin.

As he doubled over, I drove the handles of the bolt cutter upward with as much strength as the adrenaline rush gave me. One handle hit him in the face, shattering a cheekbone. The other caught him under the jaw. His head jerked back, and his gun hand swung upward.

The gun went off, the bullet hitting something metal across the room with a loud *Ping!*

He swung the weapon downward toward me.

I hit him in the side of the leg with the bolt cutter, and he dropped to his knees, firing again.

I tried to scramble backward, away from him, as he tried once more to take aim at me.

Jabbing at him with the bolt cutter, I managed to hit his wrist.

The gun fired again.

I ducked to the right.

Kulak was screaming now, in a blind rage, his eyes rolling in his head.

'Kulak! Freeze!'

'Sheriff's office!'

'Freeze!'

'Drop it!'

I heard the shouts and the shots that followed instantly.

Blood and tissue pelted me.

Alexi Kulak's body jerked and twisted above me.

He looked surprised. Shocked.

And then the light in his eyes went out, and his rage went flat, and his body dropped, falling across Bennett Walker's legs.

I dragged myself to the side on one arm, trembling violently, my heart pounding wildly. My ears were ringing. I lay flat on the cold concrete. Not six feet away Bennett Walker stared at me. His eyes were wide open, unblinking.

One of the shots from Kulak's gun had struck him in the forehead.

He was dead.

# 65

Landry ran across the garage, shouting Elena's name at the top of his lungs, knowing she probably couldn't hear him. The gunshots were still ringing in his own ears. He could hardly hear himself think.

'Elena! Elena!'

She didn't move, staring at Bennett Walker's blank, lifeless stare.

'Elena!'

He was there then, on his knees, bent over her, wiping blood splatter and tissue from her face, hoping to God none of it was hers. His hands were shaking.

'Are you hit?' he shouted, staring into her face. 'Are you hit?'

She blinked, seeing him for the first time.

'H-he's d-dead,' she said.

Landry nodded. Gently he pulled her into his arms and held her, his cheek pressed against the top of her head. It seemed they stayed there for a long time, even as deputies and crime-scene people moved around them.

His heart galloped for miles as the adrenaline slowly ebbed. He couldn't remember ever having been so scared as he had been seeing Alexi Kulak pointing a gun at this woman he now held.

What an idiot he had to be, falling in love with a woman who put herself into situations like this one over and over again. But there it was, and all he could do about it was hold her and stroke her hair, and whisper words to her that he was sure she couldn't hear.

It didn't matter. It didn't even matter what the words were. It only mattered that he said them.

# 66

For once an ER doc and I agreed: she did not want to admit me, and I did not want to be admitted.

'She's been shot, for Christ's sake,' Landry growled.

The doctor, who might have been a zygote when I was her age, rolled an eye at him. 'It's only a flesh wound.'

'Yeah?' Landry said. 'How many times have you been shot, sweetheart? This isn't a fucking paper cut.'

I got off the gurney, my arm in a sling, and started for the door.

'Elena—'

'I want to go home,' I said simply, and walked out into the hall.

'I'm going with you,' he said.

I didn't argue. Nor did I point out to him that I couldn't get home without him. I hadn't gone to Alexi Kulak. Alexi Kulak had come to me. I didn't want Landry asking me why.

'Lisbeth is there and—'

'No, she isn't,' he said.

I stopped and faced him. 'What?'

'She's not there. There was no one in the house when I stopped by.'

Half a dozen bad scenarios streaked through my head like so many comets, the worst of them being that Kulak had gotten rid of her while he was lying in wait for me.

'We have to find her,' I said.

'We'll find her.'

'No,' I said. 'You don't understand. We have to find her. She knows what happened.'

Landry squinted at me. 'What do you mean, she knows what happened? We know what happened. Walker killed Irina because she was pregnant. She was going to ruin his life. He killed her and dumped her body.'

I shook my head. 'No. I don't think so.'

'You don't think so? You've been selling Bennett Walker as a killer from day one.'

'I don't think he did it, James,' I admitted. 'I watched Alexi Kulak torture him. The only thing Kulak wanted to know was why. Why did he kill her? And all Bennett could say was that he didn't know, that he couldn't remember doing it.'

'So? Who would cop to anything that would piss off Alexi Kulak?'

'But *that* pissed off Alexi Kulak,' I said. 'If Bennett had had an answer, he would have given it up. I think he believed he did it. I think he woke up Sunday morning, found a dead girl in his pool, and convinced himself he must have done it.

'He couldn't give Kulak the answer, because he didn't have one.'

'And what makes you think Lisbeth does?'

A hunch, I thought, a feeling. A feeling that had been slowly taking root in the back of my mind as small scraps of information bonded together.

'When Barbaro recanted his statement,' I said, 'I asked him if he had seen anyone who could corroborate his statement. He said he'd seen Lisbeth. As he got back to his car at Players, she was walking across the parking lot. But Lisbeth told me she went home long before that.'

'So Barbaro's lying,' Landry said.

I shook my head. 'That doesn't make sense. Why would he lie about something so stupid? Why not just say no one saw him? It's impossible to disprove a negative.'

'And why would Lisbeth lie about being there,' Landry

said, as the picture started becoming clearer to him, 'unless she had something to hide.'

'Exactly,' I said. 'Yesterday I showed a photograph of Irina and Lisbeth to a mentally disturbed woman who hangs around Players and the Polo Club. I asked if she had ever seen Irina. She looked at both girls and said that *they* were very naughty. I think she meant "they" as in "together."'

'You think Irina and Lisbeth were involved?' Landry asked.

'I think so. I think Lisbeth thought so, anyway.'

'But why would Lisbeth kill Irina?' Landry asked.

I thought about it for a moment, replaying all the broken little pieces of memories. The photographs of Lisbeth and Irina together, Lisbeth so happy and smiling – and the photos of Lisbeth standing a little apart and uncomfortable in the snapshots of herself with men. Too many pictures of Irina on her fridge, I had thought.

I thought about how hard Lisbeth had argued with Irina about the after-party. I thought about the abject grief and the abject guilt.

'Irina was pregnant,' I said. 'She wanted a rich American husband, not a naive lesbian farm girl from East Backwater, Michigan.'

'Rejection,' Landry said.

A deep sense of sadness came over me as I thought about it. As motives for murder went, it was one of the oldest stories in the book. Unrequited love. It never ceased to amaze me that an emotion that was supposed to be so good and bring such joy so often turned so destructive.

And no matter how often life tries to teach us that lesson, we keep going back for more.

# 67

The moon was bright as Lisbeth walked along the dirt road. She didn't know what time it was. Time didn't matter. She had been walking for quite a while, though, she thought.

She had never walked into the wild countryside alone. The idea would have frightened her. But not Irina. Irina would have laughed at her fear of snakes and alligators, and teased her into going. Irina knew how liberating it was not to feel fear. Lisbeth was only just beginning to learn what that meant.

She knew where she was going because the location had been described in great detail over the last few days among riders and barn hands, on the news. It was a pilgrimage of sorts, to go to the place where Irina had been found, where her body had been destroyed. It was no less a holy place than any other for her.

She had worshipped Irina. Irina, so smart, so sophisticated, so bold, so brave.

She had loved Irina as she had never loved anyone in her life. She had needed Irina. Irina had been her big sister, her best friend, her . . . her mentor. Irina had been everything Lisbeth was not.

Lisbeth had tried her hardest to follow in Irina's footsteps – to be casual, and careless, and carefree, and elegant; to look life in the face and grin a wicked grin.

It would have been so perfect, if only it could have been just the two of them.

Funny, she thought. When she came to South Florida she had such very different ideas about what she wanted from life. She had wanted what she had been taught to want – a husband, a family – even though she had known from past experience with men that there were no happiness guarantees, that love could be a hateful, frightful thing.

And she had learned that lesson all over again . . . and again . . . and again. . . .

Irina had taken her under her wing. Irina had been her one true friend and her protector – or so she had thought.

Never in her life had Lisbeth been with – or thought she would ever be with – another woman. She had been raised to believe that was wrong. But with Irina she had felt right, and safe, and, Midwestern guilt aside, happy.

Lisbeth paused along the trail to bend over and cough and to struggle to fill her aching lungs with air. She sat down for a moment's rest on a cypress stump.

The night was clear and warm. Teeming with life, if a person cared to notice. She did. She listened to the frogs and the squawks and ratchet sounds of the marsh birds.

It was, of course, the animals that could be neither seen nor heard that came with the most danger in them. Love was an animal like that. And jealousy. And hurt.

Lisbeth sat on the stump along the oily black canal, waiting for them to come to her.

# 68

'Barbaro told me Irina wasn't shy about her plans to entertain the boys that night,' I said. 'Lisbeth begged Irina not to go, but Irina went anyway.'

'You think Lisbeth came back later to confront Irina?' Landry said. 'That was when Barbaro saw her.'

He pulled into the drive and parked next to my car near the cottage.

I felt a terrible sense of urgency as I got out of the car. The fatigue that had taken hold of me burned off on a new rush of adrenaline.

Lisbeth was alone somewhere. I had a feeling Lisbeth had been alone a very long time. I thought that was perhaps the source of my sympathy for her – that I looked at Lisbeth Perkins and saw in her all the things that life had burned out of me long ago.

I called her name as I went inside, knowing she wouldn't answer.

Sick as a dog from what she had gone through the night before, her Midwestern work ethic still had not allowed her to leave a mess in a host's home. She had made the bed and fluffed the pillows.

The note was propped against the spring-green velvet bolster, in Lisbeth's happy, loopy, girlish handwriting.

I read the message, my heart sinking deep inside me.

She thanked me for helping her.

She thanked me for being a good friend to Irina.

She apologized for everything she had done wrong, for every shortcoming she had, for every good thing she wasn't.

She wrote down the names and phone number of her parents in Michigan.

She said good-bye.

# 69

She felt so calm now. So at peace. She had fought the decision, but now that it was made, it was the only thing that made sense to her.

Elena had told her to work off her guilt, not wallow in it. In a way that was what she was doing. She was paying back in kind.

She had been looking forward to the party that night. It should have been fun. She and Irina would dance and flirt and bat their eyelashes and guys would buy them drinks, but Lisbeth had already decided she would leave early. She was done with Mr. Brody and his friends. She didn't want that life anymore.

But Irina did. Or so she had said that night when Lisbeth wanted to go home.

*'I want a rich husband, Lisbeth. You know that. And you know which one I want.'*

*'But, Irina, you know he won't marry you—'*

*'He will. You'll see. I'm pregnant. I just found out.'*

*The pain was so sharp it took Lisbeth's breath away.*

*'What?'*

*'I'm pregnant. I'll tell him later tonight.'*

*'For God's sake, Irina, how could you possibly say it's his? You've been with more guys than you can count in English.'*

*Irina's eyes flashed with anger. 'How dare you say that to me, Lisbeth? You fuck all of them too!'*

*'Not anymore. I'm done with them.'*

*'Well, good for you, Miss Goody Goody. I am not done. Bennett Walker will divorce his crazy wife and marry me. I'll make sure of it.'*

'But, Irina, what about us? I love you.'

Lisbeth would never forget the expression on Irina's face – a strange, painful mix of cruelty and pity.

'Don't be foolish, Lisbeth.'

All that night Lisbeth had replayed that scene over and over and over in her head, each time hurting worse than the last.

In some versions she saw regret in Irina's eyes, heard sadness in her voice. That was the memory she worked hard to keep – that Irina knew they couldn't be together, and her cruelty in saying no was a kindness in disguise.

Lisbeth had gone home and paced her tiny apartment, crying and fretting, wishing she had said something different, that she hadn't been so stupid and sounded so clingy. It didn't matter what kind of arrangement they had. It didn't matter if Irina had her rich American husband. Lisbeth knew firsthand that Bennett Walker had no objection to her and Irina being together. So what if he wanted to watch even?

*God, how pathetic you are, Lisbeth,* she'd thought. But in the next second she felt terrified she had already blown it, and she couldn't get to Players fast enough to mend the rift.

Everyone had gone on to Bennett's house by the time Lisbeth got back to Players. She didn't have a parking pass to get into the Polo Club, where Bennett lived, and wasn't good at convincing the guards with half-truths about who she was and why she was there. She parked at Players and walked over.

But Lisbeth never went inside Bennett Walker's house that night. Standing in the shadows, she was able to see in through the tall windows and what she saw had sickened her.

She had been at those parties herself, had done what Irina was doing, but somehow being on the outside looking in, with the soundtrack removed, she saw it all the more clearly for what it was. Degradation.

Only Irina wouldn't have seen it that way. She was laughing and wild, beautifully, stunningly naked and proud, taking everything Bennett Walker and Jim Brody and his friends were giving her and begging for more.

Lisbeth didn't know that person. That person would never have loved her.

Then the harsh words had come from within.

*How stupid could you be, Lisbeth? How naive?*

Words that had lashed her like whips many, many times in her life.

Why would she ever think she might be loved by someone?

The tears came like rain as she sat there waiting. She felt as if she were made of shattered glass. She could even see the lines between the broken pieces as she looked at her wrist in the bright moonlight.

She had spent hours that night sitting crouched against the side of Bennett Walker's house, her entire being throbbing in pain.

Sometime before dawn Irina had come out to smoke a cigarette. She sat on one of the lounges by the pool, her long legs stretched out in front of her.

*'I don't know you,'* Lisbeth said, standing beside the chair. *She stared down at the stranger she had spun into a fairy princess. 'How could you do that, Irina? How could you do that to me?'*

*'No one did anything to you, Lisbeth,'* she said. *'They all did it to me.'*

Irina had laughed at that, a hard, cynical noise as discordant to Lisbeth as pot lids clashing.

*'Grow up, Lisbeth,'* she said.

Hurt beyond words, Lisbeth had gone behind the lounge. She crouched behind it, sobbing, her hands over her face.

'I loved you,' she whispered over and over. 'I loved you, I loved you. . . .'

The pain had built and built, the pressure of it threatening to crush her lungs, and her heart, and her head.

Slowly her hands had inched around the back of the chair and her fingertips had brushed Irina's upper arms.

And then, without even realizing fully how, she had hold of the leather cord that hung around Irina's throat with a medallion hanging from it, the necklace just like her own. They had bought them together at the horse show in Wellington.

And her hands tightened on the cord.

And the pain swelled.

And her vision went red.

And she thought, *All I ever wanted was for you to love me.*

She cried aloud now, a sound so full of torment and raw pain it didn't sound human. She cried for all she had lost – her heart, her innocence. She cried for all she would never have – a future, a family, love.

And when the crying stopped, there was nothing left. She was empty, finished. It was time.

With no emotion at all, she undressed. She pulled from the pocket of the borrowed jacket a small, very sharp knife she had also borrowed from Elena's kitchen.

And with the tip of that knife, she opened a vein in her left wrist, and one in her right.

And she stepped down into the black water of the canal and poured her life into it drop by drop.

# 70

Sometimes, our best just isn't good enough – not for those around us, not for those who love us, not for ourselves.

Landry and I made it to the canal where I had found Irina in record time. But record time wasn't good enough.

Landry hit the brakes, and I think we were both out of the car before it fully stopped.

I ran as fast as I could across the little land bridge to the far bank, where the glare of the headlights shone on the little bundle of borrowed clothes Lisbeth had neatly folded and left there to be found.

I called her name and turned around, as if she would materialize before my eyes.

Landry caught me before I could turn too far and see too much. And he pulled me hard against him and held me there as tight as he could, as I cried in the only way I could – with my soul.

## 71

In a way, I felt as if I had died over the course of those few days that winter. Parts of me I thought had died long since were resurrected and purged all over again.

In Irina's death, I saw the death of dreams that never should have been. The life she had wanted, the reasons she had wanted that life, would have never brought her happiness. Just as I would never have found happiness with Bennett.

In Bennett's death, I saw the wheels of justice turn in their own time, not in mine. And the old hatred and bitterness I had harbored for him all those years simply ceased to be. I didn't feel happy. I didn't feel relieved. I didn't feel vindicated or triumphant or anything else. What I felt was the absence of feeling, and I knew it would be a long time before I fully understood what that was all about.

In Lisbeth's death, I saw too much, too close up, and it hurt so badly to look at it, I could only take it out of the most secret part of my heart and glance at it askance for just the briefest part of time before I had to put it back.

Lisbeth had been the child I never was, had worn on her sleeve the heart I'd learned to guard so carefully so very long ago. And perhaps because I had never been allowed to mourn the loss of that child in me, I felt her death the hardest of all. It left me feeling wounded in a place so deep inside, I had thought nothing and no one could ever reach it.

I didn't like being wrong.

I phoned Lisbeth's parents back in Michigan and spun them a story about their sweet daughter and a tragic accident. They had no need to know anything about how tragic Lisbeth's life had been in the weeks leading up to her death. Some truths are too cruel to pass along. I kept Lisbeth's for her.

The hoopla surrounding the shoot-out at Alexi Kulak's salvage yard would take weeks to die down. It was something to be endured, like a mosquito bite.

I gave no interviews, made no comments. I turned down an offer for a movie-of-the-week. I took a day and had a boat with no holes in it delivered to Billy Quint.

When I returned, Barbaro was at the farm waiting for me.

'I have much to apologize for,' he said, holding my car door as I got out.

'Not to me,' I said. 'You did the right thing in the end.'

'Too little, too late.'

I didn't comment.

'How are you, Elena?' he asked. He didn't look at the sling on my arm. That wasn't what he meant.

I shrugged. 'I didn't learn anything I didn't already know,' I said. 'The benefit of being jaded and cynical. It's difficult to be either shocked or disappointed.'

'I'm sorry for that,' Barbaro said. 'I'm sorry we could not have known each other in a different time, under different circumstances.'

'So far as I know, this is the only time we've got,' I said. 'All we can do is play the hand we're dealt.'

He nodded and sighed, and looked away. 'I'm going back to Spain for a while,' he said.

'What about the season?'

'There'll be another. I just wanted to say good-bye. And thank you.'

'For what?'

He smiled a sad, weary smile, and touched my cheek. Gently, I'm sure, though I couldn't really feel it.

'For being who you are,' he said. 'And for helping me to see who I had become.'

The sun was low in the western sky, flame orange and fuchsia on the low flat horizon, when Landry stopped by later that day.

I stood beside the dark four-plank fence that created a paddock for Sean's pretty mare Coco Chanel. She grazed as delicately as if she were eating cucumber sandwiches at a garden party.

Landry came over and stood beside me. We both watched the horse for a moment.

'How are you feeling?' he asked.

'I've had better days,' I said. 'I've had worse.'

'Your father gave a press conference today. Did you see it?'

'My invitation must have gotten lost in the mail.'

'He's trying to pin the whole thing on the Russian mob. According to him, Irina was part of an elaborate scheme to get Alexi Kulak hooked up with the Walker family.'

'That's why he makes the big bucks. I guess the movie people should go to him.'

'I'm sorry for you he had to be a part of all this,' Landry said.

'I'm sorry any of us had to be a part of it,' I said.

'Yeah.'

'I'm sorry he has to be my father, period. But let's not talk about him,' I suggested. 'He'll only ruin a lovely sunset.'

He nodded and slipped an arm around my shoulders. It felt good to have him touch me, to have him be there, to know that despite his many rough spots, he would be there for me when it counted. Of the lessons I had learned during that week, that was the one I decided was most important to me.

I thought of asking him what would happen to the

remaining members of the Alibi Club, but I knew the answer. Nothing. Nothing would happen to Jim Brody or any of the rest of them.

Aside from some minor recreational drugs, they hadn't done anything illegal. They would probably lay low for a month or two, or maybe for the season. But then it would be business as usual.

That's just the way of the world. Would there be more Irinas, more Lisbeths? Absolutely. But they would go into that circle of their own free will, and they would pay the price they paid. I couldn't be everyone's savior — nor did I want to be. I had my own life to go on with.

'You're no box of chocolates, Estes,' Landry said at last.

I smiled the little Mona Lisa smile. 'Neither are you.'

'Nope.'

'We must deserve each other, then, huh?' I said.

He smiled and nodded.

I sobered then and looked up at him. 'I don't know what I want, James. I don't know what I need.'

He tipped my head against his shoulder and pressed a kiss against my hair.

'It doesn't matter,' he said softly. 'We have what we have, and I won't let it go. That's what matters,' he said.

And he was right.